STONE OF INHERITANCE

COMPANY OF STRANGERS, BOOK 2

MELISSA MCSHANE

Night Harbor Publishing

For Bryan,
in thanks for the worship of Averran and delicious salmon

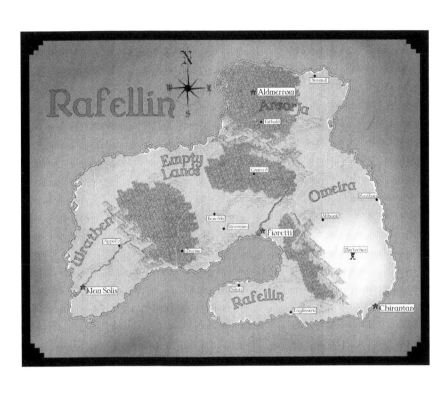

1

The cloudy gray light before the storm dulled the white marble façade of the Tombrino auction house to pearly dimness. Its many arches and gilded spires gave it the look of a temple of the avatar Gavant instead of a temple to worldly wealth. White statues topped the small round arches lining its roof, too far away for Sienne to make out details or identify who they were meant to be. She guessed long-ago rulers of Fioretti or representations of divine virtues, monitoring the activities of anyone who dared go within.

A gust of freezing wind snatched her cloak from her hands where she gripped it closely around herself. She grabbed the cloak and wrapped it more tightly to her. Winter clung to the city despite having supposedly been evicted by first summer, and rain was imminent. Sienne was grateful they were far enough south that it wouldn't be snow instead. Snow was pretty when you were indoors looking at how it covered the gardens and drinking spiced wine, but less pretty if you had to be out in it.

"Was this always an auction house?" she asked Perrin, who strode along beside her. His long dark hair was windblown, and the tip of his nose was as red from the cold air as hers no doubt was.

"It was the home of a minor noble, some hundred and seventy-five years ago," Perrin said. "Someone who plotted against the queen of that era. His fortune and lands were confiscated, his family driven into exile, and his life forfeit. I am certain it was a far more tragic story at the time, but now it is simply a cautionary tale. The Fiorus family have ever been canny when it comes to protecting their rule."

"I don't know. That still sounds sad, at least for the family. I suppose it was generous of the queen not to have them all executed."

Perrin took a drink from the flask at his hip. "Indeed. And daring, to leave alive any who might seek revenge for their father's death."

Sienne eyed the flask, but said nothing. After nearly nine months of being Perrin's companion on their scrapper team, she was used to his near-constant state of mild to moderate inebriation. The priests of the avatar Averran, whom Perrin worshipped, were expected to be a little drunk when performing their devotions, but Sienne couldn't help feeling Perrin took it too far. She'd overheard enough of his side of the prayer conversations he had with his avatar to suspect Averran didn't like it either. But any time she brought it up, even obliquely, Perrin sidestepped the issue with steely grace, and after four months she'd given up even the most subtle queries.

The entrance to the auction house was an open arch with no door, through which men and women bundled up in cloaks against the cold scurried like so many drab gray or black beetles. Perrin and Sienne followed the trickle of people through a short hall where the wind blew briskly and into a larger antechamber with a domed roof. There was no indication as to what it had originally been meant for, but the fine frescos on the walls and the doors beneath them suggested some kind of reception chamber. Scuffs on the parquet floor, which had not been waxed in some time, told Sienne this was a place of serious business that didn't have time for niceties like polished floors. Though the room was sheltered from the wind, it was still bitingly cold, and Sienne wished her magic for heating water applied to air as well. Though it was unlikely she could heat a volume of air this size.

There were only about twenty or twenty-five people in the room, standing in knots of two or three, all of them huddled into their cloaks or coats as she was. Sienne surveyed the frescos. They depicted a series of familiar fairy tales featuring talking animals that walked on their hind legs and dressed like humans. It was subject matter she would have expected to see in a nursery rather than a noble's reception chamber. Nobody else seemed to notice. "There's not many here," she said in a low voice. "That's good, right?"

"It's not bad," Perrin said. "Though we are counting on no one wanting the rather pedestrian lot we are here to bid on. But we should not discuss it in public. It may be a pedestrian lot, but we do not want to give any hint that it matters to us more than that."

Sienne nodded. Perrin was right; the knives they were here to bid on shouldn't matter to anyone but themselves, but no sense giving the game away, and possibly encouraging someone to bid against them.

It had been a long nine months leading to this point. At first, their newly acquired quest to free their companion Alaric's people from the wizard who had them in thrall went nowhere. Perrin's blessing enhancing Alaric's memory of the wizard's binding ritual had given them plenty of information, but none of it hinted at what their next step should be.

Then, three months ago, Alaric had been successful in bribing someone to let him look at the confiscated possessions of Lord Liurdi, from whose property Alaric had originally taken one of the ritual pieces, a brass goblet. According to Perrin, the city treasury made good money off letting prospective bidders do this, so it wasn't that spectacular an achievement, but it had been progress all the same.

Alaric's enhanced memory identified one of the knives in Liurdi's trove as companion to the goblet. Warned in advance by Perrin, who refused to explain why he knew so much about city policies, Alaric didn't try to buy the knife outright. Instead, he found out when Liurdi's possessions would be auctioned off. And now Perrin and Sienne were going to bid on the knife. The lot of knives, actually; there had been five knives in the ancient trunk the team had found the key to. Sienne still felt annoyed that they hadn't been allowed to keep the salvage, since they'd essentially found it, but Denys Renaldi, the guard lieutenant who'd arrested Lord Liurdi for kidnapping Sienne and a host of other crimes, had refused to break what was city custom, if not law. So bidding it would have to be.

Perrin abruptly turned away from Sienne and swore under his breath. "What's wrong?" Sienne asked.

"There is someone here I would rather not encounter," Perrin said. "Fortunately he is just as loath to meet me, but his companions might decide to force the issue. Better if they simply do not see me."

"Who—"

"It is unimportant. Someone I knew once. Someone who took exception to my conversion." Perrin raised the flask again, stared at it, then put it away with a grimace. "I must keep my wits about me, however much I would prefer to lose myself in a gentle fog of brandy. Damn him."

Sienne knew little of Perrin's past except that his family had cast him off when he converted from the worship of Gavant to that of Averran and, to make matters worse, became a priest of that avatar. She casually scanned the crowd, looking for anyone who might be paying close attention to them. Was it a relative? Another noble associated with the Delucco family?

She met the gaze, briefly, of a short, slim man wearing an old-fashioned jerkin over a bell-sleeved white linen shirt and hose. He appeared to be scanning the crowd as she was, and she wondered what he was looking for. Sizing up the competition, perhaps? A nearby woman dressed in a long gown of heavy chartreuse brocade looked warmer than everyone else, and for a moment Sienne envied her the gown. Then she thought about how awkward gowns were, and the moment passed.

A high-pitched bell rang out, a single tone that stilled the already quiet conversations. A woman dressed as Sienne was in fine linen shirt, close-fitting wool trousers, knee boots, and a form-fitting vest emerged from one of the side doors. "The auction will begin in five minutes," she said in a clear, carrying voice. "Please follow me."

Perrin hung back, Sienne guessed to avoid whoever it was he didn't want to meet. They went through the door nearly at the rear of the group, giving Sienne plenty of time to observe the others. Most of them were men wearing the colors of various Fiorettan guilds: carpenters, watchmakers, chandlers, and a few Sienne didn't recognize. There was the woman in chartreuse, and the slim man in old-fashioned clothes. A group of two men and a woman, dressed more finely than the others, might be a rich merchant's representatives or even those of a noble house. And finally, a young woman, probably in her late teens, clutched a purse to her side in both hands as if fearing thieves. Her thin nose was red-tipped as Perrin's was from the cold, and she kept her gaze focused straight ahead on the backs of those in front of her. Sienne couldn't help wondering what all these people were after, and whether any of them had, like Alaric, bribed their way to an early showing of the merchandise.

They passed through the door, and Sienne had to control a gasp. The enormous room beyond had once been a ballroom, though one at least twice the size of the ballroom at her father's ducal palace in Beneddo. More frescos, these of dancing nobles in the dress of two hundred years earlier, covered the walls and the high, arching ceiling where chandeliers still hung, dark and cobwebby. The light came not from the disused chandeliers, but from lanterns on poles scattered throughout the room. The smell of lamp oil was strong in the frigid air. This floor was also scuffed and scored with deep scratches where merchandise had no doubt been dragged over the years. It was almost criminal that they'd treated such a magnificent room so.

But what had startled a gasp out of Sienne was not the beauty of the room. It was its contents. The ballroom was packed with furniture, tables and chairs and armoires and chests and all manner of household furnishings. Wooden crates with their lids removed lay here and there, some with packing straw sticking out of the top, others gleaming with unidentifiable contents. Sienne's eye was drawn to a blocky, antique trunk atop which were piled furs, probably minks if Sienne had to guess. She and Perrin weren't interested in the trunk, though it had come from the same ancient keep that had started their quest in motion, but Sienne was tempted to bid on it, for nostalgia's sake.

Men and women in the uniforms of the Fiorettan city guard stood at attention around the room, armed with the traditional sword and knife and looking willing to use them. Sienne didn't need their deterrence to keep her distance from the wares.

The auction house employee walked to a spot near where the goods were piled most heavily and said, "Bidding will proceed as follows. An item will be presented and an initial price declared. I will call for bids, and the highest bidder will be the purchaser. All items must be paid for at auction's end. If the highest bidder lacks the cash to pay, the second highest bidder will be given the chance to purchase. Items not purchased at the end of the auction will remain the property of the city." She waited as if expecting questions, then said, "The first lot is a dining table and sixteen chairs. Bidding will start at one hundred lari."

Sienne scanned the room again. This was going to be a *very* long day.

She tried not to fidget as Lord Liurdi's possessions were auctioned off. She hadn't gone to the man's execution—none of them had—and the last she'd seen of him had been when she testified to his kidnapping of her. When she'd first met him, he'd been vibrant and confident, if unattractive. At the trial, he'd looked as if all the life had been sucked out of him. Sienne felt no pity, because he'd murdered and schemed to get the key to open that trunk, but she did feel awkward, as if she'd seen him naked and not just beaten. She'd also felt angry that the Giordas, who'd been his accomplices in murder and theft, had been given prison sentences rather than death simply because they'd testified against him. Prison was awful, true, and it was possible they wouldn't survive the term of their sentence, but it was just wrong.

The bidding proceeded. It was boring, actually, with most items going for their first asking price and some items not bid on at all. Sienne couldn't see a pattern to the order in which things were presented for auction. A sofa—a familiar sofa, she'd lain bound upon it while she listened to Liurdi and his friends plot her death!—was followed by a set of silverware, followed by porcelain bedroom utensils Sienne hoped someone had cleaned thoroughly. She let her mind drift, thinking about what Leofus might make for dinner. They were almost certainly going to miss the midday meal, the way things were going.

Perrin put up a hand, startling her. Surely she hadn't missed the knives being presented? But no, it was the pile of minks on the trunk he'd bid on. A few bids were exchanged, and Perrin was outbid. "Why did you do that?" she asked.

"Camouflage," Perrin said quietly. "And there are a few items we could use or resell at a profit."

"But what if we don't have enough for the knives?"

"This is not my first auction, Sienne. Have faith."

Sienne subsided. Perrin knew what he was doing. She was just there to keep him company and, she now realized, provide magical backup if necessary. If he bought an armoire like the one they were selling now, he'd only get it back to Master Tersus's house if she cast *fit* on it.

"Next lot," the auctioneer said. "Five knives recovered from an ancient ruin, non-magical, but in excellent shape. We will start the bidding at twenty lari."

Perrin raised his hand. "Twenty lari, do I have twenty-five?" the auctioneer said. The young woman with the thin nose let go her purse long enough to raise her hand high in the air. "Twenty-five, I'm looking for thirty." Perrin bid again. "Thirty. Thirty-five?" The young woman's hand shot up again.

Sienne examined her more closely. She was plainly dressed, but in clothes that screamed bespoke and a pair of boots Sienne recognized as coming from the bootmaker she and her companions patronized, a woman whose wares were as expensive as they were high-quality. Her hair, unusually light for a Fiorettan, hung loose to her waist in mouse-colored waves. Sienne's hands closed into fists. There weren't supposed to be any real challengers to their bid.

The bidding continued to mount. Perrin looked as calm as if this weren't crucial to their plans. Sienne didn't know how much money Perrin had brought. Surely it would be enough. She resented the young woman and her stupid intrusion into their plans. They needed that knife, damn it!

"That's two hundred lari," the auctioneer said as Perrin lowered his hand. She was trying to maintain her calm, but her wide eyes gave away her astonishment at the turn the bidding had taken. "Two hundred fifty?"

One of the merchant's representatives raised a hand, outbidding the girl. Sienne's heart sank. The unusual activity made it look like Perrin and the girl knew something about the knives' value, and now others wanted in on it. She wanted to scream, snatch the knives, and make a run for it. She wouldn't get far before the guards tackled her, but she was almost desperate enough to try.

"Two hundred fifty," the auctioneer said in a faint voice. "Three hundred?"

"One thousand lari," the girl said. Her voice was thin, but clear. The woman in the chartreuse gown gasped.

"The bid is three hundred," the auctioneer said. Her hand by her side was shaking.

"I'm prepared to pay one thousand," the girl said. "This just saves time."

The auctioneer considered her. She looked at the merchant's representative and at Perrin. Perrin's jaw was rigid. Sienne was sure they didn't have a thousand lari. "One thousand lari," the auctioneer said. "Do I have one thousand and fifty?"

No one moved. The merchant's representative shook his head. "One thousand, then," the auctioneer said. The girl came forward to accept the numbered chit, then merged back into the crowd.

Perrin stared at nothing. His hand came to rest on the hip flask, but didn't take it. Sienne couldn't think of anything to say. They'd lost, and to a girl who... what? Maybe she believed the knives had a value they didn't. Or was she an unknown enemy who wanted them to suffer? She couldn't possibly have known about their interest.

Sienne stared at the girl, who was turning the numbered chit over in her hands like it was a precious jewel. Maybe they could reason with her. Maybe they could offer her money for just the one knife.

No, that might sound like desperation, and make her inflate her price further.

"Should we—" she began.

"Let us talk later," Perrin said. "When there are fewer prying ears."

Sienne nodded.

More lots came and went. Perrin half-heartedly bid on a kitchen table, and won. "Leofus has been complaining about the old table we use now," Perrin said as he accepted the chit showing the lot number he'd purchased. "I thought this would be a nice gift for him."

"He'll be thrilled." Sienne felt empty. Of course there was no point conserving their money now the knives were out of reach, but it was so *pointless*. She didn't know how Perrin managed not to despair. Or maybe he was despairing, and concealed it well.

It was hours before the auction was over, and by the end Sienne's feet hurt from standing so long, her stomach was empty, her bladder was full, and her hands were numb from cold. The announcement of the last lot energized her, until she remembered they still had to pay for the table. After what had happened, she resented the table for keeping them one moment longer than necessary, but she waited more or less patiently with Perrin to present their chit and hand over the money. "Will you arrange for delivery?" the man who took their money asked.

"My companion will handle the details," Perrin said, walking over to the table. Sienne followed him, pulling out her spellbook and opening it to *fit*. She'd had the spell for six months and still wasn't tired of using it. Slowly she read out the syllables of the transform, envisioning the size she wanted the table to become, and savored the honey-sweet taste that filled her mouth. As the last sound left her lips, the ten-foot-long table vanished, replaced by a doll-sized table no more than a foot long. There was never any transition between the two states; objects went from one size to another with no intervening stages. Sienne closed her spellbook, ignoring the stares and whispers of the onlookers. Perrin picked up the table. "Our thanks," he said, and strode off toward the exit.

Sienne began to follow him, but a hand on her arm stopped her. It was the girl who'd outbid them. She held a bulky leather bag larger than Sienne's spellbook in her other hand. "I have something you want," she said in the same thin voice.

"How dare you taunt me!" Sienne said, jerking away.

The girl was unmoved by Sienne's anger. She dipped into her belt pouch and brought out a rectangle of pasteboard. A calling card. Sienne had once had ones just like it. She extended it to Sienne, who took it without thinking. "Be at that address at nine a.m. tomorrow. All of you." She tucked the leather bag under one arm and turned to go.

"Wait!" Sienne said. "Why—"

"Tomorrow," the girl said, and kept walking.

Perrin hadn't stopped walking, and now he returned to Sienne's side. "Sienne," he said, "why were you talking to her?"

Sienne looked at the card. It bore the name *Odela Figlari* and an address on the east side of Fioretti. "I think," she said absently, "we've just been had."

2

Perrin took the card and read its contents. "Figlari," he said. "The name is unfamiliar."

"She said 'all of us,'" Sienne said. "Perrin, this was a set-up."

"Agreed," Perrin said. He tucked the card into his belt pouch. "Back to Master Tersus's house, and we will discuss it."

He turned away, then halted. Standing in front of him was the trio of finely-dressed merchant's representatives, or minor nobles, or whatever they were. Perrin went very still. "Good afternoon," he said, all emotion drained from his voice.

"You're still in Fioretti," the oldest of the trio said. He had silver hair swept back from his face, which was handsome despite the many lines wrinkling it. Sienne judged him to be in his early sixties, and very hale.

"And why should I not be? It is my home." Perrin's right hand closed into a loose fist, and Sienne hoped he wasn't going to start a fight, surrounded by all these guards.

"You should have the decency to leave, and prevent encounters like this," the man's female companion said.

"I did not choose to speak to you," Perrin said. "Please excuse us. My companion and I have business elsewhere."

"Your 'companion'?" the older man said. His lips compressed in a tight, pale line. "You betray Cressida—"

Perrin's fist tightened. "My friend is a scrapper, as am I. And *you* are the one who annulled my vows, not I. By law, there is nothing to betray. But I am faithful as you were not."

The man snarled and slapped Perrin. The sound rang out over the murmurs of conversation. Two guards looked in their direction.

Perrin didn't retaliate. His hand was clenched so tightly it was almost white. "I think we have nothing left to say to one another," he said. "Unless you would like to include those guards in our conversation."

The man took a step backward. "Leave the city," he said. "Spare your family the humiliation—"

"The humiliation is all in your eyes," Perrin said. "Now get out of my way." He walked forward, and Sienne held her breath, certain there would be a fight. But the man and his companions stepped aside, and Sienne hurried to catch up to Perrin, who was almost running.

They emerged from the auction house into darkness and a thin rain. Night had fallen while they were inside, and the cobbled streets were slick in a way that suggested it had been raining for several hours. Sienne trotted to keep up with Perrin, and finally gasped, "Slow down, please!"

Perrin came to a stop. Sienne got a look at his face and swallowed her next complaint. He shifted the table and swiped away the water slicking his cheeks. Sienne pretended to believe it was just the rain. "My apologies," he said. "I would like to return to Master Tersus's quickly, and get out of this incessant rain."

"Me too, but my legs are shorter than yours." Sienne walked beside him at a somewhat less brisk pace, and finally dared, "You knew that man?"

She regretted her words instantly. Of course he knew him. That was the stupidest thing she could have said. But Perrin, to her surprise, let out a short laugh. "You could say so," he said. "That was Lysander Delucco. My father."

Shocked, Sienne blurted out, "He expected you to leave Fioretti?"

"He did. Disinheriting me was insufficient balm to his soul, I fear. Nothing less than my complete disappearance would satisfy him. But I was never a satisfactory son, even when he still considered me that."

"He thought you and I were a couple."

"He has a low mind, for someone so... respectable." Perrin's voice was low and bitter, and Sienne stopped short of asking him who Cressida was. She didn't need to ask; based on that conversation, Cressida was almost certainly Perrin's wife. He had a wife? Or—was she not his wife anymore? Perrin had said Lysander had annulled his vows. In either case, Sienne could guess how painful it would be to Perrin to bring her up.

"I'm sorry," she said instead. "That your father is an ass, I mean."

Perrin shot her a surprised glance. Then he laughed, heartily this time as if she'd just told the funniest joke he'd ever heard. "My thanks," he said when he wound down. "I was on the verge of feeling sorry for myself, but you have reminded me that not all my woes are of my own making." They were trudging up the short hill to Master Tersus's house, and Perrin once more wiped water off his face. "Let us hope they have waited dinner on us. I feel my stomach is trying to cave in on itself from hunger."

Sienne went through the door into the welcome warmth of Master Tersus's back hall. She hung her wet cloak on its accustomed peg and ran her fingers through her shoulder-length chestnut hair. Light, and the smells of roast beef, came from the kitchen doorway ahead, and she advanced into the room, for the moment not thinking about Perrin's tragedy or their colossal failure. She called it Master Tersus's house, like they all did, but in her heart, it was home.

Her other companions were seated at the scarred old table and looked up when she entered. Nearly empty plates lay in front of them, and Kalanath, red-haired and wiry, was the only one still eating. As usual, his staff stood propped against the wall behind him, next to the kitchen window. The young Omeiran had a healthy appetite for someone who never seemed to gain any weight.

Beside him, Dianthe had pushed her plate away with a few

morsels of potato still clinging to it. Her dark blonde hair, braided in a crown around her head, was as untidy as it always was by this time of day. Long, agile fingers held her wine glass lightly, and she thrummed the fingers of her other hand against the table top. At the moment, she was laughing at something, the merry sound making Sienne wish she'd heard the joke.

And, seated at the head of the table as usual, Alaric leaned back with his hands behind his head in a pose that said he'd thoroughly enjoyed his meal. The giant Sassaven, with his white-blond hair and pale blue eyes, was tall even when he was sitting, his broad shoulders and well-muscled chest making him look even bigger than he was. He caught sight of Sienne in the doorway and smiled a welcome. She smiled back and hoped it didn't look as foolish as she felt whenever she saw him.

"You're back!" Dianthe exclaimed. "There's food in the oven. Hurry, I want to see it—" Her cheerful smile wavered, then disappeared. "That's a table. A doll's table."

"A gift for Leofus," Perrin said. "But we failed to achieve our primary goal. I will not apologize, as it seems we were made the dupe of someone else's plan."

Alaric's smile vanished. "Sit," he said. "Tell us what happened."

Sienne got herself a plate from the warming oven. The slices of roast beef were tender and pink, the roasted potatoes sprinkled with herbs and salt, but the smell didn't tempt even her empty stomach. She sat next to Alaric and picked up knife and fork. "We were outbid. By someone who did it on purpose."

"I do not see," Kalanath said. "If you are outbid it must be on purpose, yes? Or do I misunderstand?"

"I mean," Sienne said between bites, "she intended us not to have the knives."

"She paid a thousand lari for them," Perrin said.

Exclamations went up all around. "There's no way we could have paid that much," Alaric said.

"Indeed. But then she approached Sienne afterward, informing her that we are to meet this woman at a certain place tomorrow morning to discuss... what, Sienne?"

"I don't know, exactly. She said she has something we want—well, obviously—and all of us were to come to discuss it." Sienne took another bite. It tasted like ashes. One more thing to hate the woman for, for ruining her enjoyment of Leofus's excellent meal. "I think she deliberately outbid us so she could exchange the knife—or maybe the knives; maybe she doesn't know we only want the one—for something else she wants. Something we can give her."

Alaric frowned. "Who is this woman?"

"Her card names one Odela Figlari, but that is no guarantee that is she, as she might have used anyone's calling card," Perrin said. "It is irrelevant. I know nothing of the Figlari family, do you?"

"Never heard of her," Alaric said. Dianthe shook her head. "Damn. It would be nice to know what we're walking into."

"And how did she know what we wanted?" Dianthe said. "That's disturbing."

"She only had to know we were interested in Liurdi's possessions," Alaric said, "and then show up at the auction and see what we bid on. And if she's got enough money to pay that much for the knives, she's certainly got the resources to bribe someone to learn of our interest in the auction."

"So she wants something of us," Kalanath said, pushing his plate away. "If it is a job, why does she not ask to hire us?"

"Then it's not a job," Dianthe said. "Or, worse, it's a job she knows we wouldn't take without the right incentive."

"I really don't like this," Sienne said. "She probably doesn't know why we want the knife, but what if she does?"

"It doesn't matter," Alaric said. "It's a private matter, but it's not secret. We aren't doing anything illegal in trying to discover this ritual. Even if she found out I'm Sassaven, what could she do with that?"

Sienne was sure Alaric wasn't nearly so carefree as he sounded. The Sassaven were a magical race able to take the form of horses or, in Alaric's case, an enormous unicorn, and Alaric had no desire for anyone to find this out. But she said, "I suppose that's true."

"Then we'll just have to see what she wants," Alaric said, standing and clearing his plate. "Why does Leofus want a miniature table?"

Sienne had nearly forgotten the one thing they'd gotten from the auction. "It's just shrunk. Will you help me swap them out?"

"That sounds like a signal for the rest of us to clear out," Dianthe said, taking her own plate to the sink and rinsing it. "I'll be in the sitting room for a while, reading."

"That is a good idea," Kalanath said.

Perrin cleared his place, scraping what was left of his meal into the scraps bucket. It was more than a little, Sienne noticed. "I'm for an early bedtime, myself. I shall see you all upon the morrow."

When the others had gone, Alaric sat next to Sienne as she finished eating. "Something else happened," he said. "Don't think I don't know when Perrin intends to drink himself into a stupor."

"We met his father." Sienne summed up the interaction, adding, "I think Perrin drinks to forget his family. I mean, I guessed it before, but this is a strong confirmation."

Alaric sighed. "I wish he'd find some less self-destructive way of coping. I'm certain it's not what Averran expects of him."

"Me too. But how can we tell him not to be upset at what his family did to him? Alaric, he had a *wife*. Maybe he had children. Can you imagine—" She broke off.

"Imagine what?"

"I was going to say, can you imagine leaving your whole family behind, but then I remembered who I was talking to. Sorry."

Alaric smiled. "It's not the same. Perrin was kicked out. I chose to leave to save myself. If my family could have come with me, they would have."

"What family did you have? Don't answer if it's prying."

"It's not. Sassaven don't have big families. There was my mother and father, my older brother Karlen, and my younger sister Genneva. Oh, and my father's sister and her daughter. All of them were bound except Gen, and by now, she has been, too."

His gaze grew distant. "She's the one I think of when I remember what we're trying to do. She's smart, and funny and… kind of a brat, actually, willful and selfish, but not in a bad way. I know that doesn't make sense. She was just so carefree, didn't give a damn what anyone else thought. And that's all gone now, with the binding. It makes me furious to think of all that being stripped away from her."

His hand rested on the table near Sienne's plate. If she put her hand on his, that would be all right, wouldn't it? Companionable, even? Then he looked at her, and the moment passed. She made herself smile. "I hope we meet her someday."

"So do I." Alaric stood and took her plate. "Let's move the chairs out of the way."

They rearranged furniture in silence, shoving all the chairs to one side to make a big empty space around the battered old table. With Alaric behind her, Sienne read off *fit* twice, once to shrink the old table and again to enlarge the new one. Alaric picked up the old table, doll-sized now, and set it in the hallway. "I know I've seen you do it a hundred times, but I still half expect the things you shrink to spontaneously grow again."

"I felt that way the first several times I saw it done," Sienne said, picking up a chair to put it back at the new table. "*Fit* on people is so impermanent, it feels as though *fit* on objects should be the same. But I'm glad it's not. I would hate to have to keep casting it on my boots, for one."

"We'll have to ask Master Tersus what he wants done with the old table. It can't clutter up the hallway for long."

"Something else to do tomorrow." Sienne stepped back and regarded the new table. "It feels almost like a waste of our money, when we needed the knife so badly."

"One thousand is too rich for our purse."

They stood in silence for a few awkward moments, not touching, not looking at each other. Finally, Alaric said, "I think I'll turn in."

"Me, too."

Another long, awkward pause filled the space between them.

"Good night, then," Alaric said, and left the kitchen. Sienne gave him a few seconds to get halfway up the stairs, then followed.

Safely in her room, she changed into her nightdress and put her clothes away, not bothering to turn on the lamp. Her room was chilly, and again she idly wished there were a spell to heat air. She climbed into bed, pulled the blankets to her chin, and cursed herself, thoroughly and in a whisper.

Her relationship with Alaric had started out badly, with him hating all wizards because of the one that had created and enslaved his people and her resenting him for being an arrogant ass. Then he'd started to bend, and she'd come to see his good side, and before she knew it, they were friends. And if she'd left it at friendship, everything would be fine. But he was strong, and clever, and had a funny smile, and now she had trouble looking him in the eye, for fear he could read her emotions there.

What made it worse was her increasing suspicion that he wasn't indifferent to her. Those awkward silences when they were alone together, like just then in the kitchen, were awkward for both of them. He, too, never met her gaze if he could help it, and he was scrupulously careful not to touch her, even casually as he did the others. Whatever this feeling was, she was sure it wasn't unrequited.

But they were companions, comrades in arms, and she didn't know much about scrappers, but she was damn sure starting a romantic relationship with one of your companions was the kind of thing that could destroy a team. She didn't want this team destroyed. They were family, or as near to as made no difference, and nothing was worth giving that up.

But at night, alone in her room, she couldn't help thinking about how it would feel to kiss him. Whether he would kiss her back. She'd become obsessed with his hands lately, watching him cut his food or wield his sword, how much bigger they were than hers, the nails cut short and blunt, the skin pale from winter. She'd imagine him putting his hands on her waist, pulling her close, and have to get up and go for a walk through the silent house to quell the images.

It was easier when they were out on a job. Then, she would share a tent with Dianthe, whose snoring kept Sienne anchored to reality, and she and Alaric could treat each other with the bantering respect they'd fallen into over the past nine months. Sienne fell asleep hoping this woman, whoever she was, had a job for them.

————

The rain stopped falling sometime before dawn, and the sun rose in a cloudless sky, the day warmer than it had been all week. It wasn't warm enough to dispense with a cloak, but Sienne didn't feel the need to huddle into hers as she had the previous day. She trudged along behind Alaric in her accustomed place. It was the pattern they'd fallen into when they were in the wilderness, marching across country or exploring ancient ruins, Sienne and Perrin in the center surrounded by the fighters. The habit persisted even when they were back in the city and presumably unworried about being attacked. Sienne found Alaric's hulking presence comforting, particularly when it meant he broke the crowds so she didn't have to.

All of Fioretti seemed to be out enjoying the sunshine that morning. Their little party progressed slowly eastward through the city's center, passing the famous Fiorettan market with its hundreds of semi-permanent stalls selling everything anyone might want, pausing briefly for Dianthe to throw a coin into the avatar Kitane's fountain. The great warrior's statue stood atop a pedestal rising from the center of the fountain, depicted in her moment of triumph over the Aldmerrow rebels, taking the young heir to the Ansorjan throne to safety. No statue would show her as she was only hours later, sacrificing herself for the prince's freedom; her enemies had killed and dismembered her, and while her worshippers swore by the various parts of her body, no one wanted to see a statue of a pile of body parts.

The address the young woman had given them took them to a neighborhood that, while not precisely run-down, had clearly seen better days. Palatial homes in need of fresh paint or repair to chipped marble stood far too close together, lacking the wide lawns and gardens popular among the wealthy of Fioretti. The one they'd been directed to looked as if a hundred stonemasons had worked a hundred days to produce a confection of carved arches and fluted pillars, all of which were cracked, some of which had fallen down. Cherubs with fat faces and chubby arms simpered over the front doors, which were heavy oak carved with grapes and grape leaves twining around gamboling lambs. Kalanath made a face when he saw it. "God's creature should not be mocked."

"What, lambs?" Perrin said.

"Sheep are sacred to God. We do not depict them in art. I know it is different here." Kalanath still looked like he'd eaten something nasty.

There was no bell pull. Alaric knocked on the door. "I'm beginning to wonder about this woman's wealth. How could she afford a thousand lari for knives when this place looks like it's about to come down around us?"

Both halves of the door creaked open. An elderly man in very old-fashioned clothes, blousy short pants over black hose and a full-sleeved linen shirt constrained by a brocade jerkin, stood there. He seemed unsurprised to see them, even though Alaric, irritated by the woman's behavior, had rousted everyone early for this meeting. "Please enter," he said, his voice as creaky as the door.

The dark hall beyond the entrance smelled of cheap tallow candles and the more biting scent of fresh polish. Sienne stopped to let her eyes adjust to the darkness, relieved only by sunlight coming through small round windows near the high ceiling. There were candles in tall wrought iron stands lining the hall, but they were unlit. Most of them had burned down to about an inch of dribbling yellow wax. Portraits of dour men and women in the style of a hundred years before glowered down at them. Something about the previous century had made everyone glum, at least as far as their portraits revealed.

"If you would follow me," the old man creaked, gesturing down the hall. Once more in the middle of their group, Sienne followed him to an uncarpeted staircase with balusters as ornately carved as the front door. The treads were worn pale in the middle and groaned softly under Alaric's weight. Sienne felt like tiptoeing along after him. A dread hush filled the whole place, as if it were a mausoleum and not someone's ancestral home. Someone who might well already be interred here.

3

The stairs ended at another hall, this one more brightly lit, but only because there were more and larger windows lining it near the ceiling. Doors with brightly-painted fanciful carvings opened off the hall, giving it a festive appearance completely at odds with the ground floor. The old man led them to a door halfway down the hall and opened it. "My lady, your... guests," he said, bowing.

Sienne once again had to wait for her eyes to adjust, but this time it was because the room was blindingly bright, the walls painted stark white, the furnishings picked out with gilt, the cushions upholstered in pale gold brocade. It was also cold. A fire was laid in the white hearth but not lit, and two windows taller than Alaric stood open, letting in the brisk morning air of early first summer. She suppressed a shiver and turned her attention to the young woman standing near the fireplace, watching them.

The day before, she'd been dressed casually in shirt and trousers. Today, she wore a morning dress with a long straight skirt and embroidered bodice, so modern she made her old-fashioned surroundings seem like the set of a historical drama. Her mouse-colored hair still fell loose to her waist, but was bound back from her face with a fillet of gold wire like the skeleton of a crown. Cold still reddened the tip of her thin nose. She regarded them dispassionately, as if they were all strangers meeting on foreign soil for unrelated reasons.

No one spoke for a few moments. Sienne was sure Alaric was assessing the room and the woman, working out a plan of attack. Who would speak first, and give up the high ground?

Finally, the young woman said, "I won't thank you for coming. I know you resent the situation."

"What do you want?" Alaric said.

Good, Sienne thought, *no wasted pleasantries.*

"This is about what you want," the young woman said. She walked to a table beneath one of the open windows. A breeze blew her hair into tangles, but she ignored it, opening a drawer in the table and removing a heavy leather bag. She brought it to one of the brocade sofas, opened it, and removed a knife in a tooled leather sheath. Sienne recognized it as one of the knives from the lot they'd bid on.

"A knife," Alaric said. "You think we want that?"

"Don't play the fool with me. I know you're smarter than you let on." The woman dropped the knife back into the bag. "I don't know why these knives are important to you, and I don't care. I'll let you have them if you accomplish a task for me." Her thin voice hardened. "If you don't, I'll throw them into the sea and they'll be lost to you."

"We don't respond to threats," Alaric said.

"That's not a threat. That's just how it's going to be."

Alaric took a step toward her. "We could take those knives and leave. You and that old man couldn't stop us."

"But you won't. That's not how you operate." The woman seemed unmoved by his looming menace. "I did my research. Your team is known for its integrity. Even your thief isn't a thief. So I know you won't steal from me, just like you won't hurt me."

After months of riding or walking directly behind him, Sienne could read the tension in Alaric's back as clearly as she could his face. She knew the moment when he decided to take the bait. "Show us the lot. I want to be sure you're not cheating us. We may have integrity, but we're not stupid."

The young woman shook the bag out. Five ritual knives lay scattered on the sofa. They looked like the right ones, though Sienne didn't know which of the five was the one they wanted. Alaric nodded. "What task?"

The young woman gathered up the knives and put the bag back in the drawer before she spoke. "My name is Tonia Figlari. My mother was Odela Figlari, and my grandfather was Stephanas Figlari. His father was Duke Marlen Figlari. Do you know the name?"

They all shook their heads.

"He was duke of a small holding north of Fioretti, nearly to the border. This was some eighty years ago. The Figlaris ruled for eighty years before that. It was, as I said, small, but successful. Until they had a few bad years in a row. Crops failed, the grape harvest was small and the wine bitter, and people began to starve. My great-grandfather had the resources to move everyone south, but at the cost of his dukedom. He settled with his household in Fioretti—in this house. It's not our ancestral house, but we own it outright."

Dianthe coughed and concealed it with her hand. Sienne couldn't see her face, but Tonia smiled wryly. "We are not impoverished, however it may look from the outside," she said. "My family never thought of this place as anything but temporary. It was always my great-grandfather's intent to return to the Figlari dukedom when the drought was over. But he was ill, and my grandfather cared more for pleasurable living than his responsibilities. It was my mother who kept alive the dream of regaining our title and lands. She died two winters ago. And now it's down to me.

"But we had—have—enemies. A family intent on seeing us reduced to hangers-on at court, landless and nameless. My great-grandfather failed to bring with him proofs of our possession, and this family, the Marchenas, have blocked our application to the king to see our title restored. They say I am lying about being a Figlari, even though everyone knows who I am. The king, whose friend Lusio Marchena is, continues to put off a final decision on the matter. He does not quite dare to deny me, but he will not restore my title."

"And you're going to tell us where we fit into your plan," Alaric said.

"The first Figlari duke commissioned an artifact," Tonia said, "a stone carving of a falcon, which is the emblem of our family. According to my mother, who was told the story by her grandfather, it was made to respond in some way to anyone of the Figlari blood. Great-grandfather was coy with the details, sometimes saying it cried out in a falcon's voice when a Figlari touched it, other times that it would speak the name of the Figlari aloud. But he was adamant that it was proof of our title."

"That's not possible," Sienne said. "The knowledge of the making of artifacts was lost in the wars four hundred years ago. Your ancestors took possession of the land less than two hundred years ago. There's no way an artifact could be made for them."

"It wasn't made for them. The artifact was... repurposed, I suppose you could call it. Great-grandfather told my mother the family legend was that it originally said something else, in response to some other stimulus. He didn't know how the Figlaris attuned it to themselves, but he did know they took the falcon as their emblem because of the stone, not the other way around. At any rate, the stone falcon belongs to the Figlaris now, and there are records of it in the official annals of the court. If I could bring it before the king and have it declare my identity, the king would have no choice but to recognize me as the duchess of Figlari."

"That is rather a stretch, my lady," Perrin said. "I can think of more than one way in which your enemies might yet scotch your plan."

Two pink spots appeared high on Tonia's thin cheeks. "I've spent the last year building support for myself among the nobles of the king's court. Their support, added to the witness of the artifact, will be enough. But I need the artifact."

"And you want us to get it," Alaric said. "Why us? This is a straightforward retrieval, not an exploration of an ancient ruin."

"No one who isn't a scrapper is willing to go that far north. It's not dangerous, but it is almost in the Empty Lands and people are superstitious. And the scrapper teams I've approached won't touch it because it *isn't* an ancient ruin, and there's no chance of salvage. Which leaves you."

"And you're not above a spot of blackmail," Dianthe said.

"It's not blackmail," Tonia said. "It's an exchange of favors. I'll even pay your expenses. You just have to bring the stone back, and you get your knives."

"I do not know the word that is when someone makes you do something you do not want, but I dislike it no matter the word," Kalanath said, gripping his staff tightly.

"Manipulation," Perrin said, "and I dislike it just as much."

Sienne watched Tonia closely. Her lips were set in a mulish line, but her gaze flicked from one of them to another, restlessly, and she had her fingers wound into the fabric of her skirt, twisting it tightly. Sienne knew desperation when she saw it. Despite herself, she felt the beginnings of pity for the young woman. Sienne had once been desperate, and if Dianthe hadn't shown up at just the right time, her life would be very different right now.

"How big is the stone?" she asked, overriding Alaric, who was about to speak.

"It's a circle roughly four feet across," Tonia said. "It's not a statue of a falcon, it's more of a plaque with the bird carved into it, like a bas-relief."

"So it's set into a wall?"

"Somewhere in the castle overlooking the village. I don't know more than that."

Sienne turned to Alaric. "I can't cast *fit* on magical things. It will be difficult to carry out, something that size."

Alaric glared. She guessed he was going to have some irritated things to say to her once they got home, starting with *I'm supposed to do the negotiating*. "I'm sure we can figure something out," he said instead. "This won't be a cheap expedition."

"I have plenty of money," Tonia said. "I take it we have a deal."

Alaric cast one more annoyed look at Sienne. "We do," he said. "Do you have a map? Directions? Once we know how long it will take, I can tell you how much it will cost. But we'll need pack animals, horses, supplies... as I said, it won't be cheap."

"Haritt will see to it," Tonia said. She pulled a bell rope dangling by the fire. "I know you're not interested, but you have my thanks."

"You're right. We're not interested," Alaric said.

The old man pushed open the door. "Haritt, provide these people with my great-grandfather's map," Tonia said. "Bring your requests to him, and he'll see to payment."

Haritt bowed to the room in general, and gestured for Alaric to precede him out the door. The meeting was over. Sienne risked a glance over her shoulder at Tonia, but the young woman had turned away and was standing beside the window, the cold wind blowing her hair about her face.

Instead of descending the stairs, Haritt led them to a room across the hall. It was equally bright, but warmer due to the windows being firmly shut. Sienne, who ended up next to one, felt a chilly draft blowing through a gap in the frame and shivered. If Tonia had so much money, why didn't she sell this place, which she'd implied had no sentimental meaning, and buy something newer and warmer? She thought of her parents' ducal home in Beneddo, how the chimneys smoked no matter how many times they were repaired. Some things could only be explained by inertia.

Haritt opened a wide, shallow drawer in a cabinet next to the door and withdrew a large sheet of paper. "You may look at this and any other maps you choose, but do not remove them from this room. They are very old and very fragile."

"I'll try not to crush them," Alaric said, rolling his eyes. Sienne watched him accept the map from Haritt and carry it to a table near the center of the room. His hands, so large and yet so agile—Sienne made herself stop looking at his hands. She moved with the others to join Alaric at the table.

The map was sepia with age, its lines faded, but still legible. It depicted an area bounded on the east by mountains and on the north by forest, dotted with villages but not showing any dukedoms or large cities. Sienne didn't recognize any of the names.

"The northern end of the Bramantus Mountains," Dianthe said, pointing but not touching the ancient map. "This isn't to scale, if that's meant to be the Cloud-tops Forest."

"It's close enough," Alaric said. "With a modern map, we should be able to determine Figlari's actual location. Or close enough that a blessing will get us there."

"We should not rely too heavily on blessings," Perrin said. "Remember that Averran considers the search a path to holiness."

"I was thinking we should rely on Averran's desire for us not to be hopelessly lost," Alaric said. "We don't have to be led straight there. A couple of nudges will be sufficient."

"So how far is it?" Kalanath said.

"We'll be at least eight days on the road, with some of that cross-country," Dianthe said, measuring with her fingers. "This map doesn't show Fioretti, so I can't be more specific than that. Eight days, probably more like ten."

Alaric had stepped away and was counting off something on his fingers, his lips moving soundlessly. Sienne didn't interrupt. He was probably still annoyed with her, and better she didn't remind him of her presence and distract him from planning. "Two hundred lari," he told Haritt. "For expenses. We'll return what we don't use."

"Unnecessary," Haritt said.

"Not to us," Alaric said.

Haritt raised an eyebrow. "One moment," he said, and left the room.

Alaric turned on Sienne. "I'm supposed to do the negotiating," he said.

"I know, but didn't you see how close she was to breaking? We were going to take the job. I just didn't want you to make her cry."

"I don't make women cry. And if I did, she deserved it."

"Probably, but..." Sienne faltered. "I'm sorry. I shouldn't have over-stepped."

Alaric scowled. "That's right, I... damn it, stop giving me that look."

"What look?"

"The 'Alaric killed my puppy' look."

"I have no idea what you're talking about."

"You do trade on your big eyes a lot, Sienne," Dianthe said. "It doesn't work on me because I have sisters."

"I, on the other hand, dread having it turned on me when supper is over and it is not my turn to wash up," Perrin said.

"I do not know this look," Kalanath said, "unless it is the one you use when you do not want to do a thing and I am available."

"I do *not* do any such thing!" Sienne exclaimed. The corner of Alaric's mouth twitched in a smile so comical it startled a laugh out of her. "I just—you're all mad, that's all, utterly mad. Do you really think I'm so manipulative?"

"Not that," Dianthe said. "Just efficient at using your assets. If we thought you were doing it on purpose, we'd have said something earlier."

"Now I can't look at any of you." Sienne laughed again. "I had no idea I had such power. Good thing enchantment is forbidden, or I might have made that look a weapon."

"I thought enchantment was impossible," Dianthe said.

"No, just totally forbidden. Nobody is allowed to teach the charm language, and if you're caught with so much as a single charm in your spellbook, you're stripped of your book and severely punished."

"So not forbidden the way necromancy is," Alaric said.

"No. Necromancy is evil, but it doesn't take a person's free will. I've heard there are charm spells that don't—there are stories of one that puts people to sleep, for example—but charm is so dangerous there aren't any exceptions made for those few."

"I approve of that," Alaric said. Sienne nodded. The wizard who had created and enslaved Alaric's people almost certainly had used charm spells to do it.

The door opened. "Two hundred lari," Haritt said, extending a purse to Alaric. Alaric took it without counting it. "I will show you the door," Haritt added.

Alaric muttered something under his breath, but followed Haritt, the rest of them trailing along behind. Descending the stairs into darkness felt like the sun setting. Sienne was grateful when they were outside and moving rapidly away from the crumbling old house.

"Now what?" she said.

Alaric opened the purse and took out a handful of coins, which he put into his belt pouch. "Perrin and I will negotiate for horses," he said. "We'll be traveling through civilized country for most of this, and the faster we get there, the sooner we can return." He handed the purse to Dianthe. "The rest of you—shopping. Standard equipment."

"We don't need two hundred lari to outfit ourselves for a few weeks' journey through civilization," Dianthe protested.

"No, but we do need new tents, and I don't feel bad about getting Tonia Figlari to pay for those. If I judge that map correctly, we'll be sleeping rough at least four nights, and it rains a lot this time of year. And if you can find the appropriate maps, buy those too." Alaric let out a deep breath. "Plan on leaving tomorrow morning. I want this over with as fast as possible."

The others nodded. Sienne looked back over her shoulder at the ruined house as they walked away. A pale blotch at one of the upper windows might have been Tonia, watching them go. Sienne's moment of sympathy for the young woman disappeared. They might be traveling mostly through civilized territory, but scrapping was dangerous work, and this girl had manipulated them into this job without a single thought that they could be risking their lives. Sienne might bat her eyelashes, or whatever it was this "look" of hers did, but she'd never be so callous of other people. And for what? Some ducal title to a place most of the way to the Empty Lands? Sienne, daughter of a duke, had no illusions about the value of a noble title—but then she'd left hers behind months ago, so clearly she didn't value it the way Tonia did hers. Even so, rank wasn't nearly as important as people's lives, or shouldn't be.

She turned away and followed Dianthe and Kalanath toward the market. Normally, she was excited at this point, the start of a new job. At the moment, all she felt was a bitter taste in her mouth.

4

Sienne believed she was, if not exactly an experienced scrapper, at least no longer a novice after nine months of expeditions. True, work had slacked off during winter, but she now had thirteen jobs under her belt and knew what to expect. At least, she'd thought so that morning. By evening, she'd learned that not all jobs were the same, that traveling along well-established roads was substantially different from going cross country, and that sunset looked very different when the day ended at an inn and not in a leaky tent. Though if Dianthe had done her job right, the new tents didn't leak. A bed, then, and not a bedroll on the hard ground. Sienne wasn't sure how she felt about the difference.

She handed her horse's reins over to a stable hand and removed her saddle bags, draping them over one arm. Beside her, Kalanath dismounted with a stagger before catching his balance. They hadn't ridden much over the last nine months, but even experience wasn't going to get him to love horses.

The inn's yard was damp, but not muddy, thanks to a light sprinkle of rain that had fallen mid-afternoon. Warm light made the stables, painted white, glow in the evening dusk. The inn itself, three stories tall and half-timbered in the latest style, blazed with hundreds of magical lights in glass bulbs, frosted from the magic that made them invulnerable. Laughter, and the sound of a fiddle, drifted toward them from the inn's open front door.

"Too loud for you?" Sienne murmured to Kalanath.

He shrugged. "It is one night. We are in a large town and this is what there is. It is simply not what I would choose to live in." His eyes looked glassy with tiredness, and he moved as if he ached.

"Me neither, really. I'm so used to the quiet of Master Tersus's house, this is rather overwhelming."

"Sorry about that," Alaric said, coming up behind them and startling Sienne. She had no idea how someone his size managed to move so quietly. "There's some sort of first summer festival going on tomorrow and there aren't many places available. I got us two rooms on the top floor, well away from the entertainment, and meals are included."

"That's fine," Sienne said. "It's so strange to end the day at an inn instead of a nice quiet camp."

"I hope you're not looking forward to that nice quiet camp too much, because it will be at least a week before we set off into the wilderness." Alaric beckoned to Dianthe and Perrin to join them. "Personally, I like the change of pace and a meal that doesn't feature some form of hard biscuit."

"I object. Hard biscuits are a staple of the scrapper's life," Dianthe said. "Staying in inns makes you soft."

"I'll remember that," Alaric said. Sienne sneaked a look at his well-muscled physique, nothing soft about it, and mentally slapped herself. That was a line of thought that went nowhere good. Then he held out a hand, startling her. "I'll take the bags upstairs. You all go in and get us some food."

A pair of young men, exiting the inn as they approached, saluted them with beery good cheer, and one of them held the door open. The warmth of a good fire and dozens of bodies all packed into a small place struck Sienne like heat coming off a true summer street. The taproom smelled of roast chicken, of the tang of warm beer and the mustiness of those same dozens of bodies, all mingled together with the smoky odor of a wood fire burning merrily against the dark night. Trestle tables overflowing with diners lined the long room, and serving girls dressed in identical blue dresses and white aprons moved busily from table to bar and from bar to kitchen door.

Dianthe pushed her way through the crowd to a spot at one of the tables. It was closer to the fire than Sienne liked, which was probably why it was unoccupied. She took a seat on the bench and enjoyed the fire's warmth on her back. Soon enough it would be uncomfortable, but for now it soaked into her bones and made her appreciate the fact that it wasn't outdoors.

"Four of you?" a serving girl shouted. Dianthe shook her head, holding up five fingers. "Beer, wine, or brandy? We're all out of stout," she added.

"Brandy, I beg of you," Perrin said.

"Beer for the rest of us," Dianthe said. Sienne was in the mood for wine, but said nothing. Something to relax her tired muscles at the end of a long day was what she wanted, and it didn't really matter what.

The serving girl—she was in her late thirties, so more like serving woman—nodded and sidled away past a couple of men standing between her and the bar, passing Alaric coming toward them. He took a seat, forcing two men to edge away to give him room.

"You said there was some kind of festival happening tomorrow?" Dianthe said, then repeated herself more loudly as the last of her words were swallowed up by loud cheering from the other side of the taproom.

"I didn't get the details. Something celebrating the beginning of first summer," Alaric said. "Most of the people here are traveling performers or merchants, getting in out of the cold. There are far more of them camped over the fields, the stable mistress said."

"Unfortunate that we cannot stay to see their performances, or sample their wares," Perrin said.

The sound of a violin curled out across the room. "We will see a performance now, I think," Kalanath said, turning to look in that direction.

Sienne could barely see the violinist, who was male and had long dark hair pulled back from a very handsome face. His eyes were closed as he sent the bow gliding across the strings, sending up a mournful keen that made her heart ache. "He's good," she said.

"Better than this crowd will appreciate, that's sure," Alaric said. He leaned back for the serving woman to set a platter with a whole roast chicken in front of him. "What are you four going to eat?" he joked, picking up a knife and carving meat away from the bone.

"We'll need more than one of those," Dianthe said to the serving woman, who laid out four mugs and a small glass before them and turned away. Perrin, to Sienne's relief, sipped his brandy rather than tossing it back in one gulp. This must be a good day. She accepted a chicken leg, her favorite piece, and bit into it happily. The crisp skin crunched between her teeth, and juices dripped down her chin. How nice to end the day with a meal with friends who didn't comment on her greasy face.

The crowd shifted, giving her a better view of the performer. He was slim but broad-shouldered, dressed in a brightly-embroidered vest over a pale green shirt, with shining black boots that came to his thighs. He put his whole body into his performance, looking as if he were wresting the notes bodily from his instrument. Sienne watched in fascination. She wiped her chin with her handkerchief and took a drink of beer. It wasn't very good.

She set her mug down and applauded as the violinist ended his song with a swooping note and a deep bow. As he rose, his eyes met hers, and he smiled, an intimate expression that made Sienne uncomfortable in its open appraisal of her. It had been a long time since anyone, and by anyone she meant her ex-lover Rance, now her sister's husband, had looked at her that way.

She smiled politely and turned away, taking another bite out of her chicken leg. The others continued to eat in appreciative silence. The violinist struck up another song, this one with lyrics many of the listeners knew. The singing wasn't melodious, but it was enthusiastic, and Sienne found herself tapping her toe along with the rhythm. She risked a glance at the violinist, who had his eyes closed again. She relaxed. She didn't need to be stared at by a stranger.

She finished off her chicken and put the bone on the platter with the others. Alaric was making inroads on the second roast chicken. Dianthe had finished and was leaning back facing the fire, eyes closed, cradling her mug in both hands. Kalanath held his staff awkwardly, trying to keep it out of the way of anyone passing by. Sienne didn't bother suggesting he lean it up against the wall. He still looked incredibly weary, and he'd only picked at his food. Perrin had finished his brandy and was trying to catch the eye of a serving girl, probably for seconds. It was as if they had their own peaceful island in the middle of the chaos, nobody needing to say anything. If the fire weren't becoming unpleasantly hot, it would have been a perfect moment.

Sienne turned to face the fire as Dianthe was. The fireplace was big enough for a sizable log or two, big enough that she could lie down in it if it weren't full of wood. Her skin felt parched after only a minute, and her nostrils felt dried out, making breathing uncomfortable. "I'm going to take a walk," she said, standing. "Too hot."

"Be careful," Alaric said.

Sienne patted the spellbook slung by her side. She'd made the harness herself, having grown tired of carrying the book under her vest, and now it was second nature to carry it with her. "Just follow the sound of the explosions."

She made her way around the outside of the room, skirting a couple kissing intently with no apparent awareness of anyone else, and found the door, falling on it gratefully. The chill evening air slapped her whole body, and she stepped outside and breathed it in. The sky was still overcast, hiding the moon, but the magic lights illuminating the inn made the place where she stood as bright as if the moon shone in a clear sky. It was funny how comfortable the cold was by contrast to the fire, when if they'd been camping, she would be shivering and cursing it.

She stood outside until she became chilled, then went back to the taproom. The space near her friends had contracted, with people seeking out the warmth of the fire, and her seat was now occupied by a big hairy man in a merchant's smock. He was talking animatedly with Perrin, who had an untasted glass of brandy by his elbow.

She made her way to the bar and found an unoccupied seat. No one behind the bar noticed her, and she thought about trying to attract their attention, but the noise and warmth made her uninterested in more of the second-rate beer. Instead, she sat and watched the performers. The violinist had vanished, replaced by a juggler who had a trained monkey, also a juggler. Sienne didn't care for animal acts, but the monkey was cute, dressed in short pants and a little vest and making faces at the audience. The monkey sat on its master's head and tossed marbles in a loop. Much as she admired its skill, she couldn't help imagining the man's consternation if the monkey defecated on him.

A hand holding a wine glass came into her range of vision. "You look as if you could use some company," the violinist said. "Dare I hope you'll share a drink with me?" His accent was unfamiliar, though he looked like any Rafellish man—any extremely handsome Rafellish man, that is.

Automatically, Sienne took the glass. The violinist's smile was no more than friendly, making her wonder if she'd misread his earlier expression. "I was just—the beer's not very good," she stammered.

The violinist leaned against the bar next to her and sipped from his own glass. "The wine is tolerable, but I've had better. What do you think?"

Sienne took a small drink. It was warmer than she liked, and she magically chilled it before taking another sip. "It's good. You're right, though, it's not the best."

His smile broadened. "I had a feeling you were someone who appreciates quality." He held out a hand. "Aneirin."

She clasped it lightly. "Sienne."

"What a lovely name. Are you here for the festival?"

She hesitated. Should she share her business with a total stranger? "Just passing through."

"Then I consider myself fortunate to have met you, Sienne." He smiled, and now the look in his eyes was appreciative. Without think-ing, she cast a quick glance at the fireplace. Alaric was watching her, though his attention drifted elsewhere as their eyes met, as if he wasn't that interested. It irritated her, and she didn't know why. None of her other friends were looking her way. Dianthe looked as if she'd fallen asleep, though how she'd managed that with all the noise was a mystery.

"You're very talented," she managed.

He laughed. "Come, now, we can do better than this common-place talk. If we'd met at the festival, I would ask you to dance, and you would tell me all about yourself, and I would tell you great lies of my adventures. Shall we dance here next to the bar, or simply pretend we are not strangers?"

Sienne laughed. "You are outrageous."

"Merely daring. I know what I want and I go after it. And I get it." He took a step closer. "Are you from Fioretti? We were there yester-day, having made landfall in the morning."

"Landfall? Where did you take ship from?"

"Oh, so it's me we're talking about now, is it? Very well, if it will make the lady more comfortable…" Aneirin sipped his wine. "I am from Chysegar."

"Chysegar!" Sienne had heard stories of the mysterious island, but never met anyone from the reclusive place. "Then you've come a long way."

"I have not been home in some time. I've traveled a long time and met so many… interesting… people." He smiled at her, and she blushed and looked away. Aneirin's gaze and his low, seductive tone left her flustered. Part of her loved the attention. Part of her wished she knew how to dissuade him. All of her felt as if the wine were something much stronger.

"I'm really not that interesting," she heard herself say, and inwardly winced. That was the sort of thing coquettish females said to entice flattery out of their admirers.

"I disagree. I see you are a wizard, or at least I assume so." Aneirin pointed at her spellbook. "I find wizardry fascinating. What spells are you capable of? Aside from the one you have cast on my heart."

That was too absurd to take seriously. It woke Sienne up. This man simply wanted a few minutes' harmless flirtation, and that was nothing to feel flustered over. She laughed. "I'm still a beginner. Most of my training is in confusions."

"Interesting. I wish I could see some of them. Many of the performers in the troupe to which I am attached are wizards who specialize in confusions—they are most entertaining. Will you show me one?"

"Ah... not in the middle of this crowd."

He took yet another step closer, putting him close enough that his hand brushed hers. "Then somewhere more private? I have a room to myself."

And just like that, the casual flirtation disappeared, leaving Sienne in no doubt as to what he wanted. Torn between feeling flattered and wanting to slap him, she said, "I don't think so," as politely as she could manage.

"Very well," Aneirin said, stepping back. His smile never faltered. "It was a pleasure to speak with you, Sienne. Perhaps we will meet again someday."

"Good luck in your performance tomorrow," Sienne said. She gulped down the last of her wine more quickly than she'd intended. When she put her glass down, Aneirin was gone. She felt unexpectedly disappointed. True, she had no intention of having casual sex with a total stranger, but his attention had been flattering.

"More wine, miss?" the man behind the bar asked. She shook her head and stepped away from the bar. Sleep, that would be nice.

There was a second door opposite the one leading to the stable yard. Beyond it, Sienne found a dimly-lit room with a desk facing a much larger door and stairs leading up. The inn's front entrance, no doubt. A man sat behind the desk with his feet up, napping.

She was halfway up the first flight before she remembered she didn't know what room Alaric had gotten for them. Tiptoeing back down out of consideration for the sleeping man, she had her hand on the door when it opened in her face. "Hey!" she said, skipping backward.

The napping man sat up with a snort. His feet hit the floor with a sharp crack. "Guests only," he said in a dull, sleep-fogged voice.

"We're guests," Alaric said. "Sorry. I didn't know you were there," he said to Sienne.

The door had cracked her on the toe, not hard enough to hurt through her boot. "It's all right. Are you going to bed?"

"I saw you leave and realized you didn't know where to go," Alaric said. "Unless you were planning to sleep elsewhere."

She sucked in a breath. Why would he—what kind of conclusion was that to draw? Had he been watching her? "If that's what you thought, why did you follow me?" she asked, irritation sharpening her tongue.

Alaric's eyes narrowed. "You haven't got the sense of a newborn lamb. Don't you know better than to drink something a stranger gives you? How do you know he wasn't trying to drug you?"

So he *had* been watching. It made her angry, because, as he said it, she knew he was right—Aneirin might have intended anything. Embarrassed at her stupidity, she said, "That's suspicious even for you, don't you think? I'm perfectly capable of taking care of myself."

"I don't think it's unreasonable for me to be concerned about my companions' well-being."

"Is that what this is? Concern?" How had this conversation turned into a fight? She didn't even know what she'd meant by that.

Alaric's jaw tightened. "Forget it," he said. "Our rooms are the second and third on the right after you turn right from the stairs. Third floor. You'll see your bags."

He turned, pulling open the door. Sienne opened her mouth to apologize—but what did she have to apologize for? *He* was the one who'd been presumptuous. She made herself breathe slowly and willed away the angry heat in her cheeks as the door closed behind him.

"Don't worry," the man behind the desk said.

"Excuse me?" Sienne had forgotten he was there, and now her cheeks went red again at the thought someone had witnessed that.

"He'll be back," the man said. "A little kiss and a cuddle and your fight will be forgotten."

"He's not—" Sienne shut her mouth. She felt ready to burst into embarrassed flame. In silence, she trod up the stairs to the third floor.

She found her room without any mistakes. Kindling the lamp, she sat on one of the three beds and stared at the window, which was small and square and not made to open. The walls were painted a soft blue, and there was an oval rug in front of the door. Alaric must have paid extra to guarantee she and Dianthe wouldn't share the room with a stranger.

Thinking of him made her angry all over again. Why would he think she might have agreed to sleep with a total stranger? That said terrible things about his estimation of her character. Or was he... he'd been watching long enough to see Aneirin hand her the wine glass; maybe he was jealous. No, that was ridiculous.

Sienne flung herself backward on the bed and groaned. This... whatever it was... between them couldn't go on. A romance between companions could destroy a team, but so could unresolved tension, and she was feeling incredibly tense. She ought to say something, but the idea made her cringe. Where she came from, it was the man's job to speak first, and a woman who made advances was unfeminine. It was stupid, she knew, but it was a conditioning she couldn't break. Even if all she had to do was get him alone and kiss him breathless. Even if she was pretty sure he wouldn't rebuff her.

Alaric had draped her saddlebags over the end of the bed. She undressed and put on her nightdress. Once they were out in the wilderness, she'd sleep in her clothes, but there was no point doing that while they were still in civilized country. Then she stood at the window and looked out over the commons the inn fronted on. Lights gleamed there too, specks of lanterns and the larger glows of camp-fires. In Sienne's home dukedom of Beneddo, they had fairgrounds like these, where twice a year festivals were held. She'd loved them as a child, and then she'd been sent to the dukedom of Stravanus for fostering, and when she came back, nothing was the same. Or maybe it was just that she'd changed. She shook her head and turned away.

She turned out the lamp and lay in bed, staring up at the ceiling, and tried not to think about the fight. She shouldn't have let him provoke her. She should have remained calm. But he'd as much as suggested she had loose morals… or maybe that was the sort of thing women who weren't noble born did, and no one judged them for it. It didn't matter. He'd interfered—all right, so he had good intentions, but for all she was a babe in arms when it came to scrapping, she was twenty-four years old, damn it, and had been in charge of her own life for years. And she didn't need a six-foot-seven Sassaven scrapper watching out for her. Even if the idea made her tremble with excitement.

She heard the door open and rolled on her side before whoever it was entered. "Sienne?" Dianthe whispered. The door shut, and Sienne heard Dianthe moving around, shuffling into her nightdress and slipping between the covers. There was silence. Sienne rolled onto her back again. She was just relaxing into sleep when Dianthe said, "He doesn't want any of us to be hurt."

"I can take care of myself," Sienne said.

"I know. He knows. It's just who he is."

"Then who he is needs to be less of a jackass." That was too harsh. Sienne sighed. "I didn't mean that."

"I know." More silence, as if Dianthe were trying to marshal the right words. Finally, she said, "Good night."

"Good night," Sienne said. She lay awake for an hour, replaying the argument with Alaric and wishing she'd said anything but what she had.

5

Sienne went down for breakfast the next morning before Dianthe woke. She'd had a restless night and now she wanted to eat and be on the road and away from this inn and all its unpleasant associations. The taproom was half-full of patrons eating sausages and fried eggs, apparently all that was on offer. Sienne sat at the bar rather than at a table, reasoning that people were less likely to want to converse with her if she didn't have empty seats on both sides. The sausage was greasy, the eggs overcooked, and the meal weighed heavily on her stomach, but she ate with determination, not much caring if it was good food so long as it filled her.

"*Coffee*," Perrin said to the man behind the bar, slipping in to stand next to her. "This is far too early for anyone to be awake, let alone alert, and I do not see how you manage to stomach such greasy fare."

"It's just food," Sienne said. She didn't want her bad mood to afflict Perrin, who hadn't done anything wrong. She edged her stool to the side to make room for him. "Why are you up so early?"

"Kalanath is ill," Perrin said, accepting a hot mug of coffee and waving away the cream pitcher, "and I chose not to disturb him with my presence."

"Ill? What's wrong?"

"Nothing more than a cough and an ague, I think. I intend to wake fully and pray to Averran to see if there is anything he might do for our companion."

Sienne pushed her plate away. "I'll go up. I take it we're not traveling today?"

"No, I think not. Alaric said we should take turns sitting with him, so you might inquire as to his treatment."

Sienne felt a brief annoyance that she quashed. She was used to Alaric taking charge, welcomed it even, so why did it bother her now? The remnants of their argument, no doubt. "I'll tell Dianthe. She'll want her coffee, too."

She knocked quietly at the door next to hers. It opened after a moment. "Did Perrin find you?" Alaric said. He looked as if he'd slept well, which irritated her further.

"He said Kalanath is ill," she said.

"Just a cough and a fever, but I don't think he should ride. Better to have a day of rest." Alaric held the door wider so she could enter.

Kalanath slept, but restlessly. He was flushed, and his dark red hair was damp with sweat. His breathing was a little too heavy, which worried Sienne, though she knew nothing about illness or whether this was serious. Her irritation with Alaric fled in the face of his calmness. She'd never been so grateful to have him around.

Alaric walked across to stand by Kalanath's side. "We can take turns sitting with him, so he's not alone, but... you could go to the festival, if you want, when you're not up here." He had his attention on the sleeping Kalanath, but his voice sounded too casual, as if what he was saying was at odds with what he meant.

"All right," she heard herself say, "but maybe we shouldn't go alone. You should go, too."

She focused on Kalanath's face so she didn't have to see what Alaric thought of her suggestion. "Maybe," he finally said. "Sienne—"

The door opened. "Is Kalanath ill?" Dianthe said. "What a start to this expedition! Alaric, go have breakfast. I'll take care of things here. Sienne, do you have any experience with nursing?"

"None," Sienne said, suppressing an irrational feeling of irritation at Dianthe's interruption.

"Well, it's not hard, I'll show you what to do. Alaric, go." Dianthe laid a hand on Kalanath's forehead. "It's not much of a fever, but he needs rest. Sienne, would you ask the kitchen for a pitcher and fill it with water? And if you could cool it, that would be good."

"All right. I'm glad you know what you're doing."

Sienne followed Alaric out of the room and down the stairs. "It's a good idea," Alaric said, confusing Sienne. "Not going to the festival alone. Take Perrin."

"Or you," Sienne said.

Alaric took a seat at the bar and waved to the barkeep. "Or me," he finally said, but he didn't sound enthusiastic. Sienne asked for a pitcher of water and fled with it upstairs. She worked the magic that cooled water as she trod the steps, wishing she knew what Alaric was thinking. Or, failing that, her own heart.

In the end, she went to the festival with Dianthe. They spent the morning watching Kalanath, bathing his forehead and giving him sips of water when he woke. Mid-morning, Perrin returned to invoke a healing blessing, and by noon, Kalanath was awake and lucid. Alaric commanded the women to get out of the sickroom and give themselves a rest. Sienne didn't need the urging.

They strolled across the road along the well-trodden path made by hundreds of other festival-goers. Colorful tents rose up on all sides, with brightly dressed men and women calling out to passersby to stop and sample their wares or view their performances. The air was filled with a million delicious aromas and the sound of laughter and music, and the fresh air blew away the funk of the sickroom and left Sienne feeling invigorated.

She told herself she wasn't looking for Aneirin when she glanced into every performer's tent, but when she heard the sound of his violin, she wandered toward it as if drawn by an invisible string. There was a crowd around his tent, and she felt unexpectedly awkward about pushing through to the front, so she stayed at the back and just listened. The music tugged at her heart, making her long to be on the road and headed for adventure. She didn't know the song, but it sounded so familiar she almost felt she could put words to it.

"He's very good," Dianthe said. "Why didn't you sleep with him?"

"*Dianthe!*"

"I'm serious. It was obvious he wanted to."

"That is *not* something I'm comfortable with! He's a total stranger, and I don't—I want more than just casual sex."

"That makes sense."

Dianthe's pragmatism made Sienne's head spin. She didn't think she'd ever be able to have that kind of attitude about sex, as if it was just something you did, like buying roasted chestnuts at a stall in the market or choosing a blue shirt over a red one.

"I wouldn't have either," Dianthe said, startling Sienne again. "I mean, if I didn't have Denys, I still wouldn't have. But most scrappers...the lives we lead, a lot of scrappers take intimacy where they can find it. Nobody would think less of you for taking that player up on his offer."

"*I* would," Sienne said.

The music came to an end. "Yes, you would," Dianthe said. "Let's go look at the crafters. Sometimes you can find the most unusual things at these fairs."

They wandered the crafters' booths, where Dianthe considered, but didn't buy, a bracelet, and ended up at another set of tents, these quieter. Sienne realized why when she passed the first and saw a woman seated cross-legged on a cushion, speaking in a low but intense voice. Traveling storytellers. Her steps slowed. She loved storytelling, no matter the story. It was almost better than reading.

"Here, this one's just starting," Dianthe said, tugging on Sienne's arm. The tent was big enough to fit fifty people, but was only half full. A woman wearing a bright pink dress with a lemon-yellow cloak over it stood at the door to the tent, holding a hat with a scattering of coins at the bottom. As Sienne dropped her coins into the hat, the sunlight dimmed, and she glanced up to see clouds moving in to cover the sun. Rain would spoil so many of the displays. She entered the tent and found a seat on one of the benches. Dianthe followed her.

"—not for the faint of heart," the storyteller was saying. She was dressed all in white, from the baggy cap with a white plume to the stack-heeled boots that laced up the side. In the dimness, she seemed to glow as if lit from within. "Those who've seen the carvers and lived to tell about it are rare indeed, for the carvers take prisoners and never let them go. Let my words be a caution to you, travelers." Her gaze rested on Sienne and seemed to look through her, identify her as a scrapper, and demand her attention. Sienne leaned forward. True stories were the best kind.

"There was once a man," the storyteller said, "who claimed to fear no one and nothing. From his youth, his daring deeds were legendary. This man, who the stories say was named Isidorus, traveled the land, fighting evil wherever he found it. It was Isidorus who challenged the were-lord of Bramantus and forced that creature and all his kin to abandon their foothold in Rafellin. It was Isidorus who guided the men of Tagliaveno in building the sea-wall that protected that dukedom from a wave of water fifty feet tall. And it was Isidorus who brought the rains to Seravano and broke the three year drought. These are only the least of the deeds of Isidorus.

"Great Isidorus had a beautiful wife named Laurea, who lived with their children, two boys and a girl, in a village near Beneddo. They should have been content, but Laurea was dissatisfied. 'My lord husband,' she said, 'you are never home, and when you are home, your heart is out on the road. Your children and I deserve better. Take us with you on your journeys.'"

The storyteller took a sip from a metal cup near her elbow. "Isidorus refused. He knew well how dangerous his journeys were, and he could not bear the thought of taking his beloved wife and children into that danger. But Laurea would not be mollified. Every time Isidorus returned home, she repeated her plea, and every time, he denied her.

"Laurea's sorrow at being repeatedly abandoned by her husband soon caused her to waste away, until one day Isidorus returned home and was shocked to see his beautiful wife a shell of her former self. Confronted by the reality that she might die from his rejection, Isidorus agreed that she and their children should journey with him."

Dianthe snorted. "Manipulative wench," she whispered. Sienne shushed her.

"Isidorus hoped that a single journey, during which they would necessarily suffer great privations from traveling rough, would convince Laurea that she and the children were better off at home. But Laurea made no word of complaint, and after three journeys, Isidorus had to admit that she was happier with him, even in the wilderness, than at home."

The storyteller paused and swept the audience with her gaze. "If this satisfies you, I urge you to let this be the end of the story, and leave now, before tragedy strikes. For this is not a tale with a happy ending."

No one moved. The storyteller shrugged. "Then on your own heads be it. The fourth journey Isidorus took with his family sent them north of Beneddo. Isidorus had heard tell of a pack of carricks plaguing a new settlement in the Empty Lands. The man who told Isidorus about it urged him not to go. Settling in the Empty Lands is dangerous and foolhardy, and carricks were likely the least of that settlement's troubles. But Isidorus laughed, and said that the Empty Lands were no more dangerous than anywhere else. And he and his family set off for this settlement.

"They traveled into the Empty Lands a day and a night, and set up camp two days south of the settlement, in a forest eerily free of wildlife. They pitched their tent, and settled in to sleep.

"But that night, a cold wind blew, bringing with it the smell of rotting flesh. Isidorus and his family woke to the sound of wild, high shrieks surrounding their camp. Isidorus grabbed his sword and left the tent. It was the last his family ever saw of him.

"Clinging together, Laurea and her children listened as the screams of Isidorus were added to the unearthly chorus of shrieks that made a torrent of terrible noise around their tent. Then the night went still. Moments later, knives tore through the tent, shredding its fabric, and horrible shapes fell upon Laurea and her children. In the darkness, they were little more than misshapen figures, their heads and arms unnaturally long, their shoulders hunched, their breath reeking of raw meat. The moonlight struck the silver blades of their horrible knives—the knives that give them their name. Carvers."

Sienne realized her fists were clenched tight and made herself relax.

"The daughter was the first to be snatched up," the storyteller continued. "Laurea clung to her, but the carvers slashed Laurea's face and throat, and she fell lifeless over her younger son, who lay frozen with terror. The carvers tore the girl to pieces, tossing her between themselves in a gruesome game. They took the other boy next and carried him away into the darkness. The younger son, overlooked because of his mother's dead body, lay motionless until the sun rose. Then he ran south, ran day and night, pursued by the carvers until he reached a river and swam across. Then he was safe, for carvers cannot cross running water.

"Finally he reached a village outside the Empty Lands. There, near dead with terror and exposure, he told his tale to any who would listen. No one ever dared return to search for Isidorus or the boy, or to return the bodies of Laurea and her daughter. The child grew to be a man and lived many years, and before he died, he told the tale to me. That is the end of the story of Isidorus, legendary hero."

The storyteller sat back on her stool. A few people clapped. Most murmured in disappointment. The storyteller smiled. "I told you it was not a tale with a happy ending. It is a warning! The carvers are real, and they are a threat to all who would claim the Empty Lands for themselves! Remember Isidorus, and take joy in your simple lives, for there are demons in the darkness, and the carvers know no mercy."

Dianthe nudged Sienne. "Ugh, let's go," she murmured. "I want a story with a happy ending."

They stood and left the tent, passing an elderly woman arguing with the money-taker over getting her coins back. "That's not a story, that's just disgusting," she said, shaking a fist in the pink-gowned woman's face.

"No refunds," the money-taker said, sounding bored. Sienne guessed this wasn't the first time an irate audience member had wanted a refund.

They walked around looking for another storyteller, but all of them were already mid-stream in their stories. "I hate it when story-tellers try to pass off fantasy as fact," Dianthe said. "There's no way Isidorus was real. Bringing rain to a city? A wall of water fifty feet high? Exaggeration, at the very least. And carricks don't hunt in packs."

"But all legends have some root in truth," Sienne said. "And she did say she'd heard the story from the boy who survived."

"She might have made that up. And even if there was a boy, he might have been making it up as well. It might be an effective story to terrify children into eating their vegetables, but hardly frightening in the light of day." Dianthe squinted at the lowering clouds. "What little light there is."

"You didn't think that was frightening? Carvers have always scared me."

"I'm not convinced they're anything but legend," Dianthe said. "All the stories have them as these grotesque monsters that eat human flesh, but no one's ever seen one and returned to tell about it. Even the boy who supposedly told the story to that woman—all he saw were hulking shapes in the darkness. What's to say they weren't just ordinary bandits?"

"Ordinary bandits don't eat human flesh."

"Neither do carvers, except in rumor. People are afraid of the Empty Lands because so much of them are still contaminated by loose magic from the wars, so they make up stories about what scares them most. And what scares them most is being altered by magic into some monstrous creature."

"I...guess that makes sense. Have you ever been to the Empty Lands?"

Dianthe's face went grim. "Twice," she said. "Once on my own, when I left my home for Concord. Once going south to Fioretti, with Alaric."

Sienne couldn't think of anything to say. Concord was the only city in the Empty Lands and it had a reputation for harboring criminals. But that couldn't have been Dianthe's reason for going there. Dianthe's expression told Sienne it was not something she wanted to discuss. "I assume you didn't meet any carvers," she said.

"Not one," Dianthe said, relaxing slightly. "Lots of were-creatures. A few carricks—those are nasty if you drink where they live. Mostly it's what the name calls it—empty. It's not even hard to avoid the contaminated areas, because they're visibly different. Bleached white."

"I don't think I'm interested in visiting. Beneddo isn't that far north, but occasionally we had people petition my father to make settlements in the Empty Lands, and he always gave permission. They all failed. I thought he was cruel to let them try when he knew what would happen, but he told me people have to learn from their mistakes."

Dianthe nodded. "I'm hungry," she said, "and I don't feel like waiting around for one of these storytellers to finish up. Let's go back and see how Kalanath is doing."

Kalanath was sitting up eating broth when they returned, holding bowl and spoon without help. His eyes looked less glassy and his fever was gone. "I feel foolish," he said when they exclaimed over his recovery. "It was nothing much and it delays us a day."

"Think how miserable you'd be if we'd ridden all day," Sienne said. "We're not in a hurry."

"And we got to go to the festival and listen to an extremely depressing story," Dianthe added.

"Did you pay money for this depressing story?" Perrin asked. "Because I assure you I can provide you with any number of sad tales and will not charge you a centus."

"I'd rather we had dinner," Alaric said.

The four of them trooped downstairs to the taproom. "Sorry your visit to the festival wasn't more cheerful," Alaric said to Sienne, who was at the back of the group.

"It was just the one story, and Dianthe said it probably wasn't true."

"Even so. I admit I'll be glad to be on the road again."

His voice sounded normal, just as if they'd never argued. Sienne wasn't sure it was a real solution, just pretending it had never happened, but she couldn't think of any way to bring it up without starting the argument again. So she said, "So will I," and smiled pleasantly.

Dinner was rich slices of beef in burgundy sauce with soft bread to mop up the juices. To Sienne's surprise, Aneirin was there with his violin, playing as if he hadn't spent the entire day performing to much bigger crowds. She watched him as she ate and smiled when his gaze met hers. He was definitely worth looking at, even if she had no intention of sleeping with him.

She asked for wine that night and got the same not-terrible vintage she'd had the night before. Sipping it, she fell into a daydream about traveling, and wondering where they would spend the night tomorrow. Dianthe was right, sleeping in inns made you soft; Sienne was already thinking about another comfortable bed.

"That smile of yours is most intriguing," Aneirin said, sliding onto the bench across from her. She startled, and he put his hand over hers to prevent her spilling her wine. "Would that I were the cause of it."

"You're a flirt," she said without thinking.

Aneirin laughed. "I believe I told you I know what I want, and I get it. Now that we are more than chance-met strangers, why should we not become more closely acquainted?"

Sienne glanced around. Alaric had gone upstairs to check on Kalanath. Perrin was deep in conversation with the same hairy man he'd spoken to the previous night. Dianthe was leaning back against the nearest wall, apparently asleep. "We're leaving tomorrow, and I'll never see you again," she said. "I think a closer acquaintance is a bad idea."

"Interesting. I honor you for your ideals, even as I curse you for having them. Where are you heading?"

Wary, Sienne said, "North, for a job."

"North! I, too, am going north. Perhaps we *will* meet again." Aneirin smiled pleasantly and gripped her other hand. "I'm engaged to play at the court of a minor duke for the season. The north is so much more pleasant by the time true summer rolls around, don't you think? Will you be staying long?"

"As long as it takes." She didn't like the way the conversation was going. True, his questions sounded innocent, but Sienne had been a scrapper long enough to recognize when someone was pumping her for information. Though why Aneirin would care about their job, she had no idea.

"Chary of telling tales, are we?" He stroked the back of her hand with his thumb. "That's all right. Keep your secrets."

"Her secrets are no concern of yours," Alaric said from behind Sienne's right shoulder. She snatched her hand away as if Aneirin's were on fire, and folded her hands in her lap.

"Are they not?" Aneirin sounded unconcerned despite the low, threatening bass rumble of Alaric's voice. "I didn't say they were. The lady and I were having a private conversation."

"One that's over now." Alaric laid his hand on Sienne's shoulder. "We're making an early start, Sienne, and you should probably turn in."

The irritation that had dwindled all day returned full force. "I'll go up when I'm ready," she snapped, though Aneirin's possessive touch on her hand had made her eager to get away from him.

Alaric released her. "Fine. Do what you want," he snapped back, and turned away to murmur to Dianthe.

Sienne stood. "It's been enjoyable speaking with you," she said.

Aneirin smiled. "And we're back to being cold again," he said in a low voice, once more taking her hand and raising it to his lips. "Farewell, Sienne, and I hope we meet again."

Sienne repossessed her hand and managed not to wipe it on her trousers. Dianthe had risen and was stretching. Alaric had disappeared again. "Good night," Sienne said, and left the taproom, not quite at a run.

When she reached the safety of her room, she stood at the window and pressed her face against the cold glass. Aneirin's charm had grown stale, and now that she was away from him, she wasn't sure if he'd been flirting, or had had some other intent in talking to her. Had he wanted details on their job? If so, why? He was a chance-met stranger... or maybe she was wrong about that.

The door opened. "I know you said you weren't interested in casual sex," Dianthe said, "but you were sending all sorts of mixed signals to that man."

Sienne spun around. "Were you *eavesdropping?*"

"Of course I was. You would have too, if our positions were reversed, and don't deny it." Dianthe sat on her bed and pulled off her boots. "I couldn't tell if you wanted him or not, and I'm usually good at that sort of thing."

"I do *not* want him!"

"Good, because I don't trust him."

"Neither do I. I think he was trying to get information out of me."

Dianthe stopped with one boot still in her hand. "Information?"

"He wanted to know where we were going and how long we'd be there. Casual questions, I know, but it didn't feel like ordinary interest."

Dianthe dropped her boot. "Wait a minute," she said, and left the room. Moments later she came back with Alaric. "Tell him."

"I, um, there isn't much to tell. Aneirin wanted to know the details of our job, and I don't think it was casual conversation."

Alaric came fully into the room and shut the door. "What makes you say that?"

She couldn't admit to her friends that after Rance, she was suspicious of any man who made her the object of his interest. "It was just a feeling. He asked those questions yesterday, too, and—am I just incredibly sheltered, or isn't it strange that he'd approach someone he met five minutes ago for sex?"

"Not that strange," Alaric said, "but I suppose it's not common, either. What exactly did he ask?"

"Where we're going. How long we'll be there. Where we came from."

"Did you happen to notice who this man came with?" Alaric asked Dianthe.

"Not yesterday. We saw him at the festival. He's with one of those big performing troupes that have a dozen different acts."

"Or he's pretending to be attached to them as camouflage," Alaric said, his eyes focused on something distant.

"You don't really think that, do you?" Sienne said.

Alaric shrugged. "I'm considering the possibilities. The more important question is, why would he care about us?"

"Tonia Figlari said she had enemies. Suppose one of them found out her plan, and wants to disrupt it?" Dianthe said.

"There are better ways to do that than interfering with us," Alaric said, "but it's possible. Or he's one of *our* enemies, and wants to relieve us of whatever salvage he thinks we're going after."

"We have enemies? I mean, the Giordas are in prison," Sienne said.

"Any successful scrapper team has enemies. Some of them turn that enmity into direct action." Alaric sighed. "At least it should be easy to keep an eye on this whatever-his-name-is. No performing troupe can travel as fast as we do, but it's too big to be stealthy even if they do. And if he leaves the troupe to follow us, we know what he looks like."

Dianthe nodded and began putting on her boots. "I think I'll sneak around the troupe's camp and see if there's anything obviously out of place. I think most of the big performers like Aneirin are sleeping in the inn, but if the whole troupe is in on his plan, some of that should show up."

When she was gone, Sienne said, "I hope I didn't just raise a false alarm."

"A little healthy paranoia never hurt any scrapper," Alaric said. "And I agree he's suspicious. So it's not just you."

Sienne nodded. Silence fell, during which Sienne groped for something to say, something to do that would keep him there or send him away. She couldn't decide which would be worse. Alaric finally said, "I said some things to you yesterday I'm not proud of. I'm sorry."

It wasn't at all what she'd expected, and she stared at him, slack-jawed, at a loss for words. "I was... too quick to take offense," she said. "I'm sorry."

"We're neither of us good at letting someone else have the last word, are we?" Alaric said with a smile.

Sienne smiled back. A manic chorus of *Kiss him, kiss him, kiss him!* rang in her brain, dizzying her. "No, I guess not."

Alaric sighed. "Get some sleep," he said. "I was serious about leaving early. Especially now that it might put us far out of the reach of any pursuers." He nodded and left the room.

Sienne relaxed her clenched hands, then fell face-first onto her bed and screamed into her pillow. Apologies were one thing, but she didn't feel they'd resolved what really lay between them. Unless she was the only one who felt there was something between them that needed resolving. If that was the case, she would need far more than a good night's sleep.

6

They left just after dawn the following morning, before anyone else in the inn had risen. The people who'd camped in the fields, on the other hand, were already awake and breaking camp when they rode past. Sienne looked for Aneirin, not really expecting to see him. She couldn't even see the tent he'd performed in, though that was because most of the largest tents were already down. Relieved, she rode on.

It was an unexpectedly warm day, with the sun burning off the early dew before midmorning and prompting Sienne to remove her cloak and bundle it behind her. The road wound through farmlands that at this time of year lay dormant, waiting to be tilled and planted. Some fields were being tilled already, with plows toiling up and down the rows and turning over rich dark soil that smelled of first summer. Sienne waved to a woman driving a plow; the woman waved her hat in return. It was hard not to be cheerful on a day like this.

That night, the inn they stayed at was a quiet contrast to the one they'd left behind. Alaric was his usual cheery self, teasing Sienne as if they'd never argued. Sienne determined to forget about the conflict. This was what she wanted, peace in her homemade family, and if it came at the cost of some corner of her heart, that was no great sacrifice.

They made good time over the next few days, as the skies stayed clear. The air, if not actually warm, didn't freeze the skin off your nose, and the roads were dry, if rutted from previous rains. Sienne practiced casting spells from horseback. It was likely not a skill she would ever need, but the focus she gained from maintaining her concentration while jouncing along applied to other situations as well, like running from a swarm of midges or chasing a lone were-boar. She was careful not to expend too much energy in practice; how embarrassing it would be to cast so many *imitate* or *force* spells that she lost consciousness and fell off her horse. And there was always the possibility, even in the middle of civilized Rafellin, that they might be attacked, and she would need those reserves to defend herself and her companions. But finding that balance, too, was an important skill, and one she didn't regret learning.

On the seventh day, they stopped at a middling-sized town called Uless, where they left the horses at the inn's stable. Dianthe bought staples, oats and coffee and other basic food items, at the local market. They packed their supplies on Button, the donkey, who'd traveled without complaint the whole long road, and hired a second donkey to carry the falcon emblem when they found it. That struck Sienne as cheerfully optimistic. She shouldered her pack with an easy competence she was proud of. Falling in behind Alaric, she headed north with her team, off the road and into the wilderness.

It didn't feel like wilderness the whole first day. There were still settlements here and there, lone farmsteadings with rail fences and dogs that ran along the fences and barked at them. The grass under-foot was short and fine, new first summer growth that looked as soft as a velvet fringe and greener than fresh peas out of the pod. It was easy for Sienne to shed her remaining disquiet and relax in her friends' company.

"I must say, this has been the least adventuresome adventure we have yet faced," Perrin said late that afternoon. "It is almost a pleasure excursion. I say that in full realization that we have yet to face the difficult part."

"I know," Dianthe said. "I'm having trouble taking this seriously."

"I'm not," Alaric said grimly. "That woman has the knife we need. That makes this serious."

"Yes, but it doesn't *feel* serious in itself," Dianthe pointed out. "Nothing's attacked us. We're not going to explore an ancient ruin. If it weren't for the knife, it would feel like cheating."

They walked on in silence for a few paces. "That would have been a perfect time for something to jump us," Dianthe said. "You see? It doesn't feel serious."

"Even midges would be something," Perrin said.

"Don't talk about midges," Sienne said with a shudder.

"Midges aren't dangerous," Alaric said, in a rumble that verged on laughter. "Everyone knows that."

"They are if they attack you en masse. I can still feel the bites."

"I don't think anyone in the history of scrapping has ever been taken down by a midge attack," Alaric said. "Until you."

"I did say not to talk about midges, didn't I? I'm pretty sure I heard myself say that."

"We will talk about them so long as it makes you annoyed," Kalanath said with a grin, "because it does not stop being funny."

"It's not funny to me," Sienne said, but she couldn't help smiling at the memory, which hadn't been funny at the time but was admittedly hilarious now. She'd thought she was being so responsible, going off to investigate movement during her watch, and then they'd *sprung* like so many fist-sized fleas, latching on to her arms and face and pumping her full of their venom. The bites had swollen to the size of large apples, and she'd itched for days, even after Perrin's blessing had cured her.

"It shouldn't be," Alaric said, then intoned in a deliberately pompous voice, "because it taught you a valuable lesson about always waiting for support."

"You're not funny either. And now I'm itching again. Thanks." She awkwardly scratched the middle of her back, beneath her pack.

"There's a river ahead," Dianthe said, shading her eyes, "but I don't see a ford."

"We have time. We can follow it a ways, see what we can find," Alaric said.

Clumps of trees defined the river's banks, steep and muddy. The river, swollen by the late winter rains, rushed along its course, in a hurry to reach its destination far to the south. They followed it for about a mile before they found a place they could cross. Alaric consulted his map. "It meanders across the countryside," he said. "We'll likely have to cross it a couple of times before we reach our destination."

"Could we not simply follow it, and avoid a wetting?" Perrin asked.

"We could, but it would take twice as long. At least it's not winter." Alaric folded the map and put it away. "Let's start looking for a place to camp."

They ended up camping in the shelter of a grove of trees some two hundred feet from the river. Despite its proximity, no one said anything when Sienne summoned water by magic rather than drawing from the icy flow. Even Alaric was used to her using her magic for ordinary tasks like washing up or making coffee.

Kalanath set snares, and they ate roasted rabbit from skewers in companionable silence as the sun went down. Sienne stretched out her legs to warm her feet at the fire. Her boots were waterproof, but splashing across the river ford had frozen her toes.

"We should reach the village late tomorrow," Alaric said. "If we don't make it there at least two hours before sunset, I think we might be better off making camp early and approaching the place in the morning."

"You don't think there's any danger, do you?" Dianthe asked.

"No. But I do think it will take time to find this stone, and I'd rather not have to cut our search short because of nightfall." Alaric leaned back on his hands and stretched out his legs as Sienne was doing. "And I admit to being superstitious about camping in a place that was the site of...not calamity, exactly, but certainly bad luck."

"I agree," Perrin said. "At the very least, we would be surrounded by melancholy, and I dislike melancholy when it is not of my own making."

Kalanath tossed a twig at the fire. "I do not understand," he said, "how the old duke told the entire village to leave. Does a duke have such power?"

"A duke has such responsibility," Sienne said. "Though I think many rulers would simply have abandoned their people and gone to another of their properties. It would have cost Tonia's ancestor a fortune to relocate the entire dukedom, even if the entire dukedom was just the one village. What *I* don't understand is how there's even a title for Tonia to reclaim. It sounded like the villagers dispersed to other holdings, leaving the old duke with nothing but the name and an empty holding. In that case, the king would have annulled the title and absorbed the property into someone else's dukedom."

"I don't know anything about how the Rafellish government works, aside from how the dukes all owe allegiance to the king," Alaric said. "Maybe she intends to reclaim the property and reestablish the holding. There aren't a lot of nobles interested in extending their responsibilities this far north."

Perrin took a sip from his flask. "I will feel more comfortable when we see this place. I cannot imagine the stone as she describes it, save to suspect it will not be easy to retrieve. Nor to carry out."

"I am sorry for the donkey, to be loaded so," Kalanath said with a grimace.

They all looked at where Button and his nameless companion stood hobbled nearby. "What if the stone's too heavy?" Sienne asked.

"We'll rig a sledge and have both donkeys pull it," Alaric said. "But I'm not going to worry about it yet. Time enough for that when we've found the thing."

The distant rumble of thunder made Sienne draw up her feet. "I think I'll go to bed before it starts raining."

"Regular watch rotation," Alaric said. "And don't forget your rain capes. Sounds like we'll need them."

Regular watch rotation meant Sienne watched last. In the

beginning, that had been because she was unused to walking all day and needed a full night's sleep. Now it was because she cooked breakfast. She'd been surprised to discover she liked cooking over the fire, not to mention watching the sun rise. She still wasn't tired of that. Every sunrise was different, but they all began with darkness turning to gray and then rosy gold, as if the world were waking up.

She took her waterproof rain cape into the tent with her and spread it across the foot of her bedroll, wrapped her soft woolen blanket around her for more warmth, and fell asleep as the first raindrops struck the tent canvas.

She woke to Alaric shaking her leg. The rain was coming down harder, but not in sheets, and she pulled on her rain cape before crouching to leave the tent. Alaric looked damp despite his cape. "There's nothing out in this rain but us," he said, "and I'm afraid the fire's gone out. No hot breakfast for us."

"Has it really been raining all night?"

"On and off. Makes it hard to see anything." His brow was furrowed. "But I thought..."

"Thought what?"

"Thought I saw something moving about an hour ago. Something human-sized and pale. But wisps don't come out when it's raining, so it was probably nothing."

"Weren't you the one who told me a little paranoia is healthy for a scrapper?"

He grinned. "Trust you to remember that."

They were standing close together, close enough for her to touch him—or for him to touch her. Silence fell, one of those awkward silences she was now so familiar with. Alaric's expression changed, became thoughtful. "Sienne..." he said.

Her breathing sounded like a gale in her ears. "Yes?"

She could tell the moment he changed his mind about whatever he was going to say. "Keep an eye out to the east. That's where I saw movement."

Disappointment coursed through her. "Toward the village?"

"No—wait. Yes." He looked in that direction. "I hadn't put it together, but yes."

"Don't!"

"Don't what?"

"Go off and explore by yourself."

He laughed. "I wouldn't do that. It's tempting, though. Suppose someone set up house in the abandoned village? We might be facing a real challenge."

"Then I definitely want to face it in daylight."

Alaric nodded. "I'll see if I can catch a few hours' sleep. Wake me if you see anything." He turned and ducked into the men's tent, shedding his rain cape and shaking it off outside.

Sienne paced the perimeter of the camp, trying not to walk faster on the east side. Alaric's words had made her nervous. She still didn't know the spell *cat's eye*, that would give her true night vision, and she felt the lack keenly. Probably it wouldn't be as useful in a rainstorm, but it would comfort her to know she could see anything that might try to sneak up on her.

She prodded the sodden fire with her toe. Her simple spark magic wouldn't be able to ignite anything that wet, and another thing she didn't know was a stronger fire spell, one that would dry the wood no matter how saturated it was. It frustrated her how much she didn't know.

The rain seemed to be letting up. She wiped her face, unprotected by the rain cape, and shivered. Probably she should have put the cape on over her cloak, for extra warmth, but the cape was smaller than the cloak and the cloak just would have gotten wet. She went back to walking around the camp. True summer felt like it was far more than three and a half months away.

Something fluttered past the corner of her eye.

She spun, scattering water drops, toward the movement. Nothing. Whatever it was had been pale, and moved lightly, like...like a bird. Sienne felt stupid. Sure, birds probably sheltered from weather like this, but there was no reason one might not have taken wing just then. She scanned the fields extending into misty distance away from the trees and the river. Still nothing.

Then something moved, far off in the fields in the direction of the village. Sienne held her breath. It didn't move like a bird, but like… like nothing she'd ever seen before, actually. It didn't walk, or lope, it *glided* as if it were on wheels. It was big, at least human-sized, and pale against the darkness. Then it was gone, between one breath and the next, vanished like a black curtain had fallen between it and Sienne.

Sienne took an involuntary step toward where it had been. Then her scrapper's intuition caught up with her brain, and she drew in a breath and shouted, "*Alaric!*"

"What?" came Perrin's sleep-fogged voice. Canvas rustled, and quick footsteps on the soggy ground came up behind her.

"What did you see?" Alaric said.

Sienne pointed. "Way out there, something white and big—and it disappeared."

Alaric took a few steps in the direction she indicated before stopping. Behind them, more noise indicated she'd woken the entire camp, and she flushed with embarrassment. The thing was gone, whatever it was, and she'd overreacted.

"Is there danger?" Perrin asked. Sienne looked around. Only Dianthe had her rain cape. The men were all becoming steadily wet in the last drops of the rainstorm. Alaric's blond hair grew dark with water.

"I don't know. I'm sorry. It's gone, whatever it was, it just—it didn't feel like nothing. It sort of glided across the fields for a few seconds, and then it was gone."

"That sounds like what I saw," Alaric said. "Very far away, but still noticeable. Did it come toward you?"

"No, away. It was almost like a puppet, or a piece of stage setting. It didn't move like anything natural."

Alaric stared off into the distance. "What time is it?"

Sienne fumbled out her pocket watch. "Almost six. It will be sunrise in about half an hour."

"We are all awake," Kalanath said. "And there will be no hot breakfast. Perhaps we should strike camp."

"That was my thought," Alaric said. "If there are creatures out there, or people, I'd rather come upon them on our own terms. Sienne, why don't you serve out breakfast, and the rest of us will pack up."

Sienne rummaged through the supplies and found a bag of apples and some dried meat. She heated the water in the coffeepot, not to boiling—her small magic couldn't manage that—but as hot as she could make it, and poured out cups of stewed coffee for everyone, even herself and Kalanath, who didn't like the bitter beverage. They needed *something* hot on a morning like this.

By the time the sun rose, the rain had stopped and they were well on their way. Sienne was grateful for her waterproof boots as they slogged through the wet, muddy grass. Every footstep sent up a whiff of crushed new grass and the darker, almost bitter scent of black, rich soil. Birds swept by overhead, calling to each other in twittering coos. It helped Sienne forget the fear she'd felt watching that... thing... glide past. She'd faced monstrous creatures before, but this was the first thing she'd seen in the wilderness that made her feel helpless with fear. And she hadn't even seen it up close.

She rubbed the harness of her spellbook. It was soft leather and made to open without impeding the pages turning. On a whim, she snatched it up and willed it open to *force*, then flipped the pages at speed. *Castle. Fit. Imitate. Slick.*

"Sienne, you're making me nervous," Alaric said without turning around.

"I was just practicing."

"I know. I assume if you saw something you needed to cast a spell at, you'd shout a warning first. But listening to the pages rustle, I can't help feeling we're about to be attacked."

"There isn't anything for miles," Dianthe said, gesturing at the empty horizon.

"I do not see this thing you saw," Kalanath said. "Perhaps it comes out only at night."

"I have been thinking of a blessing I might request," Perrin said. "Something that will provide extra protection to our camp at night. When we stop in an hour or so for me to pray, I will ask Averran if in his wisdom he might not grant it us."

"Not something that removes the need for us to watch?" Alaric said.

"Possibly, though I think human awareness is superior to any form of magical warning. No, it is an alarm of sorts, something that will alert us if anything above a specified size crosses its boundary. It is not intelligent enough to ward only against things intending us harm, and prone to false alarms, but ideal for warning against enemies we have difficulty seeing."

"That sounds like a good idea," Dianthe said. "I take it that means there *isn't* anything smart enough not to go off if a rabbit crosses its path?"

"I think not. Averran believes humanity benefits from exercising its God-given wisdom, and rarely provides blessings that take its place."

"I'll take whatever Averran is willing to grant," Alaric said.

Two hours later, they reached the river again, and paused on the riverbank for Perrin to make his devotions. The four retreated a few yards to give him privacy. Sienne watched the water flow past, carrying with it twigs and leaves from the previous night's storm. Perrin was right; this was the least like an adventure they'd ever had. She shivered. That felt like ill-wishing. Anything could still happen, and there was the thing she'd seen... but in the bright light of morning, it was hard to believe in monsters.

Perrin stood, dusting himself off, and came to join them. He was frowning. "Something wrong?" Dianthe asked.

"I am not sure. I received the warding blessing I asked for, and a scrying blessing. I thought we might want to examine the village from a distance."

"Good idea," Alaric said.

"But that is not what disturbs me." Perrin waved the rice paper squares of his blessings at them. "I left it to Averran to choose what else he would bless me with. There are five healing blessings."

"That is many," Kalanath said. "More than before."

"I have never received so many healing blessings at one time. I fear what it means for the coming day." Perrin rummaged in his pack for his sewing kit and his pastels. "One moment, and I will be ready to proceed."

"Take your time," Alaric said. "Let's walk carefully. It's not quite hostile territory, but we should be alert."

They waited for Perrin to assemble his blessings into a riffle of marked papers, then moved out again. The remaining clouds cleared away, leaving a blue sky through which the sun drifted as they walked. Sienne found herself clutching her spellbook too tightly and forced her hands to relax, only to have to repeat the process again and again throughout the morning. By noon, when nothing had attacked them, she was tired and edgy and ready for a rest. But Alaric handed out food so they could eat while they walked. "I want us to make good time," he said when Sienne protested. "Even if we don't reach the village in time for some exploring, we'll still need the light to choose a good campsite."

Sienne grumbled, but had to admit he was right. She tossed her apple core aside and ran her hand across the spellbook's harness. It calmed her somewhat. Everything was going to be fine. It was just an old, deserted village, not a true ruin like they'd explored so many times before. Whatever she'd seen, they'd deal with it.

A cold wind sprang up around midafternoon, prompting Sienne to put up the hood of her velvet-lined cloak. The wind blew tendrils loose from Dianthe's braid and whipped Perrin's long hair around his face. Sienne ducked her head against it and was therefore surprised when she ran into Alaric, who'd come to a stop. "Sorry," she said.

"I think that's it," Alaric said, pointing. Sienne looked and saw dark, regular shapes against the pale new grass. Beyond those rose a stone building that at this distance looked intact. No telling how run-down it actually was after eighty years' abandonment.

Perrin was sighting along his arm as if measuring distance. "I think another half-hour's walk will put it within the scrying blessing's range."

"All right," Alaric said, and strode off across the fields. Sienne scrambled to catch up with him.

Half an hour later, when they'd once again reached a stretch of river, Perrin said, "Here is sufficient," and stripped off his pack to rest it on the damp ground. He removed his riffle of blessings from his pocket and tore off one with a blue smudge on one corner. "Help me make a circle, if you please."

They tore up grass to make a lopsided circle some three feet across. Perrin dragged his toe along its outer edge to define the flat, muddy area more precisely. He stepped close to the circle, gripped the blessing in both hands, and muttered an invocation. A bright blue glow filled the space, bright enough to make Sienne squint her eyes. She blinked away tears as the glow faded. Five sapphire dots of light, like glowing beads of water, were grouped at the center of the circle, which overflowed with pale blue fog that bubbled as if the ground beneath were boiling over. They all stepped back involuntarily.

"Odd," Perrin said. "I do not know what the fog means. It disturbs me."

"There are no other people around, correct?" Alaric said.

"No other thinking minds. That includes were creatures, but not carricks or wisps or other non-sapient monsters." Perrin crouched and swiped his hand through the fog, which coiled around his wrist as if it wanted to drag him down. He pulled his hand away with no difficulty. "I think I should consult with Averran."

"You don't think he'll be upset?" Sienne asked. She sidestepped a tendril of fog that caressed her boot before fading away.

"Oh, he will most certainly be upset, but he is always upset, so I choose not to let it disturb me unduly." Perrin walked a short distance away and sat cross-legged on the ground. "O most cantankerous Lord," he began, "I—"

He stopped, and his eyes flew open. "Danger," he whispered. "We are in great danger."

The other four drew closer together, back to back. "I don't see anything," Dianthe said.

Perrin shook his head briskly. His hair flew in every direction, blown by his movement as well as the wind. "I do not understand, o Lord of crotchets," he said, and fell silent. The other watched him closely. Sienne clutched her spellbook, letting its hard edges anchor her. Finally, Perrin stood and brushed himself off. He was breathing as heavily as if he'd run ten miles without stopping. "I cannot tell if Averran will not answer, or cannot answer. I only know that his communication was of danger to us. We are not safe here."

"But there isn't anything here," Dianthe said. "And I don't want to turn around and go back when we don't know what the danger is."

"We've been in danger before," Alaric said. "It's not a reason to run away. It's a reason to be cautious." He shrugged, settling his giant sword, which he wore on his back, into a better position. "Let's set up camp here, well away from the village. Then we'll explore until just before sunset. We stay out of the place after dark, and we use the alarm blessing as well as setting watch."

They nodded agreement and began setting up the tents. Sienne helped Dianthe put up their tent, but half her attention was on the distant village. It looked peaceful in the afternoon light. Danger, Perrin had said. She had a terrible feeling they'd all find out what Averran meant before the night was over.

7

The river was deep and wide where they'd camped, so they struck out westward until they found a place they could cross. At a narrow bend in the river, crumbling pillars of piled stone showed where a bridge had spanned it once. Alaric walked to the river's edge, which was steep and muddy. "I'd like to avoid getting wet," he said. "Any ideas?"

"I can jump from pillar to pillar, and probably Kalanath can too, but that doesn't help the rest of you," Dianthe said.

"I can think of a plan that involves only Alaric getting wet," Sienne said, opening her spellbook.

Alaric eyed her dubiously. "How big can you make me?"

He was quick. "Fifteen feet? That should make the water no more than thigh-deep on you. You might want to take off your boots."

"Do it." His brusqueness concealed the fear she knew was there every time she cast a spell on him. The shadow of the wizard who'd enslaved the Sassaven was always over him, she supposed, and it made her heart ache for him. It was a constant reminder that if he hadn't run away, he would be a docile servant of an evil master, robbed of free will and tasked to protect the one who'd enslaved him.

She didn't think she could endure having magic cast on her under those circumstances.

She read off the *fit* spell three times, avoiding Alaric's eyes—it felt like an invasion of his privacy, seeing the fear he couldn't quite control. Alaric stretched newly-elongated arms and legs, then picked up Sienne by the waist and ferried her across the river, setting her down gently and without comment on the far side.

She surveyed the terrain while waiting for the others to cross. Probably this area near the river had been cultivated fields, but there was no sign of them after eighty years of lying fallow, nor of a road leading away from where the bridge had been. The rush of water and wind were the only sounds Sienne heard; not even the sound of busy insects in the grass was audible. The noise was constant and unvarying, fading into the background to fill the world with an eerie stillness that had Sienne shivering with more than cold.

Something large came up beside her. "How long until it wears off?" Alaric said. His normally deep voice sounded like thunder.

"A minute or two. I cast it at the lowest dur—"

Alaric grunted, and a moment later, he was his normal size. "Good. Give me a minute to put my boots on, and we'll move on."

Ten minutes' walking brought them to the first of the ruined houses. When they were whole, they'd had stone foundations and timbered frame upper stories with thatched roofs and stone chimneys peeking out of the thatch. Now, stone was all that remained, and not much of that. Sienne slowed to look at one of the houses whose walls had collapsed outward, as if removing the timbers had made all of them fall at the same time. Long ago, people had lived in these houses. It was difficult to imagine.

"Stay close together, and stay alert," Alaric said. Sienne kept close to his broad back, holding her spellbook ready. It felt as if they were following a road now, though there was still no sign of one; it was just how they were passing houses on both sides in varying stages of decay. Having left the river behind, the incessant wind was all the noise they heard except for the rustle of their booted feet in the grass. It was so still Sienne could hear a thrumming in her ears, like the rush of the tide, and the gentle rasp of her breath, in and out a little faster than her walking pace could account for. She thought about singing to break the horrible tension, but her singing might drown out the noise of some monstrous creature approaching. She wiped first one, then the other hand on her trousers and took hold of her spellbook again.

"The ruins are larger now," Dianthe said.

Kalanath prodded a wall with the tip of his staff and stepped back in surprise when some of the stones rattled down. The small sound was larger in the stillness. "We are near the center," he said. "Still I see nothing."

"Anything hiding here would have to be small," Alaric agreed. "No were-creatures. Definitely not carricks. Midges, maybe." For once, it wasn't a joke.

The villagers hadn't left anything behind, not even furniture, but Sienne agreed they'd passed the houses and had reached the village square. To the left she saw the remnants of a forge, the fireplace a crumbling heap of stones, the anvil missing from the oak stump near it. Posts indicated where a stable might have been.

"The road begins here," Perrin said, "or, more accurately, the part of the road they chose to pave begins here." He pointed at round cobbles making a path toward the keep, with fine new grass growing up around each stone, making them look like little bald men with green hair fringes hammered feet-first into the ground. It was an unsettling image for an unsettling place.

"Anyone see anything?" Alaric said. No one spoke. "Let's move on."

They walked slowly up the stone path toward the keep. It was a castle in miniature, with towers at three of the four corners and a peaked arch leading to the front doors. For the residence of a duke with so small a holding, it was impressively large, but by absolute standards it was little bigger than a typical Fiorettan manor. Unlike the village's buildings, it was made entirely of stone, smooth-faced tan and gray blocks the length of Sienne's forearm forming walls that rose three stories high. In this place, far from any mountains, the Figlari dukes must have spent a fortune having the stones hauled in.

Sienne stopped when the rest of them did, about a hundred feet from the keep's front door, and stood looking up at it. Its foundations and walls seemed undamaged by the ravages of eighty years of neglect. The glass windows were gone, of course, with broken shards jutting from the window frames, but the main doors hadn't shifted in all that time, and stood dark and forbidding before the companions. A frieze carved above the outer arch represented warriors going off to battle, with birds—falcons?—flying over their heads. "That's not it," she said.

"It was too much to hope it is," Kalanath said.

"I'll scout around," Dianthe said, but Alaric put a hand on her shoulder.

"We stay together," he said. "I know, that has its own dangers, but I don't want anyone alone in this place."

Dianthe nodded. "Let's circle the keep and see what we can see."

Apple trees grew close around the rear of the keep, an ancient orchard grown wild for almost a century. There were no windows at ground level, and arrow slits lay at intervals along the columns of the corner towers. It was a remarkably fortress-like keep, what with the arrow slits and the crenellations along the towers, which made sense to Sienne, given how far from civilization the Figlari dukedom was.

They ducked low-growing branches just budding with new growth, spreading out by necessity, which made Sienne nervous. Even here under the trees there were no animal noises, no birds singing or flying from one branch to another. She found herself straining to hear anything beyond the sound of their own passage, anything that might prove they were still in the real world and hadn't slipped into some dream reality—or nightmare.

On the far side, a row of window holes left the keep open to the elements. "I wish I could fly," Sienne murmured. "But I couldn't find anyone willing to trade for it."

"Let's see if we can get in via the front door," Alaric said.

The front door, two slabs of heavy oak, looked as if they weren't made to open, but a single push from Alaric and Kalanath set them swinging. "That's... unexpected," Alaric said. Sienne drew closer to Dianthe, who stood nearest her. The ease with which the doors had opened had given her a momentary image of someone hunkered down in the darkness within, anticipating their arrival.

"It is not normal," Kalanath said. "I dislike this place."

"Let's find the stone and get out of here," Dianthe said, striding forward through the doors. Sienne hurried after her.

Gray sunlight was all that illuminated the hall beyond, a small space that smelled of old, wet stone and bird droppings. Sienne still couldn't see or hear any birds, but the odor was unmistakable. She stood beside Dianthe, gripping her spellbook, and let her eyes adjust. Gradually, she made out stone stairs with no rail going up the left-hand wall to a gallery open on the front, and another door, smaller than the first, in the wall directly opposite. A rotting tapestry covered most of the right-hand wall, the details obscured by darkness and, probably, water damage.

"Up, or forward?" Dianthe asked.

Alaric considered. "Up," he said. "Tonia said the stone was set in a wall, and it's probably high up where it can be seen from far away. We need to see if we can get onto the roof."

Sienne eyed the stairs. "Those don't look safe, with no rail."

Dianthe took a few careful steps up and bounced once or twice on the balls of her feet. "They're sturdy enough, just narrow. I don't think there was ever a rail. Odd." She ran the rest of the way up and disappeared into the gallery. "This is empty."

"I'll go last, just in case," Alaric said. Sienne guessed he meant "in case my weight is too much for them." She edged up the stairs behind Kalanath, who went as easily as Dianthe had. The open space beyond the edge of the stairs sucked at her, giving her the crazy notion that if she leapt off its edge, she would drift to the floor beneath like a dry leaf. Behind her, she heard Perrin muttering under his breath something that might have been a prayer. Perrin hated heights more than she did. She pressed into the wall harder, keeping her eyes focused on the stone stairs in front of her, and almost bounded off the last step onto the balcony.

The balcony was deeper in shadow than the entry hall, prompting Sienne to make several magic lights and set them bobbing along after her companions. Their cold light revealed a long, narrow passage, its walls stained with old leaks and scabbed over with a greenish scaly growth. Closed doors at either end of the passage offered no hints as to where they should go.

"Left," Alaric said.

He sounded so decisive Sienne asked, "Why left?"

He shrugged. "I didn't have a coin to flip, so I chose the nearest one. Stay close."

Sienne didn't need the warning. The moss, or lichen, on the walls made strange patterns, almost faces, and she carefully avoided looking at them. Dianthe pushed the door open. It moved as easily as the front door had, with barely a creak. "This is disturbing," she said.

"Don't let your imagination take over," Alaric said. "Keep moving."

An empty room, nearly cubical in shape, lay beyond the door. Dust piled heavily in the corners and on the untenanted cobwebs hanging from the ceiling. Sienne brushed one aside and made her light fly higher, illuminating the room better. No windows, no furnishings, not even a stray centus, just another door in the room opposite. Dianthe opened that one as easily and they filed through. This room had a window with half its glass missing, turning it into a toothy maw. It, too, was empty.

"How many of these rooms are there?" Dianthe said.

"Old keeps were designed like this," Sienne said. "No hallways, just rooms opening off rooms. I can't imagine they had any privacy."

They passed through three more rooms like beads on a string before coming to a heavier door that stuck. Alaric put his shoulder to it, with no result. "Is it locked, or barred?" he said.

Dianthe came forward and tested the latch. "Not locked. I don't think there's a bar, it wouldn't make sense."

"I have an idea," Sienne said. "I can cast invulnerability on the hinges."

"That...strikes me as a step backward," Perrin said.

"No, invulnerability doesn't work on metal. It just weakens it. Not so much that it shatters, but it might be enough to break it down." She stepped forward and rested her fingers on the frame, concentrating briefly and picturing each hinge. It was a simple piece of magic for something with so many uses. She stepped back and said, "Try shoving it again."

Alaric once more put his shoulder to the door. It creaked, groaned, and gave at the hinges to sag open, revealing more sunlight and sending a breath of fresh air swirling past. Sienne breathed it in and relaxed. They were on the wall-walk between the main keep and its southwest tower, which rose high above the roof.

Alaric led the way across the wall-walk and forced open the tower door. Inside, stone stairs spiraled up out of sight. The arrow slits let in enough light that the tower's interior was gloomy but not dark. Alaric tilted his head back. "This should give us a good view of the roofs."

Dianthe began climbing the stairs. "Be careful, they're slippery," she said. Sienne swallowed and took a few steps after her, longing to hurry but conscious of what a bad idea that was.

She was sweating by the time she reached the top, not from exertion but from nerves, and was grateful to step away from the treacherous stairs. They hadn't reached the tower roof, but rather a single round chamber with a number of gaping windows giving a panoramic view of the keep, the village, and the surrounding countryside. It was cluttered with all manner of debris the way the rest of the keep was not. Sienne shoved aside an ancient suit of armor to get out of Alaric's way as he came last up the stairs. "By Sisyletus, look at this," he said. "What a lot of junk."

"Maybe," Dianthe said. She held up a rusted mace that even Sienne could tell had once been a fine weapon. "Armor, weapons... this was someone's armory once."

"That is odd," Kalanath said, picking over a couple of disintegrating leather jerkins. "This is not a place for an armory. Why bring these things so far up?" He prodded the suit of armor with his staff.

Perrin stepped over a sword lying loose on the floor and stood in the center of the room, hands on hips. "And there are no racks nor stands to hold it all. It is as if someone simply dumped it all here to get it out of the way."

His words chilled Sienne, though she didn't know why. "Someone... who?" she said. "And why didn't they take all this with them when they left? It's junk now, but it would have been valuable when it was new."

Kalanath, crouching over a pile of chain links orange with rust, suddenly stood and shifted the pile with the end of his staff. "This is new," he said. He bent and picked up something thin and flat that flexed like leather. He handed it to Sienne. "A spellbook, but not like yours."

Sienne took it and turned it over. Its pale birch cover had flowers burned into it in a thick pattern that had traces of red paint still in the curves. It was much thinner than Sienne's, with only eight pages, but —Her fingers went briefly numb with horror. "There are two spells to a page, front and back," she said. "People used to do it that way, for a little while, until it turned out it was less efficient. But... that was fifty years ago."

She waited. They all looked at her, waiting for her to continue. "Fifty years ago, don't you see?" she exclaimed. "This place was abandoned *eighty* years ago. So—"

"Somebody else was here," Dianthe said. "Somebody who lost her spellbook. That's not something you do voluntarily."

Sienne closed the book. "What happened to her?" She looked down at the pile of rotting leather near her feet. "What happened to all of them?"

"We need to get out of here," Dianthe said.

"But this place is clearly abandoned. We have seen no sign nor sound of anyone but ourselves," Perrin said.

Alaric had not been poking around the piles. Instead, he'd roamed from one window to the next, sticking his head out and looking around. "We're not going without the stone," he said. "I can see the whole roof from these windows, and it's not up here. And it wasn't on the outside when we walked around the keep. We need to keep looking."

"This is not a good place," Kalanath said.

"It does look like someone used to live here who preyed on scrappers," Alaric said. "Probably bandits. But they're long gone. Let's get what we came for and leave this place behind."

Sienne tucked the spellbook into her harness, behind her own book. "We have to tell Tonia what it's like here. I don't like her, but if she's planning to retake this territory, she needs to know what she'll be facing."

"Something to worry about later, but I agree," Alaric said. "Let's go back to the entry and see what's on the ground floor."

Sienne's disquiet faded as they made their way back down the tower stairs and through the connected rooms. She wished she'd thought to pay more attention to the lost spellbook's contents. Suppose it had spells she didn't? Granted, more spells had been discovered in the years since this spellbook had been assembled, but there were so many she didn't know, the odds were in her favor. Her impatience to find the falcon stone and be done with this miserable job increased.

Back in the entry hall, Dianthe tested the second door and found it unlocked. It, too, opened as easily as if the hinges were oiled. Sienne examined them just in case that was true, and found no trace of rust. "This is strange," she said, running her finger along the hinge plate. It came away damp and a little dirty, but not greasy or tinted red with rust.

She turned away from the door and found her friends clustered together in the doorway, examining the room. It was the keep's great hall, an enormous space that took up most of the ground floor. Three steps led down to the sunken floor, made of flagstones that had probably required *fit* to transport them, they were that big. Blackened remnants of rushes strewed the flagstones, but no tables or chairs remained. More shreds of time-ravaged tapestries clung to the walls, lit by the row of windows they'd seen outside.

Sienne took a deep breath and let it out slowly. The room was cold, much colder than the weather outside. She had left her cloak behind in camp, wanting freedom of movement more than warmth, but now she wished she could snuggle into it. The tapestries still showed some of their original colors and patterns, but in irregular patches, and the effect was as if dozens of misshapen eyes were looking down at her. She shuddered. Everywhere she turned, she felt she was being watched.

Dianthe exclaimed, "Look!" She pointed at the far wall, toward a dais where the duke and his family would have sat. Above it, set into the stone of the wall, was a round stone about four feet across with a ridge around the rim. Carved into the stone as if emerging from it was a falcon, its wings spread and its beak open, caught by the sculptor mid-cry.

Alaric walked toward the dais and stood with his hands on his hips, looking up. "I don't know whether to be glad we found it, or irritated that it's embedded in the wall."

Sienne came to stand beside him. "How thick do you think the block is? As thick as the wall? I mean, it's not structurally part of the wall, right?" There was something strange about it, but she couldn't identify the source of her disquiet.

"How should we know?" Perrin stood on Alaric's other side and tilted his head like an inquisitive sparrow. "My extensive education did not cover matters such as fortress engineering, which at the moment seems a shameful oversight."

"It looks like they put it in after the keep was built," Dianthe said.

"If that's true, I can use *sculpt* to shape the stone surrounding it and free it from the wall."

"I think that will work," Dianthe said, moving to one side. "You can—ah!" She stumbled and fell to her knees.

"What happened?" Alaric said.

"I tripped. There's something here. Something..." She groped along the floor. "It's round and hard, and invisible—" She jerked her hand away. "It feels like bone."

Her words sent a jolt of fear through Sienne, and she edged toward Alaric, staying clear of his sword arm. "How could—"

The air shimmered, and there it was—ivory-white, with a rounded top, rocking from where Dianthe had kicked it. A human skull.

Dianthe backed away hurriedly. "What is going on?"

Someone laughed. The chilling sound made gooseflesh rise up on Sienne's arms. She spun around and saw only Kalanath, who was also looking wildly about for the source of the laughter. The tapestry eyes mocked her terror.

Alaric drew his sword, which made a reassuring rasp of steel against leather. "Show yourself!" he shouted.

More laughter, from three different places. Then shapes emerged from the shadows surrounding the sunken floor. They had not been invisible; invisible creatures who became visible did so in an instant, not fading in as these... people... were. It was as if they'd been visible all along, but blended in with the stones until they chose to make themselves seen.

There were dozens of them, dressed haphazardly in fur and leather far too skimpy for this weather. Their skin was ice-pale, paler than Alaric's northern complexion, touched with blue where the shadows lay across their bodies. They were tall and slender and moved with a cat's grace, like hunters sneaking up on their prey. Sienne focused on the one nearest her, a man wearing fox tails like a cape across his shoulders. He was impossibly beautiful, his eyes large and dark, his face an elegant sculpture of planes and angles, his lips full and sensuous. He had his eyes fixed on her, and Sienne swallowed, her mouth and throat suddenly dry with fear.

The creatures came to stand around the pit and went so motionless they might have been statues carved out of someone's nightmares. Sienne's fingers groped for her spellbook, though her mind was numb. She couldn't think of anything to do against these otherworldly creatures.

Movement caught her eye, and she spun to face the one who came down from the dais and crossed the room toward them. She was as beautiful as the others, her eyes as blue as the icy shadows that defined her arms and shoulders, her fair hair cascading down her back to fall nearly to her knees. Unlike the others, who looked at the five with hunger, she looked curious, her head tilted to one side, her perfect brow furrowed into the slightest of lines. She approached Alaric, who stood with his sword ready to attack, but stopped some ten feet from him. Alaric was breathing heavily, his shoulders moving as if he'd exerted himself almost to his limit, but he didn't attack.

The woman raised one delicate hand, and Alaric moved, bringing his sword up to swing at her. Sienne lifted her spellbook, willing it to open to *force*. Nothing happened. A wave of lassitude swept over her, exhaustion so profound her fingers ached with it. She let the spellbook fall to swing in its harness by her side. Her eyelids drooped, and she tried to force them open, but it was like trying to hold back the tide. Beside her, Dianthe slumped to the floor, not falling so much as folding at the knees and lying gently on the flagstones. It seemed like such a good idea, sleep, that Sienne sagged to the floor herself. She wouldn't have imagined flagstones could be so soft.

She heard Alaric drop to his knees and opened her eyes just enough to see him bent over, clutching his head as if it hurt. *He should sleep, too*, she thought. She blinked once more and saw the woman bending over her. By her side, dangling from a loop of leather, was a long, curved knife stained dark with old blood. Then Sienne's eyes closed, and she knew nothing more.

———

8

Sienne's mouth tasted terrible, dry and bitter as if she'd eaten coffee grounds. Her whole body ached the way it usually only did when she was ill and had slept restlessly. She blinked, and her eyelids resisted the motion, feeling dry and crusty. Something warm and soft pressed against her cheek. She shifted, and discovered her hands were bound behind her. That brought her to full consciousness, alert and terrified. What had they done to her?

She struggled to sit up. The soft thing she was lying on was Kalanath's thigh. He was just coming awake, his hands bound as hers were. They were all crammed together in a small room with wooden slats for walls—no, it was a cage, there was a door to one side, and if her hands had been free she could have reached through the slats to whatever lay beyond. The cage was no more than five feet high and about twice that in length, and it stank of urine and vomit.

Alaric sat up abruptly and smacked his head on the roof of the cage. He grunted and swore explosively. "Is everyone all right?"

"I take it you mean aside from the minor matter of being bound and caged," Perrin said.

"If you can be sarcastic, I assume you're fine," Dianthe said. "They took my sword."

"And mine," Alaric said.

"And my staff," Kalanath said.

Sienne groped at her side. "My spellbook's gone."

"But we're all still alive." Alaric shifted, trying vainly to find a comfortable position. "Caged, so they probably want something else out of us."

"Sienne, give me your hands," Dianthe said. "I'll untie you and you can untie me. It's a start, anyway."

Sienne turned her back and held out her hands for Dianthe to pick at her bonds. "Can anyone see them?" Dianthe continued.

Kalanath pressed his face to one of the gaps. "They are eating," he said. "There are many tables now, all surrounding the sunken place. They were not there before."

"Or they were under an illusion," Perrin said. "I see too late what the scrying intended us to know. Whoever or whatever they are—"

"Carvers," Sienne said, memory striking like an icicle into her chest. "They're carvers."

"Carvers are imaginary," Dianthe said.

"All legend has basis in fact," Sienne said. "They have strange magic, they appear and disappear when they want, and the knives... I bet they've all got knives."

"It's impossible," Dianthe said. "These are just... just humans who can..."

"They all have knives," Kalanath said.

"It doesn't matter if they're carvers or not," Alaric said. "That doesn't help us know how to escape, given that no one's ever escaped a carver attack to tell about it."

"As I was saying," Perrin said, "whatever they are, they have magic that confuses the scrying. They are intelligent, but their illusions, if illusions they are, are more powerful than Averran's magic. That fills me with horror."

The ropes around Sienne's wrists fell away, and she flexed her hands briefly before beginning on Dianthe's bonds. "Are they paying any attention to us?" she asked.

Perrin joined Kalanath in peering through the slats. There was no room for more than that. "They are eating in eerie silence," he said, "no talking, no singing, no laughter. If it turns out they are, in fact, not human, I would not be at all surprised."

The ropes binding Dianthe's wrists were thin—in fact, they were from their own supplies, which made Sienne angry as nothing else had. She clung to that feeling like armor against the terrified despair the thought of carvers made her feel. She picked at the tight knots with her fingernails, loosening them slowly. Every second was one more second in which the carvers might decide to investigate what their captives were doing. Gradually, the knots became loops, and finally she pulled the last strands apart and tore the ropes free. Dianthe's hand immediately went for her boot. She sighed. "Thank Kitane they didn't take my lock picks. Now we just have to wait for them to go to sleep, and I'll unlock this cage and let us out."

Sienne sneaked a hand through the slats of the door. "There's a padlock. It doesn't—" She pulled her hand back and sniffed it. "It's not rusted. I think it's just an ordinary lock."

"This assumes they sleep," Kalanath said.

"Or that they do not have plans for us before that," Perrin said.

"Let's not borrow trouble," Alaric said. "They kept us all together, and that's good. Can anyone see where they put our things?"

Perrin shifted awkwardly. "They are on a table on the dais, next to that woman. Are we agreed in thinking she cast that spell on us?"

A spell. Sienne had forgotten the unnatural sleep. "Charm," she breathed. "She used a charm on us."

"And without a spellbook," Dianthe said. "Maybe you're right about them being carvers. What human could do that?"

"No human," Sienne said. "But it means... she might be able to do anything. Charm is so forbidden I barely know anything about it. Just a few names of spells."

"Not something we can help," Alaric said. He held up his hands for Sienne to work at his bonds. "Let's concentrate on getting free, and getting our weapons back. Then we can find a way out of this trap."

Kalanath sucked in a sharp breath. "Two of them are coming this way."

Sienne frantically tore at the ropes around Alaric's wrists. The sound of a key in a lock carried far in the still air. The door opened, and Kalanath lunged at it, coming up short when one of the men shoved a knife in his face. The other man reached past him and grabbed Sienne by the collar, dragging her out of the cage. The others shouted her name, but the man with the knife slammed the door shut and locked it again. Sienne fought, twisting and clawing in her captor's grasp, until he laid the sharp curved edge of his knife along her throat.

She went still, trying to calm her breathing. The cage was off to one side, between the door and the dais. Her captor changed his grip on her collar so he could march her to the center of the sunken central pit of the great hall. Kalanath was right, the room was full of tables surrounding the sunken area, which remained clear of anything but dead rushes and... Sienne's heart pounded harder. Dark stains streaked the flagstones, stains that had been invisible until now, and bones scattered across the floor, some small like animal bones, some unmistakably human. The smell of old blood rose from the floor, mingled with the smell of wet, ancient stone.

She looked up and met the gaze of the woman, who alone among the carvers ate nothing, but held a pewter goblet in one elegant hand and stared at Sienne as if sizing her up. Sienne glared at her, pretending she wasn't close to screaming in terror. Alaric's greatsword lay across the table beside the woman, with Dianthe's smaller sword atop it and Kalanath's staff propped against the table. Sienne's spell-book, still in its harness, lay open on its face nearby, as if the woman had been reading it and was one of those people who thought nothing of cracking a book's spine by laying it on its face. Doing that couldn't damage a spellbook, but it irritated Sienne, and she clung to that irritation as she did her pretend defiance.

The woman leaned forward like a cat sniffing a mouse it hadn't decided to eat yet. Her eyes narrowed. Sienne continued to glare. The woman set down her goblet and stood, walking around the table and descending the dais, then the three steep steps into the pit. She gestured the man with the knife away and took Sienne by the chin, turning her head one way and the other. Then she released Sienne and walked away. It was all done in complete silence, making Sienne wonder if they were even capable of speech, or if they were simply so disdainful of humans they wouldn't bother speaking to them. Or maybe they communicated some other way. If they were going to kill her, it didn't matter one way or the other.

The carver with the knife—the one who'd dragged her out of the cage; they all had knives—took hold of her shoulder and marched her toward the door. For a wild moment, she thought he was going to let her go—but she couldn't abandon her companions! But no, he merely thrust her to sit on the stairs leading up from the pit and took up a watchful pose at her side. Cold and damp leached through her trousers from the stone steps, and Sienne wrapped her arms around herself and shivered.

The woman raised her hand. Three carvers stood from their tables and walked around to the cage, then paused as if waiting for direction. Sienne watched them closely, watched the woman, and saw nothing that might be communication pass between them, but after a moment, one of the three, a woman, opened the cage, and the other two dragged Alaric out. Sienne held her breath. Big mistake on their part; Alaric overtopped each of the carvers, tall as they were, by several inches, and Sienne knew he didn't need his sword to beat them into submission.

She couldn't understand why Alaric let them drag him out of the cage until he was free. Alaric swung a fist at the nearest carver, catching her under the chin and sending her reeling a few paces back. He ducked a swing of the next one's knife and pounded him hard in the kidney, then spun and caught the knife hand of the third, using the man's own momentum to flip him over to land heavily on his back. Alaric ducked the first one's knife and rushed her, catching her around her midriff and flinging her to crash into a table.

Sienne became aware of a rhythmic thrumming sound, a heavy, regular beat she couldn't at first identify. Then she saw that the carvers seated at the tables were thumping the tabletops with their fists, *thump, thump, thump* like the tramp of a hundred boots on a wooden bridge. It was almost like... applause. Sienne clenched her own fists and shouted, "Stop it! Stop that right now!"

The thumping continued. The three carvers fighting Alaric disengaged and leaped lightly away, out of the pit and onto the tables. Alaric, his shoulders heaving, ran to Sienne's side and dragged her not very gently away from her captor. The man made no move to stop him, which frightened Sienne further.

"Stay here," Alaric said, and turned to face the woman. She'd risen again and was watching him, a smile touching her perfect lips. Alaric, his back to Sienne, tensed visibly. He put his hands to his head as if it hurt. The woman's smile vanished, and she leaned forward. She looked like someone concentrating on a difficult task who puts her whole body into that concentration.

Alaric's knees buckled, and he landed hard on the stone floor. Sienne shouted his name and ran forward. She put her arms around him and tried to help him to stand, but it was like lifting the keep itself. "Alaric," she said, "what is she doing? Don't let her—"

Alaric sagged, all the tension going out of him at once. The sudden lack of resistance bore Sienne to the ground beside him. The woman stepped back. Alaric raised his head and focused on Sienne. His eyes were dull in the dimly lit hall, and the pupils were tiny dots in an ocean of pale blue.

He raised one arm and backhanded Sienne across the face.

She had already been off-balance, and the blow knocked her off her feet and sent her skidding away, flailing to stop herself. Her jaw erupted with fire, her eyes watered, but that was nothing to her stunned horror at having been struck by someone she trusted with her life.

Alaric rose to his feet and wavered unsteadily before taking a step toward her, and another. Sienne shrieked and scrambled to her feet. She ran for the side of the pit and got one knee up on the wall before being shoved back down by a couple of carvers sitting at the nearest table. A heavy hand fell on her shoulder a second before Alaric spun her around and punched her in the stomach. She let out a *pah* of breath, ducked his next blow, and in desperation darted between his legs and under him, running for the other side of the pit and the cage above it.

She heard Perrin and Kalanath screaming words she couldn't understand, saw hands reaching out from between the slats, saw silver flash as Dianthe desperately picked the lock, and skidded to a stop before reaching them. She needed not to draw attention to what Dianthe was doing. All she could do was run, stay away from Alaric —something was dreadfully wrong with him.

She caught sight of the woman, staring at Alaric in intense concentration as he weaved across the pit toward Sienne. He couldn't keep a straight line, and he once again clutched his head as if it pained him. The woman's gaze flicked toward Sienne, and Alaric's path altered to point him more directly at her. It had to be the charm spell *dominate*, one of the few Sienne knew by name. That woman was controlling Alaric, making him do her bidding. At that moment, Sienne understood exactly why charm spells were forbidden. She wanted to weep for Alaric, his will shredded to nothing by that woman, and weep for herself, who was going to die at the hands of a friend if she couldn't figure out a plan.

Sienne again made a break for the wall and was again shoved back down. She darted to one side, but not fast enough, and a blow aimed for her stomach hit her leg instead, buckling it. She dragged herself out of the way of the next blow and got to her feet, but her leg wouldn't support her for more than a hobble. The thrumming of the pounding on the tables beat in time to the rhythm of her pounding, frantic heart, accompanied by the screams of her companions. She scrambled past Alaric again, feeling the barest tug on her hair as he grabbed for her and missed. The woman looked triumphant, her smile fierce as any predator's snarl. Beside her—

Oh. I am an idiot. Sienne hobbled as far from Alaric as she could get. Her vision went in and out of being blurry, but she could still see her spellbook, lying unattended next to the carver woman. Alaric was staggering toward her again, but his hands weren't clutching his head and his eyes looked alarmingly aware of her. She would only get one chance.

Sienne willed her spellbook off the table. It flew across the room to land in her hands with a sharp crack that stung her palms, already open to the spell she wanted. She blinked to clear her eyes and read off the evocation *force* as rapidly as she dared.

The power of the spell built inside her, burning her mouth like acid, until the last syllables ripped out of her and a bolt of pure magical energy shot away from her. It flew past Alaric's head as he reached for her and struck the carver woman square in the face, flinging her backward into the wall.

Then Alaric's hand was around her throat, and he squeezed. Sienne choked and gasped in a futile effort to draw breath. She clawed at his fist, leaving deep scratches that had no effect on his powerful grip. Dimly, she was aware of her other friends pounding at his arms, prying at his fingers, but the light was fading and she smelled blood, her own or Alaric's, she had no idea.

The grip loosened. Sienne's vision cleared. Alaric stood looking down at her, utter bewilderment on his face. His pupils were normal-sized again and his mouth hung slack, moving slightly as if he was searching for words. He let go of her, and she gasped, gagged, and coughed so hard she thought she might throw up. "Sienne," he whispered. The pounding had stopped, and her coughing as blessed frigid air poured into her lungs was the only sound in the still room. She sagged, her arms and legs unable to support her.

Alaric stepped backward, his eyes still focused on Sienne. He roared, an agonized sound that shattered the stillness. Then he was gone, and in his place was an enormous equine creature, dark brown shading to black where the shadows touched his flanks. The unicorn tossed his head, making his black horn gleam as if oiled in what little light there was. He reared back, screamed defiance, and charged.

9

"Lie still," Perrin said. His hair fell loose around his face as he tore a blessing from his riffle of papers and pressed it to Sienne's forehead. She closed her eyes. Her throat felt torn to shreds, her leg was on fire, and she was sure Alaric had ruptured something inside her with his second punch. She knew she had to fight, but she could barely rise.

"O gracious Lord, stop being a cranky bastard and be useful for once," Perrin muttered. A glorious green haze filled Sienne's vision, and warmth coursed through her like a stream of hot water. The smell of jasmine and mint came to her nose, strong but not overwhelmingly so. She blinked, and sat up. The pain was gone, and so was the fear. They were going to fight, and they were going to win, damn it.

She snatched up her spellbook, slung the harness over her shoulder, and looked around. The room was in chaos, centered on Alaric, who lashed out with sharp-edged hooves that had never been shod and a horn that came to a wicked point. He was screaming the high, furious scream of a horse in terrible pain, and it made her want to weep for him again. The carvers tried to keep their distance from him, but he ranged from one side of the pit to the other, stabbing and slashing and covering himself in pale rosy blood that came from nothing human.

Dianthe and Kalanath stood back to back, picking off carvers who fled from Alaric's wrath. Dianthe had taken a bad blow to her left arm, which dripped blood that enraged the carvers who came near. They pressed her closely enough that even Kalanath, guarding her off side with his whirling staff, couldn't keep all of them away.

Sienne threw open her spellbook and cast *force* again, and again, knocking away the carvers threatening Dianthe. She heard a thump and turned to see Perrin holding up his left arm, from which radiated the pearly gray glow of a divine shield wide enough to cover both of them.

"On my mark, move!" Sienne called out, flipping the pages of her spellbook and raising one hand. She began reading off the evocation *scream*, closing her hand into a fist as she neared the end. Perrin whirled the shield out of her way to cover her back as the last syllables erupted from her as a wave of tangible sound shrill enough that even she winced.

The four carvers caught in the blast dropped, writhing and covering their ears, which bled rosy pink. Sienne had enough time to reflect on how grateful she was that carvers were at least that close to human before she had to blast another one bent on stabbing her.

She cast *force* once more and had to bend over to catch her breath. Her mouth was raw from the evocations, and she felt dizzy, a sign that she'd cast too many spells in too quick succession. Pearly light flared, and she looked up to see Perrin once more shielding the two of them from carvers whose knives dashed impotently against the divine barrier. "Are you well?" he said.

"Well enough." Even in the heat of battle, the carvers were eerily silent. The two slashing at the shield snarled at them noiselessly, their faces contorted with anger. "Are we winning?"

"We need to retreat," Perrin said. "Follow me!"

He thrust forward with the shield, pushing the carvers back. The shield was in gray tatters from the carvers' knives, but held firm as they crossed the room to Dianthe and Kalanath. Both were bleeding,

Kalanath from a wound along his hairline that had nearly scalped him. He had to pause every few seconds to wipe blood out of his eyes.

"We have to get out of here," Perrin said in a voice pitched only slightly above normal. It made the whole situation even more surreal that he wasn't shouting, Sienne thought, and wondered why everyone was moving around so much. *No, it's me,* she realized. Her reserves were lower than she'd thought.

"They barred the door," Dianthe said, "and Alaric is out of control. We have to stop him."

"You do that, and let us manage the door," Perrin said.

Dianthe nodded, stabbed one of the carvers through what Sienne hoped was her heart, and ran off to where Alaric paced an arc of the pit, screaming and thrusting at the carvers who were trying to back out of his reach.

The shield shivered, then shattered and vanished like soap film. Perrin swore. "To the door," he said, and the three of them ran for it, dodging carvers.

A heavy oak beam barred the door, surprisingly sturdy after so many years—or maybe it wasn't so surprising, if the carvers had been here long. Sienne turned her back on the door and flipped the book open to *scream.* She heard Perrin and Kalanath shoving on the bar, and then all she could hear was *scream,* burning her lips like acid and knocking down another three carvers. It hurt, but it was bearable. She did it again, and this time she gagged on the spell as it emerged from within her. Her eyes could barely focus to read the spell language, every carver had a ghostly double emerging from them, and her stomach roiled.

She staggered, blinked, and cast *scream* again. The sound echoed through the still chamber, but no carvers collapsed. She blinked again, and realized they had all stopped outside her range. They'd figured it out. They hovered there, pacing an invisible line past which *scream* had no effect, watching her as intent as an owl hunting a mouse's burrow. She croaked out a warning.

Hands took her by the upper arms. "Keep walking. They know you are a threat," Kalanath said in her ear. He and Perrin guided her through the little entry hall and out into a crisp first summer night. The moon cast the keep's sharp shadow over them, and the fine new grass crunched underfoot.

"Where—" she whispered, then gagged again and nearly vomited.

"Coming," Perrin said.

A thunder of hooves, and Dianthe and Alaric emerged from the keep at a run, swiftly outdistancing them. Sienne tried to walk faster, but only stumbled. They had to run, they had to get away before—

The first of the carvers emerged from the keep's door. She was battered, and pink blood streamed down her right arm, but her gaze was fiercely intent on them. More followed, dozens more—had they killed *any* of them? It seemed an unending stream of tall, pale, impossibly beautiful men and women poured out of the keep, all of them wielding bloody knives, all of them moving with the fluid grace of predators who know it is just a matter of time before the prey falls to them.

Dianthe shouted, "What are you doing? Run!"

"The only thing keeping them at bay is their fear of Sienne," Perrin said. "If she turns, we are lost."

"She cannot keep going. She will collapse," Kalanath said. "She is at the end of her reserves."

Sienne heard all of this in a daze. She glanced at her spellbook. The letters danced on the page, wavering in and out of focus. She couldn't cast spells if she wanted to. She watched the carvers steadily advance, took another step backward, and hoped Perrin and Kalanath would keep her from falling.

The sound of hooves on the hard ground grew louder. Alaric's shrill, terrifying scream made Sienne stumble, and this time she went down, dropping her spellbook to dangle loose in its harness. The carvers surged forward, then scattered as Alaric thundered down upon them, spitting one on his horn and flinging him into three of his fellows.

Perrin hauled Sienne to her feet and spun her around. "Run!" he shouted, and Sienne lurched into motion.

She could barely see, her vision was so badly doubled, and she depended on Perrin, who hauled her along bodily. Everything was dark except where the moon shone, turning the pale grass into a milky sea she could walk on. She knew it was a slightly mad comparison, but nothing in the world made sense except for Alaric's sharp, terrible neighing. She clung to the sound, because it was the only clear thing she could perceive.

She tripped and fell hard on her face, skinning her palms. Someone, she thought maybe Dianthe, hauled her up again, and then they lifted her, and she was lying across something broad and warm and hairy that moved like a ship, up and down. She flung her hands out and grabbed long strands of hair, wound her fingers around them and clung as if her life depended on them, which might be true.

She didn't bother opening her eyes, which would only lie to her, just gripped tight with her hands and her knees. The air was filled with the scent of blood. Alaric hadn't been able to avoid all those knives. The coppery stench combined with the bitter tang of what had to be carver blood made her stomach churn.

In any other situation, she'd have been awestruck. How many people in all of history had ridden a unicorn? She tried not to think how embarrassing it was, not only for her but for Alaric, how awkward and intimate. That wasn't important. What was important was getting away from the carvers, who were going to chase them down until they couldn't run anymore, and then—her mind skittered away from the possible ways she and her friends could die by those horrible knives.

Something niggled at her addled mind. The river. Right. "Head for the river!" she cried, but her mouth was full of mush and she only managed to make a garbled croak. Maybe the story was right, and carvers couldn't cross running water. It was the only chance they had.

Despite her resolve, she opened her eyes, and the whirling was so bad combined with the up and down motion of Alaric's gait that she vomited all down his side. She was so sick she couldn't even feel embarrassed about it. *If I live through this, I'll never be able to face him again,* she thought.

"Just keep running!" someone shouted, and there was a terrific splash, and water rushed over her face, making her splutter and cough. She clung tighter, and moments later Alaric reared up, and she slipped toward his hindquarters, crying out in terror that she would be flung off. His muscles strained beneath her, bunched and lifted, and with a couple of bounces his gait leveled out, then stopped.

Sobbing, Sienne clung to him, feeling the heave of his flanks as he sucked in air as desperately as she was doing. Why had they stopped? They weren't giving up, were they? If this was a desperate last stand, she needed to be up and fighting. Even if all she could do was throw up on their enemies.

She heard a splash, and then a high-pitched wail that in a human might have been a scream. This sounded like the death cry of a mortally wounded animal. "It's true," Dianthe said. "Kitane's left arm, I don't know that I'd wish that on any creature."

"They tried to kill us," Kalanath said, his voice flat and vicious. "I think if they die, it is no loss."

"They cannot follow us," Perrin said, "and they have no ranged weapons. And—dear Averran, what are they doing?"

Sienne tried to sit up and failed. "They're leaving," Dianthe said. "What if they find a way across?"

"There are no bridges," Perrin said. "We are safe for now. We need to return to camp and start a fire. The river was bitterly cold, and this night is not much warmer. And we must tend to Sienne."

"Alaric, will you carry her a while longer?" Dianthe asked.

Alaric made no response. He couldn't speak in this form, but Sienne had seen him nod or shake his head the few times he'd trans-formed, and this time he did nothing. She felt the bunch and pull of muscles as he started walking, and she released most of the death grip she had on his mane. That couldn't be comfortable for him.

"Sienne, are you awake?" Dianthe said, putting a hand on her forehead. Sienne groaned. Nodding seemed like a really bad idea. "The water stopped them. One of them fell in and it boiled his skin away, down to the bone. They won't follow us."

"Let us hope they disappear and go back to the keep," Kalanath said. "Sienne was right to kill their wizard woman. It seems they have no other."

"She is not dead," Perrin said. "I saw her stir when we were fleeing the great hall. Sienne disabled her, but it was not permanent."

"It was enough. After what she did to Alaric—" Dianthe went silent. "I'm freezing. We'll need to gather wood. I think there was a fallen tree in the copse near our camp."

"Sienne can...or possibly not," Perrin said. "We will have to do it the old-fashioned way, with an axe. I will set up the alarm blessing, just in case."

Sienne tried to relax. The crisis was over, and they'd all survived. With a little rest, she would be back to normal. But Alaric...

She couldn't help wondering what was going through his head. That woman had used a charm spell on him to make him attack Sienne. He might have believed Sienne was an enemy. Or had the woman forced him to attack against his will, and he'd known it was Sienne the whole time? No, that didn't make sense, because at the end he'd looked so bewildered, like he was coming to himself after a deep nightmare. It didn't matter. The carver wizard had used him, violated his free will, and made him her tool. Alaric, of all people, wouldn't be able to live with that.

She'd never been this close to him in this shape. The unicorn's scent was a heavy but not unpleasant musk that reminded her of hearth fires and freshly-cut trees, of the humus of a pine forest floor, and it made her long to put her arms around him, not the unicorn, but the man, and give him comfort. She realized she was crying and hoped no one would notice.

Alaric stopped. Hands pried her fingers free from his mane and lifted her off his broad back. She discovered she was capable of standing, though she needed support. She risked opening one eye and flinched away from the dark shape right in front of her face. In the next second, she realized it was Alaric's head and wished she could kick herself. "Sorry," she croaked.

Alaric jerked away, tossing his mane. Then he turned and ran at top speed away from the river, away from the camp. Away from her.

She cried a protest and tried to follow him, but fell shivering to the ground. *"Alaric!"* Dianthe shouted. "No, come back!" But he was already far beyond the reach of her voice, the moonlight turning his dark flanks silver and shining on the tip of his horn.

Dianthe stood staring off after him. Her hands were clenched into fists. Finally, she said, "Fire first. You two gather wood. I'll get Sienne wrapped up. At least she didn't get as wet as the rest of us."

She helped Sienne stagger to their tent and crawl inside, kicking off her boots. She put Sienne's blanket around her shoulders, then her heavy cloak, and guided her to lie on her bedroll. "When the fire's going, I'll come for you," she said. "See if you can't get some rest."

"Thank you," Sienne whispered. Her mouth still felt raw from the evocations, her stomach was sore, and she ached as if Perrin hadn't healed her from Alaric's beating. She remembered Alaric bearing down on her, his hand around her throat, his face contorted with rage, and tears flowed helplessly down her cheeks. She wasn't sure who she was crying for, herself or him. The plain truth was that even though she knew he wasn't at fault, that it was the carver woman who'd attacked her, she was going to have trouble not remembering all that every time she looked at him.

She lay in a numb stupor, horrible images running a mad cycle behind her eyelids, until a rustling at the tent flap told her Dianthe was back. "Are you awake?"

Sienne thought about lying, but realized the alternative was continuing to lie there, watching someone she cared about try to kill her. "Yes. What time is it?"

"I have no idea. Late. Come have something to eat."

Sienne found she could rise and even walk without help, though her vision was still blurry. No more casting spells for her that night. Perrin and Kalanath had found or hewn down a slim tree with a bole about eight inches in diameter, and had cut it into sections to burn, using some of them for seating. Sienne sat on one and breathed in the smell of burning wood. Dianthe handed her a few strips of dried meat. "No time for hunting, and it's a little late for it anyway."

"I don't mind," Sienne said. She liked the dried meat, which was flavorful once you got it chewed and properly moistened. Tonight it tasted like mud. Probably nothing would have tasted good, given the night she'd had.

Perrin was eating an apple. He always ate them as close to the core as anyone could get and not be spitting seeds. He took a final bite and tossed what little was left into the fire. "I am worried," he said.

"He'll come back." Dianthe didn't sound very certain.

"Of course he will," said Kalanath. "What I do not know is how he will be when he comes back."

Sienne gnawed on her meat and said nothing. She was looking at the fire, but she could feel their attention on her, an uncomfortable pressure that made her wish she could run into the darkness to get away from it.

"He'll be fine." Once again Dianthe didn't sound certain. "We need to treat him just as we always have. It could have happened to any of us."

"But it happened to him," Sienne said. "He fled his home to keep something like that from being done to him, and now it's happened anyway."

No one spoke. Sienne was sure she knew what they were thinking: Alaric was their leader, the one they all looked to for guidance, and if he lost his confidence because of this, what then? "It doesn't matter," she burst out, surprising herself. "I mean, it doesn't matter to me. We just have to make him see that he's still himself."

"If we can," Kalanath said. "It is a hard thing to make someone believe what they do not want to believe."

"Do you think he does not want to believe he is not changed?" Perrin said.

Kalanath looked off into the fire. "I think it is a dark thing, to have your mind taken from you. I think it is worse to be made to do terrible things. I think he blames himself. He *is* changed. It is just not for the worse. I do not know if he believes this."

The meat sat like a lump in Sienne's stomach. "I still feel unwell," she said, and stood. "Is it all right if I go to sleep? Wake me for my watch."

"Don't be stupid, Sienne," Dianthe said. "You're not standing watch until you're capable of casting spells. Go to sleep, and I'll wake you in the morning."

Sienne thought about arguing, but realized she wanted sleep, and arguing with Dianthe was usually pointless. "Good night," she said, and went back to her tent, trailing her blanket and cloak. She settled into her bedroll and closed her eyes, waiting for a return of the horrible memories. But food, and the warmth of the fire, had settled her demons for now. She said a brief prayer to Averran that he would watch out for Alaric that night, and fell asleep hoping he'd be back when she woke.

10

Sienne woke to Dianthe gently shaking her shoulder. Firelight lit the front flap of their tent, but it was still full dark outside. Dianthe's face was in shadow, backlit by the fire. "Is it morning?" Sienne asked, though it clearly wasn't. "I thought you said—"

"Alaric's back," Dianthe said. "You need to talk to him."

A jolt of fear shot through her, a memory of a huge hand wrapping around her throat. She pushed it aside and said, "Why me? What do I say? You're his best friend—you talk to him!"

Dianthe sat on her bedroll and laced her fingers together in front of her. "I did," she said. "But I'm not the one he nearly killed. He needs reassurance I can't give him."

"What, that I don't blame him for having been controlled by that bitch? That can't possibly be enough! I can't make it not have happened. I can't give him back his dignity. This isn't about hurting me, you know it isn't."

Dianthe studied her fingers. "Sienne," she said, "what I'm trying to say is, he's not tearing himself up over hurting you. It's that it was *you* he hurt. You can't be so blind as to not realize that would matter to him."

It was like a blow to the chest. "Oh," she said, the little word sounding like thunder in the silence that followed Dianthe's words. "I... oh."

"Please," Dianthe said. "Just talk to him. He needs to know he's not beyond redemption."

"But he hasn't done anything wrong! None of this was his fault!"

"Then tell him that. Tell him... I can't tell you what to say. You'll know the right words when the time comes." She let out a low chuckle. "You always do."

Sienne was sure that wasn't true, but she'd never had any luck arguing with Dianthe, especially when the woman was convinced she was right. She stood, crouching under the tent's low roof, and disentangled herself from her blanket, leaving it piled on her bedroll. She straightened her shirt and put on her boots. She fiddled with her cloak, which wouldn't sit straight across her shoulders. Dianthe said, "Stop fidgeting and go." Sienne went.

Alaric sat on one of the logs, a hunched dark shape next to the fire. His breath steamed in the cold night air, but although he wasn't wearing more than a thin shirt, he didn't seem to notice the cold, or the fire. He just sat with his hands resting on his knees and his head bowed. Sienne's feet crunched on the frost-rimed grass, and her cloak dragged behind her, making a swishing sound. She hoped she was loud enough not to startle him. Not that she was much worried about it; Alaric's hearing was preternaturally acute. It just seemed more wrong, now, to startle him when he'd already suffered so much.

She could tell he knew she was there because the muscles in his jaw tensed visibly even in the dim light. He didn't turn his head, or speak, just sat there staring at the fire. In the face of his silence, she couldn't think of anything to say. She didn't know if she should go on standing, or pull up a log and sit, or turn around and leave him to his pain. Finally, she blurted out, "I'm sorry I threw up on you."

Alaric shifted, but still didn't look at her. "It washed off," he said. The deep timbre of his voice surprised her, as if she'd never heard him speak before. It was the first thing he'd said to her since hitting her.

"It was embarrassing," she said.

Alaric bowed his head more deeply. "If that's the only thing you have to feel embarrassed about, you're very fortunate."

This left her, again, with nothing to say. She felt awkward and stupid and wished she could go back to her tent and sleep until all of this went away. But she remembered Dianthe's words, told herself *This isn't about you*, and said, "It wasn't your fault."

"It was my hand," Alaric said. "My fist. Your throat."

"You would never have done that if she hadn't charmed you."

"You don't know that."

His words sounded so dismissive that anger swept away all her awkwardness. She prodded a log with her toe until it rolled close to his, then sat, tucking her cloak under her for padding. "So you harbor some secret hatred of me, is that it? I guess I'm still a wizard, and deserving of being killed?"

His head came up fast, his pale blue eyes blazing, and she almost flinched again, remembering his hand around her throat. "Of course not! Sienne—"

"Then it's that you're a monster deep down. An irrational monster just biding your time to kill all of us, and I happened to draw the short straw."

His lips compressed in a tight line. "You're being ridiculous."

"So are you. Get your head out of your ass for one moment and *listen to me*. That carver woman cast a charm on you. It made you do things you would never have done if you were in control. None of that was your fault. It was hers, as surely as if she'd struck me herself. I don't blame you, and I want you to stop blaming yourself."

Alaric was shaking his head. "It's not that simple. I can't..." He took a deep breath and looked away. "I didn't recognize you. I thought you were one of the carvers, and yet I knew, deep within me, that it was a lie. I just didn't know what the lie was. I wanted to kill... you... because I thought that would clear away the confusion. Then I woke up, and my hand was around your throat, and you looked so terrified... I never want to see another human being look at me that way. Least of all you."

She held her breath, waiting, afraid to speak for fear of shutting him down again.

"I can still feel her inside my head," he went on. "Not really, not because she's somehow still there. It's more the way a scar aches in cold weather, the memory of her. I ran for miles tonight, trying to drive the memory out, but all I could do was make it retreat a little. I'm afraid to sleep. And when I'm not thinking of her, I'm remembering how you flinched from me when we reached camp—"

"I'm sorry about that. I wasn't afraid of you, it was just that you were so close when I opened my eyes, I was startled. I'm sorry."

He waved that aside. "I'm a big man, and I know that makes some people afraid of me, just on principle. But my team—none of you should fear me. And yet she controlled me so easily, I'm afraid of *myself*. Afraid she unlocked something inside me that might surface again."

"That's not true," Sienne said. "And it wasn't easy. I don't know much about charm spells, but I do know they're supposed to work instantly and completely. That you were able to fight her at all... I'd say it's because you're Sassaven, not human, but given what you've said about the binding ritual, I think it ought to make you *more* susceptible, not less. But she had to work hard to keep you under control. Don't be afraid of yourself, Alaric. You *are* strong—strong of will, not just of body."

"You're just saying that."

"Yes, because I'm prone to telling you flattering untruths. I think —all right, you know what I think happened? I think those carvers do that with all the people they capture, make them kill their friends or loved ones and then realize that's what they've done. And I think they looked at us and figured it would be especially funny to make the big strong guy kill the smallest of our party."

Alaric flinched and turned his head away. The furtive, guilty motion made her heart ache. She went on, "But what they *got* was a wizard and someone who may possibly be the only man in the world who could stand up to that carver bitch even a little. And he turns out to be a unicorn. I wish I could have slowed time so I could see her face just before I smacked it with a *force* bolt." The image made her giggle, and she clapped a hand over her mouth to hold it back.

Alaric shook his head, but just for a moment, she saw him smile. "Why didn't you hit me with it?"

"I... it never occurred to me. I just wanted her to stop hurting you."

The smile vanished. "You are far more generous than I deserve." He turned his head away from her again. "I can't believe you can even bear to talk to me. Don't your memories burn inside you?"

"They do," she admitted, remembering what she'd thought earlier that evening. "But it will pass. I don't want to be ruled by fear."

"I'm starting to think I don't have a choice," Alaric said, his voice so low she could barely hear it.

Unshed tears burned her eyes. Her heart ached as if he'd trodden on it. Impulsively, she put her hand over his where it rested on his knee, leaned forward, and kissed his cheek, wanting desperately to reassure him.

That was her intent. But he jerked, startled, when she touched his hand, and turned to face her so her kiss landed not on his cheek, but on the corner of his mouth. She drew back in confusion. Alaric's eyes were wide with surprise. He said nothing. They stared at each other for a long, breathless moment in which Sienne felt caught between the past where they were friends and comrades and a future she could hardly imagine.

She didn't know which of them moved first, whether he came to her or she went to him, but in the next moment they were kissing, him with his hands around her waist, drawing her onto his lap, and it was the most glorious moment Sienne had ever experienced. His kisses grew tentative, uncertain, and she put her arms around his neck so he would know she had absolutely no reservations about what they were doing.

"Sienne," he murmured, pulling away, "no. We shouldn't."

"I know. Shut up and kiss me again."

"We're companions...what if—"

"What if you get controlled by a psychotic monster and try to strangle me, and everything is awkward between us? At least this way, I get to kiss you, and feel your arms around me, and if that goes wrong, well, I'd rather have had the kissing than not."

His hands hadn't moved from around her waist, he hadn't pushed her away, and it made her heart leap up for joy. "That makes no sense," he said, but he was smiling. "The only part I understood," he added, "was that you want me to kiss you again."

"More than anything."

His lips touched hers again, and this time his kiss was confident, and his hand strayed from her waist to touch the nape of her neck. "I'm sorry I hurt you," he murmured against her mouth.

"I know. I forgive you."

"I've thought about kissing you for so long."

"Me too. But I was afraid—"

"I think the time for fear is past," Alaric said, and they were done talking.

He held her, and they kissed, and talked, until the sky turned gray and then pink. Then Sienne rose and made breakfast, refusing his offer of help. "You're too impatient to make porridge," she said. "You always make it lumpy."

"I hate porridge. Are you sure there's no way to bring eggs into the wilderness?"

Sienne paused in her stirring to think. "I suppose, if you had the right kind of crate—but even then you'd have to worry about bouncing around. It would be better to use *convey*. It's a spell that moves an object from one place to another instantaneously. So if you stored a box with a dozen eggs in a particular location, you could *convey* them to your hand wherever you were."

"I like this idea. You need to find this spell as soon as we get back to Fioretti."

"Back to Fioretti?" Perrin said, crawling out of the tent. He eyed Alaric, and Sienne saw him make the conscious decision not to bring up the events of the previous night. "I dislike going home in failure, but in this circumstance I do not think we can be blamed."

"We will have to think of another way to get the knife," Kalanath said, emerging after Perrin. He, too, pretended nothing abnormal had happened, even though Alaric in the light of day looked like someone who'd spent the night running wild and then hadn't slept. "We can help Tonia Figlari regain her title some other way."

"We could," Alaric said, "but we won't." He nodded to Dianthe, who for once wasn't making pained noises about too much sunlight and not enough coffee. Dianthe shot Sienne a look. Sienne blushed. For all her bold words to Alaric, she wasn't sure she wanted her friends to know how their relationship had changed. True, they probably deserved to know, as it affected all of them, but she was a private person and it was a private thing. And there was a tiny part of her that kept screaming *Don't forget what happened with Rance! You thought he loved you, and he betrayed you! What makes you think Alaric is any different?* She wished she could find that tiny part of her and *force*-bolt it into unconsciousness.

Alaric stood and walked around the fire to where he could see all of them. "I apologize for failing you," he said, and held up a hand to forestall denials. "I don't mean in being mind-controlled. That might have happened to any of us. No, I mean in deserting you last night. That was selfish and dangerous and I should never have done it. I promise it won't happen again."

Perrin opened his mouth to say something, then closed it again, exchanging glances with Dianthe that Sienne couldn't read. "As for going home," Alaric continued, "it's true we might abandon this job and feel not a bit guilty about it. We're the first people in history to have survived a carver attack and we could return to tell everyone about it. No one would fault us for not going back. And I'm certainly not going to make the decision for all of us. But I can think of two reasons for us to finish the job."

He held up one finger. "We need that knife. Tonia Figlari may sound like a waif, but she was determined enough to put us in a position where we'd have to do her bidding. If she says she'll destroy the knife if we don't bring her the stone, she'll do it. And getting the stone means walking back in there. So that's one reason." He held up a second finger. "The other reason is more personal, but still important. You people left my sword back there with the carvers. And I'll be damned if I let them keep it."

11

Sienne smoothed the sheet of paper flat on her spellbook, dipped the nib of her pen into the dish of blood ink, and began scribing the staccato lines of the summoning *jaunt*. The unknown wizard who'd owned the flowered spellbook couldn't have been a beginner, if she had that summoning, but the rest of the contents of her spellbook weren't much different from Sienne's. Sienne had found three spells she didn't already have: *jaunt, drift,* and *mud.*

She wasn't sure about the usefulness of *drift*, which made you temporarily light as a feather. It could keep you from dying of a fall, but being able to cast the spell while you were already falling would require practice and a lot of luck. But in the nine months since she'd become a scrapper, she'd learned that unusual circumstances called for unusual solutions. She would scribe all three, and see what uses she'd find for them.

Jaunt was one she'd heard of but never been taught, on the grounds that a duke's daughter wouldn't need the ability to transport herself instantaneously between places. How short-sighted. Who knew what kind of need might develop in, say, a ball in which you wanted to escape the attentions of an obnoxious suitor? She wasn't confident she could guess how to use it, or what its limits were. Range of sight? Any place she knew well? Anywhere at all within a certain area? And were there safeguards to keep you from *jaunting* into a solid object? She dotted the last line and threw the pen into the fire. She'd been taught never to use the same pen for scribing more than one spell, but not why that was necessary. Her education had the oddest holes in it.

She set *jaunt* aside and picked up a fresh pen. "You know how boring this is," she said without looking up. "Having you staring at me isn't so much a distraction as a reminder that wizardry isn't all that glamorous."

"I've packed our tent and I have nothing better to do," Dianthe said. "Kalanath is practicing, Perrin is praying, and Alaric is pacing the riverside muttering to himself. It's watch you or watch them."

"Kalanath's practicing is beautiful," Sienne said, tracing the swooping lines of the transform *mud*. This one, she had plans for. Transforming stone to mud was less elegant than *sculpt*, but for freeing the falcon stone from the wall, it was ideal. It was unfortunate she had to be in physical contact with the stone she transformed, because none of them were sure the wall the falcon stone was in supported the keep's structure, but it was the fastest way to get it loose.

"So is your writing. What little I can see of it. If I watch for more than a few seconds, my eyes start to water."

"That's because the human mind can't comprehend magic in its pure state. You forget the first part of a spell before you get past the middle of it." Scribing spells from a book was much harder than having them dictated to you. Sienne was good at concentrating, but she could feel a headache coming on. She finished *mud* and began working on *drift*. "I want to test these before we implement the plan."

"You have time. Perrin said he thought he would have to argue with Averran over the blessings he wants."

"I hope Averran is in a giving mood." If he wasn't, *mud* wouldn't matter. Sienne drew a final curving line, tossed her pen into the fire, and gathered up the metal bowl containing her blood ink. There was a splash of blood left in the bottom. She summoned a glob of water over the bowl to fall into it, turning the dark red blood pink. Pink like carver's blood. Sienne shuddered and walked to the river to toss the bloody water away. She'd had her blood used against her by a wizard once, and while she didn't think that was likely to happen now, she never took chances.

"Finished?" Alaric said. The cold wind ruffled his loose shirt, but he didn't pick up his cloak that lay nearby, just crossed his arms over his chest. His short hair barely moved in the wind.

"Nearly. I have to make the pages invulnerable." The wind ruffled the spell pages too, pinned down by a stone from the river bed. "When they're dry."

"I don't think you should test the featherweight spell in this wind. What if someone got blown away?"

"I'm not sure it works that way, but I intend you to hold onto my wrists, just in case."

He smiled at her, his eyes alight with amusement. "You do, eh? There are easier ways to convince me to hold you."

Sienne blushed and looked around. Nobody was near enough to overhear them, except maybe Dianthe—Sienne had learned never to underestimate the range of her friend's hearing. "Should we... Alaric, I don't even know what this is between us! And I'd feel stupid announcing it to the rest of the team when I don't know what I'm announcing."

Alaric took a couple of steps toward her. "It is two people exploring their attraction to each other," he said in a low voice, "and I agree, it's a bit premature to make it public. Much as I'd love to sweep you off your feet and kiss you whenever the opportunity arises."

This close, she could smell the faint musk of the unicorn, and realized it was Alaric's own scent, if much less strong. "I'd say the same, but it's unlikely I could sweep you anywhere," she said, making him laugh. "I suppose there aren't many chances for us to explore out here, but when we get back to Fioretti..."

"Exactly. Keep thinking like that. We'll get the damned stone and exchange it for the knife, and then... actually, I haven't thought past that. Too many things could go wrong."

Sienne sighed and retrieved the pages. She concentrated briefly, and they went stiff and faintly brown. "I can't stop seeing them pouring out of the keep's front door. There are so many of them." She inserted the new pages into the back of her spellbook and closed its complicated latch.

"And one of them is a wizard. Sienne, I want you to promise me something. If she controls me again, I want you to knock me out."

"We need you fighting!"

"You don't need me fighting you. Promise me. If you can't get a clear shot at her, stop me before I hurt anyone."

His expression was so bleak it frightened her. "I promise I won't let you hurt anyone. But if Perrin is successful, it won't be necessary." She put her spellbook back into its harness, next to the flowered spellbook—she should be able to make some money off it in Fioretti—and cradled it in her arms, open to *drift*. Extending her left arm to Alaric, she said, "Hold on, and try not to let go. I don't know how this will feel to you."

Alaric took her wrist in a firm grip. His hand was dry and callused from years of sword fighting. "If you start to blow away," he said, "I reserve the right to hold you close."

Sienne smiled. "Now I'm not sure what to wish for." She read off the sweet syllables of the transform. As she read, she felt a strange bubbling sensation in her stomach that spread to her limbs, almost like the tingling of circulation returning after being cut off, but pleasant rather than painful. She felt light, as if her bones and organs no longer weighed her down. The sensation of wind blowing against her body grew more intense, but she didn't feel as if she were going to blow away, just that walking against the wind would be difficult.

She finished casting the spell and lifted one foot cautiously. It was surprisingly hard to make it move. She felt as if she had less control over her muscles now that they weighed practically nothing. She took a couple of steps toward Alaric. "Does my arm feel any different to you?"

"Not at all. You look as if you're swimming through air."

"Why don't you try lifting me?"

Alaric raised his eyebrows, but took hold of the back of her waist-band and lifted like a mother cat picking a kitten up by the scruff of its neck. Sienne squeaked as she flew upward. If she hadn't been teth-ered by his grip, she was sure she'd have sailed into the sky to hang like dandelion fluff before drifting downward. "Let go my trousers, and let's see how long it takes me to fall," she said.

"You still have mass," Alaric pointed out, "and momentum. I bet it takes some time, though."

"Astonishing," Perrin said, coming up to where they stood. He smelled of brandy, and his steps were unsteady. "Perhaps trans-porting the stone will be easier than we thought."

"It only lasts a few minutes," Sienne said, "but if I do it right, I can make the stone fall lightly instead of dropping to the floor and maybe breaking." Her words brought a memory to mind, of something odd about the stone she'd noticed just before the carvers had appeared. Or, rather, that she'd noticed something odd she couldn't identify. She still didn't know what had struck her. She decided not to worry about it. They had enough troubles without her dwelling on possibly imaginary ones.

"You're moving like a soap bubble," Dianthe said. She and Kalanath joined their little group, and everyone stared at Sienne, floating gracefully to the ground.

"I feel fizzy," Sienne said. Just as she said that, the fizzy feeling vanished, and she dropped the last two inches to land awkwardly on her feet. Alaric helped her find her balance, then released her. "That was interesting. It didn't feel like flying, because I had no control. Just floating."

"So it works," Kalanath said. "But will it work when we are surrounded by carvers who try to kill us?"

"It had better," Sienne said. "It comes down to how fast I am."

"And the protections we have," Perrin said. He waved a handful of rice paper squares and smiled in a slightly drunken way. "It took a large quantity of brandy, but Averran has been generous, if irritable at the specifics of my requests."

"Which are...?" Alaric said.

Perrin took out needle and thread and began binding the squares together at one corner. "Normally, I leave it to Averran to decide what we need. In this case, I had to explain the nature of the carver wizard's magic and ask for something that would negate it—something that would affect all of us." He knotted and bit off the thread, and drew out his colored pastels to mark each blessing according to what it did. "He was not pleased with the request."

"That seems strange," Dianthe said.

"Averran teaches that human will should be developed through challenges and trials. He seemed to be of the opinion that we should fight this wizard's dominance unaided. I had to plead and cajole to get him to understand that such fighting is beyond our capacity." Perrin carefully didn't look at Alaric. "The blessing he gave me, in the end, will not prevent our being controlled, but will give us mental clarity to allow us to fight her domination. It is, I am afraid, the best I can do."

"It's better than nothing," Alaric said. "What else?"

"I decided I should leave the rest entirely to Averran, having pestered him quite enough for one day. There are healing blessings—not many, for which I am grateful—a few shields, one of which is the full protective dome, and one I do not fully understand. It has something to do with communication, but it has lines that indicate it is to be used offensively, not as mental speech between us."

"I'm just as happy it's not mental speech," Dianthe said with a shudder. "The one time we had that was more than enough."

"Indeed. And then there is a blessing I do not recognize at all. It hints at breaking, but there is no suggestion as to what." Perrin frowned. "It will have to be a last resort."

"You're right, Averran was generous," Alaric said. "What about the other thing?"

"Hah. Averran rose to new heights of crankiness when I asked him for that guidance. In the end, the vision I received was nothing more than the sun, high in the noonday sky. I presume that the day we choose matters less than the time at which we make our assault, so we may attack today so long as it is near noon."

"That's better than I'd hoped." Alaric let out a deep breath. "All right. So we can't count on the carvers being asleep, or absent, but Perrin's vision says we'll have the best chance of success if we attack at noon. We don't know if they can be invisible while they attack—"

"If it were true invisibility, maybe," Sienne said. "But their ability is more like camouflage. I think—I don't know, maybe we shouldn't depend on this, but I think they only stay hidden so long as they're not moving."

"So it's possible, but unlikely, that we'll be fighting invisible enemies," Alaric said with a nod. "Dianthe and Kalanath, did you observe any other unusual tactics while you were fighting them?"

"They can distract you with their eyes," Kalanath said. "Until I realized this, I looked them in the eye and forgot what I was doing."

"That's how they got me," Dianthe said, rubbing her now-uninjured left arm. "It only lasts for the space of a breath, but a lot can happen in such a short time."

"We already know they're no more invulnerable than a human when it comes to their bodies," Alaric added. "So as long as we avoid their eyes, and can keep the wizard from casting whatever other spells she has on tap, we can hold them off while Sienne retrieves the stone."

They all looked at Sienne. "*Mud* radiates out from where I touch the wall," she said. "And I don't know how long it takes to turn stone to mud. The closer I can get to the falcon stone, the faster it will be. But..." She hesitated, then went on, "There was something strange about the stone I couldn't put my finger on when we saw it. There wasn't time to work it out because we were attacked, but... something isn't right."

"Something dangerous?" Alaric asked.

"I don't know. I don't think so. Just something off about the stone. It probably doesn't matter as far as retrieving it goes. I'm sure it will come to me once we've got it safely away."

"Just so long as you're sure. I don't want any more surprises than we're already certain to have." Alaric nodded. "Then the plan is to sneak up on the keep and get as far as we can before engaging in combat. Dianthe and Kalanath will fight off the carvers while Perrin defends Sienne. And I will get my sword and keep that wizard from attacking anyone else."

No one spoke. Sienne saw indecision on Dianthe's face a moment before it hardened into resolve. "Shouldn't we worry about defending against their attacks, no matter who brings them?"

Alaric's face was stony. "This is not up for debate," he said. "Sienne convinced me that I resisted her control more than anyone could be expected to. With Perrin's blessing, I expect that resistance to become even greater. I intend to keep her attention off the rest of you and, Sisyletus willing, I'll take her head."

Sienne knew that look. There was no point arguing with him when he looked like that.

"Perrin, how long will that blessing protecting us from being controlled last?" Alaric asked.

"Half an hour, perhaps a little longer. But I doubt retrieving the stone will take us half an hour, unless the mud spell is considerably slower than we expect."

"It's slow. It's not that slow," Sienne said.

"Then it's time we move out," Alaric said.

They took the donkeys and all their gear to the ford, to wait on their return. This time, when Sienne cast *fit* on Alaric to make him tall enough to ferry them across the river, he didn't look uncomfortable or afraid. His hands lingered on her waist longer than was necessary, and she smiled at him and felt warmed by the smile he gave her. He hadn't lost his confidence, he was ready to face the carvers... if not for his insistence on fighting the wizard himself, she would have thought him untouched by his experience. His reasons made sense, but she knew—they all knew—sense was not what motivated him. She wasn't sure he was wrong. If killing the wizard was what it took to exorcise his demons, she would cheer him on. And pray he wasn't so set on his personal revenge he put the rest of them in danger.

There was no way to stay hidden as they crossed the plains toward the abandoned village, so they didn't try. If the carvers had placed sentries to guard against their return, they were invisible.

Sienne hoped the carvers believed they wouldn't be so stupid as to return after being routed once. If they could catch the carvers unawares, so much the better for the success of their plan.

Once they reached the village, they moved more slowly, taking advantage of the broken foundations as best they could. Alaric was never going to be stealthy, no matter how soundlessly he moved, but he still took shelter where he could. When they reached the collapsed smithy, they paused for Dianthe to look around. "Nothing moving," she said. "I'm not assuming not seeing them means they aren't here, but I don't hear or smell anything."

"Smell?" Perrin said.

"They have a rancid odor, like rotten meat," Dianthe said. "It's very faint, but still noticeable."

Sienne hadn't noticed it, but Dianthe had skills that were beyond her. "I think they were partly visible, and we just didn't realize it," she said. "I felt we were being watched. I don't have that feeling now."

"I had that feeling as well," Kalanath said. "Now there is nothing but the silence."

"We're nearly there," Alaric said. "I think it's time for that blessing. We shouldn't talk once we're on the road to the keep."

Perrin nodded and tore a paper square with a smudge of pale pink on one corner free from the others. "Stand in a circle around me," he said. The others clustered in close. Perrin held the blessing high over his head and muttered his invocation. The paper burst into pink flames, licking Perrin's hand. Nothing else happened.

Perrin lowered his hand as the fire died away. "That was—" He shut his mouth abruptly. "Did you hear that?"

"Hear what?" Dianthe said. Her eyes grew wide. "Oh, that is strange."

"What is?" Sienne said. *What is?* echoed inside her head, a strange doubling of sound as if she had spoken with two voices, half a second apart. "Is it supposed to do that? That echo?"

"I do not—" Kalanath began. An unexpected smile spread across his face. "I like it."

"I don't hear—" Alaric said. "Oh."

"I have no idea what it means," Perrin said, "save that such a doubling might make controlling someone under that influence difficult to control. That is a supposition."

"Let's take it on faith that it works, and keep going," Alaric said. He held out his hand. "Good fortune to us."

One by one, they put their hands together in the center of the circle. Sienne tried not to think of it as a farewell. They were going to survive, damn it, no matter what they found inside that keep.

They walked up the road of rounded stones Sienne still couldn't help thinking of as tiny skulls toward the keep's front door. No one leapt from the shadows to attack them with a terrible curved knife or a spell cast without a book, something that still unsettled Sienne. The frieze over the arched doorway looked no different, though Sienne couldn't help wishing the Figlari dukes had put their family emblem there instead. So much easier if they had.

They huddled inside the arch while Dianthe listened at the closed door. She shook her head. Too thick to hear anything, or maybe there wasn't anything to be heard. Alaric nodded. He pushed on the door, which opened as readily as it had before. The carvers hadn't barred it against them, so either they weren't expecting their return, or they weren't worried about the five humans as a threat. He slipped through the narrow gap as quietly as he could, followed closely by the others.

Once again, the entry hall was empty. Sienne looked carefully at the walls and the gallery above. No sign of anyone concealed there. Alaric gestured for them to follow him. Sienne moved into position behind Dianthe, who with Alaric would be first through the door. Then Sienne, then Perrin with his shields, and finally Kalanath.

Alaric held up three fingers. Folding them away one at a time, he counted down to zero. He flung open the door to the great hall and, roaring a challenge, ran through. Dianthe followed him, and Sienne, taking a deep breath, clutched her open spellbook and dashed forward.

12

They'd caught the carvers napping. Sienne had time to observe them stirring from where they slept on the sunken floor or slumped against tables before she was across the room and darting up the steps of the dais. The carver wizard wasn't there, for which Sienne thanked whatever avatars watched over them. So much the better if they didn't have to face her, and never mind about Alaric's personal revenge.

"Help me push the table!" she cried to Perrin. Kalanath was right; once you got used to it, the doubled sound was pleasant. They grabbed both ends of the table and hauled it close to the wall beneath the stone falcon. Sienne climbed atop it and slapped her left hand as high as it would go on the wall, which was about three feet from the bottom of the falcon stone. She raised the spellbook to eye level and spoke the syllables of the transform.

The wall went spongy in an instant. Her hand, pressed flat against it, sank a fraction of an inch. Dampness rose from the smooth, hard, cold surface. The yellowish-gray stone around her hand turned brown and oozed between her fingers. The brown color spread outward like water soaking into a cloth.

She shrieked with delight and turned her head to look at Perrin, who had his back to her. As she watched, he tore free a blessing and chanted an invocation. A pearly gray hemisphere sprang up around them seconds before a pair of carvers crashed into it, knives raised.

"How fast?" he asked.

Sienne looked back at the wall. The shield's top was only inches from her head and hugged the wall, making Sienne wonder if it continued through it and was visible on the outside. The dark stain spread nearly a foot from her hand, unimpeded by the shield. "Faster than I thought," she said.

Perrin nodded and turned his attention to the carvers slashing at the shield. Sienne closed her spellbook and opened it again, this time to *drift*. The wall was starting to drip, if you could call huge gobbets of mud "drips." Mud covered Sienne's hand entirely and slid down her wrist. The stain was two feet in diameter now, and the wall looked like a child's sandcastle eaten away by the oncoming tide.

She glanced away to see how her companions fared. Kalanath had taken down the two who had been hacking at the shield, but three more had taken their place. He and Dianthe stood back to back, fending off attackers. Alaric had repossessed his enormous sword and cut a swathe through the carvers who'd been sleeping at the tables. His blade was gory with pink blood.

Sienne shuddered and turned her attention back to the wall. The dark, wet stain had nearly reached the stone. Sienne readied her spellbook to cast *drift* on the stone as soon as it began to slip down through the mud. An artifact should be able to withstand falling ten feet to the table underneath, but—

Sienne gasped. Artifact. *That* was what was wrong. The falcon stone had no magic on it.

She watched the dark stain spread to the stone and around it—and begin turning the rounded ridge of the falcon stone's edge to mud. She yanked her hand off the wall, flicking drops of mud every-where. The spread of mud stopped immediately. One edge of the falcon stone sagged and dripped. She wiped her hand on her trousers, heedless of the mess, and stared through the gray shield at the stone. It wasn't an artifact. It was clearly what they'd been sent after, but an artifact wouldn't have been affected by *mud*.

With a silent *pop*, the shield vanished. "Sienne, take care!" Perrin shouted. She ignored him. Hopping off the table, she grabbed one of the tall chairs and lifted it to the table top, then climbed on it. It gave her enough height that she could barely touch the muddy edge of the stone.

She looked around wildly for something else to climb on. It was just in time to see the door swing open and the carver wizard enter the room. She moved as gracefully as ever, but more rapidly than before, as if she were in a hurry to dispose of them and get back to whatever she'd been doing. Alaric saw her, and booted away a carver trying to disembowel him. He advanced on the wizard, sword held at the ready.

The wizard, seeming unconcerned about the oncoming threat, looked directly at Sienne. Sienne blinked, caught by the force of those blue eyes. She hopped down from the chair and jumped to the floor, flipping pages from *drift* to *force*. Alaric couldn't be allowed to hurt the wizard; this was all just a misunderstanding—

Perrin gestured, and something that blazed with orange light hit Sienne in the face like a pillow, soft and hard at the same time. She blinked. Two images were overlaid across her vision. In one, the carver wizard crouched in terror before a monstrous Alaric, and Sienne's heart went out to the woman. In the other, the wizard stared at her, willing her to attack her friend. Sienne shook the images away. *Force*, yes, but against the bitch who'd hurt Alaric.

"*Sienne!*" Perrin shouted. Sienne screamed as a carver with a sharp, bloody knife rose up before her and slashed at her throat. She stumbled backward, and Perrin dove between her and the carver. A second later, a gray shield sprang up around Perrin's arm, blocking the carver's second blow.

"Sorry!" Sienne cried.

Perrin looked up at her. "So am I," he said. Sienne gasped. Bright red blood soaked through his vest and down the arm of his shirt. She let her spellbook fall to her side and knelt beside him, searching for the wound.

"Don't worry about me," Perrin gasped. "Get the stone."

She almost told him the truth—that they'd risked their lives for nothing. But if Tonia Figlari couldn't sense magic, they might still give her the stone and get the knife. Sienne ran for the table, opening her spellbook as she went, and cast *fit* on the chair. It grew instantly, shaking the table, and she leaped on it and could easily reach the stone. Feeling dizzy from too much spellcasting, she turned to *sculpt* and read off the transform, swallowing the now-cloying sweetness of the spell.

She dropped the spellbook in its harness and plunged her hands into the stone surrounding the falcon. Kneading and shoving with both hands, she pushed the now-pliable stone away from the round edges of the falcon stone. Carefully not touching it, she reached behind it and scraped more soft stone away from its back. The falcon stone slid.

Faster than she'd thought possible, she had the spellbook open to *drift*. The falcon stone was falling by the time she finished reading the transform, but slowed in its fall before it was halfway to the table, and landed atop it with barely a thump.

Sienne jumped off the chair and picked the stone up. It weighed almost nothing, though that wouldn't last long. She didn't have the reserves to keep casting *drift* unless she felt like ending up in the condition she'd been in the last time they ran from this place. She took advantage of its current feather-light state and shoved it off the table to drift to the floor. It didn't lie flat, but canted as if it were raised on the back as well as the front.

Leaving it to lie there, she ran to Perrin, who lay semi-conscious beneath a shield two carvers were slashing at. It looked like it might fail at any moment. Sienne grabbed him and said, "You need to heal yourself!"

Perrin nodded. "Find...the right blessing," he murmured. Sienne had seen him invoke healing blessings often enough that she knew which one he needed. She snatched it up, and he took it with a bloody hand. Just then, the shield popped, and the carvers stepped back, startled. Sienne whipped out her spellbook, frantically opening it to *scream*.

Alaric came out of nowhere, sweeping his greatsword at the carvers. Pink blood flew as he took the head of one right off. The other backed away, snarling silently. Sienne turned the page to *force*, but Alaric put himself between her and the carver. "Get the stone," he said, poking it with his toe.

"Time to—*watch out!*" Sienne shrieked. It was all she had time for before the carver wizard, her face a bloody mess, strode forward and put a hand to Alaric's forehead.

Alaric stopped. His eyes closed and his mouth opened in an agonized howl. Sienne scrambled around to where she could *force*-blast the wizard, but Alaric shook himself like a dog coming out of deep water and threw himself at the wizard, blocking Sienne's shot. He wrapped his arms around the woman and bore her to the ground.

"Never again," he snarled, took her head between his hands, and snapped her neck.

Sienne gaped at the suddenness of it. Alaric dropped the dead wizard and rose, gathering up his sword. "Time to go!" he shouted.

Sienne tried to lift the stone, but *drift* had worn off, and she had to work at getting it off the ground. Then Alaric was there, sheathing his sword. He picked the stone up as easily as if it still weighed almost nothing.

A bloody hand on her arm startled Sienne. "You guard our retreat," Perrin said. He sounded as if he'd never been injured. Sienne took up a stance with her book open, though the words danced on the page and she wasn't sure she could cast spells. The carvers didn't know that.

Kalanath was suddenly beside her. "We will walk backwards together, you and I," he said, and slammed the steel-shod end of his staff into a carver's chest with a sickening crack. Sienne nodded and took a step, then another, hoping her friends wouldn't let either of them fall.

She nearly did stumble over the steps leading up from the sunken floor, and only Perrin's guiding hand kept her from falling. The carvers followed them as they had the night before, their eyes glittering—Sienne felt dazed for a moment, then remembered she shouldn't meet their eyes and focused on their hands instead.

She squeezed close to Kalanath so they could both fit through the door out of the great hall, and heard his heavy breathing in rhythm with her own. Then they were out of the entry hall into the bright sunlight. How long had it all taken? Not half an hour, probably much less. It felt like forever.

"Excuse me," Perrin said, stepping in front of Sienne and Kalanath.

"What are you doing?" Kalanath exclaimed. "You will block us."

"I have determined what this blessing does. One moment." Perrin took a blessing marked with rosy pink on one corner. "My thanks, o Lord, and if you will, stop being a cranky bastard and be useful for once."

Rose-colored flames played over his hand. Perrin jerked backward as if punched, nearly falling into Kalanath. And the massed ranks of carvers, considerably diminished from the night before, lurched and fell like puppets whose strings had been cut.

Perrin regained his footing. "We should run," he said, and took off down the road toward the village. Sienne, startled, jerked into motion and ran after him, surrounded by her friends.

"What *was* that?" she gasped. "And why didn't you do it sooner?"

"Later, when we are not running for our lives," Perrin said.

They ran without speaking then, though Sienne glanced back once and saw no pursuit. It wasn't a risk she wanted to take. Beside her, Alaric was breathing easily despite the burden of the stone. She remembered it wasn't an artifact, and the thought made her angry and bewildered all at once. If Tonia Figlari had set them up to die out here... but surely she couldn't have known carvers had taken over the

Figlari keep. Or was the story of the falcon a myth, and Tonia had been fooled as much as any of them? She concentrated on running, and on being grateful they were all still alive.

They reached the ford and swam across without waiting for Sienne to cast *fit* on Alaric. Dripping and shivering, they collected Button and his nameless companion and trudged to the nearest copse, where they started a fire and settled in to dry off. Dianthe handed around hard biscuits and apples for a noon meal. As she gave Perrin his food, she said, "So—what was it?"

"It was a blast of mental communication—in this case, the word 'fall,'" Perrin said. "Though it is not a compulsion, and likely I could have used any word. I believe it is a mental form of *scream*. As to the latter, its use occurred to me as I was dying of my injury, and I was rather preoccupied. Not to mention that its efficacy is heightened when the enemy is grouped in that manner, again like *scream*."

"I like it," Alaric said. "Very effective."

Sienne watched him covertly. He didn't seem at all disturbed by having killed someone with his bare hands. Granted, the carver wizard had been evil and not human, but she'd *looked* human, at least a little... it might be good that he wasn't upset, but maybe they should all be worried.

"And we got the stone," Dianthe said, patting it where it lay in the grass nearby.

"Well," Sienne said. "About that. It's... not what we were told."

She was suddenly the center of attention. "Don't tell me it's not the thing we were sent after," Alaric said.

"It matches the description Tonia Figlari gave us. It's the right stone. But it's not an artifact."

"You are sure of this?" Kalanath said. He prodded the stone with the tip of his staff.

"Very sure. Not only does it not have magic—that's the thing I noticed but wasn't conscious of before—it was nearly turned to mud with the rest of the wall. An artifact would be immune to a transform."

They stared at the stone. "So... what does that mean?" Dianthe said.

"It could mean several things," Alaric said. "Tonia might have lied to us about the stone, intending us to die here. She might have told the truth and just been misinformed. Or someone might have used her to get at us."

Sienne hadn't thought of that last one. "What do you mean?"

"She chose us because of our reputation, but she's no scrapper. So someone must have steered her in our direction. Which leads us back to the possibility we came up with about Sienne's friend Aneirin—"

"He is *not* my friend."

"Sienne's acquaintance, then. The possibility that one of our enemies is behind this."

"But aside from the Giordas, we don't have any enemies who would care enough to set up this convoluted plot," Dianthe said. "At least as far as we're aware. And those enemies would have had to know this job meant almost certain death. Nobody's been out here for years to know the carvers were here."

"That we know of," Perrin said. He stretched his feet out toward the fire. "But I admit it strains credulity that someone else might have come here and survived the encounter, let alone that it should be someone who wishes us ill. I cannot believe we have made *that* many enemies."

"Neither can I," Alaric said. "The simplest explanation is that the story of the falcon stone is a family legend without a lick of truth to it, and Tonia Figlari was just wrong. But..." He stared into the fire. "My instincts tell me something else is going on. I don't know if we were intended to die here, or if..." He stood and lifted one end of the stone, raising it to teeter on the rim. Upended, it revealed the back of the stone was, in fact, not flat. It looked like the tail and claws of a falcon. From that perspective, the stone resembled a falcon caught mid-flight through a slab of stone and petrified as a result.

"Sienne, cast *mud* on this again," Alaric said. His voice was distant, the voice of someone thinking hard about something.

Sienne opened her spellbook and read off the transform, swallowing the nausea-inducing sweetness. A few more spells and she would be incapacitated again. She gripped the rim of the stone and watched the dark, wet stain spread across it. Mud oozed between her fingers. "We're destroying our only chance of getting the knife," she said.

"I don't think so," Alaric said. The stain reached the falcon's body and crept over its stomach and chest. More mud dripped down Sienne's hand and wrist.

Dianthe gasped. "What is *that?*"

A green glint shone beneath the mud of the falcon's breast. Mud slipped away from it, revealing a dirty green surface that shone like crystal. Dianthe stepped forward and swept mud off the thing. Great globs of mud dripped and fell on the grass, revealing more of whatever it was.

"Help me with this," Dianthe said, and Kalanath put his hands under it, supporting it as the mud fell away. It was clearly a bird, but smaller than the stone falcon, about three feet from wingtip to wingtip. Beneath the mud it was made of something hard and green. Sienne brushed away the last of the mud and released the spell.

"Let's rinse it off," Dianthe said, and she and Kalanath took it to the river and dunked it. The remaining traces of mud went liquid and flowed away, revealing a carved figure of a falcon. They raised it, and the sunlight caught the facets of its clear green surface and blazed with light.

"Kitane's eyes, it's solid emerald," Dianthe said. Sienne didn't bother asking how she knew. Dianthe always knew about gems. "I didn't know they could be that big. Be careful with it, those wings are probably fragile."

"It won't break," Sienne said. To her wizard's eye, the falcon shone with more than reflected light. "It's an artifact. A powerful one. The stone sealed the magic in."

Dianthe and Kalanath set it on the grass. It was a deeper green than the grass and looked unspeakably gaudy next to the simple new growth. "What in Averran's name have we lent ourselves to?" Perrin asked, sounding awed.

"This is a tangle," Alaric said. "It's an artifact, but not the one we were sent after, unless Tonia Figlari was holding out on us. Sienne, any idea what it does?"

"None. And it was useless so long as it was cased in stone, so the Figlari dukes couldn't have used it as Tonia said they did. There's no way it spoke to anyone." Sienne paced to the river bank and back. "I don't understand why someone would go to all that trouble, unless it was a dangerous artifact... but why display it to the world if it was dangerous?"

"Pride," Perrin said. "A desire to lord it over the neighbors. Though Figlari has no neighbors, so perhaps not that."

"Is there any way to figure out what it does?" Alaric said.

"The avatars see everything that happens on earth," Perrin said, "so it is likely Averran knows. Whether he will tell us is another matter. And I dare not pester him further today."

"If we know what it does, that might tell us who'd want it, and why," Alaric said. "It might also give us an idea of why someone might have involved us in retrieving it." He squatted to look at the falcon closely. "We'll pack up and put as much distance between ourselves and this place as possible, camp for the night, and in the morning—"

"The late morning," Perrin said.

"In the late morning, we'll see if Averran is willing to give us a hint."

Dianthe walked over to Button and pulled out a heavy sheet of canvas. "This was meant to wrap the stone, but it will do just as well for the artifact." She wrapped the emerald falcon securely and stowed it with the gear on the second donkey. "I wish it wasn't an artifact. Do you have any idea how much we could get for an emerald that size? Carved with that kind of craftsmanship?"

"We have to focus on retrieving the knife," Alaric pointed out. "And until we know what role Tonia played in this deception, we have to pretend we've done what we were sent to do."

Sienne washed her hands off in the cold river. Her trousers were filthy with mud and might never be the same. She swiped the mud off them as best she could, then doused the fire and took up her position behind Alaric. He still didn't seem disturbed by having killed the carver wizard with his bare hands. It worried her enough that she resolved to find a way to ask him about it later. A way that didn't imply he'd turned soulless or evil.

13

Spellcasting had left Sienne dizzy and sick, but she didn't want to delay their journey; she wanted to get as far away from the Figlari dukedom as they could. She concentrated on putting one foot in front of the other, staring at the ground and then staring at Alaric's back. It felt like their first job, when she'd been a raw beginner and a day's march had exhausted her. Her mind numb, she kept walking until Alaric stopped and she almost ran into him. He turned to say something, took her chin in his hand, and tilted her head to look into her eyes. She managed not to jerk away from him, fighting her terrible memories.

"You cast too many spells," he said. "Damn it, Sienne—"

"I'm fine," she said, though in truth his outline was doubled and she wanted to throw up. "I didn't want—"

"Sit over here and put your head between your knees," he said, steering her off to one side and gently pushing on her shoulder. She sank gratefully to the ground and took a long drink from her waterskin. Bowing her head, she listened to the sounds of people making camp, smelled wood smoke from the fire, and despite her illness she felt at peace.

She heard crows sweep past overhead, and their shrill cries

reminded her of another evening, sitting in Rance's room at school in Stravanus while the raucous birds cawed outside his window. For the first time, she thought of Rance without anger or embarrassment. If he'd told his parents he wanted to marry her instead of her sister, if he had been the man she thought he was, she wouldn't now be in this place, with these people she cared about. And Alaric…she wasn't sure what would grow between them, if anything, but she already felt safer and more cherished with him than she ever had with Rance.

Dianthe shook her arm. "Dinner," she said. Sienne hadn't realized she'd nodded off, but if dinner was ready, she'd slept a while. Kalanath had brought down a small deer, enough for two meals, and she ate happily, ignoring the shivering outlines of the flames that told her she wasn't fully recovered.

"Regular watch rotation," Alaric said. "Sienne, you'll sleep through the night."

"I'm well enough," she protested. "It's not like I'm an invalid."

Alaric scowled. "Fine. But if I think you aren't capable when I wake you—"

"Yes, sir," Sienne said, grinning at him. He smiled, and there was a light in his eyes that made Sienne tingle all over. She wondered if anyone else had noticed. They would have to be careful if they wanted to keep this a secret.

She went to bed when the sun set, wriggling into her bedroll and stretching lazily. She never felt so alive as when they'd successfully completed a job, and though she knew this one wasn't over, she couldn't help feeling they'd earned their success over the carvers.

Dianthe crawled into the tent after her and sat on her bedroll, taking off her boots. "I'm so tired I can't think about anything but sleep," she said. "Even though I know this is just the beginning of a new trouble."

"Me too."

Dianthe lay down and yawned. Firelight flickered on the tent flap, interrupted by Perrin, who had first watch, walking past. The night wasn't as cold as the previous one, but it was still chilly enough that

Sienne appreciated the extra warmth of her blanket. She closed her eyes and let out a deep sigh.

Dianthe said, "Whatever you said to Alaric, it worked. Thank you."

Sienne was glad Dianthe couldn't see her blush. "I just... told him the truth."

"He killed that carver wizard. Did you see it?"

"Yes."

"I hope it gave him peace. I've never seen him kill someone with just his hands before."

"You don't think it was, I don't know, a dark thing to do?"

Dianthe sighed. "I'm not going to tell him how to slay his demons. But yes, I did. I'm not sure what to say."

"Me neither."

There was silence for a time. "I'm sure kissing would resolve the problem," Dianthe said.

Sienne rolled over to face the darkness where Dianthe lay. "*Dianthe!* Were you *spying* on us?"

"No. But you just confirmed my suspicions. You should keep your secrets closer to your chest."

Sienne groaned. "We didn't want anyone to know. I don't know what to say."

"Don't say anything. Kidding aside, I don't want to intrude on your privacy. Alaric's like my brother, and I want him to be happy. You're my friend, and I want you to be happy too. If you're happy together, well, that's doubly good."

Sienne rolled onto her back again. "I am happy. I never would have guessed this could happen, not after the way we clashed when we first met."

"Oh, I don't know. I think Alaric's problem was that you were a cute girl *and* a wizard, and his instincts were at odds with themselves. He's been pining after you for months. It was sort of pathetic, in a sweet way."

Sienne blushed again. "I wasn't indifferent to him, either. I just didn't know what to say."

"Sounds like speaking wasn't the important thing."

The arch tone of Dianthe's voice made Sienne blush harder. She'd never used to be someone who blushed at every little thing, and now...

"Seriously, though, if you can talk to him about killing the wizard, I wish you would," Dianthe said. "He listens to me, but he doesn't always take me seriously because he thinks of me as a younger sister. Even though I'm three months older. You, though, have a chance of getting him to face up to it."

"Why is that? Not because he's attracted to me?"

"That, and the two of you are alike enough that he feels you understand and aren't just telling him what he wants to hear. That's my theory, anyway."

"I'll do what I can." It made her uncomfortable, having that kind of influence over someone, particularly someone as strong-willed as Alaric. It was a responsibility she wasn't sure she was ready for.

Dianthe began to snore. Sienne grinned into the darkness. She'd never met anyone who could fall asleep so readily, or under any circumstances, as Dianthe. The snoring soothed her, and eventually she, too, fell asleep.

She woke to someone shaking her foot. "How do you feel?" Alaric said.

Sienne sat up and looked past Alaric at the fire. No shivering outlines, just the low-burning flames. "Fine," she said, pulling on her boots.

"You'd better not be exaggerating."

"I wouldn't do that."

"Yes, you would, if you thought it would get you what you wanted."

Sienne crawled out of the tent and stood. The chilly night breezes carried the scent of the fire and early morning dew to her nose. "And what do you think that is?"

Alaric put his arms around her waist. "I hope it's this," he said, kissing her.

She pulled his head down to return his kiss. He was more than a foot taller than she, a difference she'd never fully internalized until now. His lips were warm and tasted of wood smoke, and she kissed him again, reveling in the feel of his arms around her.

He released her, and she felt a pang of regret until he took her hand and guided her to the fire. "We can watch from here," he said.

"Don't you want sleep?"

He touched her face lightly. "I spent my whole watch waiting for the time I could wake you and have you join me. Sleep is nothing next to that."

"We can't spend the whole time kissing. We might as well not be on watch if we did."

"Much as I'd love that, you're right. I had in mind talking instead. I want to know more about you."

"And I—"

"What?"

She hesitated, then said, "I wanted to ask you about killing the wizard."

His hand in hers went rigid. "What about it?" he said, the teasing note in his voice vanishing.

"Never mind. It's not important."

"It must be important for you to bring it up now. You think I did the wrong thing."

"No! I—Alaric, I can imagine killing her will help you recover. I just thought... I didn't know if you'd ever killed anyone that way before, and if you thought it was different. I am in no position to judge you, and I wouldn't even if I were. But I worry."

His hand relaxed, then closed more tightly on hers. "It felt good," he said in a low voice. "It felt like I had power over her instead of the other way around. And I'm ashamed of how much I liked it. It was necessary, I don't regret it, but I don't want to be someone who takes joy in killing. You're not wrong. It's not the same as killing with a sword. And the carvers look like people even though they aren't. I've thought about it—wondered if I would feel different if I'd used my sword instead of going for her throat. But in the end, I'm just glad she's dead. I can't imagine how many people she tortured and killed, or made kill their friends."

"I don't think I've ever killed anyone, not even monsters," Sienne said. "I don't know any of the spells that kill outright. I've wondered if that's a mistake."

"Don't," Alaric said. "You disable your enemies just fine without killing them. I don't think you should have any regrets about the contents of your spellbook."

"But you and Dianthe and Kalanath kill. It doesn't make you evil."

"No, but it's changed us. And I'm not sure you want that kind of change." Alaric sighed. "You'll probably have the opportunity to gain those spells someday, and if you decide to take it, I'll support you. I just don't want you feeling inadequate because you're not a killer."

Sienne scooted over and tucked herself under his arm. "You're not a killer either, not really. You don't want humans to be afraid of you, and I'm certain you wouldn't turn on another person unless it was to protect someone else."

He squeezed her shoulders. "You have such faith in me. I fear it's unwarranted."

"Not at all," she said, and kissed him.

———

WHEN THE DARK SKY LIGHTENED, SIENNE DISENTANGLED HERSELF FROM Alaric's embrace and summoned water, then built up the fire to boil it for porridge. As she set the coffeepot to heat, Alaric stood, saying, "I'll fetch more wood. It's funny, I don't feel tired at all."

"Neither do I." They'd alternated sitting by the fire with walking hand in hand around the camp, talking of everything and nothing, and Sienne had never felt so energized. This feeling of something new beginning, her growing attraction to him and the awareness that he was attracted to her, was better than sleep.

Alaric stooped to kiss her, stroking her cheek with his thumb. "When we get back to Fioretti—" He laughed. "Sorry. I don't think we should make plans until this job is over."

"That's smart." She regretted it, though, regretted that this mysterious artifact and Tonia Figlari's hold over them interfered with their growing relationship. She wished the night watches were twice as long.

She stood by the fire until Alaric came back with more fuel, then stoked it to a nice low blaze and began pouring grain into the pot, a little at a time to keep the porridge smooth. "*Convey* will be an expensive spell," she warned him.

"I'll pay for it."

"Alaric the wizard-hater, paying for a spell? You'll be the talk of the market."

"I don't hate all wizards, just the one. The rest I'm suspicious of. And there's one I'm enjoying getting to know better." He put an arm around her waist and hugged her briefly, releasing her when the men's tent flap rustled and Kalanath emerged. Sienne felt her face grow hotter than the fire warranted and hoped Kalanath wouldn't notice her blush.

Kalanath saluted them both with his staff. "I cannot sleep longer," he said. "I dreamed about the emerald falcon. In my dream it grew larger than a tree and devoured people. It was not a nice dream."

"You don't think it had meaning, do you?" Sienne asked.

"No. I do not have prophetic dreams." Kalanath's voice was flat and hard, and his narrow eyes were closed almost to slits. He turned and walked away toward the nearby grove of trees, and shortly they heard the sound of his staff striking wood.

"That was strange," Alaric said. "Why would that suggestion make him angry?"

"I don't know. He never talks about himself or his past, you know. I wonder if—no, I can't think of anything that might provoke that reaction." Sienne added coffee to the pot of boiling water and gave it a stir. "It's funny that we're all hiding secrets, or were. You all know my secrets now. And we know yours. Unless you're secretly a unicorn prince."

Alaric laughed. "No such thing. Nobody knows why some Sassaven are born unicorns and the rest aren't, but we don't treat each other differently. Though all the people whose other selves are unicorns are as big as I am—that's really the only thing we have in common, as far as I know."

The tent flap rustled again. "Ah, what sweet aroma do I scent?" Perrin exclaimed. "And by sweet I of course mean most bitter and arousing to the senses."

"Just a few more minutes." Sienne stirred the porridge and let it drip off the spoon. "Isn't coffee at odds with Averran's, um, requirements?"

"What requirements are those?"

"The brandy."

"Ah." Perrin sat cross-legged beside the fire, near the coffeepot. "Averran encourages humanity to seek wisdom in many ways. For some, it is the blessed haze of alcohol. For others, it is the crisp sharpness of mind that coffee brings. For a few of us, it is both. I have long enjoyed a cup of steaming, undiluted coffee in the morning, but on occasion I partake of coffee liberally laced with alcohol. It is the most stimulating feeling." He took hold of the coffeepot and filled his mug, then drank it down without heed for how hot it had to be. "In fact, I believe I shall do so now." He poured a generous amount of brandy from his hip flask into the mug, then topped it off with coffee.

"Don't drink it all," Dianthe said, sitting beside him and pouring her own cup. She winced at the bitterness, but they couldn't bring cream into the wilderness any more easily than eggs. Sienne handed her a chunk of sugar, which she accepted gratefully.

"Not to be impatient, but when will you speak with Averran?" Alaric asked.

"It will yet be some hours. Averran, like all right-thinking individuals, prefers to rise late, and is most testy when he is woken before the shine has worn off the new day. I suggest we begin our travels, and I will make my prayers when we halt for a noon meal."

Sienne scooped porridge and handed the bowl to Alaric, who made a face but accepted it. She had to control a giggle that bubbled up from within. She was as giddy as a girl with her first crush—well, Rance had been her first romance, and there hadn't been anyone since then, so it might as well be her first crush. And yet there was something so different about this. Despite the fact that they'd been age-mates and kept pace with each other as they studied, Rance had never treated her with the unspoken respect that said he saw her as an equal. He'd never been interested in listening to what she had to say, always subtly turning the conversation to himself. Even his love-making had felt selfish, though at the time she'd blamed herself and her inexperience for how lackluster it had been. It had been barely more than nine months since she'd met Alaric, and already she felt he knew her better than Rance had after nine years' acquaintance.

They broke camp half an hour later and set out southward. Sienne felt rested and cheerful for the first time in days. She had to stop herself from skipping as she followed Alaric across the grassy plains. They still had a long way to go before the job was finished, and skipping was undignified as well as not yet called for. But the day was warm, finally felt like first summer, and the grass underfoot smelled green and fresh. Birds flew past for the first time since they'd left the ruined keep.

"What's that song?" Alaric asked, glancing over his shoulder at her.

"What song?"

"The song you keep humming."

"Oh! I didn't realize I was humming."

"It's pretty," said Dianthe.

"It's called 'The Robin and the Jay.' It's just an old folk song. I don't know the words." No doubt the birds flitting overhead had brought it to mind. "My nurse used to hum it to me when she put me to bed."

"You are quite cheerful today," Perrin said. "Would that we all might be infected by your good cheer." He sounded, if not annoyed, at least not in a pleasant mood.

"You're not looking forward to your prayers, are you," Sienne said.

"Not in the least. I have been a rather importunate priest these last few days, and gaining my Lord Averran's attention has become difficult." He took a drink from his flask. "I would that I might find a way to serve, to pass on some of the blessings the avatar has graced me with."

"You do not serve when you work with us?" Kalanath asked.

"My contribution to our merry band is by way of being an extension of my requests, as they are on our party's behalf. I believe Averran is dissatisfied with my exclusivity, as it were. And I have not done as much as I should to grow in my own wisdom."

"You can hardly serve others when we're the only ones around," Alaric said. "That seems unreasonable."

"Avatars have their own reasons, of which mortal reason knows nothing." Perrin took another drink. "Do not worry. I will work out my relationship with Averran on my own terms, and hope he does not choose to chastise me."

"What would chastising you look like?" asked Dianthe.

"Oh...a temporary withdrawal of his presence. A refusal to grant blessings. Overt reminders of to whom I owe everything. But I am not so lost to Averran's mercy as to be in quite so dire a circumstance, so have no fear."

Sienne thought it sounded dire. She didn't worship any avatar in particular, but she could imagine what it would be like to have a priest's relationship with an aspect of God and then have it taken away.

At around noon, they reached a rail fence, the first sign of civilization they'd seen on the return journey. Beyond it, untilled ground lay broken and lumpy from winter's rest. "We'll stop here," Alaric said, unslinging his sword and letting it fall to rest on the soft grass. "Food, and then..."

Despite his earlier words, Perrin ate and drank with no sign of concern. Most of that was probably due to how much alcohol he'd consumed since waking. He was decidedly relaxed, and he laughed louder than any of them at the story Dianthe told of a job three years earlier that ended with Alaric dangling from the crumbling eaves of an ancient fortress. "He tried to claim it was all part of the plan," she said, chuckling, "but I don't know that any plan requires you to cover yourself in pigeon crap and leap from a second-story roof."

"It was too subtle for you," Alaric said. "I am a subtle thinker."

"You once held Conn Giorda off a roof by his ankles and told him if he didn't leave that girl Tressa alone, you'd find out how high he could bounce," Dianthe said. "You're not subtle."

Alaric managed to convey wounded pride with a single shrug. "I am in no way changing the subject," he said, "but if Perrin is ready, I think we should proceed."

Perrin nodded. He withdrew a handful of blank rice paper squares from inside his vest and set them on his lap. "If you don't mind, please withdraw a few paces. I am afraid the sound of your collective breathing might be a distraction."

They all took several steps toward the rail fence. Perrin closed his eyes and settled into a pattern of rhythmic breathing, his chest moving lightly, his face relaxed. "O good and recalcitrant Lord," he said, "I come before you with a simple request. We have found an artifact we do not understand, and as you, Lord, see all that passes on earth, I ask merely that you share your wisdom with me in instructing me in its use."

Perrin went still. His breathing became more labored. "I understand, o Lord, but this artifact is simply a means to an end. We do not intend to keep it, but to make disposition of it as—" A trickle of blood ran from his nostril to his lips. Perrin didn't lick it away. "Yes, great Lord of crotchets, and were I capable of doing so, I would not trouble you—no, I don't think—"

Perrin's face contorted in rage. "*I am not a drunk!*" he shouted. "You in your infinite wisdom should know my heart, and if you accuse me —" He swayed, and put out both hands to steady himself. "If not me, then who?" he said in a quieter voice. "O Lord of ill humor, my request is simple. Show me what this artifact is meant for, and I will endeavor to put it to proper use, whatever that use may be. And I will take—no, do not refuse me, please, this is most urgent."

He went silent, but Sienne could see his face, and whatever struggle he waged with his avatar was visible in his countenance. It was a look of mortal agony, and she wished she dared interrupt and spare him the pain he was enduring. Alaric had his enormous hands clenched into fists, and leaned forward, as intent as she was on the conflict. The artifact couldn't possibly be worth this.

Perrin's face relaxed, and just as Sienne realized it meant he was unconscious, he slumped to the ground, scattering rice paper squares everywhere. They all lunged forward to support him. "Back up and give him air," Alaric said, putting a gentle hand under Perrin's head and easing him to lie straight. Sienne gathered up the rice paper and squared it neatly into a stack.

Perrin's eyelids fluttered open. "Such concern," he joked weakly. "I am deeply touched." He tried to sit and was restrained easily by Alaric. "I think perhaps you are correct, and I should lie here for a moment."

Sienne glanced at the squares of paper. "Um," she said, "none of these are marked."

"I chose not to ask for blessings, given that my request was an extraordinary one." Perrin held out a hand for the papers. "And Averran was rather more irritable than usual. I am unsurprised that he did not grant me blessings of his own volition."

"Did he tell you what the artifact does?" Dianthe asked.

Perrin nodded, winced, and lay still again. "In general terms. The thing is a weapon of great power, and if I understand correctly, it is not a weapon against which there is a conventional defense."

They all looked at the canvas-wrapped bundle on the nameless donkey's back. Sienne could guess what they were all afraid to ask: had Averran revealed how to use the weapon? She wasn't sure she wanted to know, except for fear of setting it off accidentally.

"All right, I'll ask," Alaric said. "How does it work?"

"That, he would not tell me." Perrin stirred and sat up, then hugged his knees and pressed his face against them. "And I am not certain I want to know, save that it would tell us just how powerful the weapon is, and how afraid of it we should be."

"There's no point being afraid of weapons," Alaric said. "It's the wielders of weapons you have to fear. But a weapon we can't use might as well not be a weapon at all."

"It's an awkward weapon, too," Dianthe said. "Big and bulky. It can't be for close fighting, because swinging it like a sword would never work. Maybe it emits a poison gas? No, that would kill whoever triggered it. I don't know. Random guessing won't help."

"We'll get it back to Fioretti, talk to Tonia, and proceed from there," Alaric said. He extended a hand to Perrin to help him rise. "The thing doesn't even have to leave its wrapping."

Sienne fell into place behind Alaric. To her left, the nameless donkey walked with the same dispirited, weary tread it always had no matter how well rested it was. She eyed the wrapped bundle. Alaric might be right that weapons weren't to be feared, but Sienne couldn't help thinking a weapon that didn't look like a weapon, a weapon of great destructive power with no obvious means of use, was something any reasonable person might be afraid of.

14

The skies continued clear and sunny, but Sienne felt as weary as if they threatened rain instead. Her awareness of the emerald falcon not five feet from where she walked pressed down on her, an emotional weight that made her want to fling off its wrappings and smash it to radiant shards. Which was impossible, because artifacts that radiated magic as this one did were indestructible, or at least impervious to any spell or physical force Sienne was aware of. Perrin's words—*no conventional defense*—frightened her, because that implied power like nothing she'd ever heard of. And it was riding along on the nameless donkey, wrapped in a stained canvas.

They passed more farmsteadings, grouped more closely together, and this time nearly every field was occupied with people and plows turning up the good dark earth, readying it for planting. Sienne waved half-heartedly at the farmers and their cheery salutes. How eager would they be to wave at them if they knew what the companions carried?

Sienne blinked. *That* was too much. This wasn't some kind of death sentence. They had a powerful artifact, yes, and it was a dangerous one, but it wasn't as if it would suddenly spring to life and begin attacking people, Kalanath's dream notwithstanding. She stood up straighter and told herself to stop being an idiot. They'd figure this out, just like they always did.

By sunset, they'd reached Uless and the inn where they'd left their horses. Genuinely weary now, Sienne leaned on the fence of the stable yard and watched men and women pass through the gate. Some led horses and clearly wanted a place to stay for the night. Others held hands with the look of sweethearts out for an evening's entertainment. The inn's bustling yard smelled heavily of anxious horses and told Sienne they might have trouble finding rooms for the night.

"Alaric's been gone a while," Dianthe said. "That means nothing good."

"It means we will sleep elsewhere, I think," Kalanath said.

A young girl ran toward them and skidded to a halt before the donkeys. "Take your animals, miss?"

"Not yet," Dianthe said.

The girl sized them all up. Her eyes lingered longest on Sienne, examining her. Sienne thought about making a face and decided she wasn't juvenile. "No loitering," the girl said, and ran off through the gate and down the road.

"No loitering," Dianthe scoffed. "As if we weren't paying good money to stable our horses here."

"Here he comes," Perrin said. "He looks displeased."

Alaric's frown was visible from yards away. "One room," he said when he was near enough not to shout. "One room with three beds. That's all they can do for us."

"Why is it so crowded?" Sienne asked.

"Hiring fair. People come from all over to get work on the farm-steadings for first summer." Alaric scratched his scalp, disordering his short blond hair. "All the inns in town are full. And by 'all' I mean the two of them. It's not a large town."

"We could see if there's a farmer willing to let us camp in his field," Dianthe said.

"I asked about that. Apparently the fields are full of migrants too.

I think, all things considered, we're better off in a room we can secure against thieves."

"It is true," Kalanath said. "You took this room with three beds? I will sleep on the floor."

"They're big beds. We can double up." Alaric took Button's lead rope and led him into the yard. Dianthe followed with the nameless donkey, which had perked up when it smelled home.

"You again," the stable master said. He was a portly fellow a little shorter than Perrin, with black hair covering his arms and face. "Any luck?"

"Some," Alaric said. "Can we rent space for our gear for the night?"

"Sure. Most of these folks for the hiring fair came in on shank's mare, so the stable's not as full as the inn. Don't suppose you want to bed down with the horses?" The man laughed, a sound that came from deep within his belly.

Alaric laughed with him. "We've been in the wilderness four days. I'm done with sleeping on the ground, however well-padded with straw it is."

"Fair enough. There's an empty stall at the end. Have no fear, we set watches all night."

"My thanks." Alaric led Button to the indicated stall. Sienne helped him unload while Perrin and Dianthe did the same for their hired donkey. Kalanath stood alert and watchful with his staff at the ready. "You expecting trouble?" Alaric said.

"I think it is that we should be cautious, even here," Kalanath said. "I do not like this thing and I will be happier when it is gone." His voice was flat and hard again. Sienne remembered what he'd said about his dream of the falcon destroying people. She had no reason to believe he was prone to prophetic dreams, but it had certainly upset him. She felt prone to a little paranoia herself.

She turned to find Dianthe handing her a bundle wrapped in canvas. She nearly dropped it. "What—?"

"We can't leave it out here, no matter how good their watchmen are," Dianthe said in a low voice. "And the rest of us need our hands free in case we're attacked. So you're the lucky guardian."

Sienne scowled and tucked the thing securely under one arm. "Is this also because I'm a wizard, and we have a special affinity for artifacts? Because I can tell you right now that's not true."

"We may not know how to work the thing," Alaric said in the same low voice, "but as a wizard, capable of seeing its magic, you have a marginally better chance of figuring it out than the rest of us. But mainly it's because you only need one hand to hold your spellbook. So stop griping." He smiled to show it was a joke and shouldered both her bag and his own. Sienne sighed and followed him to the inn's door. She was conscious now, as she usually wasn't, of her friends grouped close around her, guarding her. It made her more nervous than if she'd been walking alone.

The inn's taproom was muggy with heat and the smell of warm beer and warmer bodies, all packed together and shouting for the attention of the overworked serving women. Alaric broke a path through the crowd, waving away the young woman who swam toward them against the current of drinkers. Sienne hated these inns where the only way to the rooms was through the taproom. It was cynical of her, but she couldn't help feeling the design was intended to get people buying as many overpriced drinks as possible.

The hall beyond the taproom was cooler and dimmer, lit by a couple of magic lights in frosted invulnerable glass bulbs. At the end of the short hall, stairs rose into darkness, smelling sharply of fresh varnish. The inn had only two floors—no wonder all its rooms were let—and their room was at the far end of the hall. By the sound of it, it was over the taproom. Noise leaked through the floorboards like water through a sieve, not loud enough for conversations to be intelligible but loud enough to be annoying. "We're not going to get any sleep tonight, are we?" Dianthe said.

"It was all they had," Alaric said.

"That wasn't a criticism." She dropped her pack on one of the beds, which were, as promised, big enough for two—or one and a half if Alaric was one. "Should we leave someone here to guard it?"

"I think we're safe," Alaric said.

"Even so, I think I should cast a confusion on it," Sienne said.

"I thought artifacts couldn't be altered by spells," Dianthe said.

"This will be on the canvas, not the artifact." Sienne knelt and shoved the artifact under the bed that stood against the far wall, back deep into a corner. She opened her spellbook and laid it on the floor, crouched so she could see both the pale canvas and the spellbook, and read off the confusion *camouflage*. Darkness spread like pooling ink across the pale canvas, blending with the shadows under the bed. She read the spell again, giving the canvas the almost-invisible grain of the wall and floor. "Take a look."

Dianthe crouched. "I can barely see it, and I know what to look for. Nice."

Sienne closed her spellbook and put it back in its harness. "Now I'm hungry."

They trooped back down to the taproom, which was, if anything, busier and noisier than before. A group of men, probably farmers by their dress, gathered near the fireplace, drinking and shouting to be heard above their fellows. A couple of musicians valiantly sawed away at their fiddles, but it was impossible to hear more than the highest notes. An exhausted serving woman passed them, rolling her eyes when Perrin put a hand on her shoulder to stop her. "Wait your turn," she said.

"I will be happy to wait, if it means waiting on you," Perrin said with a smile.

It charmed a tired smile out of the woman. "Be right back."

"How do you do that?" Kalanath said. "It is a surprise every time."

"There is no surprise," Perrin said with a shrug. "People respond well to kindness when it is sincere, and I am always sincere."

"It certainly doesn't work for me," Alaric rumbled.

"Your size mitigates against it, I think. Yours to intimidate, mine to charm."

The serving woman returned. "What'll it be?" She addressed all of them, but her eyes were on Perrin.

"Brandy for me," Perrin said, "beer for my companions, and whatever delicious-smelling thing is served for dinner, if you please."

"See if you can find a table, and I'll bring you your drinks." She looked around as if hoping a free table would appear out of nowhere.

"My thanks," Perrin said with another smile. "You're most generous, given how busy you are. I hope not every night is like this one."

"Every year at this time, for a good three nights. You picked the wrong time to stop here." She smiled, showing a dimple that made her look younger than she was.

"Well, we are in no hurry."

Sienne's stomach chose that moment to growl, audible even over the noise. The serving woman laughed and turned away.

"Over here," Alaric said, pushing through the crowd. A man and woman sat at a round table that was otherwise unoccupied, wrapped in each other's arms and kissing so intently they didn't notice when Alaric sat down. It was almost too small for the seven of them, forcing the companions to sit close together. Sienne managed to sit next to Alaric. She put her hand on his knee beneath the table and squeezed gently, enjoying the look of surprised pleasure that crossed his face.

It was hard not to watch the kissing couple. Sienne turned her attention to the musicians, but she couldn't make out what they were playing and was pretty sure they didn't know, either. Kalanath looked at the couple with obvious interest. "It is not a thing we do in Omeira, to make affection in public," he said. "It is sacred to God."

"Interesting," Perrin said. He, too, was watching the couple with his elbow propped on the table and his chin in his hand. "I wonder that these two do not find a quieter place to share their affection."

The man disengaged long enough to say, "Get lost."

"He speaks!" Perrin leaned forward. "I admire your singleness of mind, both of you. Have you been wed long?"

The woman giggled. "None of your business," the man snarled.

"I think they are not married," Kalanath said. "Else they have a house to go to."

The man let go the woman and stood, looming over Kalanath. "You wanna say that again, Omeiran scum?"

Alaric rose. "You might want to reconsider saying anything else."

The man's eyes widened. Alaric sitting looked big. Alaric standing looked *enormous*. The man took the woman's hand and pulled her to her feet, clearly wanting to hurry away but afraid to turn his back on Alaric. Alaric smiled pleasantly and made a shooing motion with one hand. The couple fled.

"I do not need protecting," Kalanath said with a smile, "except that this place is too small for staff fighting. I would have to use hands and feet, and I prefer not." He scooted his chair away, giving the others room to spread out.

"Mine to intimidate, eh?" Alaric said, taking his seat. "I enjoy getting the better of bullies."

The serving woman appeared with a huge platter of tarnished silver from which came the most heavenly aromas of fresh beef and sautéed onions. "Hope you like steak," she said, setting out plates.

Sienne's stomach growled again. She loved steak, and these were particularly beautiful—properly browned, marbled with fat and flowing with dark juices, piled high with sweet-smelling onions in loops and curls across the beef. She picked up the fork that lay across the plate and took out her belt knife. "Is this really what they're serving tonight?"

"It's what I'm serving to people I like," the woman said, smiling at Perrin.

"We thank you for your generosity," Perrin said, bowing slightly. "My companions and I have not eaten so well in days."

"You're scrappers?"

"Indeed."

"That's so exciting! Find anything good?"

"Alas, no," Perrin lied, "and our adventures were such that your lovely hair would go white at the telling, so I dare not abuse your hospitality so."

The woman laughed. "Let me know if I can get anything else for you." She turned and sidled through the crowds toward the bar.

All eyes turned on Perrin, who took a large bite of steak and onions. "What?" he said through his mouthful.

"Were you *flirting*?" Dianthe said. "I'm sure you weren't flirting."

"I was not. I was merely being my usual charming self." The smile was gone. Sienne had a sudden feeling they shouldn't press him on this issue.

"I wonder why they have such good meat on hand," she said, forestalling whatever Kalanath had been about to say. "I doubt most of these people can afford to eat like this even now and again."

"The last time we were here, one of the ranchers to the south was about to slaughter cattle," Alaric said. "I don't know anything about ranching, but the man I talked to said he had to cull his herd sooner than he expected. Might be a lot of good beef on the market."

"How unfortunate that we cannot take it with us," Perrin said, chewing placidly. He downed the contents of his brandy glass in one gulp and signaled the serving woman for another.

Sienne glanced at Alaric, whose expression when looking at Perrin was impassive. He said, "I'd like us to get an early start, so let's not stay up too late drinking."

"Was that directed at me?" Perrin said.

"It was directed at everyone. Is there some reason you think it should be directed at you?" Alaric shot back.

Perrin pushed his half-eaten meal away and stood. "What I do is my own concern. If I intend to enjoy a few glasses of brandy, well, there's no harm in that, is there?"

Alaric's body tensed. "What's Averran's opinion?"

Perrin slammed his fist on the table, making Dianthe, sitting nearest him, jump. "My relationship with my avatar is none of your business, and I will thank you to keep out of it." He shoved his chair back. "I will see you all later. I intend to find a more congenial place to drink." Pushing through the crowds, he made his way to the door and slammed through it.

Alaric sighed. "I shouldn't have said anything."

"You weren't wrong," Dianthe said. "It's why he's angry. He knows he has a problem."

"I think... he didn't like the accusation of flirting," Sienne said. "I'm not blaming you," she went on hurriedly as Dianthe opened her mouth to protest. "It's just... I think he's still faithful to his wife, in his heart, even though they can't be together."

"He has a wife?" Kalanath exclaimed.

"Didn't I say—oh. He met his father at the auction house—"

"His *father?*"

"There's a lot I haven't mentioned, isn't there?"

"Just a bit," Dianthe said. "Go on."

"Anyway, his father as much as accused him of cheating on his wife with me, and Perrin said it wasn't his choice that his vows were annulled, and that he was still faithful. I think Perrin gets drunk whenever he thinks about his family."

"It's what I suspected," Dianthe said. She looked at the door Perrin had left by. "My heart goes out to him."

"Yes, but he's going to destroy himself if he keeps this up," Alaric said. "You heard his prayers. I think Averran has been after him about his drinking. You'd think if an avatar told you to stop, you'd do it."

"But if an avatar can't change him, what can *we* do?" Sienne exclaimed.

"Be patient, and wait for him to speak," Kalanath said. "It is what I would want."

"That's right," Alaric said. He resumed eating. "He's our companion, and more than that, he's our friend. We have to let him know we support him."

"But—"

"He's a grown man, Sienne. We can't force him against his will."

Sienne scowled. "There has to be something more we can do."

"If you think of it, let us know," Alaric said.

Her delicious steak had lost its aroma. "I'll be back," she said, rising.

"Where are you going?" Alaric asked.

"Just out back to the facilities." She cleaned off her belt knife and sheathed it before pushing her way through the crowd, past the bar and out the door.

The inn had three outhouses around back, set well away from where their stink would inconvenience customers. The sun had set, and the nip in the air chilled Sienne. She hurried to the one on the end whose door hung ajar. It didn't smell as bad as she'd expected, given the number of patrons the inn served that night. She made a magic light, then wished she hadn't, as the floor of the outhouse was mucky and disgusting. She'd almost have rather it smelled bad. Quickly, she did her business, then stepped outside and summoned water to wash her hands.

She examined her boot soles. Nasty muck she hoped was dirt clung to one of them. She crossed the yard and the street in front of the inn to a strip of grass that ran alongside the road. Dragging her foot along its softness, she wiped off as much filth as she could, then went back to the stable yard and kicked her feet against one of the fence posts, knocking off more. Satisfied she wouldn't be trailing the outhouse stink across the taproom, she hurried back to the inn, wishing she had her cloak.

She reached the door just a pace behind someone else who was wearing a cloak, the hood pulled up against the cold night air. "Excuse me," the man said, holding the door for Sienne.

Sienne nodded thanks and was about to enter when she stopped, stunned. "What on earth?" she exclaimed. *"Aneirin?"*

15

Aneirin's brows rose. "Sienne!" he said. "What a pleasant surprise!"

"A surprise, at least," Sienne said. "What are you doing here? Didn't you say you were engaged to play for a duke for the first summer season?"

Aneirin wrinkled his nose as if he'd eaten something rotten. "Unfortunately, that engagement fell through," he said, "and I'm at loose ends. But let's not stand in the doorway chatting. Allow me to buy you a drink."

Still stunned, Sienne let him lead her to the bar, where he found an empty stool for her. He shrugged off her suggestion that he sit, too. "I don't mind standing," he said, gesturing to the barkeep for two glasses of wine. "As to my predicament, well, it seems the duke in whose home I intended to reside had two very lovely daughters, both of whom appreciated my many skills."

"I bet they did," Sienne said.

Aneirin laughed. "I'd forgotten how keen your wit is. It's true, I practiced my more amatory arts on them, but of course I intended it as harmless flirtation. They, alas, felt otherwise, and when the duke tried to prevail upon me to marry one of them, I decided it was time for me to take my leave. My savings brought me this far, and now I play for my supper and a few extra soldi at the other inn every night, and come here for a companionable drink afterward. Easier not to play, so to speak, where I work." He sipped his wine. "But now I insist you tell me of your adventures. Have you returned from the wilderness so early?"

Sienne thought fast. It was beyond coincidental that Aneirin was here, never mind the story he'd spun. He'd confided in her so she'd feel comfortable opening up to him. The question was, how much should she tell him? "What makes you think we've already gone? We might well be on our way out."

"You left with such alacrity, I assumed you traveled at the same speed. But you're right, that was simply a guess on my part. I don't know anything about scrappers, except that there's one I'm interested in getting to know." Aneirin smiled and put his hand over Sienne's. She kept from jerking it away.

"We're headed back to Fioretti," she said. "So your guess was right."

"Then you were successful?"

Sienne made another lightning-fast decision. "We were. We're going to report to our client and get paid."

"And what does success look like, for a scrapper like you?" Aneirin stepped closer, not letting go of her hand. Standing, he loomed over her on her stool, and she had to work at not flinching. She felt no sense of menace from him, but he was still bigger than she was, and the greatest dangers were the ones you didn't see coming.

"It means whatever makes the client happy, or brings us the best salvage," she said. "Sometimes both."

"What did your client want?"

"I'm not at liberty to say. I can say she'll be satisfied with what we bring her." That was a lie, since Tonia Figlari didn't want an emerald falcon artifact that might be capable of destroying thousands with a touch, or however it was activated. But Aneirin didn't need to know the truth.

"Well, I won't press you for details. I'm more interested in knowing if you've changed your mind." Aneirin's face was very near hers, and she smelled mutton and wine on his breath. She was about to ask what he meant when he leaned closer and swift as thought pressed his lips to hers.

She jerked backward, bumping into the person seated next to her, who grunted reproof. "How dare you!" she exclaimed. She wiped his kiss off with the back of her hand.

Aneirin looked puzzled. "My apologies," he said. "I thought... but I was mistaken. Forgive me my blunder?" He smiled that same winning smile that had attracted her attention from the beginning.

"Does that work on every woman?" Sienne asked.

"Sadly, no," Aneirin said. "It failed to work on you, clearly. I really am sorry. I enjoy flirtation, but I have never made a habit of kissing unwilling women."

Despite herself, she felt sorry for him. "I believe you."

Aneirin glanced over her shoulder. "Ah. Your Ansorjan companion is looking at me as if he wishes he could gut, clean, and butcher me. I might have guessed your relationship was rather closer than that of companions."

Sienne kept a blush off her face. "He's just protective. We're not together."

"Really? Then I need not sleep with a knife under my pillow." Aneirin caressed her cheek, so briefly it was over before she could protest. "Farewell, Sienne. Will you be here tomorrow night?"

"No," she said automatically, then wondered if she shouldn't have stayed close-mouthed. Well, it wasn't as if he couldn't find out their travel plans elsewhere, if he really cared.

"Such a shame. Then—here's to chance meetings." Aneirin saluted her with his glass, drained it, and left it on the bar. Sienne watched him until the door was safely closed behind him, then finished her wine and crossed the room to once more sit with her companions.

Perrin was still gone. Kalanath had asked for, and gotten, seconds on the steak and onions. Alaric looked as if he were ready to explode. "What was *that* about?" he said. "Where did he come from?"

"It *is* a huge coincidence, isn't it?" Sienne said, taking a seat next to Alaric. "He says his performing agreement fell through, and he's been staying here trying to earn money to move on, but I don't believe him."

"And yet the alternative is believing he was waiting here for us," Dianthe said. "That he's been after us ever since we left Fioretti."

"If he is an enemy of Tonia Figlari, that makes sense," Kalanath said. "What I would like to know is how much an enemy knows of her plans."

"Meaning, does Aneirin know what Tonia hired us to do?" Sienne said. "It's impossible to say. Is it better for us to assume he does, or that he doesn't?"

"Better to assume he knows," Alaric said. "If he didn't, he'd ask different questions and he'd have snooped around us more. So let's say Aneirin knows Tonia sent us to the Figlari dukedom to retrieve the falcon stone. Sienne, did you tell him we had it?"

"Not in so many words. I told him we were successful. Was that wrong?"

"I don't think so," Dianthe said. "If he knows what we were after, he'd probably assume you were lying if you told him we were unsuccessful."

"I still feel stupid. I shouldn't have said anything."

"Don't worry about it," Alaric said. "We're still guessing at this point, and we can't begin to know what he intends to do with the knowledge. I think it's a safe bet that he has comrades in the shadows, which means someone powerful hired him and them. So the next thing he'll do is report in. After that..." He shrugged. "That's when fighting becomes likely."

Dianthe pushed away from the table. "I'll see if I can follow him," she said. "Don't wait up."

"Don't take too long," Alaric said.

Sienne glanced covertly at him. He hadn't met her eyes the whole time since she'd returned to the table. "I'm going to bed," she said, yawning dramatically. "How about you two?"

"I am not yet finished," Kalanath said.

"I'll join you," Alaric said, rising.

He led the way through the taproom, diners and drinkers making way for his impressive bulk. Sienne's nerves felt frayed to the breaking point. He'd seen Aneirin kiss her, so he must have seen her reaction, and he couldn't think it had been a welcome kiss. If he did, well, they hadn't made any promises to each other and he had no right to be upset... or did he?

He held the door for her and she immediately went to her knees to look under the bed. The illusion was intact. "I was a little worried, though I probably shouldn't have been," she said.

She rose and met Alaric's glare. "All right, let's hear it," she said.

"Hear what?"

"You're upset because I talked to Aneirin. Did you see him kiss me?"

Alaric sat on the bed, making it creak. "I could see you didn't want him to," he said, "and it infuriated me. I don't like seeing anyone take liberties with you."

Sienne sat on his lap and put her arms around his neck. "You know," she said casually, "forty-eight hours ago we were nothing more than friends and companions. And now you're fast becoming the person I most want to spend time with."

The glare faded. He put his hands around her waist. "We really shouldn't do this," he said. "Anyone might come in."

"I could lock the door."

"They don't have locks."

"That seems like an oversight," she said, and kissed him. His mouth tasted of beef and beer, but unlike Aneirin, it enticed her, made her long for more. He pulled her close with one hand and slid the other up her back to stroke the soft skin beneath her hair. She murmured, "Don't stop doing that."

"I wasn't planning on it," he replied, trailing kisses along her jaw and throat. She ran her fingers down his spine and was delighted to feel him shiver. It felt amazing that this powerful man was so responsive to her touch. She almost felt sorry that they'd only gotten one room, though the idea of more than kisses made her uncomfortable. She'd regretted sex with Rance, who'd seen her as a pleasurable interlude and nothing more, and she had no intention of making the same mistake with Alaric. *But it would be an incredible mistake*, she thought, and laughed at herself.

"Something funny?" Alaric murmured in her ear.

"Just me." She kissed him, long and sweet, then turned her face away. "You're right. We really can't risk someone coming in."

Alaric kissed her forehead. "You're very sensible. Should I leave while you change into your nightdress?"

"Would you mind? Then... I want you to tell me more about your home. If it's not too painful."

"Telling you things makes them less awful," Alaric said, rising and crossing the room to the door. "I—"

The door flung open in his face. The serving woman stood there, breathing heavily. "Your friend," she said. "The Omeiran. A fight—"

Alaric shouldered past her and ran for the stairs, Sienne racing at his heels. The taproom was virtually empty, the door to the outside hung open, swaying slightly in the cold wind rising outdoors, and from nearby came the shouts of angry people cheering the mob on. Alaric cursed and went for the door. Sienne took her spellbook in both hands and hoped she wouldn't need to use it.

In the light from a dozen magic-lit lanterns, the stable yard was nearly as bright as day. A mass of people surged first one way, then the other, following the motion of a few men at its center. Sienne was too short to see who it was, but she could guess. Alaric tore into the crowd, heaving people bodily out of his way, and Sienne followed him as closely as she dared. He burst through half a step ahead of her and kept going, a force of nature roused by human misdeeds and ready to wreak havoc on the offenders.

Sienne stopped inside the ring of onlookers, gaping. Kalanath stood there, balanced lightly on the balls of his feet. His staff was missing, his shirt was torn, and there was blood on his sleeve and a bruise starting high on one prominent cheekbone, but he was smiling as if this were the best fun he'd had all week. His opponents, three burly men, circled him at a distance—and then Sienne saw the two men unconscious on the ground that Kalanath's opponents had to step around or over. One of the unconscious men was the man who'd insulted Kalanath in the taproom, the one who'd been kissing the woman not his wife. No mystery as to how this had started, then.

Kalanath saw Alaric approaching and waved him off. "This is nothing," he said. "A child could take them with a thing that rattles."

"Think so?" one of the men said, and charged.

Kalanath dodged, got the man by the shoulders, and used his own momentum to propel him into the watching crowd. A roar of approval went up. To Sienne's surprise, everyone seemed to be cheering the Omeiran on. Apparently even this far from the capital, not everyone was bigoted.

The two other men took the opportunity of Kalanath's preoccupation to attack, one from each side. Kalanath punched one in the stomach, and when he folded, struck him in the face with an open-hand smash that made him scream and clutch his nose. He half-turned and kicked the second man in the chest and then the throat without losing his balance, astonishing Sienne further. The man fell, both hands holding his throat. Kalanath swept the other man's legs from beneath him, dropped, and jabbed his chest, making the man gasp for air.

The first man, who'd fallen into the arms of the onlookers, turned around with their help and barreled down on Kalanath. "Look out!" Sienne screamed, but it was an unnecessary warning. Kalanath turned, dodged out of the man's way again, and performed a flying kick to a part of his anatomy that made even Sienne wince. The man dropped, curled up in his private world of pain. The crowd shouted with excitement.

Kalanath, breathing heavily, turned in a slow circle to survey his fallen victims and the watching crowd, which gradually fell silent. "If there is another here who would like to start a fight, come now before I become bored," he said. No one moved. Kalanath brushed his hair out of his face and walked, limping slightly, past Alaric and Sienne and through the crowd to where his staff was propped near the door. Sienne hurried after him.

"You're not badly hurt, are you?" she asked. "Because Perrin doesn't have any healing blessings today."

"He is not here," Kalanath said. "I think I will look for him. Do not worry, I am well." He picked up his staff and limped away down the street.

"Is that a good idea?" Alaric said.

"I think he just proved he can take care of himself."

"I was thinking of the possible mayhem if someone else picks a fight. Five men, for Sisyletus's sake."

"Maybe he can talk sense into Perrin." Sienne yawned. "I really am tired now. All that tension, watching Kalanath fight...you would have stepped in if it had gotten serious, right?"

"As he would have to defend me. Or you."

They filed back into the taproom with the rest of the onlookers. From what Sienne could hear of their conversations, that fight would be the stuff of legends in a week's time.

She trudged up the stairs and then, alone in the room, took out her nightdress, and went still. She looked around the room carefully, then dropped to the floor and scanned the corner. The faint misalignment where the disguised canvas met the wooden walls hadn't changed.

She rolled away from the bed and stood, hurrying to let Alaric in. "Someone's been in our room," she said.

Alaric scanned the room, his eyes narrowed. "How can you tell?"

"I left my bag unfastened, and it was fastened just now. *And* it was on a different bed, before you ask if I'm sure I left it unfastened."

Alaric opened his pack and looked into it without taking anything out. "My things have been rummaged through. The falcon's still there?"

"It doesn't look any different, but..." She fell to her knees again and dragged the bundle out, unwrapping it. Sparkling green emerald that glowed with magic peeped out of the canvas folds. Sienne let out a deep, relieved breath. "It's still there." She wrapped it again, shoved it under the bed, pulled out her spellbook and cast *camouflage* again. The first one wasn't likely to fade for hours, but it made her feel better.

"Suddenly Kalanath getting jumped by five hick farmers makes sense," Alaric said. "Somebody wanted us out of this room."

"And none of my things were stolen, just rearranged. You?"

"The same."

"So either we didn't have anything the thief found valuable, or he was looking for something he didn't find."

Alaric sat on the bed and let his pack fall to lie at his feet. "What do you think the odds are that two people are snooping around this inn after us?"

"Not good. But if Aneirin was able to get in and out without raising an alarm, what happened to Dianthe? Wasn't she going to follow him?"

They looked at each other in growing alarm. "We need to find her," Sienne said. "Now."

"Don't worry, I'm here," Dianthe said, pushing the door open. She sat on the bed nearest the door and said, "Kitane's left eye, but I'm tired. I climbed the outside of this building without being seen, and let me tell you, that is not as easy as it sounds."

"It doesn't sound easy at all," Sienne said. "Why did you climb the building?"

"I caught up with Aneirin as he was goading on our amorous friend and his acquaintances, encouraging them to attack Kalanath. I think money exchanged hands, but I doubt it needed to. The guy was pretty mad at Kalanath." Dianthe leaned back against the wall and worked her boots off. "Then Aneirin said something to our serving woman that sent her up the stairs. *Then* you came down like a couple of polecats with firebrands tied to their tails, and Aneirin sneaked away to the stairs. I couldn't follow him covertly, so I ran around to the side, where there's a low porch roof, climbed up it, and shimmied across to our window. It was an informed hunch."

"So he *was* the one in our room," Alaric said.

"He was good, if a little sloppy. Checked under the beds and everything. That must be some confusion." Dianthe saluted Sienne with a boot. "Then he put everything back mostly the way it was and left. I climbed down and followed him as far as one of the houses. This town is set up with the important businesses and all that on the main street, and houses on the little side streets. Then beyond that, you get the ranches and farmsteadings. Anyway, there are some decent-sized half-timbered houses to the south and west, and he went to one of those. Went right in without knocking, so I assume it's either his or belongs to someone he's very friendly with."

"Can you show us the one?" Alaric said.

"I could, but it wouldn't be a good idea. Right now, he thinks... well, he might think we suspect him, but he certainly thinks he's ahead of us because we don't know for sure he's an enemy. I was only able to get close because I'm experienced. You would rouse suspicions. We need every advantage we can get, and that means letting him believe we're clueless."

"So what do we do?" Sienne asked, somewhat plaintively. "Because we *are* clueless, at least as far as knowing what's going on goes. If he really was thorough enough to check under the beds, he might have searched with his hands and not just his eyes. So why didn't he take it?"

"I'm going with him not being all that thorough. It makes more sense. But it doesn't matter what his game is. We head south, just as we intended," Alaric said. "He'll probably follow us, but it's not like he can do anything in broad daylight on the highway in the middle of Rafellin. We keep the falcon close and don't go off—" He stopped, closed his eyes, and cursed. "Kalanath and Perrin are off on their own."

"Let's go find them," Dianthe said. "And hope Perrin isn't so drunk as to be lost to all reason."

The town's second inn was larger than the first, but just as busy. Sienne was so tired of taprooms and noise and the smell of stale beer. She wished they were home, rid of the emerald falcon and free to do... well, whatever they wanted. Whatever she and Alaric wanted. She shook the image away. Now was not the time to woolgather.

Perrin and Kalanath sat near the fire next to an alarming number of empty shot glasses. Both men sat relaxed and boneless in their chairs, heads tilted back. Sienne thought they were asleep, despite the noise of the taproom, but Alaric said, "We have news. You'd better both be sober."

"I am sadly sober," Perrin said without opening his eyes. "I tried to rectify the situation, but Averran's priests are somewhat immune to the fruit of the vine, so to speak, and I find I cannot get as drunk as I would like."

"I am sober too," Kalanath said, his words slurred enough to give him the lie.

"It doesn't matter," Alaric said. He grabbed a nearby chair and sat. "Our room was searched. Aneirin set up the attack on Kalanath to give himself time to search it. He didn't find anything, but we need to be more careful. Starting with staying together."

Perrin opened one eye, barely visible past the fall of his dark hair. He closed it again. "I apologize for running off," he said, quietly enough that Sienne could barely hear him. "Please, let us speak no more of it."

Alaric looked as if he wasn't ready to let the subject drop, but he said nothing. "It's not important. *Everyone* does it sometimes," Sienne said, glaring at Alaric, who had the grace to redden. "But what if those men who attacked Kalanath had been more seriously armed? He was all alone."

"I promise they are not a threat, Sienne," Kalanath said, sounding amused. "Even with weapons."

"All right, but you see my point. Aneirin was willing to get you injured and maybe dead for the sake of his distraction. I know he looks harmless, but we should take his threat seriously."

"He's almost certainly not alone, too," Dianthe said. "There were other people in the house I followed him to."

Perrin opened his eyes and stood, a trifle unsteadily. "Let us return to the inn, then, and no longer provide this Aneirin with opportunities to catch us unawares. I take it the plan is as it was—to go south?"

"Right. Traveling in company as best we can," Alaric said.

They left the inn, gathered a little too close for comfort. The cloudless sky gave the air a chilly bite that woke Sienne from the funk the still, muggy air of the taproom had put her in. High above, the waning moon shed nearly as much light as it had when they'd fled the carvers the first time. It seemed like ages ago. Sienne tucked her hands under her arms and shivered. For once, the idea of sharing a single room with her companions didn't annoy her, but made her feel safe. It was seven days from here to Fioretti. Seven days in which anything might go wrong.

16

Sienne's horse seemed happy to see her after five days' absence. She snuffled Sienne's hand, smearing slobber across her palm. Sienne wiped her hand clean on the mare's neck and turned to saddling and bridling her. She wasn't a horse lover like her older sister, but she liked them well enough, and they'd rented Spark often enough that she'd finally purchased her outright.

"Such a pretty day," she confided to the horse. "You can almost believe in first summer on a day like this. Clear skies, bright sun... maybe not as warm as I'd like, but warm enough." She smoothed Spark's mane and tugged once more on the straps securing the saddle, then draped the saddle bags across the horse's broad back, balancing the weight.

"Mount up, and I'll give you the last of your load," Alaric said.

"What do you mean, the last—oh." Alaric held the stained canvas bundle. "We can't put it on Button?"

"I'll feel better if one of us is monitoring it more closely." Alaric handed it up to her. She settled it in front of her, where it nestled against Spark's neck as securely as if it had been meant for that perch.

"*I'll* feel better when we know what we're going to do with it," Sienne murmured.

Alaric shook his head. "I have some ideas, but much will depend on Tonia Figlari's reaction. If she doesn't accept our story, or doesn't care, we'll have to come up with some way to get her to give us the knife. And *that*, I'm still working on."

"If I still had my family's connections, I might be able to talk to the king. My father and mother are... I don't know if they're friends exactly, but they have influence with King Derekian."

"Don't worry about it. It's unlikely their influence is greater than that whatever his name was, the Marchena lord. And you'd risk someone telling your family where you are." Alaric smiled. "Not that I'd let them drag you back to Beneddo, kicking and screaming."

"I know. I'd just as soon it wasn't an issue." Sienne patted the falcon. "It's not going anywhere. And I haven't seen anything of Aneirin this morning. I'm going to indulge in some optimism and say we won't have any trouble today."

"I'm too superstitious for that." Alaric squeezed her knee gently and turned away. Sienne petted Spark's mane again as she watched him go. He moved, not gracefully as Kalanath did, but like a force of nature, like someone who was so used to other people getting out of his way he was completely unconscious of it. She wondered how that would feel, never worrying about having to move aside for anyone.

It took another few minutes for all of them to be ready to leave. Perrin's eyes were bleary and squinted against the clear morning light as if they pained him. Maybe he had trouble getting drunk, but he suffered all the aftereffects anyway. She hesitated to ask when they would stop for him to make his devotions. He hadn't said anything about it at breakfast—hadn't said much of anything—and she felt awkward bringing it up. But if Perrin's relationship with his avatar was on shaky ground, didn't that affect all of them? She just didn't think nagging him, even if it wasn't meant as nagging, would help.

Alaric guided his large gelding toward the gate. "We'll stop at Harchow around noon for a meal, then press on to Verrone to spend the night. That second leg of the journey will be longer, but there's no helping that unless we want to camp somewhere instead of staying at an inn."

"I'd rather an inn," Dianthe said.

"Did you not say it makes you soft?" Kalanath teased.

"I did. It does. I'm soft. And I don't care."

"Ride on," Alaric said, and they trotted out of the stable yard together.

The streets of Uless were crowded with plainly-dressed men and women headed for the commons south of town. A couple of carriages, one finely decorated and gilded, the other plain and black, made even less progress against the tide of humanity than Sienne and her friends did. The road cleared substantially when they passed the commons, where booths flying the standards of various large farms and ranches dotted the fine new lawn. "What is it they do?" Kalanath asked.

"Hiring fair," Dianthe said. "People come from all over for jobs on local farms or those ranches—over there, to the south, you can see one. It's usually a big party time, though it looks like today is strictly business."

"My father always turns it into a major event," Sienne said. "They have a festival, and they crown the Queen of First Summer, and he and Mother and all us children would have to go around and be nice to the major land holders. I didn't like that part much, but I was young then—I left for Stravanus when I was fourteen. I liked the harvest fairs better. So much amazing food." She giggled. "Though the first summer festival does have the greased pig contest. All those young men, falling over themselves to catch a well-oiled piglet..."

"Why would they do that?" Perrin asked.

"Well, they get to keep the pig, for one. A good pig can provide a lot of food, come winter. And it's funny." Sienne giggled again in memory. "Nobody has any dignity when they're half-naked, covered in mud and grease and chasing a pig."

"You had a remarkably rural upbringing for a duke's daughter," Perrin said. He sounded amused, and it cheered Sienne that he might be coming out of his funk.

"My father loves the land," she said, "and he makes it a point to know his landholders and their problems. And he has a country estate he likes to putter around in. People come from all over to look at his roses. So I spent most of my youth outside the city."

"I can't even imagine that," Dianthe said. "City girl, born and bred. I was even more out of my element the first time I traveled rough than you were nine months ago."

"I, too, am a creature of the city," Perrin said. "Though I find I enjoy our excursions into the wilderness. It is a contrast that increases my pleasure at my return to civilization."

"I'm never really comfortable in the city. It's stifling," Alaric said, shrugging to adjust the position of the sword slung across his back. "So which do you prefer, Sienne?"

She almost said *Wherever I'm with my friends*, but discarded it as being terribly sentimental. "Oh, I like both for different reasons. I like cooking over the fire, and I like a bed with a mattress."

"Not things you can have at the same time," Alaric said. "Unless there's a spell for that, too."

Sienne grinned. "*Convey* again, but I'm not sure I could manage something as large as a bed, even if I had the spell."

"Kalanath, you've been quiet," Dianthe said, turning to look over her shoulder at where he rode near the rear of their group. "Everything all right?"

"I did not sleep well," Kalanath said. "Bad dreams."

"Not about the falcon again?" Sienne asked.

"I will be happy when it is gone." He looked, Sienne realized, as tired as Perrin, his skin sallow as if he'd been shut away from the sun for weeks. His attention never strayed from the bundle Sienne carried in front of her. She wanted to ask what he'd dreamed about, but had a feeling he wouldn't answer.

A rattling from behind them announced the approach of a carriage, and they moved to one side to let it pass. It was heavy, painted a plain, unadorned brown, and the windows were closed and curtained. That was a shame, given how beautiful the day was. Sienne waved at the driver, who ignored her, his gaze focused straight ahead. "I'm glad we're not cooped up in a carriage," she mused aloud.

"Yes, you don't know how lucky you are. Alaric is a terrible traveler. He gets sick in enclosed carriages," Dianthe said.

"I do not."

"You do so. There was that trip to Glorenze, five years ago—"

"I had food poisoning."

"I ate everything you did, and I didn't get sick."

"Just bad luck." Alaric scowled at her.

"And then there was—"

"Could we talk about something else? Perrin, when do you want to stop for prayers?"

"In half an hour." Perrin didn't sound enthusiastic. He also didn't sound even a little bit drunk. Sienne, who was riding beside him, didn't see his flask at his waist or anywhere else. Should she mention it? Surely he knew what he was doing better than she did. She was seized with an irrational anger that she had to step so lightly around people she considered friends—couldn't ask Kalanath about his dreams, couldn't ask Perrin about his flask. It was stupid.

"Perrin, why does Averran want his priests to be a little drunk when they approach him?" she asked.

Her sudden aggressive inquiry startled him. "Ah—well, it is to lower our inhibitions and to give him greater access to our minds, for better communication. It is not necessary, as Averran can speak to his followers whatever their state of sobriety, but Averran himself was fond of liquor. He claimed it unlatched the gate of his soul, though he might have spoken that in jest. He rarely spoke so poetically unless he meant it as humor, or as rebuke to those who thought too well of themselves."

"But you've said before it's hard for a priest of Averran to become truly drunk."

"Is there a point to this inquisition?"

"I just want to understand why, if he wants you to be drunk, he'd make it hard."

"Sienne," Dianthe began.

"He allows his priests the dubious gift of consuming liquor while remaining in only a slightly inebriated state," Perrin said stiffly. "Do you intend to criticize me for my overindulgence, too?"

"Perrin, what makes you think we're critical of you? You're our friend. We're *concerned*. If Averran thinks—"

"I don't—" Perrin said loudly, then squinched his eyes tight shut and let out a deep breath. "My relationship with my avatar is my business and mine alone. I do not expect an outsider to understand it. Particularly one with no religious affiliation of her own."

"Well, maybe it takes an outsider to see things clearly. If you don't—"

"Sienne, that's unnecessary," Alaric said. He glared at Sienne over his shoulder. She glared back at him. *Somebody* needed to brace Perrin with his problem, and sooner was better than later.

"I have changed my mind. This field, now, is as good a time and place as any," Perrin said, steering his horse over the verge and into a grassy meadow to the left of the road. Sienne dismounted and led Spark to one side of the road, following Alaric.

Perrin handed his reins to Dianthe and rummaged in one of his saddlebags, finally coming up with the missing flask. He took a long drink and made a face as if it were medicine rather than fine brandy, which Sienne had seen him filling the flask with that morning.

"Please excuse me," he said, hooking the flask to his belt.

The field's fine new grass was the brightest yellow-green Sienne had ever seen, dotted with white flowers the size of her pinky nail. Perrin strode across it, crushing grass and flowers alike under his boots. There were millions of tiny flowers, and it would be impossible to cross the meadow without destroying some of them, but to Sienne's eyes Perrin walked as if he wanted to crush as many as possible.

She tried not to feel guilty at haranguing him. He had a problem, and he needed to face up to it. *So what makes you responsible for that?* she asked herself, and felt even guiltier. She needed to apologize, but he was already yards away and settling down cross-legged on the grass.

The rest of them stopped at a distance and watched Perrin take another drink from his flask, then place a handful of white rice paper squares in his lap and settle his hands loosely on his knees. "O Lord of crotchets, it is I," he said, his voice carrying clearly to them on the breeze. "Please hear my petition, and grant me your blessings according to your will."

He fell silent. Sienne shifted her weight restlessly from one foot to the other. The silence stretched, broken only by the sound of a blackbird singing to an unseen neighbor, *twit-a-twit, twooo.* The breeze returned, carrying with it the scent of a distant river. Still Perrin said nothing. His face was still, his eyes closed, and he did not appear to be under the strain he sometimes was when making an extraordinary request of Averran.

Perrin took in a deep breath. "O Lord, I ask again, please grant my request." Again he fell silent. Then his face contorted in pain, and he let out a breath as if he'd been punched.

Kalanath took a step toward him and was restrained by Dianthe's hand on his arm. Perrin's hands closed into fists so tight the tendons stood out. His breathing went ragged, the sound of someone exerting himself to the utmost. Sienne found herself leaning forward, willing him to speak or cry out, anything to release the pressure he must surely be under.

Perrin let out another deep breath, sagging forward. His hair spilled across his face, concealing it, and his hands relaxed. When he didn't immediately stand, Alaric crossed the distance to him, followed by the others. Alaric knelt by his side. "Are you all right?"

Perrin shook his head without looking up. "I am not dead, which I suppose is cause for rejoicing."

"You could have died?" Dianthe exclaimed.

"Unlikely. I meant, rather, that so long as I live, there is hope." He raised his head and looked at Sienne. "Was it so obvious, the path I was treading?"

"I don't know what you mean," Sienne said, though a horrible suspicion grew inside her.

"It seems Averran has finally lost patience with me. He was... rather vocal about my flaws. Apparently my justifications, while satisfactory to myself, are not good enough for an avatar. And since I knew this and pretended not to, he was even testier than the situation warranted."

Silence fell again, this one heavy with unspoken words. Finally, Alaric said, "Does this mean you're no longer a priest?"

"More accurate to say I am a priest under chastisement. Averran's displeasure does not extend to casting out his erring worshippers, as that is contrary to his belief in humanity's capacity for increasing in wisdom and faith. But I will not receive any more blessings until Averran forgives me." Perrin smiled a crooked half-smile. "I realize this makes me useless to you."

"You are *not* useless," Sienne retorted. "You're one of us no matter what you can or can't do. You wouldn't kick me out if I lost my spell-book, would you?"

"Sienne's right," Alaric said. "Now, what will it take for you to gain forgiveness? And how can we help?"

Perrin blinked at him. Then he laughed. "Oh, my friends," he said when he finally regained control of himself, "I had forgotten what true fidelity looks like, having seen so little of it in my own family. It will take time, but I know not how much. Give me another moment, and I will humble myself to inquire."

"We'll wait for you with the horses," Alaric said. "Take your time."

Sienne tried to avoid stepping on the flowers as they trudged back across the field. It was impossible. She wanted to march into Perrin's father's house and shake him until he saw sense. What kind of person disinherited and banished his son just because he found a different path to God? Sienne's father worshipped Gavant as Perrin once had, so she knew a little of that avatar's worship, and Gavant would never demand that of his followers. He didn't seem to care that Sienne's mother worshipped Kitane, and that only three of the eight Verannus offspring had followed in their father's footsteps. If Perrin drank too much, it was all down to Lysander Delucco being arrogant, or narrow-minded, or both. Though according to Averran, it didn't really matter why Perrin was a drunk, just that he was. And that he was capable of changing.

She petted Spark's mane for a while, trying to ignore Kalanath's intent gaze. He wasn't looking at her, just at the artifact, but since she was in the way, it was she who got the full brunt of his stare. Alaric said, "What are we going to do?"

"We're in the middle of civilization, so it hardly matters whether he has healing or protection blessings," Dianthe said. "And we're well enough off that we can afford not to take any jobs for a while."

"It's the guidance about the artifact I'm worried about. I was hoping we could get Averran's advice about a solution." Alaric scratched his head. "I don't think it's safe to sell it to a collector when we don't know what it does. And we aren't capable of destroying it."

"We shouldn't worry about that until we've found out what it does," Sienne said. "Maybe it's not as bad as Perrin thought. Maybe it can only be activated under certain conditions. That would make it less powerful."

"Still optimistic today, eh?" Alaric said. "Do you want to see if you can make it work?"

"Not right now, but when we stop for the night, yes." She sounded more certain than she felt. The idea of experimenting with the emerald falcon filled her with dread. But they needed to know more about it, and with Perrin unable to get answers from Averran, she might be the only one who could.

"Take care," Kalanath said. "It is a dark thing, and dangerous."

"I won't take chances," Sienne said.

The sound of footsteps in the grass alerted them to Perrin's approach. He looked more cheerful than he had, though his eyes were reddened as if he'd been crying. "All is not lost," he said, taking out his flask and unscrewing the top. "Though the depth of the regret I feel at doing this suggests that I am rather farther gone down the wrong path than I thought."

He tipped the flask over, and a thin stream of amber liquid poured out. Sienne sucked in an audible breath, and Perrin looked at her and smiled.

"Have no fear, I will not die from lack of spirits, either alcoholic or natural," he went on. "I intend to gain control of myself, and this is the first step."

Sienne looked at her friends. Nobody seemed to know what to say. Perrin shook out the last few drops and screwed the top back on. "Let us proceed," he said, mounting and guiding his horse away without waiting for the rest of them.

Sienne hurried to mount, adjusting the artifact's position so it wouldn't dig into her thighs, and urged Spark after Perrin. Anything she might say to him would sound fatuous or insulting—*Good for you! You can do this!*—and she felt she'd already harassed him enough for one day. Timidly, because she wasn't sure she had the right, she composed a mental prayer to Averran. *He gave up everything to serve you,* she silently prayed, *and I think he's in pain. Be generous with him, please.*

A quiet peace settled over her, centered on her chest and radiating outward. She chose to take it as a good sign.

17

More carriages, and a couple of horses, passed them going north, but the companions were the only southbound traffic on the highway. They rode in comfortable silence, none of them feeling the need to talk. It was one of the things Sienne liked best about her team, that they could go for miles without a word and still feel as close as if they'd talked and laughed the whole time. The only sour note was Sienne's sense of Kalanath staring at the artifact and, by extension, her. She didn't have to look over her shoulder to know he was doing it. It increased her resolve to figure out how the thing worked, if only to give him some peace of mind.

Traffic increased whenever they drew near a village, mostly men or women driving ox carts and a couple of youths with switches and dogs herding sheep. One of the latter drove them off the road for a while around noon, the young shepherd chewing on a blade of grass and ignoring everything but his woolly charges. The dogs kept a tight hurdle on the sheep as if they were constrained by ropes. Sienne had been allowed to watch a sheep shearing when she was nine and it had been both fascinating and utterly boring. Sheep really weren't very interesting, maybe not even to their owners. But the dogs—*they* were interesting, how they appeared to know what to do without instruction from the shepherd. Sienne liked cats better than dogs, even though it was a cliché, wizards and their cats, but she respected working dogs like these.

Kalanath edged forward until he was next to her. "It is beautiful," he said, gesturing at the flock. "God's beloved, all in one place."

"You said before that sheep are sacred to God. Why is that?"

"For many reasons. Because when God called all the animals of earth together to hear Her commands, the sheep were the only ones who came." He let out a deep breath. "We do not eat their meat, and only the holy ones wear their wool."

Ahead, the flood of sheep turned off the highway and headed east around a small village. "That's Harchow," Alaric said. "Anyone hungry?"

Kalanath urged his horse forward. Sienne followed, eyeing the wool of his cloak. Did he mean only the holy ones in Omeira wore wool? Or was there something he hadn't told them? He was too far ahead now for her to gracefully ask him. She filed the question away for later consideration.

Harchow only had one inn, but it was large and looked prosperous. Half-timbered with small red bricks filling in the spaces between the beams, its many windows caught the noon light and reflected it back at the travelers. Well-pruned rose bushes lined its walls, waiting for first summer to give way to true summer so they could bloom and fill the air with their sweet scent. A tidy fence separated the inn yard from the road, twined with flowering clematis.

Alaric led the way into the yard. A stout older woman came to greet him. "We're just stopping for a meal," he told her.

"Of course, Master Alaric," the woman said, bowing. "We are at your service."

Alaric blinked at her. "Excuse me?"

"Please allow us to care for your mounts. Vervinia will show you where you can wash up." The woman held out her hand for Alaric's reins. More stable hands approached, smiling and bowing. A handsome young man came to Sienne's knee and extended his hand to help her dismount. Stunned, Sienne took it, though she didn't need any help. She had the presence of mind to snatch the artifact off Spark's neck and tuck it under an arm.

"Let me care for your belongings, Mistress Sienne," the handsome young man said with a smile.

"Um, no, actually I think I'll... hold onto this," Sienne managed. She gave him Spark's reins and backed away, nearly tripping over Kalanath. He looked as surprised as Alaric.

"They know our names," she murmured.

"They knew we were coming," Kalanath replied in the same low voice. "What mystery is this?"

The others drew near, huddling together for protection against the stable hands' strange behavior. "This is bad. No one should know we were coming," Alaric said.

"What do we do? Should we ride on?" Dianthe asked.

Alaric hesitated. "I don't like leaving a mystery at our backs," he finally said. "Let's talk to the innkeeper."

They followed Vervinia, who turned out to be a gangly adolescent who wore her dark hair in two long tails down her back, to a small door at the rear of the inn. It opened on a little room with a pump and basin, much cleaner than Sienne expected from a stable yard. With Vervinia looking on like a schoolmistress watching her pupils for signs of cheating, they washed their hands and faces and dried them on a very clean cloth. Then they followed their guide around to the front of the inn. The inn's front room was spacious, with two staircases at opposite ends of the room and a large desk with key cubbies behind it. Doors to the left and right hung ajar, emitting the most delicious smells of soup and chicken and ham.

A woman who looked like the stable mistress's younger sister stood just inside the front door, hands folded in front of her. She came to attention exactly like a soldier whose general has just appeared and said, "My dear, honored guests, it is such a... an honor to host you this noon! My name is Laetizia Tavano. Please, enter, make yourselves at home."

"Thank you," Alaric said. Behind him, Sienne and Dianthe exchanged glances. Nobody was ever this happy to see them, not even their landlord Master Tersus, who was close to being a friend. "We would like a meal, if it's not too much trouble."

"Everything is laid out. Your companion is waiting in our private dining room." Mistress Tavano bowed and waved to the door on the left.

Sienne looked at Dianthe again. *Companion?* Dianthe mouthed. Sienne shrugged.

"Thank you, Mistress Tavano, I see our companion has preceded us," Alaric said, not betraying the confusion he must surely feel. "We appreciate your hospitality."

Thoroughly bewildered now, Sienne followed Alaric through the door and into the inn's private dining room. It was richly decorated with maple paneling stained dark to match the floorboards, which were covered by a blue and green woven carpet. A single long table that could seat twelve but was set for six filled the center of the room, illuminated by a lovely brass light fixture that hung from the ceiling above it. The table bore six or seven covered dishes of brightly polished silver, and each of the places was set with fine porcelain that, if not the height of fashion, could not embarrass Mistress Tavano's pretensions to elegance.

A woman seated at the head of the table rose as they entered. She was tall, fortyish, and had the beginnings of middle-aged spread setting in around her cheeks and throat. She wore her dark hair piled high on her head in a businesslike twist, and her gown was simple in the way only the very wealthy achieved. Hazel eyes looked Alaric up and down, then swiftly assessed the rest of them. Sienne wished she had some way to hide the artifact where this woman couldn't see it, even concealed as it was.

Alaric said nothing, just stood with his hands clasped loosely behind his back. The woman smiled. "I'm so glad to meet you," she said, her voice a low, melodic alto. "Please have a seat. My name is Georgina Marchena."

"Mistress Marchena," Alaric said. "Or... Lady Marchena?"

Georgina Marchena inclined her head. "Lady. But I insist you call me Georgina. I feel as if I know you, and I cannot be so formal with anyone I know well."

"I'm afraid I can't extend you the same courtesy. I know you only in passing."

The name sounded so familiar. Sienne couldn't bring it to mind. She hoped Alaric could.

"I'm not offended. Really, do sit. The meal should be excellent. I paid the innkeeper enough to ensure that." Georgina took her seat and gestured with an elegant hand at the table.

Alaric hesitated only a moment longer, then drew out a chair at Georgina's left side and sat. Sienne and the others quickly followed suit. She hesitated, dithering over what to do with the canvas-wrapped artifact, but in the end set it in her lap, where it stuck out on both sides, not quite touching Alaric and Perrin, who flanked her.

Georgina withdrew the cover from what turned out to be a beautifully glazed ham, tangy and sweet-smelling. "Would you carve? I insisted we be left to ourselves for this meal. I hope I didn't insult Mistress Tavano terribly by refusing her service."

"I don't mind. Why don't the rest of you see what else Mistress Tavano has provided?" Alaric picked up a knife and carving fork and started cutting slices away from the ham. Sienne uncovered the dish closest to her; it was a tureen filled with fresh new peas, one of her favorite foods. She helped herself without waiting for further instruction.

Georgina had clearly led Mistress Tavano to believe there were five times as many of them as there were. In addition to the ham and peas, there was a roast duck, a bowl of mashed potatoes big enough to be called a vat, a tureen of gravy, a standing rib roast, and a huge dish of creamed spinach. Sienne accepted a slice of ham from Alaric and a cut of the roast from Dianthe, took a large helping of mashed potatoes and a tiny scoop of spinach, just to be polite, and settled in to eat. She hoped the stranger would give some hint as to who she was and why she knew them all so well. Marchena. She was sure she'd heard the name recently.

Georgina filled her plate and began eating. Sienne watched her covertly and noticed she took the smallest bites and chewed every-thing thoroughly. For a moment, Sienne feared poison, but the woman wouldn't have eaten even a bite if she'd poisoned it. Georgina must have some other reason for eating so lightly, and Sienne was sure it wasn't that she was already full.

"I trust you've had a good journey this morning?" Georgina said to the table at large.

"Very good," Alaric said. "Yourself?"

"I find *ferry* exhausting, actually." Georgina looked at Sienne. "Are you familiar with the spell?"

Sienne swallowed a mouthful of half-chewed peas. "I don't have it, if that's what you mean, but I have experienced it a few times. Are you a wizard?" She hoped that question didn't reveal too much of her ignorance.

"No, not I. Or I would have used *jaunt,* isn't that correct?"

Sienne tried not to blush. *Ferry* was for taking others along in instantaneous travel; *jaunt* was for the wizard alone. "Not if you brought a companion. Are you saying you came alone?" she said, trying to turn the conversation back on Georgina.

"I don't think this conversation requires more than just the six of us, yes?" Georgina turned her attention back to Alaric. "Let's not dance about any longer, shall we? I'm sure you're wondering—oh, so many things. How I know you. What brings me here to meet with you. What I want."

"I don't dance," Alaric said. "And I'd prefer not to interrupt this delicious meal, if you don't mind. Questions can wait."

Georgina raised an eyebrow. "Very well."

Sienne felt like kicking Alaric under the table, conveying the message *How can you stand to eat without knowing what she's up to? Doesn't it drive you mad with curiosity?* But she was sure that was too complex for a kick. She trusted Alaric to have a plan, but she really wished she knew what it was.

Alaric ate unhurriedly, helping himself to seconds of everything and driving Sienne nearly mad with impatience. She sipped her wine and noticed Perrin hadn't served himself anything to drink. She wondered how long he could abstain before it was too much for him to bear. For his sake, she hoped it was a long time.

Finally, Alaric wiped his mouth with a fine linen napkin, dropped it into his lap, and said, "What relation are you to Lusio Marchena?"

Georgina smiled. "He's my second cousin."

That name struck a chord. Lusio Marchena, enemy of Tonia Figlari. The one who was so friendly with the king. Sienne opened her mouth to speak and a foot ground hers into the floor. She closed her mouth abruptly and glared at Alaric, who wasn't paying her any obvious attention.

"I take it Lord Marchena is interested in the results of our expedition," Alaric said.

"So direct. I find that refreshing. Yes, Lusio has an interest in scrapping, and in your expedition in particular. I won't insult you by pretending it's coincidence."

"That's fortunate," Alaric said. "Then I won't pretend we weren't successful."

"How nice that we can treat together as equals. Would you care for more wine?"

"Please," Alaric said. "So, what specifically is Lord Marchena's interest in our find?"

"It's simple," Georgina said. "He would like to buy it. I'm prepared to offer you five thousand lari for the stone falcon."

Dianthe choked on her wine and turned it into a cough. Georgina ignored her. Sienne, seated across from her, could tell by her expression that five thousand lari was a lot even for a non-artifact emerald falcon, let alone for the stone Georgina believed they'd found.

"Interesting," Alaric said. "What makes you think we're interested in selling?"

"It's not as if you intend to keep it as a wall decoration. You're selling it to Tonia Figlari, yes? We're asking you to sell it to us instead."

"We're contracted to give it to Lady Figlari."

"You're a practical man. The stone falcon means nothing to you except a payment. What difference does it make who gives you that payment, so long as it's the most lucrative one?"

Dianthe's eyes narrowed. She opened her mouth, and then jerked as if someone had kicked her under the table. Alaric said, "That's a valid perspective. But I'm afraid we're not interested."

Georgina leaned back, wine glass in hand. "Seven thousand."

"Better. But... no."

"Ten thousand. That's the best offer you'll get. And I'm certain the Figlari woman won't be able to match it."

Alaric set his glass down with precision and rotated it slightly, as if lining it up with some detail on his plate. "You say you feel you know us," he said, "but that's impossible. If you did, you'd know our reputation. We don't renege on contracts, and we don't deal behind our clients' backs. You're right, ten thousand lari is more than Lady Figlari can pay us. And if Lord Marchena had thought to approach us at the beginning, we might have agreed to work for him instead. But we have a contract, and we don't intend to break it."

Georgina didn't look upset at this. "Are you certain? This is the only offer you'll receive. Maybe you should discuss it—or are your companions satisfied that you speak for them?" She shot Dianthe a look that said she knew how Dianthe felt about the sum offered.

Dianthe swallowed. "Alaric speaks for all of us," she said, "and we'd rather have our reputation than ten thousand lari."

"I imagine it cost you much to say that," Georgina said with a smile. "Very well. I'm sorry we couldn't come to an arrangement."

"Thank you for the meal," Alaric said, pushing back his chair. "Give our regards to Lord Marchena."

Georgina remained seated. "I'm sure he appreciates your integrity. Perhaps he'll hire you someday."

"Perhaps."

Sienne followed Alaric out of the inn and around to the stable yard. "Say nothing until we're well on the road," Alaric said, for their ears alone. Perrin looked like he was bursting to speak, but managed to stay silent.

They received their horses from still-obsequious stable hands and trotted out of the yard. High, thin clouds had come up to cover the sun, and the remaining light was oddly gray and cast unusual shadows. They passed through Harchow without speaking. Sienne felt as if every passing pedestrian and ox-cart driver wanted to hear their conversation. It had been such a strange interaction. Lusio Marchena would apparently do whatever it took to prevent Tonia from regaining her dukedom. She almost wished she could meet the man. Anyone that bent on destroying someone else was... not *interesting,* precisely, but unusual.

Traffic on the highway thinned until they were once more the only travelers on it. The road dipped below the level of the surrounding fields until they were walking in what was almost a tunnel, the sides of the road level with Sienne's eyes. Alaric reined in his horse and turned to face the rest of them. "Perrin has been dying to tell us something for the last fifteen minutes," he said. "Namely, that there is no one named Georgina in the Marchena family."

"I—yes, actually," Perrin said in astonishment. "How did you know? I did not believe you knew anything of the Marchenas."

"I don't. But I guessed she wasn't who she claimed to be when she offered to buy the artifact for ten thousand lari." Alaric shook his head. "Nobody pays that much for abstract revenge. She didn't want to deny Tonia her birthright, she wanted the artifact for itself. My instincts told me she was using the Marchena name as cover."

"I do not know the Marchenas to speak to," Perrin said, "but I know of them, and they are a small family. No doubt it is as you say— whoever she actually is, she counted on Tonia to have told us of the Marchenas' enmity, and wished to conceal her interest behind the feud."

"Then who is she?" Sienne asked. "And how did she know about the artifact, or who we are, or that Tonia hired us?"

"At a guess, our old friend Aneirin," Alaric said. "He would have reported his conversation with Sienne to his employer, even if he couldn't prove we had the artifact. And it's not as if we're unknown as a scrapper team. Though I don't know how he discovered that Tonia Figlari hired us. But that's irrelevant. What matters is that there's a third party out there with an interest in this artifact, assuming the real Marchenas also don't want Tonia to have it, and one with considerable resources."

"Ten thousand lari is beyond considerable," Dianthe said.

"We couldn't sell it, Dianthe."

"I know that, but my heart is going over all the things it could buy with its share of ten thousand lari and having trouble discarding those fantasies. Assuming the offer was legitimate."

"It is not just money," Kalanath said. "She said she was brought here by magic, yes? So she can afford to hire a wizard, and probably to keep him... it is when you pay and someone works for you when you ask."

"On retainer," Perrin said. "Do we think she is the interested party, or does she work for another?"

Alaric scratched his chin. "I think she was the negotiator," he said. "People who command those kind of resources don't generally take part in initial negotiations."

"What do you mean, initial?" Sienne said.

"If this person was willing to pay that much, and could transport his negotiator magically to the middle of nowhere to meet with us, he's not going to give up just because we said no," Alaric said. "That's bad news."

Sienne was about to ask why when the answer struck her. "You mean he'll try violence."

"Right."

They all fell silent. Perrin said, "I cannot provide protection. I regret this more than I can say."

"It's all right," Alaric said. "Sienne, how does *ferry* work?"

"It's like *jaunt*, except you can take one other person with you. I don't know any more about the specifics than I do *jaunt*, how far a range it has, how precise it is. What you're really asking is how quickly that person's wizard can amass a fighting force to come after us."

"Right."

"Well, it would have to be slow, unless..." Sienne chewed her lower lip. "There's a form of *jaunt* called *transport* that lets you take a lot of people all at once. But I don't know how many 'a lot' is. And there's no guarantee that wizard knows it. If I had to guess—"

"I'll take guessing."

"—I'd say we don't have to worry about being attacked for at least a day, probably more. That assumes the enemy is in Fioretti and doesn't have *transport*. If we're careful, if we travel off the road, we could avoid them indefinitely."

"Except this person, whoever he is, has access to at least one priest as well," Perrin said.

"How do you know?" Dianthe asked.

"Unless the person—can we call him our enemy? It seems fitting —unless our enemy was in Uless, and why would he be if he had someone working for him there, Aneirin had to communicate with him at a distance. That means Aneirin was either in company with a priest, or had been given a means of communication by a priest. And if a priest works for our enemy, he or she will be able to track us by means of scrying, and I am in no position to counter that." Perrin sounded bleak. His fingers twitched toward a flask that wasn't there, then stilled.

"So it is dangerous for us to travel away from the main road," Kalanath said, "out where anyone can attack and kill us without being caught."

"Right," Alaric said. He looked around. "We should keep moving. The enemy may not be able to bring his forces against us today, but there's no sense dawdling."

Sienne nudged Spark into motion. The horse had been grazing on tufts of grass growing out of the bank, but seemed unperturbed at being dragged away from her snack. "So how do we defend against this attack, if we don't know when it will come or from which direction?"

"It will come from the south," Alaric said. "They'll want to set up an ambush rather than attack us openly, so they won't want to chase us down by, for example, sending all their fighters to Harchow. And they'll want to attack us well away from any settlements. We'll look at the map tonight and see if we can't identify the most likely ambush spots."

"And I'll try to figure out how to work the artifact tonight." Sienne laid her hand on the bundle. "I wish I could *jaunt* back to Fioretti and put it somewhere safe. But I'd probably end up in the middle of the Jalenus Sea."

"One thing at a time," Alaric said.

18

The clouds darkened as the afternoon wore on, though no rain fell. The road rose back to ground level and unrolled straight as a furrow through the grasslands. It was hard to imagine anyone being able to ambush them, and Sienne said so. "We won't reach the forest for several miles," Alaric said, "and once we're past that, it's back to plains and farmland, as you remember from the trip out."

"So if we can make it through the forest, we're safe."

"Unless our enemy is more desperate than I imagine, yes."

"Maybe he is far *less* desperate than we imagine, and our refusal has deterred him," Perrin said with a smile that said he didn't believe his own words.

"Do you suppose he knows what the artifact does, and how to operate it?" Dianthe asked.

"What *I* wonder," Sienne said, "is whether he thinks *we* know what it does and how to operate it. That would have to affect how he approaches us, right? If he believes we might use the artifact on his people?"

"Let's hope that makes them cautious enough to give us an edge," Alaric said.

The sun set about half an hour before they reached Verrone. With the overcast covering the moon, the road was dark enough that Sienne tried creating magic lights to illuminate the way. All they did was make the blackness more complete by comparison. She hunched over the artifact, feeling obscurely that she might protect it with her body from some nameless attack out of the darkness.

Night insects chirruped all around them, a high-pitched chorus that threaded its way into her ears and down her spine, increasing her tension. The low, long *hoo* of a hunting owl made her jump and nearly sent the artifact to the ground. She grabbed it and clutched it as tightly as if it were delicate porcelain.

"Are you well?" Perrin asked in a low voice. He rode beside her as usual, but sat erect in his saddle where she was bent over.

"Just... tired," she said, "and ready to be indoors. I know they can't reach us yet, but I feel so exposed."

"Understandable." They rode a few more paces, and Perrin added, even more quietly, "You were right. And I was rude. Pray, forgive me."

It took her a moment to understand him. "No, I shouldn't have attacked you—"

"You were concerned, and you were right to be. Perhaps, if I had listened—no. I think I have been on this path a long time." He sighed. "I told myself I deserved oblivion because the pain of what I lost was so great. I think there is never a time when that is true."

"Do you... you must miss your wife terribly," Sienne dared.

Perrin sighed again. "She agreed with my parents that my choice put me beyond the pale. I thought... Cressida and I loved each other from childhood, and I would have sworn she trusted me more than any other. It seems I was wrong."

She wanted desperately to ask if he had children, but knew it was a selfish desire that could only add to his pain. "I don't understand," she said instead. "Didn't you know how your family would react to your conversion?"

"I had some inkling, yes."

"Then why did you do it? If all it did was bring you misery?"

There was a long silence in which Sienne wondered if she'd

pushed him too far. Finally, Perrin said, "My life until a year ago was a long, long string of doing what other people told me was right, no matter what my own intellect and instincts said. I worshipped on holy days and paid my offerings according to tradition and never thought about religion on all the days between. When I learned of the teachings of Averran, it was as if windows opened up inside me, revealing a world I could not have dreamed of." He bowed his head and studied his hands gripping the reins. "And the first time I spoke to the avatar, and heard his voice responding to mine, I became the man I believe I was always intended to be. I could not give it up, do you see? I simply could not give it up."

Sienne wasn't sure she did see, but she nodded.

"You had to be true to yourself," Dianthe said, startling Sienne, who hadn't known she was listening. Perrin seemed unsurprised.

"It is a facile way of putting it—no offense to you, because I understand your meaning, but being true to oneself has for centuries been used to excuse all manner of bad behavior."

"Yes. I meant you couldn't keep your integrity and go back to being a casual worshipper of Gavant."

"That is it exactly. I might as well have broken my marriage vows —it would have been as damaging to my soul."

"I hope Averran is listening to this," Sienne declared, making all of them laugh.

"He embodies wisdom in its most perfect form, so of course he hears us," Perrin said. "And he knows my heart. It is simultaneously my greatest hope and my greatest fear that he will take my intentions into consideration. And—what's that?"

Sienne looked past Alaric's dark bulk. Ahead, lights twinkled. "Please tell me that's Verrone."

"We're here," Alaric said. "And I hope we don't have the kind of warm reception we had at Harchow."

Verrone was considerably larger than Harchow, nearly a city in size, and the highway broadened as they neared it. Sienne relaxed when tall, half-timbered buildings with stone foundations surrounded them, most of them bearing sign boards with names or pictures painted on them. Maybe she did prefer civilization, after all.

Dianthe chose their inn based on criteria Sienne wasn't privy to. She hoped they had to do with the place's impregnability in case of a siege. It was tall and narrow, with a stable yard behind and well off the street, and occupied a corner lot where two wide roads, busy even at this hour of evening, intersected. Sienne, alive to the possibility of pickpockets and tense enough to worry about the artifact being stolen off the horse while she sat there, kept one hand on the canvas bundle as she followed Alaric and Dianthe around to the stable. She dismounted, held onto Spark for a moment while her legs remembered how to support her, and removed the bundle from Spark's neck.

"Inside," Dianthe said in her ear. "We're going to negotiate for rooms while the others handle the horses and gear."

"Shouldn't we stay together?"

"We're safe here, Sienne. Relax."

It was easy enough for her to say that, Sienne thought, when she didn't have a deadly artifact tucked under one arm. She went with Dianthe through the back door of the inn and through the kitchen to the tap room, where Dianthe found the owner serving drinks. A few coins changed hands, and they returned to the yard to meet the men just entering the inn. "Two rooms, guaranteed lice free," Dianthe said. "I was afraid to ask why that had to be specified."

"Let's drop off our things and get some food," Alaric said. "I'm starving."

The rooms were on the top floor, and it turned out Dianthe had requested them intentionally. "I like having the high ground," she said when Sienne complained at the third-floor landing. One room had two beds, the other four, and Sienne sank gratefully onto her bed and set the artifact beside her.

"I'm not very hungry," she said. "I'll stay up here and see what I can make of this thing."

"You have to eat, Sienne," Alaric said, "and it's not safe for you to try to activate it without anyone around in case of an accident."

"I was thinking it might be safer not to have anyone around, in case it shoots poison darts or something." She stretched. "Bring me back some bread and cheese. I'll be fine."

Alaric looked like he wanted to argue the point a while longer, but only pressed his lips together in a thin, disapproving line and followed the rest of them out of the room. Sienne leaned back against the wall and closed her eyes. She liked Spark, but it was so nice to sit on a surface that didn't move.

She unwrapped the canvas to reveal the emerald falcon, but didn't touch it. "So, you're dangerous and there's no conventional defense against you," she said. "You're an artifact, so you need someone to operate you, which means, I assume, you won't kill your operator when she uses you."

The thing stared up at her with a flat, glassy eye. It tilted to one side, propped on its right wing. Its claws were partially curved as if the creator had transformed a real falcon in the act of stooping on its prey. Sienne closed her hand around its... were they still ankles if it was a falcon's legs they were attached to? At any rate, she took it around the legs just above its feet, with those wickedly sharp talons she was careful not to touch, and lifted it so its eyes and beak were level with her chin. She turned it around to face away from her.

"If it were me, I wouldn't design a weapon with a face unless I intended that face to be a crucial part of that weapon," she went on. Good thing her friends weren't there to hear her talking to an emerald artifact. "Maybe you do an extra-powerful version of *scream*. I've heard there's one that knocks people unconscious, and it's hard to defend against an attack made of sound. Or *force*? It could blast from your beak, I suppose."

She prodded the back of its head and neck, looking for moving parts. There was a groove a few inches deep and about a hand span wide at the base of its neck, and she ran her fingers through it. It was smooth and warm, warmer than the falcon's surface, but nothing changed when she touched it. She ran her hands over the wings and tail, checking every feather. None of them moved. She tested the point of a talon against her thumb; it pricked her sharply, nearly drawing blood, which made her wonder if it needed blood to activate. She'd heard of artifacts that did. Grimacing, she raised her left hand to the thing's beak and drew her thumb across the point, then squeezed a drop of blood into the falcon's mouth and braced herself for an explosion. Nothing happened.

Sienne set the falcon on the bed and sucked on her thumb. It was a weapon. It couldn't do damage in an area all around, or it would kill the wielder. Therefore, it had to do damage in a line or a burst of some kind. She picked it up again and examined the groove. It looked a little like a hand grip, curved inward as if made to match the contours of a hand...

She took a deep breath, then curled her right hand around the groove. Instantly the falcon grew warm to the touch, not just where her hand fit the groove, but where she gripped its legs and along its back where her right arm rested.

She let out a little shriek and nearly dropped it, but it didn't do anything else. Cautiously, she released the groove, and it cooled off immediately. She gripped and released a few more times before setting it on the bed again. She'd gotten a reaction out of it. She just didn't know what it meant.

Someone knocked on the door. "I brought food," Alaric said. "Despite my feeling that I shouldn't encourage you to neglect your physical needs for the sake of that artifact."

"Thanks."

He offered her a napkin-covered plate containing some beef in gravy and a pile of limp green beans. "The food's not much, but it's better than going hungry."

"I made it do something." Sienne dug into the beef. "It's a start."

"What, already? Isn't that unlikely?" Alaric picked up the artifact by one wing and let it dangle.

"There's really only so many ways you can design a weapon for human use. The real unlikelihood is that we'll figure out the conditions for activating it."

Alaric took a seat next to her on the bed, making it groan under his weight. "I thought you had a chance at doing that, because you're a wizard."

"I'm hoping, because it's a weapon, it was made for anyone to use. Artifacts can have the oddest requirements, like only working in the light of a new moon, or you have to be a virgin—"

"You're kidding."

"No. Anyway, this one—hold it by the ankles and see if you can fit your other hand into that groove."

"Are they really ankles, if it's a bird?" Alaric wedged his fingers into the groove. "I don't feel anything."

Sienne touched the falcon's side. It was cool. "Maybe your hand is too big. Let me show you." She traded him the plate for the bird and gripped it properly. Instantly, it heated up. "Touch the side."

"So you activated it!"

"Part of it, anyway. There must be some other step." She set the falcon down behind her and went back to eating. "We just have to be prepared for the possibility that it's a step we can't fulfil."

Alaric leaned back against the wall and looked at the thing. "All this trouble over Sisyletus knows what."

Sienne scraped her plate clean and laid it and the fork on the floor. She moved the bird aside and leaned back next to Alaric. "It's not what Tonia wanted. If we weren't concerned about what it might do, we could have sold it to that fake Marchena for ten thousand lari."

Alaric slid his arm around her waist. "I could do a lot with a fifth of ten thousand lari. What about you?"

"Buy more spells, I suppose. A nice dress to go dancing. Would you go dancing with me?"

He shook his head. "I look like a performing bear when I dance. But I could watch you dance."

"With other men? You wouldn't enjoy that."

"I would enjoy seeing their faces when you left them at the end of every set to join me." He pulled her closer and kissed the side of her head.

"You sound awfully certain of yourself. How do you know I'd come back to you?"

"Because," he said, tilting her head up so she looked at him, "none of them will ever kiss you the way I do."

His lips touched hers, first lightly, then with a growing insistence that made her tingle all over. She put her arms around his neck and drew him closer, and they kissed, gradually shifting until they were lying on the bed, entwined together. Alaric shifted his embrace to pull her tightly to him, kissing her breathless. Sienne hooked one leg over his, feeling desperate to be as close to him as possible.

Something hit the floor with a chiming *thunk*. Startled, Sienne drew back, then laughed. "It's the artifact," she said. "What a duenna."

"Yes, I think we were a little carried away," Alaric said. He helped her sit, then kept hold of her hand as she picked up the falcon with the other. "I don't think we're ready for that."

"Certainly not when Dianthe could come back at any moment." Sienne examined the falcon for cracks, or any sign it had been damaged by its fall, though she didn't expect to find anything.

"Does Dianthe know there's something between us? She gave me the strangest look when I said I'd bring you food."

"She guessed. Were you really pining after me?"

"Is that what she said? I was *not* pining. I was secretly longing from afar."

"That's the same thing as pining."

"No, it isn't. It's far more manly."

Sienne laughed and punched him lightly on the arm. "I think it's sweet. Though it's far sweeter that you're not pining anymore, and I'm not dithering, and—"

He interrupted her with a kiss. "Dithering, eh? I'm glad that's over."

Someone knocked lightly on the door. "It's me," Dianthe said, opening it a few inches. "You'd better not be naked."

"*Dianthe!*"

"Just kidding." Dianthe came fully into the room. "Any luck?"

"I can make it heat up, but still have no idea how to use it as a weapon." Sienne removed her hand from Alaric's and picked up the falcon in both hands. "Take it by the ankles and put your hand in the groove."

Dianthe did as she was told. "I don't feel anything."

Puzzled, Sienne laid her hand along the falcon's faceted side. "That's strange. I thought Alaric couldn't make it work because his hand is too big, but maybe you have to be a wizard to activate it."

Alaric stood. "I'll get the others. We can test that theory right now."

When he was gone, Dianthe said, "I hope you were kissing at least some of the time. Wouldn't want you to waste any of the privacy I engineered for you."

"It would be indelicate of me to comment."

Dianthe snorted. "Meaning you did. Good for you! Alaric needs some fun in his life, and you could stand to think about something other than magic."

"I think about plenty of things other than magic!"

"Really? Like what?"

Sienne gaped. "I... the fact that I can't think of anything right now in no way validates your opinion."

The door swung open. "We want to try something," Dianthe said to Perrin and Kalanath.

The artifact remained inert for Perrin. Kalanath flatly refused to touch it. "It will not work for me either," he said. Sienne didn't push.

"So it needs a wizard to activate it," Alaric said. "That's good news. It eliminates nine out of every ten people from being able to use it."

"But our enemy knows a wizard," Kalanath said. "Someone who will use it at his direction. And if our enemy knows how to make it work, he will send that wizard after us to retrieve it."

"True, but there's nothing we can do about that." Alaric took the falcon from Perrin and wrapped it in its canvas again. "Dianthe, do you have the map?"

Dianthe rummaged in her pack and came up with a map tube. Alaric unrolled the map and spread it out on Dianthe's bed, where he and Kalanath held its corners down. "Verrone is here," Alaric said, letting a corner of the map curl up when he released it to point.

Sienne held it down. "Thanks. The highway south goes through a bunch of little towns, and then Terrius, which is the last city before the road heads into the forest. It will take us a day and a half to get that far. The forest is where they'll have to ambush us." He jabbed the map with his finger. "It's a stretch of road about twelve miles long, with only the one town, Muskey, at the eight-mile mark. Muskey isn't very big and we can't count on it dissuading them from attacking us. Our best bet is to stop at Terrius until the next day's dawn, then ride like mad through the forest and hope to outrun them."

"I wish I had *cat's eye*," Sienne groused. "We could sneak through at night. Or the kind of *force* that blasts several people at once."

"I'm more worried about Kalanath's point that these people will probably have a wizard with them," Dianthe said. "If he can cast that *ferry* spell, who knows what else he might be capable of?"

"*Ferry* is powerful. It could be a lot," Sienne said.

Perrin stepped back. "I intend to go to my room and pray," he announced. "I think it unlikely that Averran has forgiven me after less than a day, but perhaps he will take pity on the rest of you." He left the room, shutting the door quietly behind him.

"We should not disturb him," Kalanath said. "I will go to the tap room and meditate."

"I'm going to have another beer," Alaric said. "Do you ladies want to join us?"

"I'm ready to sleep," Sienne said. Dianthe nodded.

"Then we'll see you in the morning," Alaric said. He looked at Sienne as if he wished he could kiss her good night, then followed Kalanath out the door.

Sienne tucked the canvas bundle under her bed, then cast *camouflage* on it. It was probably pointless; Dianthe might be a snorer, but she slept lightly, and no one would get more than a few steps into their room without her waking. When she stood, Dianthe was already in her nightdress and settling into bed. "Perrin will be all right, won't he?" Sienne said.

"I wish I could say yes," Dianthe said. "But our need for a priest isn't as great as his need for healing. It might be a while."

Sienne changed into her nightdress and climbed into bed. She sent a magical breeze toward the lamp, blowing out the light. "I wish there were something we could do to help."

Dianthe responded with a gentle snore. Sienne smiled into the darkness and rolled to face the wall. She thought about composing another prayer to Averran, but if he was as crotchety as Perrin said, he might not like non-worshippers pestering him. Instead, she thought of her family. She was as isolated from them as Perrin was from his, but in her case, she'd chosen to leave. At the time, she'd been angry and hurt and willing to make them angry and hurt too. Now she could think of her parents and her sister Felice with only a trace of the pain she'd felt nearly a year ago. If they'd cast her off instead of the other way around, would she miss them the way Perrin missed his wife? Sienne didn't think it was at all the same. Even so, she fell asleep almost, but not quite, regretting her actions.

19

The next two days' travel was uneventful, though Sienne couldn't quite shake her unease at carrying the artifact so casually before her pommel. She rode with the reins clasped lightly in her left hand, resting on the falcon, and her spellbook loosely held in her right, ready to fall open to *force* or *scream*. But no one attacked them. The roads weren't well traveled at this time of year, and every time they saw a group approaching from the south, Sienne tensed. It was never the promised ambush. By the second day, when they reached Terrius at around two o'clock in the afternoon, she was so worn out Alaric took the artifact from her and sent her to bed. She went without a fight and fell gratefully into a deep, restful slumber.

The next morning dawned gray and wet. Sienne stood at the window in her nightdress and looked out at the rain slicking the cobbles. "Maybe they'll stay home," she said. "This isn't good ambush weather."

"Of course it is," Dianthe said. "Visibility is low, everyone's hunched into their hoods trying not to be rained on, they're thinking about other things and distracted... weather control is impossible, right? Because I'd almost suspect their wizard of arranging things to suit them otherwise."

"There are evocations for calling a wind or creating lightning, but that's the most anyone can do to change the weather. And I was thinking about how hard it would be to sit in the rain for hours, waiting for their prey to stroll by. They've got to be distracted, too."

"They probably cancel each other out." Dianthe rose and got dressed. "I couldn't sleep last night. Kept going over possibilities for avoiding this confrontation, none of which were viable."

"If I knew how to use *jaunt,* I could go back to Fioretti and find someone to sell me *transport,* and then I could take us all home in a heartbeat. Or several heartbeats, I guess. The only thing I know about spells like *jaunt* and *transport* is they're not instantaneous."

"Well, my conclusion was that there's no point fretting about this. We know they're waiting for us somewhere, and that will have to be enough of an edge. It's probably too much to hope for that they think we're oblivious."

Sienne pulled her shirt over her head and picked up her trousers where they lay across the foot of her bed. "I was thinking I should ride in front."

"Really? Alaric will never go for it."

"If I'm in front, I can cast *scream* and disable some of them before it comes to close fighting. I can't do that if Alaric is blocking my view."

"That's true. We can suggest it. He might even see sense."

They were the first to the tap room for breakfast. The serving woman offered them a choice of eggs or hashed potatoes. Dianthe took eggs. Sienne asked for potatoes. They were eating peacefully when the three men entered. Only Kalanath looked fully awake. Perrin's eyes were bleary, and he refused food in favor of black coffee. Alaric looked as if he hadn't slept well, but took both eggs and potatoes.

"Don't eat too heavily," he warned them. "We need to be alert, not logy with food."

"What do you call *that?*" Dianthe asked, pointing at his over-flowing plate.

"That *is* lightly, for me. I wanted twice as much." He took a drink from his coffee mug and added, "I have no idea where they'll strike.

My guess is somewhere past Muskey. It's too small a village for them to have stayed there overnight so they could come north to attack us as we enter the forest. But the forest road is more over-grown north of Muskey, with better opportunities for an ambush, so I could be wrong. So, unfortunately, we'll have to stay alert the whole way."

"I was thinking I should ride in front," Sienne said.

"Out of the question," Alaric said.

"She can cast *scream* to incapacitate some of the enemy," Dianthe pointed out.

"And if their wizard casts spells, she will see the magic first," Kalanath said.

That was something Sienne hadn't thought of. "You'll be close behind," she told Alaric, who looked torn. "And we'll all be in danger no matter where we ride."

Alaric's lips thinned in irritation. "All right," he said. "But you fall back when we encounter them, after casting *scream*, all right? You and Perrin can't get into hand-to-hand range."

"I appreciate the warning, and will try not to feel resentful that it is necessary," Perrin said with a grimace.

"They'll try to stay hidden, to let us walk into the middle of them so we're surrounded," Alaric said. "As soon as we see them, we ride hard as far as we can until it comes to fighting. Kalanath, are you comfortable fighting from horseback?" It was a polite way of saying what Sienne knew he was thinking, which was *Are you going to fall off your horse if it comes to a fight?*

Kalanath scowled at his plate. "Staff fighting is not good for horses. But I will do my best. Do you think they will be mounted?"

"No. Hard to stay concealed when you have horses to worry about. If you have to dismount to fight, that's just how it has to be. But the idea is not to engage with them if we can help it. The idea is to break their ambush and ride south. Stopping to fight is a distraction that could get someone hurt."

"But we stay together," Dianthe said. "Nobody runs ahead, nobody gets left behind."

Nobody could think of anything to say to that. They finished their meals in silence.

Alaric came to Sienne's side as she was saddling Spark. "I'm not happy about this," he said.

"I know."

"If that wizard throws something big at us, you'll be the first hit."

"I know." She settled the artifact on Spark's neck.

"Don't get hurt."

"I wish I could promise that." She looked up at him. "It's not just me, is it? You'd willingly throw yourself in front of any of us if it meant protecting us."

"That's true." He smiled. "It might be extra true for you."

She'd never more wanted to fling her arms around his neck and kiss him. "Thank you," she said.

"For what?"

"For caring. And for letting me ride first anyway."

He clasped her hand briefly. "We'll get through this."

She mounted, wheeled Spark around, and headed for the gate. Around her, her friends did the same. She took a moment to look at each of them: Perrin, his face still drawn and tense; Kalanath, looking calm but with one hand on his staff; Dianthe, seemingly unconcerned about what came next; and Alaric, fiercely scowling at nothing. Her friends. Her adopted family. She tried not to feel superstitious about her moment of sentimentality.

It was so *strange* not having Alaric's looming back blocking her view. Terrius was large and old, one of the oldest cities in Rafellin, and its age showed in the archaic wattle-and-daub houses and narrow streets that forced them to ride single file. Men and women in modern dress looked out of place against the buildings with their tiny glass windows and the streets whose sidewalks were the merest curbs defining the gutters. But it was clean, the gutters free from refuse, and had the day not been overcast it would have been a pleasant ride through an attractive city.

Sienne smiled tightly at a child who gaped up at her, tugging on his sister's sleeve to point out the scrapper team riding through their streets. They were deliberately riding into an ambush. It had to be the stupidest thing she'd ever done, far stupider than investigating a midge hive on her own. She relaxed her grip on the reins and practiced breathing to calm herself, in through the nose, out through the mouth. By the time they left Terrius behind, she was more relaxed. All she could do now was be prepared to cast spells at the first sign of trouble, and not get hurt. She hoped it would be that easy.

It took half an hour's riding to reach the beginnings of the forest. They'd passed a number of travelers, some in wagons, others walking, going north, and it cheered Sienne. Their enemy wouldn't attack them if there might be witnesses. She ignored the tiny voice that suggested the enemy would just kill any would-be witnesses. They didn't know how ruthless he was. All he wanted was the artifact; their deaths were unnecessary. She clung to this theory. It helped her stay relaxed.

Thunder rumbled as they moved deeper into the forest. With the overcast, it was particularly dim beneath the branches. Sienne's gaze roved across the road from side to side. Was that a man? No, just a broken tree. She stayed alert for any sign of magic, or the sound of someone casting a spell. Raindrops began striking the canopy of leaves, pattering lightly like someone tapping their fingers on a table top. She put up her hood as the first drops of water made their way between the foliage.

"We can move a little faster," Dianthe said from beside her. She hadn't put her hood up and looked alertly ahead and to the sides.

Sienne nudged Spark into a trot. At that gait, it was hard to hold the reins *and* her spellbook *and* keep the artifact from slipping off. She opened the spellbook to *scream* and cradled it in the crook of her arm. Rain struck its impervious pages and rolled off like water on glass. The clop of Spark's hooves on the road became more of a squish as the earth soaked up the rain. Sienne stroked Spark's wet mane and wished for both their sakes this was over already.

Minutes passed. Sienne tried not to feel impatient with their enemy for not ambushing them immediately. The waiting would kill her. She wiped rain out of her face. A gray mist rose up from the ground, curling around her horse's hooves. Visibility was getting worse. Sienne peered into the fog. How could it be foggy if it was raining? That seemed impossible.

Impossible fog. She caught her breath. "It's *fog*," she whispered.

"I can see that," Dianthe said.

"No, not natural fog, magical *fog. Mehla.* It's them."

"Can you clear it away?" Alaric murmured.

"No."

"Then *ride!*" Alaric shouted, spurring his horse forward.

Sienne kicked Spark into a gallop and careened into the fog bank rising up before them. She brought her spellbook up to just below her chin and stared vainly for a target.

A gust of wind came out of nowhere, blowing so hard Sienne nearly dropped her spellbook. The fog turned to tatters and then was gone. Men, too many for Sienne to count at the speed she was going, appeared in front of her, weapons at the ready. She leaned wide of Spark's head and read off the evocation *scream,* feeling it burn her mouth as it built to a terrible shrill volume.

As the spell left her lips, a light grew ahead and to the left, a warm orange glow like the sun setting, except it was far too early and the wrong direction. It rushed toward her, growing brighter and hotter, and she barely had time to get her spellbook in front of her face before the fire struck her and Spark nearly head-on.

Spark let out a terrified scream that Sienne echoed. The fire was everywhere, clinging to her clothes and her hood, filling her nose with the smells of burnt hair and scorched fabric. It hurt as nothing had ever hurt before. Spark reared up, and Sienne lost her seat, falling heavily to the ground. She rolled frantically, remembering vaguely that this was what you did with someone on fire. She couldn't see anything but the lightness of the pages of her spellbook, and tears came to her burning eyes, tears of terror that she'd been blinded.

After what felt like an eternity, she realized the pain had lessened, and she couldn't smell fire anymore. She pushed herself up and nearly screamed again at the pain in her hands. Their backs were red and blistered from where she'd held the spellbook in front

202 | MELISSA MCSHANE

of her face. She blinked away the tears and the world swam into focus. The harness was ruined, but her spellbook had saved her face and her eyesight. She clutched it to her chest and drew great sobbing breaths.

She became aware of sounds, shouting and the clashing of weapons. She looked around frantically for her friends. She'd gotten turned around and had no idea which direction was south, but Alaric and Dianthe were slashing away at their attackers somewhere ahead of her, Kalanath had dismounted and was smashing his way through more of the enemy toward them, and Perrin was running her way, screaming something and waving his hands. *Behind you,* it sounded like—

Sienne twisted around. A man wielding a sword was fifteen feet from her, bearing down on her rapidly. Without thinking, she opened her book to *force* and blasted the man as he swung his blade at her head. She threw herself to one side, screamed again as she landed on her burned wrist, and then Perrin was there, helping her up. "You have to find the wizard," he shouted.

"Where—"

"He hit us all with that fire and hasn't cast anything else—look out!"

An enormous warrior strode out of the dimness, armored in heavy plate mail and wielding a sword as big as Alaric's. Sienne scrambled to stand and cast *force* again. The blast took the man in the chest and bounced off, not stopping him. Terror struck Sienne as hard as *force.* She'd never seen anyone stand up to that spell before.

The warrior continued to advance, bringing the sword up for a powerful swing. No light gleamed along the edge of the blade. No light...

With an effort, Sienne turned her back on the warrior. "*Sienne!*" Perrin screamed. "What are you doing?" He grabbed her around the waist and bore her to the ground, out of the way of the warrior's blade that swept through the air above them.

Sienne struggled free of his grasp and stood. "It's *phantom,*" she said. "Terrifying images meant to paralyze with fear. But it's not real.

And if that's the best that wizard can do, he's not as powerful as we imagined."

The warrior struck again, swinging his blade hard and fast. It passed through Sienne harmlessly.

"You took an awful chance," Perrin said. He was breathing heavily and his eyes were wide.

"Where's Spark?" Sienne asked. Another jolt of terror went through her. The artifact was still on Spark—unless it had fallen when Sienne did. She turned in a wide circle, looking for her horse. Spark was gone. A short distance away, a white lump growing dark with rain lay on the ground. Sienne ran for it. Charred holes in the canvas revealed its precious glittering contents. Sienne snatched it up, ignoring the pain in her burned hands, and tucked it under her left arm.

"Sienne, *move!*" Perrin shouted. Something long and dark flew at her, striking her in the stomach and knocking her backward as the air whooshed out of her. Her spellbook slipped from nerveless fingers. A flying tree. The wizard had hit her with a tree. Sucking in air desperately, she thought *I need his spellbook. Wonder if he'd like to trade?*

Perrin helped her stand. "It was from that direction," he said, pointing. "You—" His eyes widened again, and he shoved her to the side just as fire erupted all around them again. His shove had sent her out of the worst of it, but again she dropped and rolled on the ground, clutching the artifact to her chest. Her spellbook, where was her spellbook? When her vision cleared, she looked around for it, felt with her right hand in case she was blinder than she thought. It was gone.

The canvas wrapping the artifact was in shreds after the second *scorch*. Sienne tossed the remnants aside. It wasn't as if concealment mattered now. Perrin lay nearby on his back, his face blistered and his clothing burned badly. She ran to his side and knelt, leaning over to put her cheek near his mouth. She couldn't tell if he was breathing. Sobbing, she shook his shoulder. "Perrin, get up. Get up!"

Steps alerted her to someone's approach. The fingers of her right hand curled reflexively into the groove at the falcon's neck. Instantly it grew warm. She stood, putting Perrin behind her, and turned to face the man coming toward her. He was short, with a dark beard and silvery hair, and he carried a spellbook open at waist level. Her mind numb with fear and pain, Sienne watched him come to a stop about twenty feet from her. All around them, fighting raged, but where they stood everything was still.

"Give it to me," the wizard said.

Sienne clutched the falcon around the ankles and held it close to her chest. "You'll have to take it."

He smiled. "I hoped you'd say that. How would you like to die? Fire, or ice?"

"You're giving me a choice? How thoughtful." She had no spellbook, no convenient friends, nothing but a useless artifact that might be the key to her salvation if she only knew how to activate it. She looked down at it, willing it to give up its secrets. Not blood, not a hidden switch. She might use it as a melee weapon, battering him with its beak or clawing with its talons—

Its talons. Curved, like it was about to grab hold of something.

"No, it will be fire. It's quicker. And I don't want you to suffer needlessly."

She ignored him. Could it be that simple? "Then do it," she said, and let go of the falcon's ankles to raise her burned left forearm horizontally across her stomach. She brought the bird down so its feet rested on her arm like they were gripping a branch.

The talons closed convulsively on her arm, piercing her flesh and digging deep. A brilliant emerald glow began deep within the artifact and grew until the falcon radiated green light. Sienne strangled a scream and lifted the falcon to chest level, keeping a tight grip on the handhold at its neck. The thing burned now, hot as *scorch* but smaller. She brandished it at the wizard. Nothing happened.

The wizard stared at her in growing horror. He began reading off an evocation, stumbled, began again. She took a step, two steps, toward him, ignoring the terrible pain in her arm. Still, nothing happened. The wizard continued to read, flicking his gaze at her between syllables. If this was another *scorch*, she wouldn't survive even if she turned and ran now.

If you're going to save me, now would be a good time, she thought at the bird. It didn't react—but it was just an artifact, not a creature, so what else did she expect? The absurdity of it made her angry. She directed her anger into the artifact and felt the heat swell to an almost unbearable level. How dare this wizard try to kill her and her friends just because his master wanted the artifact? How dare he believe this entitled him to kill?

Orange light grew and coalesced around a point above his spell-book, straining to fly free. The wizard spat out the last syllables of the evocation, and it flew at Sienne. She screamed and instinctively raised the artifact to protect her face. The *scorch* slammed into the artifact, making Sienne step backward to keep her balance, but instead of agonizing fire, she felt—nothing. The fire vanished, absorbed by the artifact.

Sienne lowered her hands, which were shaking. The wizard's mouth hung open in shock. His expression of surprise, as if she'd done something unthinkable, filled her with unaccountable rage—anger at being attacked, at the pain she felt, at the sheer stupidity of it all. She brought the falcon up to chest height again and aimed it at the wizard.

A beam of light, pale green like new grass, shot from the falcon's beak to strike the wizard in the chest. His eyes went wide and aston-ished. The green light spread from the point of impact to cover his body, turning him green for an instant, then vanished.

The wizard dissolved into ash.

20

Sienne blinked. She looked around, thinking there must be some mistake. He'd run away, or fallen, or... her mind stuttered to a halt. She sank to the ground and cradled the falcon against her chest, ignoring the blood running down her arm to stain her shirt. There was a ringing in Sienne's ears, the sound that comes just before unconsciousness. *Rasapadi*. It couldn't be anything else. The lost spell *rasapadi*. And she'd used it to turn a man to ash.

She realized she was shaking again and made herself stand and walk. Alaric needed to know about this. They all did.

Perrin still lay unconscious on the ground nearby. She needed to get help for him. She didn't know what to do if the healer was the one who needed healing. Though Perrin had no healing blessings, so what did that make him? Her addled brain was having trouble keeping everything straight. Find Alaric and Dianthe and Kalanath, get them all free of the ambush—

A dark shape ran at her, someone who raised a sword and shouted things she couldn't understand. She raised the falcon and directed her fear and anger and self-loathing into it. It was easier this time. The man disintegrated just a foot away from her, the light wind carrying his remains to cling to her ruined shirt and trousers. She felt no sorrow at his death. She couldn't feel anything.

More shapes with swords came at her. She turned them to ash, one at a time, marveling in her trancelike state at how easy it was to bring death when you had the right tool. Soon they were running the other way, some of them throwing down their weapons. How interesting, that they wanted to protect their swords from being disintegrated with their bodies. She couldn't imagine caring that much about a sword.

She raised the falcon and aimed at the one figure still trying to attack her. The person ducked, caught her around the knees and bore her to the ground. "Sienne, Sienne, it's me," Alaric shouted. "They're running. You can stop. Put it down."

Alaric. Definitely she should not disintegrate him. She shook her head, feeling the numbness in her mind fade. "Get it off me," she whispered. "It hurts."

Alaric touched her arm lightly and swore. "Somebody help me!"

More running footsteps. "Sienne, you have to let go," Dianthe said in her ear. "Relax your hand."

"It's dug into me."

"Your other hand. Just relax."

Sienne remembered she had two hands. She released her right one from its grip on the hand hold. The talons immediately retracted, and she jerked away from the falcon, not stopping it from falling to the ground. It wasn't as if that could hurt it. Nothing could.

"That doesn't look good," Perrin said. "The burn should not be covered, but we must stop the bleeding."

Sienne couldn't bring herself to look at the bloody mess that was her left forearm. "Is everyone all right? Perrin was..."

"I am well. The last fire knocked me unconscious briefly, but did not singe more than my face and clothes," Perrin said. He took a handkerchief from inside his burned vest and wrapped it tightly around her forearm, covering half the deep puncture wounds. "Anything else—yes, thank you, that should do nicely." Kalanath handed him a yellow scarf that Perrin used to bandage the rest of her arm. Finally Sienne felt she could look at it.

Perrin removed his flask from his hip. "Water," he said when they all stared at him. "I believe Sienne is the worst burned of us. She took the wizard's first shot most directly." He poured cool water over the burn on her right arm, soothing it enough that she wished she had a stream to lay it in.

She accepted her spellbook in the tattered remains of its harness from Dianthe, then looked at her friends, reassuring herself that everyone was well. Every face was scorched to some degree, and burns marked all their clothes, but no one was glassy-eyed with pain. Well, no one except her, and she'd done it to herself.

"Spark," she suddenly exclaimed. "Where is Spark?"

No one answered. Dread touched her heart. "She's not dead, is she?"

"She took the same direct fire you did," Alaric said. "She's hurt badly. If we're lucky, she'll make it through the forest and we can find someone to care for her. But you won't be able to ride her."

Rage burned inside Sienne, and without thinking she put her hand on the artifact and felt it pulse in recognition of her anger. "How many of them were there?"

"Many," Dianthe said. "If you hadn't... done what you did... we would all be dead now. We were only barely holding them off." Sienne realized Dianthe was holding her arm stiffly, Alaric had blood on his jerkin, and Kalanath had limped heavily walking to join them. They weren't unscathed, after all.

Sienne cast her gaze toward the artifact. It felt cool to the touch and, aside from that one pulse, completely inert. "It's called *rasapadi*," she said. "It means 'ash.' It's one of the lost spells, the ones the ancients had in the before times that were lost in the rebuilding. We don't know what all of them were, but we have descriptions and names for some of them. That's one."

They sat silently around her, all staring at the artifact. "We can't give that thing to *anyone*," Dianthe said. "Even if only a wizard can use it, there are a lot of wizards in Fioretti alone. And even if we give it to a school, or a wizard with an impeccable reputation, that doesn't keep it from being stolen by someone less savory."

"And it cannot be destroyed," Perrin said. "Except by itself, presumably."

"Not even then," Sienne said. "*Ash* can't destroy anything that's invulnerable—it left the wizard's spellbook untouched, but everything else he wore or carried is gone. And an artifact is basically invulnerable. But it doesn't matter. I don't think it can be turned on itself."

"A mirror? No, it would destroy the mirror first," Perrin said.

"Then we'll have to dispose of it some other way," Alaric said. "But first, we have to get back to Fioretti."

"Aren't we safe now?" Sienne asked, feeling dread return.

Alaric shook his head. "Too many of the attackers escaped with the knowledge of what the artifact does. If our enemy didn't know that before, he will now. He was willing to kill us for it before, and I doubt this will change his mind. We have to get this thing to Fioretti and find a way to keep it out of his hands."

"But how?" Dianthe exclaimed. "Burying it won't work if he's got a priest who can scry. It can't be destroyed. And locking it up somewhere just means having to defend against thieves for the rest of our lives." She picked it up gingerly, as if she thought it might turn on her.

"I was thinking," Alaric said, "we might dump it in the sea."

"The... sea?" Sienne asked.

"Yes. If we put it somewhere deep enough, it won't matter if someone can scry for it, they won't be able to get at it. Unless you can think of a spell that would make that possible."

"Well..." Sienne chewed her lower lip. "*Vortex* makes a spinning body of water that leaves a clear space at its center, but it can only be eight feet tall. That wouldn't be enough if we left the artifact in the deep ocean."

"It's the beginnings of a plan, anyway," Alaric said. "But one thing at a time. We need to get through the forest to the next big town and hope there's someone there with a restorative blessing."

"Restorative? Restore what?" Sienne asked.

Alaric and Dianthe looked at each other. They were the kind of looks that said each wanted the other to be the bearer of bad news. In the silence, Kalanath spoke. "The horse was hit in front and the side. Her face is burned and one eye is destroyed. The skin on her side is gone in places all the way to the fat below."

Numbness descended upon her once more. "Poor Spark," she said. "But she's alive—that means she'll be all right, doesn't it?"

"It's hard to tell how much pain she's in," Dianthe said, "but she can barely stand. There's nothing we can do for her here." She looked away. "It might be kinder if we... put her down."

"*No!*" Sienne blinked away tears. "We have to at least try to get her help!"

"Sienne, nobody would blame you—"

"Muskey isn't that far away, right? She can make it that far!"

"Muskey isn't much more than a hamlet. They don't even have a priest in residence. Sienne—"

Alaric put a hand on Dianthe's shoulder. "Sienne's right. It's only about ten miles to Manetto. If the horse can make it that far, there's hope."

Sienne nodded. "Then let's go—no. There's something else I have to do."

She retraced her steps, avoiding the traces of ash on the ground growing damp and mushy in the drizzling rain, until she reached the wizard's spellbook. The rain had stopped falling, but drops still fell from the branches above, beading the book's invulnerable cover. She picked it up and brushed it clean. The ash stuck to her damp fingers. Ash that had once been a person. She gagged, went to her knees, and vomited up everything that was in her. She barely heard the exclamations around her, was conscious only of someone holding her hair off her face and her stomach convulsing as if it wanted to turn itself inside out. If only it were so easy to rid herself of memories.

Finally, shaking and gasping for breath, she spat out the last remnants of bitter bile and wiped her streaming eyes. "Sorry," she said.

"Do not apologize," Perrin said. "Can you ride?"

"Spark can't carry me."

"You'll ride with me," Alaric said. "Paladin is big enough to carry two."

She let him lead her to his enormous gelding and pull her up to ride behind him before urging Paladin on. She took hold of his waist, careful not to let her burned skin rub against his shirt. They'd stripped the saddle off Spark and given her a simple rope halter that still had to be agonizing against her face, but there was nothing else they could do. Sienne didn't know if a priest would condescend to use a healing blessing on an animal, or if an animal could even be healed that way. Tears burned her eyes again, and she blinked them away. She couldn't even wipe her eyes without hurting her burned hands.

A few bodies lay in the road and off to the side. The enemy hadn't left anyone living or injured behind. Maybe those men she'd used *scream* on had escaped. Or maybe they'd been killed while they were helpless. Death came so easily. She'd never realized that before.

"Stop it," Alaric said in a low voice pitched for her ears alone.

"Stop what?"

"Feeling sorry for yourself."

"How do you know that's what I'm doing?"

"I know how you think. You've never killed before, and now you've done so in what you probably think is the most horrific way possible. And you think that makes you a bad person."

"Doesn't it?"

"I killed at least three men back there. Does that make me a bad person?"

"Of course not!"

"What's the difference?"

She had to think about it. Thinking was so *hard*. "You were defending yourself."

"And you weren't? Sienne, I find it difficult to believe you turned the artifact on those people because it felt like fun. Any one of them would have killed you if he'd had the chance, starting with that wizard. How does it make it anything but self-defense?"

She pondered that for a while. "You said you were ashamed of how you enjoyed killing that carver wizard," she finally said. "I think my blood triggered the artifact—woke it up, maybe—but that wasn't what made it cast *ash*. My emotions did, I think. I just know I was so angry... angry enough that it was almost a tangible thing, fighting to get out of me. It's like my anger is what killed them. And I'm ashamed of that."

"I understand. I don't know what it was like for you growing up, but the Sassaven teach their children, early on, to master their emotions, because for us, it's a shameful thing to strike out at someone in anger. Maybe it's to prepare us for the binding, and maybe it's just that Sassaven like me are so strong, losing our temper can cause serious damage. I don't know. The point is that losing control is... like you said, you feel ashamed. And when you actually hurt or kill someone on top of that, it can fill you with such guilt you can't help blaming yourself for everything, even if you acted rightly."

"Yes. That's it. Bad enough that people died, but I can't stop remembering how angry I felt, and I shouldn't have let it take me over."

"Maybe. If that was the only way to get it to work—"

"I don't know. It drew my blood and started glowing. But then I had to... I still don't know what I did, except I had to direct it. It didn't immediately start turning people to piles of ash." She cringed inwardly at how flippant that had sounded.

If her tone disturbed him, Alaric didn't comment on it. "And it's not something you can really experiment with."

"It hurt so much. It still hurts. Maybe that's on purpose. Maybe whoever made it didn't want people using it frivolously." She leaned into him. He was warm and solid and comforting, and she felt her numbness fade.

"That would certainly guarantee it." He patted her knee. "You're not evil, Sienne. An evil person would be working out how to use that thing without getting her arm torn up, or plotting who to threaten or kill to advance her personal desires. I can't tell you this doesn't change you, because you'd know that was a lie. But it's not a change for the worse. If I know you, it will make you more compassionate and more sensitive, now that you know how fragile life really is."

She sighed. "Thank you."

"For telling you the truth? Always."

"No, for reminding me that I'm not special."

"Did I say that? Are you sure that's a good thing?"

She put her right arm around his waist. It was such a comfortable position. "I'm not the only person in the world who's taken a life in self-defense. I don't have any right to carry on as if killing is somehow worse just because it's me doing it. As if I'm too... perfect, maybe, to sin."

"I don't think it's sinful."

"But you know what I mean."

"I think so, yes."

She gently ran her fingers over his chest. "So... thank you."

"You would do the same for me. Did, actually." He squeezed her knee again. "If it helps, Dianthe was right—you using that artifact saved all our lives. So you were defending five people, not just one."

"I guess you're not the only one willing to bleed for the rest of us," Sienne said. Alaric laughed.

"We could all use a joke right now," Dianthe said.

"Not a joke, just... it's not important," Alaric said. "We survived. We learned how the artifact works. We should be celebrating, not moping about."

"I find myself surprisingly unable to celebrate, given that I cannot restore us to full health," Perrin said. Sienne's heart ached at how bitter he sounded.

"You don't think we're upset about that?" Dianthe said.

Kalanath said, "No one thinks worse of you, Perrin."

"I think worse of myself enough for all of you," Perrin said. "But I realize those thoughts will not restore me to my Lord's good graces. So I will attempt to find the good in this situation."

"What's that?" Sienne said, then felt embarrassed, because she'd made it sound like there wasn't any good to be found.

"It is good to trust in Averran's protections. It is not good to be so dependent on them that we cannot fend for ourselves. We survived that fight despite our lack of protective shields, proving that we see Averran as a partner in our endeavors rather than a paternal figure to run to when danger approaches. And while they are no substitute for divine healing, my increasing skills in medical treatment allowed me to tend to Sienne's wounds rather than simply bemoaning my lack of blessings. That is something Averran smiles on, an increase in wisdom and knowledge. In truth, if I berate myself for falling into chastisement, it is because this poor horse is suffering and need not do so if I were a priest in full fellowship with Averran."

Sienne craned her head to look at Spark, walking just behind her and Alaric. The animal plodded along without a trace of the liveliness she usually exhibited. Patches where the skin was burned down to the subcutaneous layers showed an unnatural glistening white surrounding large areas of black. Sienne couldn't see the side of Spark's face where she'd been struck full-force by *scorch*, but she remembered the raw look of her flesh and the sunken lid where the eye was gone, and she wanted to cry for Spark, who couldn't cry for herself. For one moment, she wondered if she was doing the right thing in forcing Spark to walk all these miles when she had to be in such pain. But she imagined them killing Spark, even kindly, and could not bring herself to agree to it.

"Just a few more miles," Alaric said. "By Sisyletus, I hope none of our attackers fled this way. I don't think I'm up to another fight."

"Most of them went north, away from Sienne—sorry," Dianthe said.

"It's all right. *Ash* is terrifying." Sienne shook her head. "It never occurred to me that the artifact might be a lost spell. Everything I imagined is so much smaller by comparison."

"It is a kind of devouring," Kalanath said, his voice sounding distant. Sienne remembered his dream and said nothing.

"Why would anyone create an artifact that injures its user?" Perrin said. "Such a thing violates all common sense."

"The ancients did all sorts of things that don't make sense to us,"

Sienne said. "They made artifacts to do the most mundane tasks. Like sweeping floors. They had one of those in the school at Stravanus."

"Did it save time sweeping?" Dianthe asked.

"No. It was terrible at sweeping in corners and it left piles of dirt everywhere. Not that the housekeeping staff used it—it's too old and precious. They would bring it out to show the new students every year, sort of a reminder that the ancients' ways were inscrutable, and that magic can't and shouldn't solve every problem."

"You must have failed that class," Alaric muttered. Sienne curled up a fist to punch him, but it hurt too badly, so she scowled at his back instead.

"There will always be things humans do better on their own," she said. "Crafting things, inventing things. Sweeping floors, apparently. Even *sculpt* can only produce rudimentary shapes, not fine statues." She looked back at Spark again. Was it her imagination that the horse's head drooped lower now?

"We'll get there in time, Sienne," Alaric said. Sienne nodded, but he sounded too certain, and she wasn't sure he was telling the truth. She looked over his shoulder, focused on a spot between Paladin's ears where the road disappeared into the distance, and willed Spark to keep going. The alternative was too dreadful to imagine.

21

They passed through Muskey without stopping. Dianthe was right; it was small, without even an inn, just a collection of houses for the woodcutters who lived there and an unusually large smithy. It was Sienne's imagination that Spark looked hopeful when she smelled the hot, crisp scent of the smithy, and dejected when they didn't stop there.

Sienne hurt all over. Her burned skin felt as if it wanted to peel away from the bone, and her left arm throbbed with a hot, wet pain. She avoided looking at the blood spreading across the makeshift bandages. Her head ached, her stomach was sore from vomiting, and gripping Paladin's sides with her calves was harder than riding Spark because he was a good deal bigger. As the miles passed, the pain in her head increased until she had to close her eyes and rest her head on Alaric's shoulders with her arms around his waist. It was a somewhat intimate gesture, but she didn't care what the others thought so long as she didn't fall off the horse.

With her eyes closed, sounds became, not louder, but more intelligible. The horses' hooves on the mushy ground thumped in a rhythm like rain falling, if rain were made of stone and not water. Wind rustled the leaves, occasionally showering Sienne with water.

Twittering songs filled the air as birds emerged from shelter and picked up where they'd left off singing when the rain began. Sienne didn't know much about birds and had always had trouble identifying them by their songs, but now she could tell there were at least four different types of bird in the trees surrounding them. She still didn't know what birds they were, but she felt it was a step in the right direction. What did the songs mean? The birds could be reporting on the battle they'd witnessed, telling their friends about the excitement. Maybe they were sharing gossip about other birds. Maybe they ranked each other on brilliance of plumage and flight acrobatics.

Just as she realized this was a slightly mad line of thought, and that she was growing light-headed despite her closed eyes, the sounds changed. The sounds of the horses' hooves became louder and sharper. The rustling of the leaves in the wind became a hollow whistling sound, echoing through canyons. The birds flew away, possibly for warmer climes. A murmur like the sound of a hundred ducks quacking filled her ears.

Sienne opened her eyes to tall brick and wood buildings lining a cobblestone street thronged with people all pressing in around their horses. She sat up and looked around. It was a market, with improvised stalls filled with household goods and a few brave early vegetables. She slewed around to check on Spark. The horse's head hung low and her knees trembled, but she was still upright. "Is there a temple in Manetto?" she said.

"No temple. A few chapels. A sanctuary to Averran, I think," Alaric said. "We want a priest of Lisiel."

"Lisiel? But—surely Kitane, or Sisyletus—"

"The priests of Lisiel believe there is a solution for everything, even if it's a sideways one," Dianthe said. "If anyone's willing to spend a healing blessing on a horse, it will be a priest of that avatar."

"The only chapel I know about is down this way." Alaric turned into a narrow alley, taking them away from the noise and bustle of the market. "It's to Sisyletus, but all the divines know each other, and they'll be able to tell us where to go."

The alley smelled of the recent rainstorm, with only the faintest hint of refuse reaching Sienne's nostrils. It was narrow enough that they had to go single file, with Alaric and Sienne in the lead. Sienne sat up further and looked over Alaric's shoulder. She caught glimpses of broken boxes and a flash of movement that might have been a cat or a very large rat. She hoped it was the former.

Paladin splashed through puddles with no sign of discomfort. He wasn't as big as Alaric was in unicorn shape, but he was still very large for a gelding, tawny like a cat and placid-tempered. Sienne wondered if Alaric ever looked at horses and saw similarities to people he knew.

The alley opened on a much quieter street, one with small houses whose slate-shingled roofs gleamed wetly after the storm. At the far end, a larger building stood, its plain red bricks giving it the appearance of a toolshed despite its size. It had no door, just a gaping dark opening, rectangular and as plain as the bricks. The unglazed windows, small and equally dark, gave no hint as to the place's interior.

Alaric halted before the door and dismounted, then swung Sienne off the horse as easily as lifting a kitten. She swayed when her feet touched the cobbles, and he put a steadying hand on her elbow. "You need healing, too," he said.

"I can wait. We have to save Spark."

"You're almost as injured as the horse. Your hands are blistered badly and your hair is singed, and your arm is still bleeding. It's pure luck your face didn't get burned with your hands."

"Spark is worse off than me."

"That doesn't lessen your need." Alaric released her, and she found she could stand on her own. "Wait here, I'll go speak to the divine."

"We can't come in?" Sienne said.

"You can, but it's small and dark and cramped in there, and we'd just crowd Dorcas." Alaric ducked under the low lintel and vanished into the darkness.

"This is the strangest chapel I have ever seen," Perrin said. "I know little of the worship of Sisyletus, but surely they do not insist on their divines living in poverty?"

"Sisyletus was a bond servant all his adult life," Sienne said. "His priests, and the divines who maintain the chapels and temples, value simplicity and plain living. I was taught the chapels are made in the image of the house Sisyletus lived in during his indentured servitude."

"Alaric worships Sisyletus," Kalanath said. "He does not live in poverty."

"The Sassaven worship God differently," Dianthe said. "They were created before the avatars came to earth, and they're so isolated their form of worship hasn't changed for five hundred years. Alaric was drawn to the worship of Sisyletus when we were living in Concord. I think the idea of endurance through the greatest of trials appeals to him. But there's no requirement to give up worldly comforts. One of our clients, years ago, was a very wealthy woman who supported the temple of Sisyletus in Marisse almost single-handedly. She had some kind of disorder, something healing couldn't fix, and she always said it was given to her to endure the trials life gives us, and that Sisyletus understood that better than anyone."

Footsteps approached, and Alaric appeared in the doorway behind a short, skinny woman with gray hair and a wrinkled face. "Dorcas, this is my team," he said. "Everyone, this is Dorcas, a divine of Sisyletus."

"I wanted to see these people Alaric speaks so highly of," Dorcas said, her voice creaky with age. Her smile was pleasant, and she stood straight, unbent by the years. "And this horse you care so much for."

"We couldn't abandon her," Sienne protested, feeling defensive.

"Of course not." Dorcas stepped forward and walked around Spark, examining her. "She's come a long way. Endured much. I think... wait a moment." Dorcas laid her hand on the horse's nose, careful not to press too hard. Spark jerked her head away, making Dorcas smile.

"I won't hurt you," she said, and clasped her hands together. Closing her eyes, she said, "O Lord whose strength is of the mountains, rooted deep, manifest your greatness and take pity on this creature."

A powerful wind whipped down the street, chill and penetrating Sienne's cloak. Green light, deeper and more vivid than the falcon artifact's disintegration, surrounded Spark. The horse took a couple of involuntary steps back, bumping into Sienne, who put her hand on Spark's back to steady herself. The green light, by contrast to the wind, was warm and smelled sweet like melted honey, and was so thick Sienne thought it would stick to her hand and arm. The light poured over her, up to her shoulder and across her chest to her other arm. She heard Dianthe gasp, but the light filled her eyes and she saw nothing but dim green shapes, unrecognizable as human or horse or anything else.

Then the light faded, and she flexed her unburned hands and let out a deep breath. Spark's coat was glossy and undamaged, her face free of blisters, and she held her head high. Sienne unwrapped the bloody bandages and ran her hand across smooth, unwounded skin. The pain was entirely gone.

Tears came to Sienne's eyes. "Thank you."

"Thank the avatar," Dorcas said. "He was most generous to include you in the healing."

"Generous to heal the horse at all," Perrin said. "I have never seen anyone invoke a healing blessing without prepared papers."

Dorcas eyed him speculatively. "You serve... Averran?"

Perrin's eyes widened. "How do you know?"

"There is a look his followers have, a certain recklessness in the eye. I attribute it to the effects of liquor. You must be new to his service." Dorcas smiled again. "If you grow in your faith, you will see many things that are now impossible to you."

"We are grateful to Sisyletus," Alaric said. "It's not what I asked of you. Of him."

"Which is no doubt why he granted it." Dorcas took hold of Spark's chin and gently turned the horse's head. "I can do nothing for her eye. You will need restoration for that. There are priests of Kitane and Lisiel in town who might do it. I suggest approaching Kaethe at the chapel of Lisiel. But take care. She is... odd."

"How so?" Perrin asked.

"Oh, the priests of Lisiel are all a superstitious lot. She'll want to test you before granting any requests, but if she sees something in you—some quality or behavior or even just that you have the right color eyes—she may give you more than you asked for. Or she may kick you out. It's hard to say with Kaethe."

"Thanks again," Alaric said. "Do you need anything?"

"A few coins to help fix the roof."

Gold passed from Alaric to Dorcas, forestalling Sienne, who'd gone for her purse. Dorcas's eyes widened. "This is more than you—"

"Take it," Alaric said. "Use it to bless others who come this way."

"As you wish," Dorcas said.

They had to keep leading Spark because her saddle had been badly damaged in the attack and they'd left it in the woods. Sienne couldn't stop looking over her shoulder at the horse. Except for the ruined eye, she looked as fresh as if she'd never been wounded. It made Sienne want to hug her, though she was sure Spark wouldn't appreciate that.

A few inquiries brought them to the chapel dedicated to Lisiel. It looked much more as Sienne imagined a chapel should: old gray stone, a high, peaked roof, tall, narrow windows of leaded glass, and a door set in a deep archway bearing a metal plaque. Alaric dismounted and peered at the plaque. "Closed," he said. "We can come back this evening."

"Let's find a place to stay," Dianthe suggested. "We need to rest before moving on."

"Is that safe?" Sienne asked. "Won't our enemy be able to find us?"

"Eventually, yes," Alaric said, "but we can't go on indefinitely or we won't be able to defend ourselves. And we need to take some time to form a new plan."

"I saw an inn at the last turning," Kalanath said. "It is large enough that our enemy cannot attack it without being challenged. I think he does not want notice."

The inn was large, and new, its roof gleaming with more than the remnants of the rainstorm, its walls freshly whitewashed and its yard clear of refuse. While Alaric negotiated for rooms, Sienne helped settle Spark in her stall. "I hope you forgive me for getting you hurt," she whispered, laying her cheek against the horse's hairy one. "Soon your eye will be fixed, and everything will be all right." She was careful to stand where Spark could see her, not wanting to distress the horse further.

Their rooms were on a corner on the second floor, three rooms with two beds each, small but well-appointed. Sienne sniffed the flowers in the vase on the dresser and felt herself relax. Yawning, she said, "We should discuss our next move."

"*You* should take a nap," Dianthe said, giving her a little push toward one of the beds. "I plan to." She handed the emerald falcon, now wrapped in Alaric's spare shirt, to Sienne and sank down on the other bed.

"But what if they find us, and we're sleeping?"

"No one's going to find us this afternoon. Sleep. We can plan when we're alert."

Sienne tucked the emerald falcon under her bed and lay down. She was asleep in seconds.

She woke slowly out of pleasant dreams of fields of wildflowers, drifting to consciousness like coming out of a deep pool. She felt rested and perfectly relaxed. The healing had taken care of her sore muscles as well as her burns and the puncture wounds. She lay on her back and stared at the ceiling, which was painted eggshell blue. She'd never seen an egg that color, but it was what her mother always called it.

Someone knocked on the door, and Dianthe came awake abruptly, jerking upright. "Who is it?"

"Perrin. Supper is ready, if you'd care to join us?"

"Is it that late?" Dianthe sat on the edge of her bed and touched her hair, which was a frizzy mess coming unbound from her customary braid. "Give us a minute."

Sienne sat up and ran her fingers through her own hair. "I'll conceal the artifact, but it might not matter."

"Why not?" Dianthe freed her hair from its braid and dug through her pack for a hairbrush.

"If one of the men who escaped got a good look at it, a priest could...it's not exactly reading his mind, more like perceiving his memory. Anyway, a priest who got a good enough image of it could scry for it. And knowing where it is would defeat *camouflage*." Sienne knelt by the bed and read off the spell anyway.

"I really do think we're safe for tonight, but we'll take extra precautions." Dianthe laid the brush down and pulled on her boots. Sienne did the same, then ran her fingers over her left forearm. She could still feel the artifact's grip, the weight of it bearing down on her arm. She shuddered and followed Dianthe down the stairs to the dining room.

The meal was good, but they all ate too quickly to really enjoy it. Sienne couldn't help feeling aware of the artifact hidden under her bed. She watched everyone who left the dining room by the inner door that led to the inn's rooms for let, assessing their potential as agents of their unknown enemy. Finally, unable to stomach one more bite, she pushed back her chair and said, "I'll be right back. I can't stand leaving it unguarded in my room." Nobody argued with her.

22

It was nearly six o'clock in the evening when they left the inn for the chapel. Sienne found herself once more surrounded by her friends, clasping the artifact to her chest. Nobody paid them any attention, so likely they didn't look as strange as Sienne felt. The air was chilly and damp, but the storm had blown past and the skies were clear. Everyone they passed was bundled up as if it were still winter, though Sienne felt comfortable in her heavy cloak over her relatively thin shirt. They ought to buy a length of fabric to wrap the artifact in; Alaric's shirt was large, but Sienne had to keep tugging it over the wings to keep them concealed. They'd already been through so much, and the journey wasn't over. She resented the stupid falcon and the unknown enemy who was willing to kill to get it.

The chapel's door was open this time, and warm light glowed beyond it. Alaric led them through the chapel's entry chamber, which was small enough to be crowded when all five of them stood inside, and into the nave. Eight backless stone pews with kneelers lined both sides of the aisle, occupied by a few people sitting rapt in their own thoughts. Lanterns as tall as Sienne hung from the peaked roof, their glass frosted with invulnerability magic. They cast a yellow glow over the chapel that made it feel warmer than it was.

Sienne was used to her mother's chapel to Kitane, which had an altar at the head of the nave and a statue of Kitane as warrior behind it. This chapel, dedicated to Lisiel, had no altar, just a series of paired doors with grilles at head height lining the rounded wall of what in a Kitane chapel would be the apse. No priests or divines were in evidence.

Alaric came to a halt in the center of the round space and looked around. "I don't know what to do next."

One of the doors opened. A man wearing a hooded cape drawn far over his face emerged and brushed past them, letting the door swing almost shut. The room beyond was a mere cubicle, meant to fit only one person at a time, and Sienne, who wasn't claustrophobic, shuddered at the thought of having to sit inside.

The door next to it opened as well, and a middle-aged woman poked her head out. She had coppery brown hair cut short to frame her face, which bore a scar along the jawline. One of her eyes was blue; the other was a greenish color. She examined each of them in turn. Sienne managed not to squirm under her regard, though it was like facing down a teacher when you didn't know the answer to a basic question.

"Well?" the woman said. Her voice was high and sharp, almost a shrill sound.

"We're looking for Kaethe," Alaric said. "Dorcas sent us."

The woman rose from her seat and stepped out of the cubicle, unfolding like a stick insect. She was tall, nearly as tall as Alaric, and though her white robe, full length and full-sleeved, concealed her arms and legs, her hands were bony and her neck was thin. Sienne's own neck ached looking at her, and she wondered how the woman held her head up. She looked as if someone had warmed her over a fire and then stretched her out like softened wax.

"I'm Kaethe," the woman said. "Dorcas sent you? I wasn't expecting anyone."

"We didn't plan to stop here," Alaric said. "We're sorry if it's inconvenient."

"Lisiel expects the unexpected. Convenience isn't important. What do you hold there, young lady?"

The direct inquiry startled Sienne. "Ah... it's personal."

"Not a dedication, then?" Kaethe strode forward and took hold of the fabric wrapping the falcon before Sienne could step away or stop her. She twitched it aside. Her eyes grew wide. "Lady of Darkness," she breathed. "Are you *sure* you don't want to dedicate it?"

"Could we discuss this in private?" Alaric said. Sienne gave him an imploring look. Discussing the artifact was not something she wanted to do. Alaric shrugged, a somewhat helpless gesture.

"All right," Kaethe said. She waved at a larger door to the left of the cubicles. "Back there."

The door led to a room about the same size as the entry, but made more crowded by a desk and a couple of chairs. "Make yourselves comfortable, if that's possible," Kaethe said, taking a seat behind the desk. "Now. Tell me what you want to know. I can put a value to that thing, if you mean to sell it."

"It's not why we came. We just need a restoration blessing," Sienne said, tucking the artifact close to her chest.

"Restoration for what? None of you look injured."

Sienne swallowed. "For... for my horse. She lost an eye."

Kaethe laughed. Her laugh, unlike her speech, was deep and resonant, and it went on long enough that Sienne grew first uncomfortable, then angry. "A horse's eye," Kaethe finally said. "That's a new one."

"If it's too much for you—"

"Don't get upset with someone you're asking a favor of, young lady, it's rude." Kaethe straightened. "Tell me about the emerald, and we'll see about the restoration."

Sienne shot another glance at Alaric. Lying to a divine was probably a bad idea, not to mention sinful, even if she didn't worship this woman's avatar. Alaric gave her the tiniest nod. She set the falcon on the desk and unwrapped it, prompting a gasp from Kaethe. "It's an artifact," she said. "A weapon. We're taking it where it can't hurt anyone."

"A weapon?" Kaethe had been reaching out to touch it, but pulled her hand back as Sienne spoke. "What kind of weapon?"

"An ancient spell. One that's been lost for centuries." Sienne didn't want to go into detail, and hoped Kaethe wouldn't press her.

"It looks like a damned big emerald to me. Are you a wizard?"

Sienne nodded.

"Then I'll take your word for it. Did you steal it?"

"Of course not!"

"There's no 'of course' when it comes to artifacts. Besides, Lisiel would look favorably upon you if you had." Kaethe scratched her head. "It can't be destroyed. Where will you take it?"

"Begging your pardon, but we can't tell you that," Alaric said. "The fewer people who know about this thing, the better."

"I see." The divine leaned back in her chair and propped one elbow on the armrest, resting her chin in her hand. "Then why did you bring it to me?"

"We didn't," Sienne said. "We just don't like leaving it unattended."

"That's what you think." She stood, unfolding again as if all her joints moved independently of one another, and removed a riffle of blessing papers thicker than Perrin's usual one from her sleeve. They were grubby and looked as if they'd been handled frequently, and there were tattered edges where individual blessings had been torn out. Kaethe flipped through the bundle until she found one she liked. "*Lady of Darkness, guide my eye*," she intoned, her voice suddenly deep.

Pale blue light shimmered over her fingers clutching the blessing, which went up in a lick of blue flame. Kaethe's blue eye radiated the same light, covering it from white to pupil so it was one solid color. She let out a long sigh like the hiss of a tea kettle just before it whistles.

"*Pursuit draws ever near*," she said, her voice still unnaturally low. "*The seeker wishes to call evil good, and good evil, but she knows not what she desires. Free the captives and your quest will be rewarded, but not with money or power.*

Sienne gaped at her. Carefully, she picked up the falcon and wrapped it up again. Kaethe shuddered, then let out another sigh, this one silent. She blinked. Her eye was back to normal. "What did I say?"

"Ah... should we have remembered it?" Perrin said. He was trying too hard to sound casual.

"Pursuit draws near, the seeker calls good evil and evil good, free the captives, our reward is not money or power," Alaric recited. "What does it mean?"

"I have no idea," Kaethe said. "It's not given to me to interpret prophecy, only to relay it. Lisiel must be in a less capricious mood than usual to have granted such a relatively straightforward prophecy."

"But... why a prophecy at all?" Dianthe said. "It wasn't what we asked for."

"I don't know that either. I just know when Lisiel has a message for someone." Kaethe resumed her seat. "As to the other thing...give me answers, and we'll see."

"What answers?" Alaric said.

Kaethe raised her eyebrows. "What do you fear, big man?"

Alaric's brow furrowed. "I don't—"

"*True* answers, or you get nothing."

Alaric nodded. "I fear losing myself."

Kaethe nodded in return. "Wizard," she said, and Sienne quickly thought over her fears. But Kaethe said, "Why won't you forgive your young man?"

Kaethe didn't say Rance's name, but Sienne knew who she meant as surely as if she had. "He's not my young man," she said, unable to stop herself flashing a glance at Alaric. "But—he made me feel worthless, and if I forgive him, it's like I agree with that."

"Intelligent words. You—why don't you go home?" Kaethe directed the question at Dianthe, who blanched. Sienne was sure she'd refuse to answer the question, though she herself was dying to know the answer.

"I... don't want to face my punishment," Dianthe finally said. Her face had gone from bone white to dull red, and she stared at the divine as if she wanted to grab her and throttle answers out of her.

"Not quite true, but I think you don't know the answer yourself yet," Kaethe said. "Why are you a hypocrite?" she asked Kalanath.

Kalanath shot a puzzled look at Perrin. "She means your actions are at odds with your beliefs or words," Perrin murmured. Kalanath's eyes went wide.

"I am not," he began, stopped, and visibly gathered himself. "I live as I was taught," he said, "and if that is wrong, there is nowhere else for me to go. I still believe I will know truth someday."

"Brave words." Kaethe turned her gaze on Perrin. "You, priest whose avatar has abandoned you."

"I have not been abandoned," Perrin said.

"You lack your avatar's blessing. What would you call it?"

Perrin drew in a deep breath. "I have faith," he said, "that I may yet hear my Lord's voice again. His chastisement will give me greater strength, and I will be restored to him someday."

Kaethe's gaze never wavered. "And if you're wrong?"

"Then at least I will be a better man for having strived to live worthily."

She pursed her lips and nodded. "I believe that day will come sooner than you think." She fixed each of them with her gaze once more, then tore off another blessing from the riffle of papers and stood. "Come with me."

They passed through the chapel, where Kaethe gave a "wait here" gesture to a woman standing near the doors with grilles holding a large burlap sack, and out a door on the other side of the apse. It led outside, where darkness had fallen during the time they'd spoken to her. Beyond a small yard, bare of growth at this season, lay a stone cottage with dark windows and a lamp glowing beside the door. Kaethe made another gesture indicating that they should wait and disappeared into the cottage. After a moment, light bloomed behind the windows.

Sienne tucked the artifact under her arm and pulled her cloak close against the rising wind. She both wanted to talk about Kaethe's questioning and hoped no one would ask her to elaborate on what she'd answered. It had been just enough information to make her curious, and aside from what Perrin had said, she didn't know what to make of the answers. She looked at Alaric, who had his eyes focused on the door. Did he fear losing himself the way that carver wizard had taken his will, or was it something else?

The interior light went out, and Kaethe returned. Instead of the blessing paper, she held a somewhat withered carrot. "Feed this to the horse, and its eye will be restored," she said, handing the carrot to Sienne.

"What can I pay you?" Sienne asked.

"You've already paid our Lady who sees in darkness with answers. But if you dedicate your next find to the temple of Lisiel in Fioretti, that will be enough." Kaethe suddenly looked very tired. "Off with you. And try not to get killed."

"Our thanks," Alaric said.

They walked around the chapel to the street and back to the inn. Sienne clutched the carrot in her right hand. Such a small thing, bought at such a small price. She looked at Dianthe, who still looked pale even in the light of the lanterns lining the street, and at Kalanath, whose expression was remote and withdrawn. Maybe she was wrong about how small a price it was.

23

Spark took the carrot happily, scattering small chunks of it everywhere in her enthusiasm. Sienne watched her sunken eyelid. Would the eye just manifest spontaneously, or would it grow? She hoped it wouldn't hurt poor Spark further.

"We should have asked how long it would take," Dianthe said from behind her.

"Surely not long," Perrin said.

"Look!" Sienne pointed. Spark lifted her head, shifting to nose the chilly wind that blew in from the stable yard. She shook her head again as if chasing away a fly. Rich green light outlined her damaged eye, and between one blink and the next, the eye was restored. It showed no sign that it had ever been gone. Spark turned her head from one side to the other, then bumped her nose against Sienne's arm. Sienne laughed and stroked her soft face. "All better," she whispered.

"That's a relief," Alaric said. "And now we need to make a plan. Back inside, everyone."

Perrin and Kalanath were sharing the largest of the three rooms, one on the corner with two windows instead of one. With all of them inside, it was comfortably cozy rather than cramped. Sienne sat next to Dianthe on one of the beds and watched Alaric pace, three steps in one direction, then three steps back the other way. All right, maybe it was a little cramped.

"Some of our attackers escaped," he said, "so we have to assume our enemy knows we survived and, more importantly, that we can activate the artifact. It's barely possible this will dissuade him from coming after us again, but it's more likely this will just make him more eager. Regardless, we have to act as if we expect another attack."

"Only this time, we have no idea where it will come from, or when," Dianthe said.

"Are we agreed that our goal is to drop the artifact in the deep sea?" Alaric asked. Sienne nodded with the rest of them. "We'll be back in Fioretti in three days, assuming nothing goes wrong and our enemy waits to attack us until then. Longer if we have to fight off another attack. We can get passage on a ship easily—there are always ships leaving Fioretti even at this time of year—and it will take another day or so to reach a place where we can get rid of the artifact. Five days, barring incidents, and it will all be over."

"But then we have to think of something to convince Tonia to give us the knife," Sienne said. "If we don't have the artifact to show her—"

"Even if we do, it's unlikely it will matter to her," Alaric said. "But that's not as important right now as keeping away from our enemy and ridding ourselves of the artifact. We'll think of something."

Sienne thought that was overly optimistic, but held her tongue. "We'll stay out in the open, surrounded by people," Alaric continued. "Assuming our enemy still wants to keep his involvement a secret, it will be harder for him to attack us if there are witnesses. We travel in company if we can, stay at large inns, and take precautions in our sleeping arrangements. We stand watches as if we're in the wilderness, too."

"I can cast *slick* on the windowsills," Sienne said.

"I've got a few ideas for alarms," Dianthe added.

"These rooms at the end of the hall are highly defensible," Perrin said. "I think we are well protected."

"Then—regular watch rotation, and let's get through this night," Alaric said.

Sienne decided not to sleep in her nightdress, feeling superstitiously that if she was underdressed, that would be the time someone would choose to attack. She felt better about her decision when Dianthe also didn't change into her nightdress. "Do you really think they won't attack tonight?" she asked.

"We can't know for sure," Dianthe said, "but whoever this is, whatever resources he has, it takes time for him to get them into position. And he's not omniscient. None of the ones who attacked us in the forest were priests, or they would have had defensive shields. So they couldn't communicate the news of their failure right away. That's time in our favor. Then they'd have to move more men to where we are. That's more time. I don't think they can even reach us until tomorrow. But that's not what worries me."

"It worries me plenty!"

"I'm concerned that they will try something other than a direct assault, now they know we can use the artifact. Something we won't see coming."

"I'm not using the artifact again."

"They don't know that. And are you really sure you wouldn't? If it meant saving our lives, or your own?"

"I—" Sienne shut her mouth. "I don't know."

"You should think about it. If you make the decision now, you won't waste time dithering over it when the crisis comes." Dianthe lay back and crossed her arms behind her head. "If it helps, I don't think I could use it either, even for that. You looked like death when we got it off you."

Sienne lay down and curled on her side. *Could* she use it again, knowing how painful it was? How easy it was to kill? Dianthe let out a small snore, and Sienne rolled over to face the wall. Dianthe was right: Sienne needed to make that decision now rather than later. *But not right now*, she told herself, and tried to relax into sleep.

Unlike that afternoon, she slept fitfully, waking when Dianthe got up to take her turn at watch and then not being able to fall back asleep immediately. When Alaric shook her shoulder a few hours later, she came awake with a start, grabbing his wrist to steady herself. "It's just me," he said in a whisper. "Come outside."

They stood in the hall together, hands clasped. Sienne felt simultaneously weary and agitated, too emotionally overwrought even for kissing. "Everything is quiet?"

"No disturbances at all," Alaric said. "Are you going to be all right? We should err on the side of caution, but I don't want you *force*-blasting someone whose only crime is wanting an early morning snack."

"I'm fine. Go get some sleep."

He stroked her cheek gently and squeezed her hand. "Take care."

When he was gone, she settled her spellbook comfortably in the crook of her left arm and made a magic light to illuminate its pages. Leaning against the wall, she stared into the darkness at the far end of the corridor. Five days, if nothing went wrong, until they were rid of the artifact. *If* nothing went wrong. That was a big caveat to hang their safety on. And they didn't have anything to give Tonia Figlari. It worried Sienne because she couldn't come up with an idea, either. She was starting to fear they'd have to steal the knife, since all their news was bad: no falcon stone to declare Tonia's legitimacy, and the Figlari dukedom was overrun by carvers.

Sienne shifted her weight. Would the carvers stay without their wizard? She'd looked like their leader, too. At the very least, the Figlari keep wasn't an inviolate sanctuary for them anymore; that might drive them out. Maybe Tonia wouldn't care. If she had enough money, she could hire an army to take out the carvers, who without their wizard's charm spells were just good fighters with a few tricks. Maybe that would be enough for her.

Or... Sienne might go to the king in her parents' names and get him to restore Tonia's title. It would mean revealing her location, and her parents would probably send people after her, but it might be worth it if they got the knife. Alaric and the others wouldn't let her be taken away, she was sure of it. It was a possibility, anyway.

She flipped the pages of her spellbook idly, practicing her speed at moving between spells. She had all the spells' locations memorized, and it was just a matter of opening to the right page. Some of her friends in Stravanus notched their pages before making them invulnerable, then memorized the notches, but Sienne hadn't thought of that and it was too late once the invulnerability was cast. Besides, her memory was good enough she didn't think it was necessary.

Something shifted in the darkness at the end of the corridor.

Sienne launched a light toward the movement. It lit up the walls and doors as it flew, sailing in an arc like an apple tossed down the hall. When it reached the far end, it stopped, hovering about a foot above the floor. Light played across the stairwell, casting funny shadows where the banisters curved out of sight going up and down. There was no one there.

Sienne calmed her breathing and took a step or two toward the light. Then she caught herself and retreated to her sentry position. If there was something, maybe something invisible, she needed not to let it get behind her. Too bad seeing invisible things was a priest's magic. She opened her spellbook to *scream*. It would both disable an enemy and alert all her friends to danger. Of course, it would wake the rest of the inn, too, but that didn't matter.

Nothing else moved. The floating light by the stairs gradually drifted to rest on the floor just above the top step. Sienne stared in its direction, not directly at it, but beyond it, until her eyes ached and she was certain no one was there, invisible or not. She checked her pocket watch. Another half-hour and she could wake everyone. She stretched tired muscles and yawned. Just half an hour.

She amused herself making and extinguishing magic lights and trying not to daydream about when this was all over. Alaric had to have been joking when he said he'd be content to watch her dance with other men. And exaggerating about looking like a performing bear. She'd convince him to go dancing with her, or walking in the hills above the palace, and it would be wonderful.

She sent another light arcing down the hall, and heard the floorboards creak. Funny how all these old inns had the same creaking floorboards—

—except this inn wasn't old. It was so new it still smelled of paint.

Sienne froze, straining to hear more. Nothing moved, nothing creaked, but she was certain someone else was in the hall with her.

She straightened and brought her spellbook up to chest level, ready to read, then hesitated. If this was nothing, she didn't want to wake the entire inn. How certain was she?

The lights hanging in the air quivered, as if someone had breathed heavily on them to make them move. Sienne began reading off the evocation *scream*. Footsteps sounded on the floorboards, someone scrambling toward the stairwell. Sienne read as fast as she dared without disrupting the spell. Whoever or whatever it was pounded down the stairs, the footsteps trailing out of earshot.

Sienne interrupted the spell three syllables from the end and lowered the book. Someone had been there. Someone invisible. Her heart was pounding so hard it hurt her ribs.

It was only ten minutes before the end of her watch, but she didn't feel like waiting. She knocked on Alaric's door and waited for him to answer. "There was someone," she said. "An invisible someone. He ran before I could blast him."

"Wake the others," Alaric said.

Once more gathered in Perrin and Kalanath's room, they listened to Sienne's story. "That was *fast*," Dianthe said. "Getting someone in position... and it wasn't a full assault..."

"It sounds like a test," Kalanath said, "to see if we are alert."

"And now we know an invisible enemy is possible," Perrin said. "I think they gave away more than they intended."

"We have to be even more careful than we thought," Alaric said. "Since we have no way of seeing through invisibility."

Nobody looked at Perrin. He lowered his head. "I think I will forego breakfast," he said. "I intend to pray most devotedly this morning. We are in greater danger the longer I am under chastisement."

"Don't despair," Dianthe said. "It will take as long as it takes. We don't condemn you for it."

"I condemn myself," Perrin said. "Now, if you don't mind, I would prefer privacy for this."

The rest of them trooped down the hall to the stairs, Sienne once more carrying the artifact. She extinguished the magic lights as she came to them. "It's creepy, knowing someone was standing just feet from me and I couldn't see him."

"Who knows how long he waited there," Kalanath said. "It is an unpleasant thought."

"Likely it wasn't all that long, if none of the rest of us heard anything during our watches," Alaric said, "but even a little while is enough. Maybe we need to double up on watches."

"That would just exhaust us," Dianthe said. "We need to be prepared for invisible attackers."

Alaric said nothing, but the way he looked at Sienne, as if he wanted to bundle her away where no attackers could get to her, both warmed her heart and made her annoyed. She was mostly sure he wouldn't try to overprotect her, but only mostly.

———

WHEN THEY RETURNED TO THEIR ROOMS TO PACK THEIR THINGS FOR THE day's journey, Perrin's eyes were dark-ringed and his left hand trembled. He drank down the black coffee Dianthe brought him without comment and wouldn't meet anyone's eyes. Sienne's heart ached for him. Despite her earlier resolve, she composed a silent prayer: *O Lord Averran, he's trying so hard. Be merciful.*

A quick inquiry by Alaric to the stable master revealed no one who didn't belong there had entered the stables that night. Sienne checked Spark carefully, chilled at how she hadn't thought the horses might be in danger. Spark gave Sienne her usual friendly nudge and seemed not at all distressed, which gave Sienne hope that there really hadn't been an invisible man in her horse's stall. Still, she saddled the horse with more than usual care. The new saddle wasn't precisely new, but it hadn't been used much and Sienne found it comfortable. She hoped Spark felt the same.

They left Manetto in company with a prosperous trader traveling with two wagons and a handful of outriders. It meant they traveled slowly, but Sienne didn't mind; the day was beautifully warm, and the trader's people were friendly. One of them in particular, a young man with bad skin and a lovely smile, rode next to Sienne and teased and joked with her. She teased and joked back, maybe a little more aggressively than she might otherwise have because her nerves were still on edge and she was too aware of the artifact riding in front of her saddle. But Borris's friendliness helped her relax, and by the time they reached Annis in the early evening, her worries about being ambushed again had disappeared.

Dianthe sidled up to her when they were settling their horses for the night. "Are you sure you want to be that friendly with the kid?"

"Why not?" Sienne's worries resurfaced. "You don't think he's a threat, do you?"

"I was thinking... never mind."

"Now you have to tell me or I'll imagine the worst."

Dianthe sighed. "It's your business who you flirt with—"

"*Flirt?* I wasn't flirting!"

Dianthe arched an eyebrow at her. "What would you call it?"

"I—he's funny, and he kept me distracted. Why would you think it was flirting?"

"Never mind. I was wrong." Dianthe sighed. "Look. You should... I don't know what's passed between you and Alaric, and his feelings aren't your responsibility. But he cares about you, and I'm pretty sure watching you and that Borris kid was painful to him."

Stunned, Sienne said, "But he has to know... he said he'd watch me dance with other men."

"What?"

"Nothing. I mean, couldn't he tell it was nothing serious?"

"I don't know what he thinks. Just that he's scowling and short-tempered, and he kept looking at you all day when he thought no one would notice. And... you're the first woman he's been interested in in over two years, and I think he's forgotten how that feels. Just be kind to him, all right?"

Sienne looked over the stable yard. Alaric towered over the stall where he was busy removing Paladin's tack. It was something he always did, even when there were stable hands whose job it technically was. Sienne shouldered her pack, tucked the artifact under her arm, and patted Spark's shoulder one last time. "I'll meet you inside."

She walked down the line of stalls until she came to Paladin's. Alaric was giving the horse what to Sienne's eye was a completely unnecessary brushing. No one else was within earshot, but Sienne found she didn't much care who heard this. She dropped her pack at her feet and said, "What makes you think I'm at all interested in other men when you're available?"

Alaric scowled. "Dianthe," he muttered. "She needs to stop interfering. I didn't think that."

"Then why are you moping?"

"I am *not* moping!" He turned away from the big gelding and crossed his arms over his chest. "It's none of my business who you talk to. You've made me no promises."

"I didn't think you were insecure. What about all those men you were going to watch me dance with?"

He shook his head, and a smile touched his lips. "It's not the same." He sighed. "I don't know who our enemy is, I don't know where he'll strike next, and the thought that he has an invisible assassin on a leash might make me go mad. Particularly since the invisible assassin might have killed you last night. All those things have me keyed up to the point that I don't know what to think about anything. I realize it's irrational, but all day I watched you ride with that spotty kid and thought about making him disappear. I'm sorry."

Sienne gaped at him. Then she laughed. "No, don't get upset, I'm not laughing at you," she said when his scowl deepened. "I was feeling keyed up myself, and Borris let me forget about it for a while. But he is rather spotty. I shouldn't laugh at that, it's not his fault, but... Alaric, don't you think I would rather have ridden beside you? That I'd prefer you were the one teasing me?"

"Then why didn't you?"

"Because you and the wagon master were having that long

conversation about the journey north, and I had nothing to contribute." She took his hand and drew him out of the stall, letting the door swing shut behind them. "Would you like to know what *I* was thinking about all day, when I wasn't laughing at Borris's jokes?"

"You did a lot of laughing. Was there time for anything else?"

"I was *thinking* that it's been a long time since you kissed me, and I was planning how I might find a private spot to do something about that. I guarantee you Borris and his spots weren't on my mind in the least."

The corner of Alaric's mouth twitched in another smile. "So you're saying I was being stupid, is that it?"

"I would never call you stupid. Logic-challenged, maybe."

He laughed. "You're very generous."

"No, just suffering from a lack of kisses. If I called you stupid, that condition might go on far too long."

"I wouldn't let that happen." He squeezed her hand, then released her. "I have a room to myself again."

"That might be a little too private."

"Then—" They were standing at the end of the stalls, next to a corner where the stable and a storage shed met. Alaric took her arm and drew her back into the corner, away from prying eyes. "This will have to do," he said, put his arms around her waist and lifted her to brush her lips with a kiss. She squeaked, laughed, and kissed him more firmly. She loved the musky smell of him, how it reminded her of walks in the forest and freshly-cut wood. They kissed for a while, forgetting the outside world, until Alaric said, "They'll come looking for us if we're any longer."

Sienne pressed her forehead to his. At that distance, his pale blue eyes blurred together into a single one above his nose. "I have no regrets."

"Neither do I." He set her down and hugged her briefly. "I promise not to be stupid again."

"It's all right. Borris is really very nice. Don't be mean to him."

"I'll do my best."

The inn's taproom had long trestle tables and was still mostly empty at this hour, with only Sienne's companions and the traders they'd traveled with seated for an early meal. Borris waved at Sienne from across the room, indicating a seat next to him. She smiled and shook her head, pointing at a place across from Dianthe and shrugging in a way she hoped conveyed a need to sit with her friends. She sat and tucked the artifact between her feet, resisting the urge to clamp down on it. Alaric sat beside her, not quite touching, but close enough to feel companionable.

Dianthe, Perrin, and Kalanath were already eating, and bowls of beef stew were at Alaric and Sienne's places. Sienne took a bite. It was rich and savory, with chunks of perfectly seasoned beef and roasted roots and tubers. Sienne was usually suspicious of stew served at inns, since most of the time it was made to disguise the fact that the cook was using the tag ends of things gone slightly bad, but this was delicious. She took another bite. It had an unfamiliar tang to it that she liked.

"Marko is going on again tomorrow, and doesn't mind us tagging along," Alaric said. He'd already made serious inroads on his stew. Now he took a long drink of beer and added, "I think he's used to traveling the Empty Lands and can't stop expecting bandits to leap out and attack. We're a welcome protection for his caravan, as he sees it."

Sienne took a drink from her own beer and blinked away a wave of dizziness. It was stronger than she'd expected. One would have to be her limit.

"So far, so good," Dianthe said. She scraped up the last bites of stew. "It's been a long day, and I feel surprisingly tired, given that we didn't push ourselves."

"I agree," Perrin said. There was no mug in front of him, just a glass of water. "I hope I can stay awake for my watch."

Across the room, Borris stood and waved at Sienne. She nodded back, making the room swim. Definitely too strong a drink for her. She watched Borris walk toward her, smiling, and doubts surfaced. Had *he* thought she was flirting? It had been friendly fun as far as she was concerned, but if he thought differently... maybe Alaric hadn't been wrong to be disturbed, if it looked like more than it was.

Borris staggered and caught himself on a table. It seemed the beer was too strong for more than her. He took another step, and his smile vanished. Closing his eyes, he collapsed, his knees bending, his shoulders relaxing, until he folded entirely. Sienne stood as he hit the floor and had to catch herself to avoid following him down. "Somebody help him!"

Dianthe rose, then sank back into her seat. "I feel dizzy," she said. "The beer was too strong."

Dianthe shook her head. "Not the beer," she said. Her words slurred together. "In the food…drugged…"

Alaric stood, gripping the table with both huge hands. "We have to get out of here," he said. The rest of the men and women at the trader Marko's table lay fallen over their bowls, one of them half on the floor where she'd slid off the bench. Sienne took Perrin's elbow and tried to help him up. He looked up at her, closed his eyes, and slumped into his bowl. Kalanath's staff lay on the floor where it had slipped from his limp hand.

Sienne turned with some effort to see Alaric wobble and then fall to the floor, not even trying to catch himself. She tried to say his name, to say all their names, but her lips were numb and her jaw felt locked tight. Her knees wobbled, sending her flailing to the bench. She stayed upright solely because of her grip on the table's edge. No one in the room was still upright but her. She called out for help, and to her relief saw a man come to the kitchen door. He stared at them all in horror, then disappeared again. Right. Not everyone in the inn would have eaten the stew. But why would the cook poison them?

She realized her eyes were closed and tried to open them. Nothing happened. Everything was so difficult, including staying upright. She felt herself falling, hit her head on the table, and knocked the bowl still half-full of stew across the table to land on the floor beyond. The sound of wood hitting wood echoed hollowly in her ears, followed by the sound of someone gabbling incoherently—

or maybe it was normal talk, and she was the one who couldn't understand it.

Someone took her under the arms and hauled her off the bench. *Good,* she thought, *help is here*, but staying awake was too much effort, and she fell unconscious just as a second person put his hands around her ankles and lifted her into the air.

24

Sienne drifted into consciousness to a ringing in her ears and the sound of someone clapping. Not the rapid patter of applause, but a slow, measured beat, three or four sharp claps every minute. Her arms were raised above her ears and ached horribly. The ringing subsided, and the clapping turned into the sound of water dripping on stone, echoing off unseen walls. She knelt on a cold, wet, rough surface that smelled of dirt. The smell, and the lingering nausea from the drug, made her want to throw up. She didn't know how long she'd been there, but it was long enough that the wet had seeped into her trousers.

She opened her eyes to dim, blurry light, the yellow-gold of a lantern burning somewhere to her right. The light illuminated a cavern, its pendulous ceiling twenty feet high in places, hollowed out not by man but by some long-lost underground river, based on how irregular its shape was. Its walls bulged and dripped with moisture, though the echoing drip was invisible, and they gleamed an unrelieved black that sparkled where the light struck them.

Across the cavern, perhaps fifteen feet away, Dianthe slumped against the stone wall, unmoving, her arms stretched out above her head and chained to the wall. Kalanath leaned against the wall some distance from her, his arms similarly restrained. As she watched, he shifted slightly and let out a low moan. She couldn't decide whether to be relieved that he was alive, or frightened that she couldn't see Alaric or Perrin.

She shifted her weight, and heard metal scrape against stone. A heavy iron cuff circled her wrist—both her wrists, she discovered—and chains attached to the manacles dragged her arms above her head, connected to rings in the wall behind her. She shivered, and could not stop shivering. The room, or cave, or wherever this was, kept the chill of winter locked inside it, a damp chill that made her think of tombs and catacombs. But her shivering had nothing to do with the cold.

Footsteps approached, drowning out the echoing water. "Don't try to stand," a woman said. "You'll just fall over."

Sienne pushed herself up with her feet to kneel erect on the stone floor and looked up at the woman. She was middle-aged, slim, with dark hair threaded with silver piled atop her head and hazel eyes unmarked by crow's feet. Her gown was rich burgundy velvet, over which she wore a cropped vest embroidered with silver and tiny winking gems that were black in the low light. She cradled the emerald falcon in her left arm and regarded Sienne dispassionately, the way someone might look at a dog or a horse they were considering buying. Sienne matched her stare for stare, though her heart was in her throat and her mouth was dry. She didn't need the woman's warning; she was sure her legs would not support her.

"You should have sold the artifact to Winifrey," the woman said. "It would have saved everyone a world of trouble."

"Who are you?"

"Does it matter?"

Sienne cleared her throat. "I like to know the name of the person threatening me. Unless you're ashamed of what you're doing."

The woman laughed. "Hardly. My need for secrecy will soon be over. But if you insist... my name is Lady Pyrenna Nerus."

"Where is Alaric? And Perrin?"

"Here." Lady Nerus gestured vaguely in the direction of a fold in the wall that blocked Sienne's view to the left. "It's irrelevant. You are in no position to rescue yourselves, if that's what you're hoping. They're chained as you are, and my trusted servants are watchful." She waved a hand, and Sienne realized some of the shadows were people, guards in plain black jerkins over red tunics, leather trousers, and leather caps, armed with longswords and daggers. They stared straight ahead, not looking at Sienne or Lady Nerus, and their expressions of alert disinterest made Sienne's stomach churn again.

She said, "You want the artifact."

"How nice that you aren't going to play the ignorant ingénue," Lady Nerus said. "I *have* the artifact. You will teach me to use it. And then I will let you go. Not immediately, of course. Not until I've achieved my goals. But soon."

Someone coughed, out of sight to the left. "We're not stupid," Alaric said, and despite herself Sienne's heart leaped. "You can't afford to let us live."

"Is that what you think?"

"You let us see your face," Sienne said. "That says you think we're disposable."

Lady Nerus smiled. "Aneirin said you were clever—too clever to give away your secrets. He was impressed that you perceived his presence despite his invisibility. But you don't have all the facts. I really don't need your deaths. There's nothing you can do to stop me getting what I want, and unlike some people, I don't enjoy killing for its own sake. I even choose to forgive you for Caberri's death."

"Who?"

The smile disappeared. "You weren't introduced. There wasn't time before you destroyed him with the artifact. His magic wasn't strong enough to defeat you."

"I—" Sienne remembered in time that giving information to the enemy was stupid, and shut her mouth. "He tried to kill us. I won't apologize for defending myself."

"As I said, if you'd sold Winifrey the artifact, all of this could have been avoided." Lady Nerus stood and walked away, out of Sienne's sight. "Why didn't you? You can't possibly have any loyalty to the Figlari woman."

Sienne opened her mouth to reply, but Alaric said, "Then you don't understand anything. We don't deal behind our client's back."

"I don't believe you. Scrappers sell their services to the highest bidder. You must have had plans for the artifact. Who were you going to sell it to?"

"Tonia Figlari."

"That's a lie. Tell me the truth. You will eventually. Save yourself some pain."

Alaric said nothing. Sienne saw Dianthe stir and sit up. Now only Perrin was unaccounted for.

Lady Nerus came back toward Sienne, shifting her grip on the falcon. "It doesn't matter. Whoever your buyer was is doomed to disappointment. Now, I want you to tell me how to activate the artifact."

Sienne glared at her, but said nothing. Behind her defiant façade, panic gripped her insides. This woman was no wizard and wouldn't be able to use the artifact even if Sienne told her how it worked. Sienne wasn't entirely sure *she* knew how it worked. Telling her the truth didn't matter. But if the woman had another wizard available, Sienne didn't dare risk handing Lady Nerus such a powerful weapon.

Lady Nerus smiled again. "People are so predictable. Of course you won't tell me. You probably think I'm the villain here. That I'll use the weapon for evil."

"You tried to kill us and you kidnapped us. I think that makes you the villain," Sienne said.

"Such a limited understanding. I've attacked you, so of course I must be unrelentingly evil. As if your little concerns mattered at all in the grand design. I'm trying to save this country from a tyrant who treats it as his own personal playground."

"Are you talking about King Derekian? He's not a tyrant!"

"I'd expect a scrapper to think that. Your understanding is so juvenile. If you were noble, if you'd ever been to court, you'd know how wrong you are. Derekian isn't the even-handed, compassionate monarch he wants people to see him as. He gives preference to his favorites and plunders the treasury to pay for his lavish entertainments. He's whimsical and disregards the laws when it suits him, which is always. Rafellin deserves a ruler who cares about its people more than his own desires."

Sienne yanked on her chains. They gave not at all. "I take it that's you."

"Why not? Again, it's not like I expect you to realize my superiority to the clown who currently sits on the throne. You're just a scrapper who's in over her head. But I assure you, my rule will be far more even-handed. I'll use the artifact wisely—"

"That's impossible. I don't care if you're the next avatar of God Herself. The artifact is too powerful for anyone to use wisely. If you're so convinced you'll be a better queen than the king, go ahead and try your coup. You'll have to do it without the artifact."

Lady Nerus smiled in a pitying, supercilious way. "You really don't see it, do you? The artifact will let me destroy the few key individuals who stand in my way. No mass bloodshed, no armies fighting armies, just a couple of clean, quick deaths. Rafellin will have a better ruler, and you'll go free to do whatever it is scrapper wizards do."

"I won't help you," Sienne said, desperation giving her words an edge.

Lady Nerus looked down at her and shook her head. "I was hoping you'd see reason. Do you want money, too? A bribe, in exchange for your knowledge?"

Sienne shook her head. "I won't do it for anything."

"I wouldn't be so quick to declare that. Last chance. Tell me how it works."

Sienne shook her head again.

Lady Nerus bit her lower lip in thought. "You, Ansorjan," she said. "Tell her to comply. You're the leader of this scrapper team, Aneirin tells me—it's in your best interests to do as I say."

"She wouldn't obey me if I did," Alaric said, "and she's right, we won't help you."

"Very well. I didn't want to do it this way, but you have to under-stand—I need this weapon, and you *will* give it to me. Get her up."

Two of the shadowy men detached themselves from the wall and moved to stand on either side of, not Sienne, but Dianthe. They hauled her to her feet and forced her to stand spread-eagled with her back against the wall. Dianthe cried out weakly. Chains rattled, and Alaric shouted, "What are you doing? Let her go!"

"That's entirely up to you," Lady Nerus said, setting the artifact at her feet. She gestured, and a third guard stepped forward and handed her his long knife. It had a wide blade that tapered at the tip and was sharp on only one edge, as the woman demonstrated by laying the dull edge along her palm. "Let's see what you value more—this arti-fact, which matters nothing to you but some abstract sense of what's right, or your companion's hands."

The third man grabbed Dianthe's left wrist and pressed her hand open against the wall. "I'll start small, to give you plenty of time to think about it," Lady Nerus said, laying the blade against the first joint of Dianthe's pinky. Dianthe screamed and struggled against her captor's grip. Sienne leapt to her feet and strained against the chains, screaming to match Dianthe. Kalanath was at the end of his chains, shouting and flailing to reach her. Sienne sobbed Dianthe's name and tried to use her invisible fingers to snatch the blade away, but Lady Nerus's grip was too tight. The woman pressed down hard on the back of the blade, and Dianthe's finger disappeared in a spurt of blood. Dianthe screamed again, longer this time.

"Stop!" Sienne screamed. "Stop, I'll tell you, just stop!"

"Sienne!" Alaric shouted.

"I can't let her hurt Dianthe anymore," Sienne sobbed. "It's not—you can't tell me you wouldn't choose the same."

"Sienne is right, the artifact is not important," Kalanath said.

Sienne wasn't sure that was true. Giving Lady Nerus a weapon of that magnitude might be disastrous. But the alternative was watching her chop Dianthe's fingers off, a little at a time. Sienne couldn't bear that. She hated herself for her weakness, but she couldn't do anything else.

"That was easier than I'd expected." Lady Nerus sounded pleased. She signaled to the guards to release Dianthe and withdrew a handkerchief from her sleeve, which one of the guards wrapped tightly around Dianthe's maimed finger.

"All right, tell me how to activate it," Lady Nerus said, picking the artifact up and returning to stand in front of Sienne.

"What do you know about artifacts?" Sienne asked.

"Are you stalling?"

"No. Do you understand artifacts have requirements you have to meet to make them work?"

"I'd heard that, yes. You'd better not be about to lie to me about this one's requirements."

"That would just get me or my friends hurt. But you won't like this one. You have to be a wizard to activate it."

Lady Nerus blinked. "Impossible."

"I can prove it if you give it to me."

"Hah! And give you a weapon against me? Not a chance." She gestured. "I'll take the rest of the woman's finger."

"*No!*" Sienne lunged for Lady Nerus, who stepped back, smiling and running her thumb over the dull edge of the blade. "I swear it's true!"

"If you touch her again, I'll make it my mission in life to destroy you," Alaric snarled.

"Hmmm." Lady Nerus pursed her lips in thought. "You leave me with a conundrum. I can't let you demonstrate, because I'd certainly be your first target. But I don't think I want Winifrey handling it, either. She's loyal, but who knows what might happen if she got her hands on that kind of power. On a third hand, I have to trust Winifrey, as Caberri is dead." She absently wiped the blade on the nearest guard's jerkin and handed it back to its owner. "Someone send for Winifrey. Her duties can wait. Tell her this is a royal command."

Sienne wanted to snap something nasty about Lady Nerus not being royal yet, but it would have been pointless. She leaned against the wall and looked at Dianthe, who was pale and sweating but otherwise composed. Kalanath strained against the limits of the chains tethering him to the wall. They were attached to iron rings embedded in the stone as hers were, probably with *sculpt* based on how the stone bulged over it. The whole thing had an impromptu look to it.

Sienne pulled against the chains. They were short enough that Sienne couldn't quite reach her opposite wrist. The manacles were held closed by a simple pin, no lock. She tried her invisible fingers on it, but the pin was heavy and hooked in a way that was too complex for that small magic. The knowledge filled her with more despair than anything else. To be so close to freedom…!

Sienne.

Perrin. She'd forgotten about him; he'd been so quiet she'd thought he was still unconscious. But that had clearly been his voice, if distant and echoing.

Don't speak. She'll hear you.

Confused, she looked around. She still couldn't see him. Lady Nerus stood about ten feet away from Sienne, toying with the hem of her vest. She didn't seem to have heard Perrin.

Just think. I will hear your response.

Sienne lowered her head in case her confusion was evident on her face, and the woman might see it. *How are you doing this?*

We can discuss that later. Can you weaken the chain connected to your right wrist? With the invulnerability magic?

Yes. Why?

Just be prepared for Alaric to move. When he does, stretch that chain taut against the wall. Understand?

She didn't understand. She also didn't care. *I need about one minute. And a distraction.*

You have it.

"So you intend to take the throne," Perrin said aloud. Sienne couldn't understand how she hadn't realized he'd been in mental communication with her before; his voice sounded so much fuller now. "Do you expect the rest of the nobles to simply fall into line?"

"Power in this monarchy is concentrated in only a few individuals," the woman said. "With those individuals gone, I can easily take control. It helps that so many of my fellows believe as I do, that Derekian's reign is tainted."

Sienne looked at the chain attached to her right wrist. She folded her fingers and tried to touch the manacle, but it was out of reach. She could still cast invulnerability on something she couldn't touch, but it took longer and wasn't as precise. She focused her attention on the links just above the manacle, pictured the magic wrapping around them, weakening the chain. Surreptitiously she tugged on it, and felt no give. Well, she wasn't strong enough to break an iron chain, even a weakened one. She wondered in passing where her spellbook was. If she had that, this woman wouldn't stand a chance against her.

"But are you certain none of the others will try to take the throne for themselves?" Perrin was saying. *Are you ready, Sienne?*

Ready.

"I have the advantage of being prepared for this event," Lady Nerus said, "and I—"

Chains rattled. Men Sienne couldn't see shouted, and she heard the thump of weapons hitting the ground. A high, shrill whinny shook the air. Lady Nerus's eyes went wide, and she staggered backward into Dianthe's arms, dropping the artifact, which hit the floor with a dull chime. The unicorn came around the fold in the stone, his massive body maneuvering into position with his hindquarters facing Sienne. In that moment, she figured out the plan. She stretched her arm to its limit, pulling the chain taut, closed her eyes and turned her head away. *Please don't let him miss.*

A breath of air whooshed past her face, and something cracked hard against the stone just inches from her ear with a tone like a chiming bell. Her arm fell loose to her side. She opened her eyes, but Alaric had already moved on, rearing up to strike down a guard whose sword was raised. In the next moment, he was human again, snatching up the fallen man's sword and bringing it up to block the next man's swing.

Sienne scrabbled the pin of the other manacle free and raced to

Kalanath's side. He was up and balanced on the balls of his feet, his attention focused on Alaric's fight. Sienne freed him and he darted away. Sienne moved to Dianthe. Dianthe had Lady Nerus in a choke-hold, her eyes fierce and her lips moving in a constant stream of muttered invective. As Sienne hovered, wondering what to do, Lady Nerus went limp, and Dianthe dropped her and held out her hands for Sienne to remove the manacles. "That felt *good*," Dianthe said.

"I can imagine. Where's Perrin?"

"Just over there. Did he speak to you?"

"Yes. How did he—"

"I'm trying not to be too hopeful." Dianthe shook her head and massaged her wrist. "Go free him. I'll keep an eye on the bitch."

Sienne hugged the wall, staying out of the way of the fight and hoping no armed guard would notice her. Perrin sat cross-legged against the wall, his arms extended above his head and his eyes closed. Sienne fumbled with the pins of his manacles, and he smiled without opening his eyes. "What a magnificent day," he said.

"Are you... is everything all right?"

Perrin stretched and stood. "I choose not to ask that question. Let us get free of this tangle, and leave the philosophy for later."

His eyes widened, and he grabbed Sienne and yanked her into his embrace, flinging up his left arm. Pearly light flared as a shield sprang into being in time to catch the descending sword of one of Lady Nerus's men. The guard snarled and hacked at the shield, making shreds of pearly gray fly.

"I think we have a problem," Perrin said. Sienne looked around frantically for help. Alaric was fighting two men at once, Kalanath had just downed one and ducked a blow from another, and Dianthe, despite her brave words, looked about to fall over, probably from the delayed effects of shock. The shield shivered, but held strong. For now.

Sienne cast about for another solution. On the far wall hung a lantern with an iron frame and frosted invulnerable glass panels set into it. She lifted it with her invisible fingers. It was heavy, almost too heavy for her to manage, but she got a firm grip on it and dragged it

254 | MELISSA MCSHANE

toward herself, building momentum as she went until it was practically flying.

The sword bit deeply into the shield, the shield burst, and the lantern slammed into the guard's skull. He dropped his sword and swayed, putting a hand to his head. Perrin tackled him around the waist, shoving him backward until the guard tripped and went down with Perrin atop him. Perrin grabbed the man's hair and slammed his head into the stone floor. The guard went limp.

Sienne picked up the lantern, which was undamaged from its collision with the man's head, and looked around. Alaric had one of the guards backed against a stone outcropping, and as Sienne watched, the guard threw down his sword and flung his hands up in surrender. Kalanath, not even breathing heavily, punched his opponent in the stomach, making him bend in time to meet Kalanath's knee coming the other way. He dropped like a lead weight. Nothing else moved in the cavern. Sienne breathed out a long, relieved sigh. They'd won—for now.

25

Alaric gestured to the lone conscious survivor to take a few steps to the right, where manacles hung, their pins intact. Alaric must have been held there until his transformation. Sienne wondered how that had looked—those manacles couldn't have restrained an ordinary horse's hoof, let alone one the size of Alaric's. Alaric directed the man to put his hands up, then secured the manacles around his wrists. The guard endured this in silence, his face expressionless. Alaric gave the chains a little yank, testing them, then walked back to join the rest of them where Dianthe crouched over Lady Nerus's unconscious body.

"Now what?" Dianthe said. "We still have to get out of here. We don't even know where 'here' is!"

"We have an excellent hostage," Perrin said.

"That wizard she summoned, Winifrey, she'll be here any minute," Sienne said. She picked up the artifact and hugged it close to her chest. "I don't want to use this thing again."

"They don't know that," Alaric said. He knelt and slapped Lady Nerus, not gently, then shook her by the shoulders. "Wake up."

Lady Nerus stirred and blinked. She focused on Alaric's face, just inches from hers. "What are you?"

"Something you shouldn't have trifled with," Alaric said. "You're going to escort us out of here. We're taking the artifact. And if you come after us again, your life is forfeit. Understand?"

Lady Nerus licked her lips nervously. "You don't understand," she said. "I want what's best for Rafellin. I swear I won't use the artifact for more than that. I've spent years to reach this point, everything's in readiness—I just need the artifact for an hour. Half an hour."

"What you plan is murder," Alaric said. "We won't be party to that."

"Not murder. Justice. Derekian needs to be stopped, don't you see?"

"Then figure out another way to stop him." Alaric hauled her to her feet and kept one large hand on her elbow. He held his confiscated sword in the other. "Now we're leaving."

"Then you condemn hundreds to death," Lady Nerus said. "Thousands, maybe. I *will* go to war if I have to, and I *will* see Derekian toppled. That artifact—"

"Start walking," Alaric said, dragging her along. The others fell into place around and behind him. It was so comforting to have his bulk between her and danger, Sienne thought, except when—

"Where's my spellbook?" she asked.

Lady Nerus ignored her. Sienne smacked her across the back of her head to get her attention. "Where is my spellbook?"

"I gave it to Winifrey to make use of," Lady Nerus said. "I imagine she's in the process of copying out your spells. You'll have to take it from her. I warn you, she's a formidable wizard. She won't let you walk out of here unchallenged."

A narrow passage led out of the cavern, gradually sloping up. They had to go single-file, with Alaric pushing Lady Nerus ahead of him and keeping a tight grip on her arm. The passage was unlit, and as Sienne had left her lantern weapon behind in the cavern, the only light came from the small magic lights she made to hover over their heads. The lights gave everyone a pale, ghostly appearance and made Alaric, already fairer-skinned than the rest, look three days dead. Sienne followed him, not too closely in case it came to fighting again, and tried not to fret about her spellbook. If that Winifrey had—well, she couldn't hurt it, but she could copy out Sienne's spells, and that infuriated Sienne more than it probably should.

The passage curved right, then left, and grew even narrower. Alaric had to hunch not to knock his head on the roof. His steps grew awkward, slower, and he turned sideways, bringing his sword arm back. "Watch it," Sienne said.

Alaric turned his head toward her. "Sorry," he said. "Maybe—"

His left arm jerked forward, and he stumbled and cursed. Sienne heard running footsteps. Alaric cursed again and sped up. "She pulled free," he said, sounding disgusted with himself. "I should have left the stupid sword behind."

Sienne trotted after him, wishing she had her spellbook so she could shrink him, or *force*-blast Lady Nerus, or anything not to feel so utterly useless. The light was increasing, more than could be accounted for by the magic lights she threw up as they ran, and warmer, gold instead of white. Moments later they were out of the passage and into a cool first summer evening, lit by the last rays of the sun. The ground immediately outside the passage sloped steeply downward, and Sienne stumbled and slid a few feet before catching herself. Green hills surrounded them, rising from a valley floor carpeted with new grass. It took Sienne a moment to realize they were in the hills outside Fioretti, and that the barest glimpse of the city was visible to the west.

Lady Nerus was halfway down the hill and accelerating. Alaric and Kalanath raced after her, and Sienne hurried to catch up. The artifact was an awkward burden, and she finally resorted to carrying it head-down by the ankles. Maybe she could beat Lady Nerus senseless with it.

A long string of short, curt syllables rang out, and something smacked Sienne in the back of the knees. She tripped, her feet tangled in something sticky. She went down hard, losing her grip on the artifact, which bounced and came to a stop in a patch of new growth a few feet from her face.

"What is going on here?" a new voice said. Sienne fought to get free of the sticky tangles around her legs. Rolling onto her back, she looked up at the speaker. It was the woman who'd called herself Georgina Marchena, clad this time in plain dark trousers and shirt. The woman bent to pick up the artifact and examined it closely.

"Put it down, it's dangerous," Sienne panted.

"Oh, I know it's dangerous. So am I." Georgina—no, Winifrey—smiled and ran her hand over the emerald head. She must have used *jaunt* to enter the cavern and come out behind them. Sienne craned her neck. Perrin struggled against the same sticky webbing she'd been caught in. She couldn't see Dianthe anywhere. Alaric and Kalanath had tackled Lady Nerus, but they were yards away and in no position to help her.

Sienne yelled a warning. Winifrey opened her spellbook again, leisurely, and flipped the pages. Alaric had turned at the sound of Sienne's voice and was running back up the hill toward them. "He's dangerous, too," Winifrey said. "I think he needs to die." She began speaking again, her words now the sharp-edged syllables of an evocation. *Scorch*. It would hit Alaric full on. Sienne screamed a warning, but Alaric kept coming straight for them.

In desperation, Sienne lifted herself off the ground with both hands and pivoted, swinging her bound legs like a hammer into the woman's calves. Winifrey staggered, the evocation cutting off mid-syllable. The falcon slipped from her arm and fell, landing beside Sienne's head. She snatched it up, clutched the hand grip, and without a second thought raised its talons to rest on her left forearm. Agony shot up her arm as the talons closed on it, digging in deep, and the falcon burst into emerald radiance. She aimed the artifact at Winifrey's head. "Back away," she panted, "or you'll go the way your friend Caberri did."

Winifrey regained her balance and turned her attention on Sienne. She spat out the first syllables of *scorch* again before comprehending what Sienne held. She backed away, lowering her spellbook. "Stop," Sienne said. "You can't outrun this."

Pounding feet heralded Alaric's approach. "Sienne, no," he said.

"It's all right, Alaric. She's not stupid."

Alaric bent to cut the webbing away from Sienne's legs. It stuck to his blade, making him curse. "It has to be burned," Sienne said. "Just give me a minute. And take that woman's spellbook from her." She concentrated, and a little spark danced along the lines of the webbing, spreading like fire consuming a dry field. It scorched her boots, which irritated her, or would have if she weren't in so much pain. Just keeping her attention focused on the spark felt like dragging herself through a mire.

Finally, she stood and faced Winifrey, whose eyes were wide. Her gaze flicked in every direction, like a small animal looking to avoid the wolf. "Lady Nerus," Sienne said, not turning to look at the woman who was approaching, escorted by Kalanath. "This is how the artifact works. Watch."

Winifrey cried out and covered her face with her arms, but Sienne wasn't aiming at her. She let her anger over Dianthe's injury and being captured and the whole stupidity of Lady Nerus's plan feed into the falcon, and a beam of pale green light shot from its beak past Winifrey's head to impact against the side of a hill. The green light spidered outward from the point of impact until it covered an area about fifteen feet in diameter, then vanished along with a huge mass of dirt and stone. Lady Nerus stared at the crater left behind, filling with wisps of ash blowing away in the evening breeze.

"I don't know if your cause is just, and I don't care," Sienne said. "Maybe I should. But this artifact makes killing far too easy. Suppose we let you have it, and you do only kill those few key individuals you've identified. What happens a year or five down the road, when your rule is threatened? You use it again, maybe? And then some bard writes an unflattering song about you, so you kill him too—no fuss, no mess, just one less bard to trouble your sleep. It's too dangerous, Lady Nerus. We can't let you have it."

"So you'll keep it?" Lady Nerus said. "Dispense justice for yourselves?"

"We're going to dispose of it," Alaric said. "We're not in the justice-dispensing business."

"You said thousands will die in your revolution," Perrin said. He still had bits of web clinging to his legs. "Are you really justified in making that choice? In sending Rafellin up in flames?"

Lady Nerus shook her head. "You don't understand. I will *save* Rafellin—"

"At what cost?" Perrin said. "Will Rafellin thank you for saving it?"

"It doesn't matter to us," Alaric said, holding up a hand to forestall Sienne's objection. "Give us back Sienne's spellbook, and the rest of our gear, and you can go your way. I suggest you get as far away from Fioretti as you can. Your wizard there can probably cast *ferry*."

"You'll inform on me." Lady Nerus's voice shook with anger. "You said it didn't matter to you."

"Politics doesn't matter," Alaric said. "Stability does. We'll give you a day to gather your things and escape, but then we tell the authorities what you intended."

"You don't care what the misbegotten king does?"

Alaric sighed. "You were right about one thing," he said. "We're just scrappers, and the relative merits of our rulers are beyond us. Maybe you'd make a better ruler than the king, maybe not. What we *are* sure of is that you'd destroy this city to bring about the change you're so eager for. This is *our* city. We live here. We have friends who'd suffer if we let your plan come to pass. So no, we don't care about the misbegotten king. Now. Our things."

Lady Nerus looked like she might fly at him and claw his eyes out. She made a tight gesture, and Winifrey held out her hand for her spellbook, which Dianthe handed over after a glance at Sienne. Winifrey let the spellbook fall open, keeping a close eye on Sienne. Sienne tried to look fierce, though she was on the verge of passing out from the pain that had gone from sharp agony to a dull, throbbing ache that made her arm feel twice its normal size. She raised the artifact threateningly as Winifrey began reading, but it was only *convey*, and in a moment Sienne's spellbook thumped to the ground beside her. A few more *conveys*, and the gear they'd had on them at dinner lay in a small pile atop the spellbook. During that time, Alaric took a few steps closer to Sienne and surreptitiously put his hand on the small of her back, supporting her. She tried not to look like she was leaning on him.

Finally, Winifrey beckoned to Lady Nerus to stand beside her. "Oh, and one of your guards is still locked up in that cavern," Alaric said. "Don't let him die there."

Lady Nerus sneered. "I don't abandon my people."

"I'm sure that makes you all kinds of noble."

Winifrey took Lady Nerus's hand and read off one more spell. It was longer than the ones Sienne was familiar with, a more complicated summoning that flecked Winifrey's mouth with blood. As it built to a peak, the two women's images shuddered, flickered like candlelight, and they were gone between one breath and the next.

Sienne sagged, and Alaric's hand on her back became his arm around her waist, holding her up. "Get it off her," Alaric said.

This time, when the falcon was removed, Perrin put a hand over her bloody arm and bowed his head in silence. Deep green light, darker than that of the artifact, welled up around his fingers. It felt cool and fresh and smelled reassuringly of jasmine and mint. When he removed his hand, all that remained was drying blood. The puncture wounds were gone.

Sienne let out a deep, relieved breath. "All right," Alaric said, "how in Sisyletus's name are you doing that? Are you no longer under chastisement?"

"And without blessings? How does that work?" Dianthe asked.

Perrin shook his head. "The details of my communication with my Lord are too complicated, and too personal, for me to share. Suffice it to say that this was by way of a... promise, perhaps. Or a glimpse of the future. Averran deigned to work directly through me because he, too, disliked the idea of revolution, or so I understand. In the morning, I will return to requiring prepared blessings, and how grateful I am for my Lord's forgiveness. But I am on probation, so to speak. I must constantly prove myself and my resolution to overcome my weakness."

"So you can't drink at all," Sienne said.

"Not one drop. It will make my prayers more challenging, though who is to say I might not someday have that restriction—but I dare not even think that, for fear my desire for alcohol will lead me back into justifications."

"That seems impossible," Alaric said. "To go from... well, where you were to nothing—"

"I choose to take it one day at a time," Perrin said. "True, it is a near-impossible task—I have been over-fond of liquor for years, and I have no illusions as to my own strength of will when it comes to drink. But my Lord is generous with human frailty when he is not in an ill humor, and with his divine help, I have faith that it will all work out. And speaking of faith, I believe Averran may yet have one more miracle in store for this day."

He reached out and gently took Dianthe's maimed hand, removing the handkerchief and tossing it aside. "O Lord of crotchets, have mercy upon me, and upon this woman," he said.

Green light flared around the missing finger. Slowly, like a seedling sprouting, new flesh emerged from the wound, growing upward until the finger was wholly restored. Dianthe looked at it in wonder. "There's no nail."

"Ah, yes. Restoration is supposed to be perfect, and as I have no reason to believe Averran incompetent in this respect, I can only surmise that he wishes you to remember from what source your healing arose."

"I don't think that's something I'll forget, but I'm not going to argue with an avatar." Dianthe flexed her finger. "It's getting dark. Let's get home before we can't see our feet."

"I can make lights," Sienne said.

"True. But I want to get home nonetheless."

"But we left all the rest of our gear, and our horses, back in Annis."

"Something to worry about another time," Alaric said. "I think we should sleep, and take passage on a ship in the morning. Once we've gotten rid of the artifact, we can take our time retrieving our gear."

Sienne hoped the innkeeper in Annis wouldn't sell their things when they didn't show up. On the other hand, he might have been complicit in their kidnapping. Maybe his guilt would keep him from acting precipitously. If he sold Spark, she was going to make him suffer.

"Should we have let Lady Nerus and that wizard go free?" Perrin said. "She might attempt assassination another time."

"Remember the prophecy from Lisiel?" Alaric said. "'Free the captives and your quest will be rewarded.' They were our captives."

"I had forgotten that, yes." Perrin shrugged. "Far be it from me to disregard a prophecy."

"But what reward?" Dianthe said. "Getting rid of the artifact is hardly rewarding, at least not in the usual sense."

"I'm hoping it means we'll find a way to convince Tonia Figlari to give us the knives, since it did say we wouldn't get money or power," Alaric said. "But at the moment I'm tired enough not to care. We can worry about that later."

They came out of the hills to find Fioretti spread out before them, glittering like a million jewels cast on the shore. The darkness of the Jalenus Sea defined the edges of the great city, curving away out of sight. Somewhere in the distance on the far shores was the dukedom of Sileas, and beyond that, Tagliaveno, and beyond that the southern continent few Rafellish had ever visited. Somewhere out there, they'd drop the artifact into the depths, and it could lie on the ocean floor for the next millennium and longer.

Sienne trudged along the streets of Fioretti after Alaric, barely noticing the bright colors and movement that characterized one of the many street festivals celebrating the turn of the seasons. The excitement and terror and pain had all worn off, leaving her too exhausted to care that she was carrying the emerald falcon openly through the streets. She adjusted her spellbook under her other arm. That other wizard's spellbook, belonging to that Caberri who had died so awfully, was missing. It had been tucked inside what was left of the harness, but it was gone when Winifrey returned the book to her. She felt a moment's regret at losing it, but only a moment. Taking the spells of a man she'd killed felt morbid.

Master Tersus's neighborhood was quiet, with lights burning in some of the houses' windows and in the spell-lit lanterns along the street, but no one was abroad even at this relatively early hour. Alaric unlocked the side door and let everyone in. The smell of roast duck filled the hall, making Sienne's stomach growl, but the thought of digging out leftovers, however delicious, made her more tired. So she merely followed Alaric up the stairs and went into her room.

The soft sound of boots scuffing floorboards told her someone was in her room the moment before they grabbed her. She opened her mouth to scream, but someone shoved a cloth into it and pinioned her arms behind her back. The artifact fell to the floor with a hard thump. Sienne fought the hands immobilizing her, but there were too many of them, at least three people flinging her face-first onto her bed, binding her hands. Someone blindfolded her, pointless in the darkness, and that scared her more than anything else.

She kicked out and heard a pained grunt, but the hands didn't release her. They lifted her off the bed, holding her tight against her struggles. Someone muttered the long, complex syllables of *ferry*, and suddenly the air was warm, almost hot, and smelled of wood smoke and, more faintly, a fruity perfume too sweet to be pleasant. The hands shoved her down onto something soft, a chair or a sofa, then withdrew.

Sienne struggled to sit up and listened frantically for anything that might give her a clue as to her surroundings. She heard movement, a shuffling, rustling sound, and someone grunting as if trying to speak through a gag. She wasn't alone here, wherever it was—maybe the others had been captured, too. She hoped that wasn't true.

Footsteps sounded on a wooden floor. "So," a man's voice said, "you intend to bring down a king, do you?"

26

The cloth in her mouth prevented Sienne from replying, not that she knew what to say. Bring down a king? They'd *stopped* that from happening! Anger and fear warred within her, anger at the complete unfairness of this, fear of what this person might do if he really believed she was complicit with Lady Nerus.

Someone plucked the cloth from her mouth, and she swallowed to rid herself of the dryness it left behind. Behind her, someone coughed, and then Perrin said, "You are sadly misinformed. I have no interest in attacking Rafellin's government."

"You met with Pyrenna Nerus in secret. You delivered her this artifact. I think you are lying." The man had a noble's accent and his words drawled, like he was considering each before he spoke it.

"Lady Nerus kidnapped us and stole the artifact," Alaric said. Relief washed over Sienne. He and Perrin were here, likely the others were too, and they'd figure a way out of this, whatever it was.

"Something a liar would say to defend himself," the man said. "What proof have you?"

"We still have the artifact," Alaric said. "We took it back from Lady Nerus."

"So you intend to kill the king yourselves."

"That was Lady Nerus's plan. We're not in league with her, and we intend to put the artifact where it can't be used by anyone."

"And where would that be?"

Alaric went silent. Sienne guessed he was worried he was giving too much away. "None of your business," he finally said, "since we don't know who you are or what you intend. You might be interested in killing the king yourself."

"You are in no position to withhold information." The footsteps sounded again, pacing away from Sienne, then back toward her. "Your only hope is to tell me what I want to know, and hope I believe you."

"Who are you?" Sienne asked.

"Someone who dislikes stubbornness in his captives." A hand slapped Sienne so hard her head snapped back. She cried out in surprise and pain, and heard Alaric shout her name.

"Hitting a helpless woman," he snarled. "My desire to be helpful just vanished."

"I'm not interested in what you want," the man said. "I care more about the safety of this country and the stability of its government than I do about your petty little lives."

"You bastard," Dianthe cried. "We stopped Lady Nerus from killing the king!"

"Then why did you not bring her to the palace for questioning? Instead, she's free to plot against the government and possibly try her assassination attempt again in future."

Sienne opened her mouth to speak and realized anything she might say would only make them look more guilty. Not turning Lady Nerus in now seemed like a stupid idea.

"Lady Nerus thought she was doing what was best for the country," Alaric said. "I chose to give her exile rather than death."

"You did, did you? And what entitles you to make that decision? You're not even Rafellish."

"Because I couldn't tell her she was wrong to want better for the country. I don't know if she was right about the king being selfish and greedy, but if she was, her intentions were good. I thought that was deserving of a second chance."

Sienne realized he'd been using *I* instead of *we* and her heart sank. He was trying to take all the blame himself, probably so he could take all the punishment himself.

"That's not your concern," the man said. "You have no authority."

"That's true." Sienne waited for more, but it seemed Alaric was done talking. It was no use. They were all dead. She only wondered why this man had even bothered talking to them instead of killing them outright.

More pacing. The cloying fragrance was making Sienne feel ill. "How does the artifact work?" the man said.

"We won't tell you that."

"Still recalcitrant, even though I can have you executed?"

"We won't give that power to anyone, least of all a stranger who can have us executed."

"I can also have you tortured."

Sienne held her breath. If he started torturing her friends, she'd tell him. She had no strength of will about that.

"You can," Alaric said, "but it won't help. That artifact needs to disappear."

The man came to Sienne's side and hauled her to her feet. Sienne bit back a gasp. What they did not need at this point was for Alaric to transform into his other self when they had no idea where they were or who this man was, and if he thought she was in danger, he might do just that. "You are a wizard," the man said. "You understand magic. How deadly is this thing?"

"Deadly," Sienne said. "It destroys with a touch, living or inorganic, it doesn't matter. The only thing preventing it from leveling armies is its limited range. Please, let us take it where it can never be found. No one should have this kind of power."

The man released her. "Not even a good man? Someone who'd use it virtuously?"

"How could it possibly be used virtuously? It brings only death, and that too easily. Anyone who used it often would forget how terrible death is because it would be so simple to cause it. Trivial, even. I don't think lives should be trivialized."

"And you think Pyrenna failed to understand that?"

"She thought she could bring down the government with a few chosen deaths. But it wouldn't have stopped at that."

"So you supported her decision to overthrow the government, just not with the artifact?"

"*No,* damn it," Sienne exclaimed, overriding a chorus of protests from her friends. "We're not qualified to decide how good the government is. We just wanted to protect the city from destruction."

"I see." The man walked away. Sienne remained standing, not sure where the sofa was and afraid of falling if she tried to sit. "Letting Pyrenna go does not help your cause."

"That was my responsibility," Alaric said. "They had nothing to do with it."

"We agreed," Kalanath said, speaking for the first time. "We could have stopped you if we chose. Lady Nerus was not bad, just... it is when you think something is true and act on it, but it is false."

"Misguided," Perrin said. "We are scrappers, not murderers."

Sienne tried not to think about the deaths they'd caused in defending themselves in the forest and in the cavern, or the beam of pale green light destroying men at her hand. She hadn't wanted Lady Nerus dead, or turned over to people who might kill her, because she was sick of death. But she was afraid to say any of this, because it made them all sound guilty.

"So, if I understand your defense correctly," the man said, "you refused to give Pyrenna the artifact, but let her go free because you sympathized with her cause. You will not tell me how to use the artifact because you think I will use it to kill indiscriminately. And you expect me to let you walk out of here with the artifact so you can supposedly dispose of it where it will never be found."

Sienne ground her teeth. So many misconceptions! She heard someone rise from another sofa or chair near her. "We sympathized with Lady Nerus's intentions, not her cause," Alaric said. "We didn't want any more deaths on our consciences. I judged she was harmless without her support and without the artifact and didn't want to see her executed. If we'd agreed with her, we would have helped her in her plan. And we have no idea who you are, but we're convinced no one, no matter how well-intentioned, can use this thing for good. That's the last I'll say on the subject. If you're going to kill us, make it quick."

Sienne held her breath. Then, to her shock, she heard the man laugh. "You have balls of solid brass to admit to being willing to kill your king under any circumstances," he said. Someone took Sienne's bound hands and slipped a cold knife between them. The ropes fell away.

Sienne pulled the blindfold off and blinked blurriness out of her eyes. The overheated room was a formal parlor, decorated in the simple, unadorned style of a hundred years previous. Sofas and chairs crowded around the fireplace, which burned high and bright. The mantel held rows of sappy porcelain figures painted in rose and pale blue, the kind of figures Sienne associated with elderly women with too much time on their hands.

She turned to survey the rest of the room. Her friends all stood or sat on chairs nearby. Perrin and Dianthe were rubbing their wrists, and Kalanath had just removed his blindfold. A short man dressed all in black velvet was just cutting the ropes around Alaric's wrists. As he straightened, the firelight fell full upon his face, illuminating its strong lines, the neatly trimmed black beard outlining his jaw, the bright hazel eyes that gleamed with intelligence. Sienne's jaw dropped.

"Your Majesty," she said.

King Derekian glanced in her direction, sheathing his knife. "Sienne Verannus," he said. "Your parents have been looking for you. In all the wrong places, apparently."

"But—why—"

"Have a seat," the king said. "I would apologize for the manner in which you were brought here, but I genuinely was not certain whether you were revolutionaries."

Sienne groped for a chair and sat, unable to take her eyes off the king. Derekian turned his back on Alaric—*brave man, that*—and went to stand in front of the fireplace, clasping his hands behind his back.

"You should have taken Pyrenna into custody and handed her over to my guards," he said. "No, don't repeat yourselves, I understand why you didn't. But you have to admit it looks bad."

"We're not in league with her," Alaric said. "Your Majesty."

"I believe you. Gavant save me from noble idiots." Derekian shook his head. "I'm slightly more disturbed that you thought Pyrenna's motivations were pure. What exactly did she tell you about me?"

Sienne looked at her friends. Now that they were facing the king, Lady Nerus's justifications were hard to repeat. "She claimed you give preference to your favorites even when it's not justified," Sienne said. "That you spend government funds on your own pleasures, and that you disregard the laws when it suits you."

Derekian laid a finger over his lips, tapping them in thought. "That is how it appears, yes," he said. "I'm not sure I need to justify myself to you."

"I'd think you'd want to defend yourself," Sienne said. "Why should ordinary citizens trust you to protect them if you're venal and selfish?"

"You're bolder than I imagined," Derekian said with a laugh. "Your father's messages suggest you are unfamiliar with the ways of the world and potentially in great danger. From what I can see, that's not the case." His laughter died, and he started pacing in front of the fire. "None of you have the knowledge to understand the political situation in Rafellin. Suffice it to say that my government is constantly under threat from the nobles who wish to increase their personal power at the cost of everyone else. Those favorites I supposedly give preference to are the only men and women I can trust not to betray me. My spending is carefully directed at increasing the stability of the government. And the laws I disregard are outmoded ones passed years ago to govern situations that no longer exist in Rafellin."

"What of Lusio Marchena?" Perrin said.

"What of him?"

"He has persuaded you to ignore Tonia Figlari's claim to her ancestral dukedom despite her evident right to it. How is that anything but an abuse of power?"

Derekian's eyes narrowed. "Your face is familiar. Are you a Delucco?"

"I was. My father disinherited me."

"I remember. Perrin Delucco, I think." He sighed. "The Marchenas are a persistent thorn in my side. I've had to keep them close to prevent them joining the coalition against me. Frankly, I should be grateful Pyrenna acted alone. Had she worked in company with anyone else, we would likely not now be having this conversation. At any rate, pretending to give heed to Lusio has kept the Marchenas at bay for over a year while I built my forces to deal with them more permanently. The time will soon come when I'm no longer obliged to endure his inane chatter." Derekian smiled. It was an unpleasant smile that boded ill for Lusio Marchena.

"So you expect us to believe you're not as Lady Nerus described?" Alaric said.

"As you expect me to believe you don't intend to assassinate me," Derekian said. "I think we all need to exercise a degree of faith."

Alaric nodded once. "Understood... your Majesty."

"Don't bother to bow," Derekian said drily. "You're free to go. If you'd like to be transported to your lodgings, I can arrange it."

"What about the artifact?" Sienne said. "We need to dispose of it."

"What was your plan?"

"To drop it in the sea." Keeping that secret from the king was pointless.

"Clever." Derekian smiled. "I think I can come up with something more permanent than that."

"But—it's our responsibility—"

"Not anymore," Derekian said. "I intend to make certain no one ever sees it again. You'll have to trust me," he added, when they all began to protest. "I assure you no one is more invested in making it disappear than I am. Now, if you'll follow me—"

"Wait," Sienne said. "Your Majesty, please don't tell my parents where I am."

"They're very worried about you, Sienne."

"In the way that says they'll drag me home for my own safety. This is my life now. I don't mind if you tell them I'm safe, but... *please*, your Majesty. I'll go home when I'm ready."

Derekian shrugged. "I doubt they'd believe me if I said you prefer to be a nobody scrapper than a duke's daughter. Very well."

"Thank you."

"We should probably go to Annis, if your wizard can do that, your Majesty," Dianthe said. "We left all our things there."

"I think my wizards can manage that."

"Then there's just one more thing," Alaric said. "A question of payment."

Derekian's eyebrows lifted nearly to his hairline. "I was right. You *do* have balls of solid brass."

"We prevented your assassination. I think we're due a little consideration." Alaric's voice was cool, but his stance said he was willing to force the issue.

"I see." Derekian nodded. "How much would you like?"

"Not money," Alaric said. "I had something else in mind."

27

I t was late afternoon two days later when Sienne and her friends plodded into Fioretti. It had been an uneventful two days of beautiful, warm weather, but Sienne was tired of traveling and wanted only her own comfortable bed in Master Tersus's house. Spark, too, seemed eager for her own stall, and Sienne had to tug on the reins to keep her from taking the familiar turning. They still had one thing left to do.

Tonia Figlari's mansion looked, if anything, more rundown than it had the first time they'd seen it. But new green sprouted between the cracks in the stone pavement, giving the place an appearance of simultaneous freshness and decrepitude, and the smell of first summer wafting up wherever Spark's hooves crushed the grass heartened Sienne. She still wasn't entirely convinced Alaric's plan would work, but it was worth trying. They'd run out of other options.

A servant, not the elderly Haritt but a young woman, answered the door. She looked surprised to find five strangers on the doorstep, leading five horses. "Yes? Are you expected?"

"Sort of," Alaric said. "Would you tell Tonia Figlari that her hired scrappers have returned? And have someone watch our horses?"

The servant nodded and held the door wide, gesturing them

inside. The hall was as dark as Sienne remembered and still smelled of tallow and polish. This time, the portraits lining the wall looked anticipatory, as if they'd expected their arrival and were eager to see what the scrappers had brought.

Footsteps on the uncarpeted stairs announced Haritt's arrival. The old man walked slowly, with one hand on the banister. He, at least, seemed unsurprised to see them. "Welcome," he said in his creaky voice. "My lady will see you now."

Alaric handed Haritt a small sack. "The remainder of the two hundred lari you paid us."

"That's unnecessary. It's yours."

"I'd rather have my honor," Alaric said. "We took this job under duress. We won't keep a centus more than we used."

Haritt shrugged. "As you wish, sir."

They trod up the stairs, making them groan softly. Sienne hesitated to touch the elaborately carved balusters, though she was curious about what they represented. It was hard to see details in the dimness, but they appeared to represent mythical figures, satyrs and dryads and other beasts of the natural world no one had ever encountered. True, people had thought carricks were mythical until about a century and a half ago, so there was no reason other creatures might turn out to be similarly real. Sienne examined a goat-legged man with two horns and a sensual smirk, and hoped that one stayed mythical.

The brightly-lit hall, and the white room beyond it, felt warmer today, with the windows closed and a small fire burning in the hearth. Tonia Figlari reclined on one of the gilt-edged sofas. Her nose was red again, but so were her eyes, and Sienne judged she had a nasty cold. Tonia set aside the blanket covering her and rose. She wore casual trousers and a shirt embroidered across the yoke and cuffs with daisies, and was in her stocking feet. Rather than appearing embarrassed at her state of undress, she held her head high and clasped her hands in front of her.

"You're back," she said. "I didn't know when to expect you, but I thought it would take longer than this."

"You're wondering if we were successful," Alaric said.

Her chin lifted higher. "I am."

"Let's sit," Alaric suggested, and took a seat near Tonia's sofa without waiting for an invitation.

Tonia raised an eyebrow, but sat, bundling the blanket beside her. Sienne sat next to Alaric and watched the others find places. She folded her hands in her lap to stop them trembling. This could still go horribly wrong.

"We have bad news," Alaric said. "The Figlari dukedom is over-run. We encountered carvers who'd taken up residence in the keep and barely escaped with our lives."

Tonia's eyes went wide. "I thought carvers were a story."

"Definitely not that. We killed some of them, including their leader. Whether that will make them move on, we don't know. But it's a consideration."

"I don't see the falcon stone. More bad news?"

Alaric took a deep breath and let it out slowly. "The story your grandfather told of the falcon stone was untrue. It wasn't an artifact and it never spoke to anyone."

"You're lying!" Tonia exclaimed. "My grandfather—how *dare* you call him a liar!"

"It's unlikely he was lying. Probably he believed the story. But our wizard—" Alaric indicated Sienne—"assured us the stone was not an artifact, and proved it by destroying it."

"You had *no right* to do so! Haritt!"

"I'm not finished," Alaric said. Sienne marveled that he could stay so calm when Tonia was ready to throw them out. "The falcon stone concealed something else. An actual artifact."

Tonia stopped mid-word calling for Haritt again. "So you did find the artifact!"

"Not the one you sent us after. This was completely different. Sienne?"

Sienne clasped her hands tighter. "We don't know at what point the artifact was encased in stone," she said, "but it was long before the Figlaris acquired it. It was hidden the whole time your family occupied the dukedom."

"Then—it belongs to me. Where is it?"

"It was a powerful weapon, too powerful to belong to anyone. We...disposed of it. Put it somewhere no one will ever find it." Sienne prayed briefly to Averran, as she had every night since meeting the king, that Derekian had been true to his word.

Tonia's mouth hung open. She swallowed. "So what you are telling me," she said in a level voice that promised an eruption was on the way, "is that you destroyed the proof of my identity, you got rid of a powerful artifact that belongs to my family, and you left me with nothing."

"That's not quite true," Alaric said. He reached into his pack and brought out a black leather scroll case. "In exchange for disposing of the artifact, we got this." He handed the case to Tonia.

Puzzled, Tonia opened the case and shook its contents into her hand. She unrolled the sheet of creamy parchment and read its contents. She blanched. "This is..."

"Patents of nobility," Alaric said. "Declaring you duchess of Figlari and restoring your property and titles."

Tonia was silent. Perrin said, "It is properly signed and witnessed. However, you must keep this concealed, revealing it to no one, until tomorrow. If you do not, the title is void and you will never again have the chance to restore it."

The king had been very clear about this. "I need a few days to bring the Marchenas to heel," he'd said, "but if you can assure me Tonia Figlari can control herself, I'll give you the papers now. No offense, but I'd rather not see you people again."

Dianthe had suggested they wait a day to give the scroll case to Tonia, just to be sure, but Alaric had said, "This will prove whether Tonia has the willpower to do what else it takes to regain her status— to herself, if no one else. And we've already waited long enough."

Now Tonia scanned the parchment once more before allowing it to roll up in her hand. "You were supposed to bring me the stone falcon," she said, and Sienne's stomach knotted up. If Tonia was going to balk at the letter of their agreement...

"Those papers are what you wanted, ultimately," Alaric said. "The falcon was just a means to an end. This way, you don't have to negotiate with the king and risk him turning you down no matter what proofs you have."

Tonia stared at him. "An artifact that powerful must be worth a lot of money," she said. "And you traded it away for this. Are those knives worth so much to you?"

"The artifact was priceless," Dianthe said, "which is the same as saying it's worthless, in the sense of being able to sell it. We got for it exactly what it was worth."

"We've fulfilled our end of the bargain," Alaric said. "We'd like what you promised us."

Tonia still looked stunned. Rising as if in a dream, she walked to the table beneath the window and withdrew the leather bag. She returned and handed it to Alaric. Alaric opened it and checked the contents. "Thank you," he said. "Don't call on us again, if you don't mind."

"Thank you," Tonia said. She gestured toward the door.

"What will you do about the carvers?" Sienne asked.

"Now that I have a right to the Figlari dukedom, I can fight for it," Tonia said. "Mythical creatures or no, it sounds like you've proved they die like anything else." A cunning smile touched her lips. "I will take back what's mine."

"Good luck," Sienne said, and meant it.

Outside, Sienne drew in a deep breath of untainted air and mounted Spark. "Home, finally?" she said.

"The stables, then home," Alaric said. "And then the real work begins."

———

SPREAD OUT ON LEOFUS'S NEW TABLE, THE FIVE RITUAL KNIVES LOOKED, not mysterious and alluring, but old and tarnished. Each was sheathed in leather in varying stages of decrepitude, most of which had once had designs impressed on them. One sheath was capped with rusted steel. All five were the same length, about nine inches long from hilt to tip. The grips of two of them were wrapped in leather strips that were falling apart; the others had lost their wrappings years, perhaps centuries ago. The only things that set them apart from ordinary knives were the decorated stones in the pommels. Each bore a semi-precious cabochon stone engraved with a stylized animal. Sienne reached out to touch a delicately carved badger, but withdrew her hand quickly when Alaric reached over her shoulder and picked one of the knives up.

"This is the one," he said. It was missing the leather wrapping for its hilt, which was made of bone, its sheath was scarred and scratched from years of neglect, and the red jasper stone bore the carving of a cat. "The others may have use in other rituals, so I don't think we should get rid of them."

"We paid too high a price acquiring them," Perrin said. "I am reluctant to discard any."

"If we repair them, maybe they will be useful," Kalanath said, picking up a knife with a lapis lazuli stone in its hilt and touching its pitted edge gingerly.

"We'll store them for later," Alaric said, holding out the bag for the others to put the knives away. He set the bag to one side and laid the cat knife on the table, beside the brass goblet incised with Ginatic characters. "One step closer."

Sienne ran her finger over the words on the cup. After nine months, she knew them by heart.

"'From the center, to the heart,'" she recited, "'to open what is closed, I am forever faithful.'" She traced the line around the base of the goblet. "'That the center will accept the offering, let this cup by my hand open the gate.'" Or door, or path—that was a word she hadn't been sure of. That she'd been able to decipher so much was a miracle.

"The knife the wizard used was newer," Alaric said, prodding the cat carving with one finger. "But the red stone, and the carving, and the shape—they're all the same."

"So we have two objects that were used by the wizard to bind the Sassaven *and* were part of some other ritual in the south, for a purpose we don't know," Dianthe said. "Is that progress, really? I mean, I don't want to sound discouraging, but there's still so much we don't know."

Alaric picked up the goblet and regarded it distantly, his eyes unfocused. "That memory blessing was effective. I can still remember the ritual as clearly as if it were happening now. The wizard picked up the goblet and held it to Mauden's lips for him to drink. He pricked his finger with the knife and drew a symbol on Mauden's palm, then cut Mauden's finger and had him repeat the symbol on his —the wizard's—palm. Then they clasped those hands, and one of the other participants looped a silver chain around their wrists, and Mauden and the wizard recited the lines on the cup."

"Except there was an extra line in the middle," Dianthe said.

"Yes. 'To bind and seal what is broken by the chain of forgetting.'"

"And that is all you remember," Perrin said.

"It's all I witnessed. I was there those three times as escort, not participant. Only Sassaven who'd undergone the ritual, who were full Sassaven, were allowed to take part in the rest. Some had unicorns as their other selves, the rest didn't, but all of them were bound."

"But you heard some of the rest," Sienne said. "Slow, lots of vowels—that's enough for me to identify the spells the wizard cast as transforms."

"And I'm sure the liquid in the goblet was some kind of sedative, because it smelled of varnwort, and I remember collecting that every fall and taking it directly to the wizard's chambers. It's a relaxant," Alaric explained. "I don't know what else went into the drink, though."

"Then it sounds like we need to discover that next," Dianthe said. "If the recipe was written down in some book somewhere, that book might contain information about the ritual or rituals it was used in."

"I wish I'd heard more of the spells he cast. That would tell us a lot," Alaric said.

"You wouldn't be able to remember them if you had, no matter how well your memory was enhanced," Sienne pointed out. "The human mind isn't made to comprehend the magic languages for more than a syllable or two at a time. So it doesn't matter that you weren't included in the ritual. Knowing they were transforms already limits our search substantially."

"Then we must search books," Kalanath said. "It may take a long time. I am not good at reading Fellic."

"And I still don't dare use the university library. You don't suppose the king would feel it was his duty to tell my parents where I am?" Sienne's hand closed into a fist under the table.

"I doubt it. He didn't sound like he thought it was his business," Dianthe said. "I'm still stunned that we were face to face with royalty. And some of us were rude to royalty." She glared at Alaric.

"He's not my king," Alaric said. "And he never apologized for hitting Sienne. I don't give a damn if he's the king, that's not behavior that will endear him to me."

"At any rate, we have no guarantee that the book we seek is in Fellic," Perrin said. "It might well be in Meiric, or Sorjic."

"And I'm not nearly so fluent in Meiric as I should be," Sienne said. "I didn't think I'd ever need it."

"I didn't know you spoke Meiric," Alaric said.

"Pay attention, Alaric, Sienne specialized in linguistics at her fancy school," Dianthe said.

"*I speak Sorjic very well, though,*" Sienne said in that language.

Alaric's eyebrows rose. "I hope I've never said anything you shouldn't have overheard."

"You're very discreet." Sienne grinned, and added in Sorjic, "*And very handsome.*"

"*Me say in Sorjic some,*" Dianthe said. "*Think you be careful.*"

Sienne blushed, and Alaric roared with laughter. "Sorry, no more talking in languages you don't understand," he said to a mystified Perrin and Kalanath. "Let's all be grateful we have the continental languages covered, so we aren't likely to miss the recipe we need for lack of understanding."

"Then tomorrow, we begin a new search," Perrin said, sweeping the bag up. "I will hold on to these, in case they become important."

Sienne handed Alaric the goblet. "It's still an hour or two before dinner. I think I'll go to the market and see if I can sell this spellbook we found in the Figlari keep, maybe trade for *convey* or *cat's eye*."

"Let me put this away, and I'll go with you," he said.

They walked through the streets of Fioretti toward the great market, close enough that the backs of their hands brushed occasionally. Alaric was silent in a way that stilled Sienne's desire for conversation. Sometimes it was nice to just walk together, not needing to speak. It was funny how a month ago they'd been awkward companions, uncertain of each other, and now... well, Sienne still wasn't sure what they were to each other, aside from more than friends. It wasn't just the kissing; she loved talking to him about anything and everything, felt safe in his company, and looked forward to seeing him every morning. Given time, who knew what this might turn into?

"How can you find out how to use the *jaunt* spell?" Alaric said, breaking the silence and startling Sienne out of her reverie.

"Oh, there are books... Madalynna probably has something in her library. That should be the first place we go to research the varnwort potion, and I'll ask her then."

"Good. That could be a useful spell."

"Not quite as useful to the team as *ferry*, but it will do."

His hand brushed hers again. Then he curled his fingers around her hand and squeezed gently.

She twined her fingers with his, not daring to look at him for fear of breaking the spell his gesture had cast over them both. His hand was large and firm, callused from years of swordplay and clearly capable of crushing hers, which made his gentleness even more endearing.

"I was attracted to you the moment I first saw you," Alaric said, his voice quiet enough that she had to strain to hear him over the noise of the crowd. "Even though you were a wizard."

"I wish I could say the same, but I thought you were an ass."

He laughed. "And now... I don't want this to hurt our team, but I can't bear the thought of going back to what we used to be."

"We're both sensible. That won't happen."

"I'll hold you to that."

They walked along in silence a few paces more. "You really don't have to worry, you know," Sienne said.

"Worry? About what?"

"About me being interested in other men, like poor Borris. I'd rather be with you than anyone."

Alaric smiled. "I was stupid, remember?"

"Logic-challenged. And Borris..." She looked over Alaric, his height and the breadth of his shoulders, thought about his quick wit and dry humor and everything else that made him what he was, and laughed. "Borris never had a chance."

He squeezed her hand. "That fills me with happiness."

They'd walked without paying attention to their surroundings, and Sienne realized they had passed the wizards' "streets" and gone all the way to the scrapper jobs board at the center of the market. Feeling shy, she pointed at the board, where all manner of job requests were posted. "Maybe we should take a job while we're researching. We didn't make any money off Tonia's job, and we may need to pay to look at some of these libraries."

"Sienne," Alaric said. She turned to look up at him and was startled by the intensity of his gaze. He took her other hand and gripped it lightly. "I don't know where this is going," he said, "but I think you should know—you're already the person I want to see first in the morning, and the last one I want to say goodnight to. If your parents do come looking for you, I swear they'll have to fight me to take you away. You know I'd put my life on the line for any of my companions, but that goes doubly true for you."

Peace, and happiness, made her heart swell. "That's exactly how I feel," she said, and pulled him down for a kiss.

SIENNE'S SPELLBOOK

Summonings:

Summonings affect the physical world and elements. They include all transportation spells.

Castle—trade places with someone else

Fog—obscuring mist

Slick—conjure grease

Evocations:

Evocations deal with intangible elements like fire, air, and lightning.

Force—bolt of magical energy, hits with perfect accuracy

Scream—sonic attack, causes injury

Confusions:

Confusions affect what the senses perceive.

Camouflage—disguise an object's shape, color, or texture

Cast—ventriloquism

Echo—auditory hallucinations

Imitate—change someone's entire appearance

Mirage—visual hallucinations

Mirror—creates three identical duplicates of the caster

Shift—small alterations in appearance, such as eye or hair color

Transforms:

Transforms change an object or creature's state, in small or large ways.

Break—shatters fragile things

Cat's eye—true darkvision

Fit (object)—shrink or enlarge an object; permanent

Fit (person)—shrink or enlarge a person; temporary

Gills—water breathing

Sculpt—shape stone

Sharpen—improve sight or hearing

Voice—sound like someone else

The Small Magics

These can be done by any wizard without a spellbook, with virtually no limits.

Light

Spark

Mend

Create water

Breeze

Chill/warm liquid

Telekinesis (up to 6-7 pound weights)

Ghost sound

Ghostly form

Find true north

Open (used to manipulate a spellbook)

Invulnerability

ABOUT THE AUTHOR

In addition to the Company of Strangers series, Melissa McShane is the author of more than twenty fantasy novels, including the novels of Tremontane, the first of which is *Servant of the Crown;* The Extraordinaries series, beginning with *Burning Bright;* and *The Book of Secrets,* first book in The Last Oracle series. She lives in the shelter of the mountains out West with her husband, four children and a niece, and four very needy cats. She wrote reviews and critical essays for many years before turning to fiction, which is much more fun than anyone ought to be allowed to have.

You can visit her at **www.melissamcshanewrites.com** for more information on other books.

For news on upcoming releases, bonus material, and other fun stuff, sign up for Melissa's newsletter at http://eepurl.com/brannP

SNEAK PEEK: MORTAL RITES (COMPANY OF STRANGERS, BOOK THREE)

Sienne stood at the villa's window and looked out over the Jalenus Sea at where the ocean met the sky, two shades of blue blending into one another. Waves far below crashed against the rocky cliff, their ebb and flow a soothing rush of noise that harmonized with the higher notes of the constantly blowing wind. One pane of thick, bubbly glass remained in the window; the rest were long gone. The glass transformed the vista into a dreamscape in which bulbous waves humped and bulged their way inland, tinted rosy pink. Sienne preferred the unaltered landscape. It wasn't as pretty, but at least you knew where you were.

She inhaled deeply, closing her eyes to enjoy the scents of sun-warmed air and salt breezes tinged with the sweet smell of the tiny pink flowers that covered the short stretch of ground from the house to the cliff's edge. They were strongly scented for something so small, and she wished she knew their name. Her father might know, dedicated gardener that he was in his spare time, but if he were standing beside her, he'd be more interested in criticizing her choices than in delivering a horticulture lecture. She scowled and turned away. And it had been such a pleasant day, too, until her past intruded on it.

"I take it you have had as little luck as I," Perrin said from across the room. The small library only had a few hundred books, but when each had to be examined closely, that was a daunting number. Perrin had made three neat stacks of books on the floor beside him, and was in the process of beginning a fourth.

"The owner loved plays," Sienne said, returning to the bookcase she'd cleared of most of its books. "They're easy to eliminate, but I admit to becoming bored. I didn't know there were so many ways to retell the story of the Seven Pilgrims."

"I have found histories. Very dull ones." Perrin flipped open another book, skimmed its pages, and set it on the new pile. "But this collection is so disorganized it is impossible to simply ignore a shelf on the basis that one has found five histories there, and therefore the other books must be the same."

Sienne reached the end of the final shelf. The last book was slimmer than the rest, bound in magenta-dyed leather that time and the sea air had worn to pink along the spine. "Poetry," she said. "*Sappy* poetry."

"I take it you are not a lover of verse."

"Not modern verse. I like old long-form epics about the before times." She set the poetry book back and stooped to gather up her piles to restore them to the bookcase. It probably wasn't necessary, since nobody was likely to come along insisting they clean up their mess, but she'd been too well trained at school in the dukedom of Stravanus to be able to leave books on the floor.

She heard footsteps overhead, making the ceiling creak. Alaric, probably, searching the upper floor for more books. The previous owners had let their collection spill over into every room in the house, and on the ground floor they'd found, in addition to the actual library, decorative shelves in both formal sitting rooms, a pile of cookbooks in the kitchen, and a couple of loose volumes of the epic *What Dreams Remain* in the outhouse. Missing pages from the latter indicated it hadn't been used for reading material, or at least not ultimately so.

Sienne began on the next bookcase. There were eight in total, all of them packed full. Exposure to the damp, salty air had caused most of the books to swell, compacting them further. She wormed her fingertips between the first and second volumes, stretching high to reach the top shelf, and pulled out a book. "*Desert Plants of Omeira.* That bores me just thinking about it. Honestly, I don't know why we're bothering. It's unlikely Penthea Lepporo left any necromantic treatises lying around where anyone might find them."

"How better to hide something dangerous than in plain sight?" Perrin swept his long, dark hair out of his face and began shifting his piles back onto the bookcase. "And the manner in which she left the house suggests she did not have time to hide any books that might draw the attention of the guards."

"I think it's sad that her family never came back after she died. It's not as if she died here, and it's a beautiful house. Or was, thirty years ago." Sienne closed her book with a snap and stared out the other window, the one that overlooked the overgrown patio and concrete urns that once held tiny fruit trees. The trees had all died from neglect, but creeping vines had taken over their corpses, their white star-like flowers giving the dead trees a false impression of life. Since they were at the Lepporo estate looking for evidence of necromancy, it seemed an appropriate image.

Their quest to find a ritual that would free their companion Alaric's people, the shape-changing race called Sassaven, had taken an unexpected turn four weeks earlier. Having acquired two ritual objects, they'd begun searching for the recipe for a potion containing the sedative herb varnwort, in hopes it might lead them to evidence of the ritual itself. Almost immediately, they'd discovered that varnwort was used in many, many rituals. All of them were necromantic.

Sienne had pointed out that so far as anyone knew, the only rituals that had survived from the wars that had all but destroyed civilization four hundred years ago were necromantic, so that was no real surprise, but it had still been disturbing. They were looking for a ritual that would invert the one binding the Sassaven to their evil creator, not one that would raise the dead. But it was their only lead.

So for the past four weeks, they'd turned their search toward finding a necromantic ritual that both used varnwort and had something to do with binding. It was delicate work; studying necromancy wasn't illegal, only the practice of it, but the law didn't always discriminate between the two, and people who studied necromancy didn't advertise the fact.

They'd found Penthea Lepporo's name in the correspondence of a known necromancer who'd died forty years ago, and Alaric had gotten permission from Penthea's son to examine the Lepporo library at the abandoned estate. Which was why Sienne was digging through old, damaged, boring books when she could be back in Fioretti reading something exciting.

She set the book down and reached for the next. It was taller than the others on its shelf and wedged tightly in place. Cursing softly, Sienne stepped back and tried using her small magic called invisible fingers on it, tugging at it without touching it. It stayed stuck as solidly as if the shelf had been built around it.

She cast about the room for a solution. Two armchairs positioned near the window looked as if they'd break if she put even her slight weight on them, but the table between them, low and square, looked hewn from granite rather than built of solid oak. She dragged it over to the bookcase and hopped up. This put her at eye level with the shelf and the row of books. Grabbing hold of the offending tome, she wiggled it back and forth, trying to loosen it.

Something snapped, and the book came free so rapidly she nearly lost her balance. "By Averran," Perrin exclaimed, "what did you do?"

"This book was stuck, that's all."

She glanced down at Perrin, who had his hand on a bookcase neither of them had examined yet. "That is not all," he said. He took hold of the bookcase's side and pulled, making it swing gently toward him. A gaping square hole in the base of the wall lay beyond it, dark and smelling of dust.

Sienne and Perrin stared at each other. "This is far more interesting than poetry, epic or not," Perrin said. "Shall we investigate?"

"Are you kidding? It would be the midge hive all over again."

Sienne drew in a breath and shouted, "Alaric! Dianthe! Kalanath! We found something!"

Hurried footsteps sounded on the stairs, and Dianthe appeared in the doorway. "Found—oh, by Kitane's left arm," she said, staring at the hole. "What is it?"

"There was a secret switch Sienne cleverly found," Perrin said.

"Just so you didn't go in there on your own. Remember the midges?"

"Is no one going to let me forget about them?" Sienne demanded.

More footsteps announced Kalanath's arrival, followed immediately by Alaric, who had cobwebs in his short blond hair. "Attic," he said. "But this is far more promising. Sienne, you didn't go down there alone, did you?"

Sienne rolled her eyes. "I *am* teachable, you know. What should we do?"

Dianthe crouched next to the hole. "There's a ladder going down, and it smells like a large room. Sienne, why don't you make some lights, and I'll see what I can see."

Sienne concentrated, and half a dozen white lights the size of small apples popped into existence, floating around her head. She directed them into the hole. Dianthe leaned farther forward. "It's definitely big, and the ceiling is remarkably high. Wait here." She turned and descended the ladder, disappearing out of sight. The others gathered around the hole and peered after her. Sienne couldn't see anything but the ladder and, far below, a black wooden floor that in the magic lights was shiny as if highly varnished. Dianthe's boots made sharp tapping noises that quickly receded to nothing.

"What do you see?" Alaric called out.

"We have our proof that Penthea Lepporo, or someone who lived in her house, practiced necromancy," Dianthe said. "Come on down. Whoever it was didn't leave any nasty surprises."

"Probably didn't have time," Alaric said, moving back to allow Kalanath access to the ladder. "Penthea's illness came on suddenly, her son said, and they all left for Fioretti with her."

"Yes, and don't you think that's strange?" Sienne said. "That they never came back to retrieve all their things? I realize the Lepporos are wealthy, but even wealthy people aren't generally wasteful."

Alaric shrugged and offered Sienne a hand. "Their town house is far more opulent than this, remember?"

"I remember." It had been opulent enough to make Sienne uncomfortable, despite her upbringing as a duke's daughter. She'd feared knocking over some priceless vase or smearing mud on an antique rug. "Even so."

"Who knows why the rich and powerful do what they do?" Alaric held her hand a few moments longer than necessary to help her onto the ladder, and she smiled at him and received a smile he reserved only for her. It still made her giddy when he looked at her that way, weeks after they'd acknowledged their mutual attraction. Giddy, and something deeper and warmer she hugged close to her heart. Falling in love with Alaric had been unexpected, and wonderful. But he never gave any indication that he cared more for her than casual affection, and she wished she knew if he was concealing some more profound feeling. She was the last person in the world who'd know love when she saw it. Her ex-lover Rance was proof of that.

She hurried down the ladder into a space several degrees cooler than the house above, which was warmed by the afternoon sun of late first summer. Dianthe was right, the ceiling was surprisingly high, at least ten feet—much higher than Sienne would have expected from a basement. The walls were painted the same black as the floorboards, providing a stark contrast to the white lines of script covering them. A wooden butcher block table stained with dark residue occupied the center of the room. Dianthe stood at the room's far side, next to a couple of flat-topped chests fastened with leather buckles. Sienne crossed toward her as she unbuckled the first one and opened the chest.

"Ugh!" Dianthe exclaimed, stepping back and pinching her nose shut. A foul stink like rotten meat wafted to Sienne's nostrils, and she imitated Dianthe's gesture. "That's far too ripe for something that's been locked away for thirty years."

"What is it?" Kalanath asked, prodding the chest with the tip of his steel-shod staff.

Dianthe leaned over, her nose still plugged, and shook her head. "I can't tell. I think it might have been a trap. But it doesn't look like the contents of the trunk are damaged, so I'm not sure what the point was. Take a look. I'll be more careful opening the other one."

Sienne walked over to the wall and examined the lines of script. They'd been painted on rather than written in chalk or ink, and in places the letters were too blurry to make out. Alaric came to stand beside her. "What does it say?" he asked.

"Nothing," Sienne said. "It's gibberish. Maybe it's a code? Or it could be a necromantic ritual, except all the ones I know about use actual Fellic words."

"This appears to be a list," Perrin said. He stood a short distance away, looking at another patch of writing. Sienne and Alaric went to join him. "A list of ingredients. Varnwort is not on it, before you ask."

Alaric let out a sigh. "I didn't expect this to be easy, but I still hoped—"

"Me too," Sienne said.

"Come and look at the books," Kalanath said.

The trunk was, in fact, full of books, jumbled together in no particular order. Kalanath handed them out to the others while Dianthe circled the second trunk, muttering to herself. Alaric whistled. "Necromancy books."

"And a journal," Perrin said, flipping the pages of one of the smaller books. "Whoever it was kept detailed notes."

Sienne shivered. "It's really cold in here. Let's take everything up to the library. There's better light there."

Alaric began stacking books in the crook of his arm. "Dianthe, what's in the other trunk?"

"I don't know. I'm afraid to open it. There's something off about the latch that I think is another trap—a nastier one." She shivered. "Sienne, can you give me a little more light over here?"

Something slammed nearby, making Sienne jump. A patter of

sharp thumps followed. The room grew marginally darker. "What was that?"

Kalanath crossed to the ladder. "The hole is covered. Something fell over it."

Alaric set down his armful of books. "I'll get it open."

The short stack of books shifted, then tumbled over, spilling across the floor. As Alaric crouched to pick them up, they rose into the air, circling him like a pack of wary dogs. "Sienne, stop that!"

"I'm not doing it!" Sienne exclaimed.

One of the books flew at Alaric's face. He batted it away as two more dove in after it. Sienne's armload of books darted away to join their mates, and the air was suddenly full of flying books, wildly careening in all directions. Sienne covered her head with her arms and cried out as a large book cracked her on the back of the skull, making her vision go blurry briefly. She ducked away from another assault and ran for the ladder. A bookcase had fallen face-first diagonally across the hole, dumping a bunch of books down it. They showed no signs of movement. That was something.

She turned to tell Alaric to get the bookcase out of the way, and froze. Behind Alaric, emerging from the second trunk, was a wispy, nearly invisible figure of a child about seven years old. It wore an old-fashioned night shirt that floated around it as if blown by an intangible breeze. The contours of its body shimmered, here one moment, gone the next, giving it the appearance of a sketch by an artist who couldn't make up her mind what to draw next. Its small face was drawn up in a silent wail, and its hands scrubbed invisible tears out of its eyes.

"Alaric, look out!" Sienne screamed. Alaric looked up, then turned, and the child grasped his shoulders and wailed. This time it was audible. The shriek filled the chamber, sending the flying books to the floor and making Sienne clutch her hands over her ears in a futile attempt to block it out. She could barely hear, over the sound of the wail, the exclamations of her friends. Alaric flailed at the thing, unable to get a grip on it even though it held him solidly in both small hands.

Kalanath stepped forward and swung his staff at the child's body. It passed through, making the form ripple with its motion but otherwise having no effect. At the same time, Dianthe drew her sword and thrust at it, but was forced to pull up sharply when she met no resistance and nearly skewered Alaric. Her eyes watering, Sienne snatched up her spellbook where it hung in its harness at her side and brought it up and open to *force*.

The child wailed again, and Sienne gritted her teeth and wiped tears out of her eyes. Taking two long strides to the side for a clearer shot, she read off the evocation *force*, feeling it burn like acid inside her mouth. As the last syllables left her lips, a bolt of magical energy blasted away from her at the creature. It struck the thing in the side. This time, its wail was one of pain and fury. It released Alaric and flew straight for Sienne.

Made in the USA
Lexington, KY
27 November 2019